# Captive
## The Shadow Atlas Book Three

**Jenny Sandiford**

VELIKOR
PUBLISHING

# JENNY SANDIFORD

Contact: jennysandiford.com

Cover designer: Miblart

Editors: Mandi Oyster

Proofreader: Amy McKenna

ISBN (ebook): 978-0-6454449-9-5

ISBN (paperback): 978-0-6459796-0-2

ISBN (hardcover): 978-0-6459796-1-9

First Edition: December 2023

*To my sisters, Lucy and Rosie—always willing travelers to magical lands.*

# Inanna's Descent to the Underworld
## A Sumerian Myth

*Thousands of years ago there were two sisters*, Inanna, goddess of love, sex, and war, Queen of the Echo Dimension, and Ereshkigal, goddess of death and the dead, Queen of the Shadow Dimension.

Ereshkigal mourned the death of her husband, Gugalanna, and invited her sister Inanna to her realm to witness the funeral rites.

Inanna agreed to make the journey and flew on her white dragon to the entrance in a hidden cave, but her motives were not pure. As she passed through the seven gates of the underworld, she shed her lapis lazuli rod, her glorious crown, her white and gold robes, her beads, and her precious gold bangles. She left all that she owned until she arrived naked at the banks of the inky Eridan River.

At the water's edge, her sister waved from the other side, dressed in black mourning garments with an obsidian crown and eyes lined in kohl.

But Ereshkigal knew of Inanna's plot to steal her throne. Ereshkigal watched her sister cross the churning river in the Maglium Boat. But when Inanna stepped to the shore, Ereshkigal killed her with Shadow Magic—the hand of death—and hung her corpse on a hook by the Eridan for all to see.

Inanna was mourned by mortals and gods alike, though not by her husband, Dumuzi. The god Enki summoned two strong gallu to retrieve Inanna's body, and they revived her with mystical waters.

Ereshkigal cursed and raged, but she could not defy Enki's wish. She made a deal that Inanna could leave, but to maintain balance, one must take her place.

Inanna offered up her husband, Dumuzi, the shepherd god, as he clearly had no love for his wife. Returning to her position as Queen of the Echo Dimension, Inanna left Dumuzi to spend half the year in the Underworld. The other six months, his sister, Geshtinanna, the goddess of agriculture, took his place. It was her absence and return that created the cycle of changing seasons within the mortal world.

Inanna and Ereshkigal remained manipulative and untrusting rivals for thousands of years. But a shift in the dimensions heralded great change...

# SHADOW MAGIC HOUSES

*Dark Magic. Source: Shadow Dimension*

### HOUSE OF SNAKES

*The Goddess Ereshkigal*

Spirits and Necromancy

### HOUSE OF WHITE DEER

*The Goddess Gula*

Healing Magic

### HOUSE OF RAVENS

*The God Zakar*

Sleep and Dream Magic

### HOUSE OF WINGED BULLS

*The Goddess Nanna*

Divination

# ECHO MAGIC HOUSES
## *Light Magic. Source: Echo Dimension*

### HOUSE OF OWLS
*The God Enki*
Mind and Water Magic

### HOUSE OF PHOENIX
*The God Utu*
Fire Magic

### HOUSE OF EAGLES
*The God Enlil*
Air and Weather Magic

### HOUSE OF BEES
*The Goddess Ninhursag*
Plant Magic

**FULL GLOSSARY AT BACK OF BOOK**

# Chapter 1

A knock thundered at the door. Azalea's eyes shot wide open, and the red light beaming from the window brought memories of the previous night hurtling back. Pain. Betrayal. Death. Azalea gripped her throat, swallowing against the bone-deep horror. Erik's broken body. Her stomach twisted. The Echo Dimension gate... it was open. Her chest tightened. The bond...

She squeezed her eyes tight, the flood of emotions overwhelming her. Had she really taken on Torin's father and had they knocked out the Archmage with their weird new magic?

All she wanted to do was burrow back into the cozy blankets and the warmth of Torin's arms and forget everything. Wait. Torin's arms?

Her breath hitched as she looked over to see Torin lying right next to her. He lay on his back with one leg out of the blanket, wearing just his boxers, giving her a clear view of his tattoo, a white snake skeleton that coiled around his toned thigh and contrasted his brown skin as if it was alive enough to jump off his body. Nice. Very nice.

His chest rose and fell with an uncommon calmness, and his eyebrows, one marked with a silver scar, weren't frowning in his sleep.

"Azalea!" Van's muffled voice sounded from the other side of the door.

"Shit." Azalea jolted upright. She shook Torin's shoulder, hoping he wouldn't think she was an assassin or something. At least there was no time to feel awkward about waking up in her apprentice master's bed. Though she couldn't shake the thought of him kissing her. *Stop it Azalea, no time!*

"Torin, it's morning," she hissed.

He mumbled something, and she threw off her blankets, chewing the inside of her cheek while looking for her warm socks, still dressed in her black t-shirt and jeans from the night before.

Was last night a moment of weakness for him, admitting he wanted her? He was messed up—that much was clear from his jumbled emotions colliding with hers. She couldn't tell who was feeling what, though she was pretty sure she was nervous, verging on panic, and for a good many reasons.

Number one right now was the loud knocking on the door.

"Coming," she yelled as she padded across the floor.

"Who is it?" Torin sat bolt upright with a momentary rush of fear that spiked through Azalea's chest, hard and fast. She couldn't tell from looking at him. His face was almost serene, his skin wasn't sunken or drawn like it had been other times when he'd hit the magic too hard. His brown eyes were bright and alert, the opposite of the night before when Azalea had used his sleep magic against him somehow.

"It's just Van." She waved her hand for him to relax. She bet she didn't look as rested as him. They'd both used a ridiculous amount of power last night, not to mention whatever that new crazy magic was they'd conjured up between them, and she was feeling it.

She flicked her long brown hair, still gritty with sand, over her shoulders, so it hung loose down her back. Her skin felt tender from being sandblasted, and she swore each individual muscle cell quivered from the magic that was pushed through her as she creaked her limbs toward the door.

It groaned against its hinges as she peered through the crack.

Van's warm brown eyes danced with relief, and she dragged Azalea onto the narrow landing at the top of the stairs and into a massive bone-crushing hug. She smelled of smoke and fresh soap.

"Thank the gods you're in here. Lucky guess. I did not want to be the one to tell your family you'd gone off on some ridiculous quest to fix this fucked-up situation." Van stepped back with a weak smile, her hand resting on her heart.

"I'm okay, Van. Turns out I needed sleep after all." Azalea pulled the door half-shut behind her.

Van was still wearing the same clothes she'd had on last night, and her eyes were bloodshot, the surrounding skin laced with thin, black veins—she'd been using healing magic recently—leaving her skin paler without its usual layer of makeup.

"How are you doing, Van? Is Jade and everyone alright?"

"This is Mage Dumont's room, Azalea." Van ignored her question and craned her neck to try to peer through the crack in the door.

"I am well aware of whose room it is." Azalea moved her head to block Van's view inside. Now was not the time to get into this. "Why were you looking for me? Is something wrong?"

Van gave Azalea a sly look and stepped back. "No more wrong than when we went to bed. Just world-ending stuff." She shrugged. "Your uncle and your mum want you downstairs now. The meeting is about to start, and I had to cover for you. Now tell me what happened in there last night." Van grinned.

"Shit!" Azalea's heart rate shot up. She didn't want her uncle to come looking for her right now. Finding her in Torin's room would be the last straw for him. "Not what you're thinking, Van. Can you just tell them I'll be down in one minute?" Azalea turned to the door.

"Not so fast, missy. I bought you a bit of time, so just chill. Thought I might take a gander up here, and what do you know, I was right." Van caught Azalea's hand before Azalea could get in the door. "What happened with Mage Dumont? Last night he could hardly look at you, and now I find you waking up in his bed. What changed?"

Azalea swallowed. How could she explain something she didn't even understand? Even now, her emotions were so entwined with Torin's. She thought about him constantly, but how could she know if it was love or lust or just their bond? All she knew was she couldn't let him die and couldn't live without him. Once that was clear, nothing else had mattered.

"We made up." Azalea squeezed Van's hand and tried to keep her voice steady, wanting to believe it was true. But maybe in the light of day, he would forget what he said. Her heart crashed against her ribs, remembering his words that changed everything: *I want you, Azalea.*

"Made up alright by the look of it. Did you—?"

"Van!" Azalea cut her off. "If you must know. No, we did not. I haven't forgotten I'm his apprentice. I know the rules." *We're just choosing to bend them. It's not like we have an illegal soul bond or anything...*

"Just be careful, okay?" Van said kindly.

"Just don't listen to all the talk about him, okay?"

"I would never." Van dropped Azalea's hand and enveloped her in an all-encompassing hug. "Just be prepared, is all I'm saying."

Footsteps sounded behind the door, and it swung open.

"Are you two done whispering?" Torin leaned on the door frame.

Azalea slid to the side, still able to feel the warmth of him and his magic so close. "Yup." She scraped a hand through her hair.

He stood super casual with his face unreadable, but Azalea felt the waves of tension rolling off him, the anxiety that tightened all his muscles like an animal ready to bolt. Hopefully, that wasn't because of her. She hoped it was because he was in the house where he had murdered her father. She hoped it was because her uncle had vowed to kill him. She hoped it was because the world was collapsing around them. Selfish thoughts, but ones she needed to believe.

"I was just telling Azalea that the meeting is about to start and thought I better warn you two. No need to thank me." Van grinned at Torin, but her smile wavered, giving away the exhaustion she was doing her best to hide.

He frowned. "We need to get moving. Azalea, you can't be here."

"I know. I just want to know how everyone is. Van didn't answer me before."

Torin folded his arms.

Van shrugged. "Oh, you know us. We're fine, just getting on with it. Quite a few people turned up in the night. I've been helping where I can."

"Don't overdo it, yeah?" Azalea said. Van was so dedicated to her apprenticeship as a healer she'd run herself into the ground before she put herself first. "Where are your family? Will they be safe?"

Van offered a shaky smile. "Mum and Dad are healers and researchers at The Pitié Salpêtrière in Paris. It has solid wards, so they will be fine. Even if I'd been able to warn them, nothing would drag them away from their work."

"Just like Maiken." Azalea's words were heavy on her tongue. Maiken was still at the Tower of London, separated from Danni and the girls who had made it here safely.

The warmth of a hand folded over Azalea's shoulder, and she couldn't help but lean into the intoxicating pull of his magic. She didn't need to look at Torin to know he wanted her closer. A spark of hope rushed through her. He still wanted her.

His hand fell away as if he realized it, too.

Van didn't seem to notice the shift as Azalea crossed her arms over her chest.

"I hope Isaac's okay." Van rubbed her arm.

Azalea nodded and didn't look at Torin. She hoped for the same thing. "I'm sure he is." An acute chill shimmied up her body. Her thin t-shirt was not suitable for standing around in the drafty stairwell.

"We better get moving." Torin twisted away.

Van got the hint and gave Azalea a quick hug. "It'll be alright, hun. They'll fix this. See you downstairs." Van perked up with what Azalea suspected was fake optimism.

Azalea slid back into the room after Torin. Her mouth went dry, wondering what she should say to him.

"What a fucking mess." Torin ran a hand across his shaved head as she hunted for a hint of what he might be thinking.

Her heart raced. Was he going to take it all back? Go back to hating her? Blaming her for not letting him shut the Echo

Dimension gate? In the light of day, would he turn back to sensible Torin and remember he was her apprentice master and that they weren't meant to be doing anything to encourage their soul bond? Their bond forming might have been an accident, but the high council and anyone with magic would not see it that way.

"Torin, about last night…" She trailed off as she felt the tension building in him.

This was it. He was going to take it all back. Azalea held her breath, waiting for him to crush her. To announce he had some new, ridiculous way to sacrifice himself to save everyone else.

"You stayed." He looked up, and his warm brown eyes melted the icy fear that clenched her heart.

"Of course I did." Azalea's voice shook. She remained by the door, unsure what to do next.

His gaze softened. "I'm glad you did." He shut the door behind her.

"Me too." Not daring to let herself smile. Not daring to hope he would kiss her again. She stepped toward him, like a cat cautious not to scare its prey.

He did the same, and before she could think of anything to say, his lips met hers. Simmering magic hummed between them. Not sharp and electric like the night before, but comfortable and powerful. The kiss was slow and deliberate like he was trying to make it last. Like he wanted to remember this.

Her eyes flashed open, and she pulled away as she felt a shift in his feelings. "You think we're going to die?"

He raised her hand entwined with his and turned over her palm as if studying an artifact. "We aren't glowing anymore."

She shook their hands. "Don't change the subject."

"The lack of glowing is a good sign. I don't think we're going to die."

"Then what has you so worried right now?" she asked, feeling like she was intruding on his thoughts, but they were hard to ignore.

"Kira was right." He shook his head and looked down.

"About?" Azalea wasn't sure she wanted to know.

He lowered their hands. "It was in a book we had when we were kids. It said whenever someone was gifted the hand of death, it always resulted in some sort of cataclysmic event. I think this qualifies."

"I think you're being paranoid. They are totally unrelated, and you haven't used the hand of death in years. You can control it now." She held up her hands in his to prove her point. "I'm not dead."

"You're right. I can control it. We just need to be careful." His forehead creased.

"I can be careful," she said.

Torin raised an eyebrow and tucked a loose hair behind her ear. "Let's just stay two feet apart at all times when in company. I know what your version of careful is."

"Hey." She crossed her arms. She'd actually been serious that she could be careful. But when she felt the brief flicker of happiness jump from Torin to her, she relaxed.

Torin was one confusing man. His emotions changed like a flick of an invisible and out-of-reach switch.

"We need to get moving. We need to fix this mess." He kissed her then picked up his sweater, leaving the gray coat on the back of the chair.

Unsure where to put them, Azalea clasped her hands in front of her. "See you at the meeting, then."

He slipped his elemer into his belt. "I'll come down with you."

# Chapter 2

Azalea's legs protested as she made her way down the narrow attic staircase and onto the second floor where most of the bedrooms were located. Torin was right behind her.

Her little black cat, Faraday, sat outside her bedroom door opposite the stairs, licking his paws. He shot her a glare that might have said 'where have you been,' if he could speak.

"Where have you been, Farry?" She picked him up and cuddled his soft black fur into her cheek.

He rumbled a greeting purr, then kicked his way out of her grip and took off down the long hallway lined with pale yellow wallpaper.

"You need anything from your room?" Torin nodded toward the door.

"I'm good. The Shadow Atlas is under my pillow. As soon as this meeting is over with, I'm asking it for ideas." The relics were all in her bag, but Torin didn't know that yet.

Torin stopped. "After everything it's put you through, you're still trusting that book?"

"Yes, and it will know how to shut the gate."

"Just how it knew how to find the relics to open the gate? If we hadn't found them, we wouldn't be in this mess. Why would you listen to it? We haven't even worked out what it is yet."

He might not have, but it had told Azalea what it wanted, and for some reason, it didn't scare her. *You will be the one to release me to my true form,* that's what the book had said the night before. Part of her wanted to help it, to free it and see its true form. Not that she would tell Torin just yet.

"I just trust it, okay? I can't explain how. I just know."

"Because it's brainwashing you. Maybe I should just hand it over to your uncle," he grumbled.

"No! You can't do that." She turned back and frowned at him.

"Keep your voice down. Let's just get this meeting over with, and we'll discuss it later."

That was Torin, right back to teacher mode, as if last night hadn't even happened. Was this what it would be like?

Azalea did her best not to sulk as they made their way down the stairs to the grand entranceway.

They got to the bottom, and Azalea considered the hotel-like selection of hallways that led off the lobby.

Cutlery clanging in one direction forced her attention down one way. "Maybe it's down there?"

"It's this way, come on." Torin marched off like he knew where they were going.

Azalea's heart squeezed in her chest—he knew the layout of this house. She knew how his mind worked. He would have studied every detail of the house, people's movements, the schedule of that night, all before he was sent in there to kill her father.

Her throat was uncomfortably dry, and Torin tensed. He didn't stop, but a fresh wave of guilt trickled off him.

Now she felt guilty for making him feel guilty. How long could they keep this up?

It felt like time stopped as they entered the dining room. Her hand went to her elemer. This wasn't the sort of danger she had been in the past few days but was just as scary.

A solid wood dining table stretched the length of the grand room which was decorated in deep blues and golds with sparkling chandeliers. She didn't even notice faces as she glanced over the many people already in there, all looking in their direction.

The clinking of cutlery on plates stopped, and someone coughed.

Her eyes locked on Uncle Fabian's at the head of the table at the far end.

Judging from the death stare he was aiming at Torin, he was still pissed off. Understandably so. She had brought his brother's murderer to his house and given him no option about Torin staying. But even Fabian would have to admit they needed Torin to fix things.

Azalea pulled her gaze away from him, hunting for a friendly face. Some people wore thin metal gloves, the type butchers wore when cutting meat, presumably iron, to prevent them from accidentally using Echo Magic, which told her these mages were from other Houses of magic, not just the House of Snakes.

"Over here, Petal! I saved you seats by me." Leda jumped up and drew Azalea into a warm hug when she reached her.

Azalea let herself relax for a split second, but a meltdown was brewing just below her skin. It would be too easy to sink into her mum's arms and let all her problems fall away. But she couldn't do that. She needed to be the one to keep it together so she could help fix this mess and close the gateway.

The high-backed chair scraped against the stone floor as she attempted to sit down.

She glanced at the chair next to her, not sure if it was a good idea to sit that close to Torin and try to keep her hands to herself.

"Sit down, Torin, no one's going to bite." Leda's eyes darted around the table like she wasn't so sure of that.

Azalea felt Torin's heart racing as if it were her own, but he stood motionless, his eyes scanning the faces in the room, and didn't move to sit.

"Torin? This man is Torin Dumont?" A man with white combed-over hair and snake tattoos creeping onto his hands threw down his cutlery and sent a withering stare at Fabian. "You allowed this man to enter your home, Fabian?"

"Trust me, Nigel. I didn't allow it," Fabian said with obvious bitterness.

The man, Nigel—who certainly looked like a Nigel with that sour face—stood up and glared at Torin. "You have the nerve to come back here after what you did. In the very house where you murdered our leader and had a good go at us, too. My friends are dead because of you," he barked.

Others agreed loudly. Azalea noted the ones that were House of Snake mages as several had snake insignias on their clothing or cufflinks. All had blazing eyes directed toward Torin.

Torin remained behind the high-back chair, his hands resting on top of it. "You all hate me. I know this. And you have every right to. But I apologize for what I did. I won't make excuses. I knew what I was doing."

Azalea gripped the edge of her chair. That was a gods-awful apology.

Torin continued, "I am sorry. I cannot undo the past but my intention here is only to help. I hope we can find a way to work together." He pulled out the chair and sat down.

Judging from the seething expressions around the room, that hadn't been the apology they were looking for. Fabian glowered but also was obviously glad he had some people on his side in this. It was only then Azalea noticed the small skeleton of a snake weaving around Fabian's neck like it was alive.

A woman with curly black hair stood up and slammed her hand on the table. "I'm with Mage Skeffington. I refuse to work alongside this man. Not when justice hasn't been served."

Danni stood up and glared at the woman, her red hair fanned out around her. She was dressed in her practical agent clothes, a blue zip-up jacket with PJU on the breast, gloves, and black trousers. Azalea felt a sudden lightness knowing Danni was here and on their side.

"Torin has more than served his sentence. He went to prison for eight years, and he indebted himself to the Archmage to bring down his father. He went from one tyrant to another. Cut him some slack and make use of his skill." Danni's gloved hands clenched into fists.

"Now everyone, let's stay calm." Azalea's grandmother, RoRo, made a gesture for everyone to sit.

Azalea didn't look at Torin but felt the discomfort rolling off him. She had to give him credit for walking into the room with these people.

A plate of food appeared in front of her. She glanced up to thank whoever delivered it, but she was already marching off. It looked like Mrs. Yates, Mary, the woman who had brought them tea last night. She probably hadn't slept either, and now she was making breakfast for at least twenty people—what a legend.

Azalea focused all her attention on her food but remained far too aware of Torin sitting so close. She could feel his magic calling to her. His leg brushed against hers, and she couldn't help but smile to herself and do her best not to look at him.

She double-checked her hands to make sure they weren't sparking, glowing, or throwing out shadows—they were fine. Letting out a quiet exhale, she studied her breakfast: fried tomatoes, bacon that wasn't too crispy, mouthwatering sausages, baked beans, fried potatoes... even the over-done fried egg made her want to grab them and shove it all in her mouth.

She selected a small potato to nibble while Torin straightened his knife and fork and arranged the glasses in front of him into a line. Faraday bounced up onto Torin's lap and sat there like he was waiting for the meeting to start. Azalea felt Torin relax a little as he stroked Faraday's sleek black coat.

RoRo rose from her chair. "I'll give you a chance to eat your breakfast while I update you on the current situation. But first, introductions."

Azalea bit into a sausage and took the chance to look around the table. Her gaze caught Jade's, who was on the end near the door. Jade gave a small wave. Azalea smiled and waved her sausage fork at her.

"I am Mage Rowena Sharp of the House of Bees. I allied myself with Fabian and the House of Snakes some time ago, so we may work together in bringing down Korbyn Dumont and the House of Ravens."

Azalea felt Torin flinch at the mention of his father's name.

"Our host, Mage Fabian Blackbourne—" RoRo gestured to Fabian next to her, whose scowl turned into a false smile as he leaned back and gave a half-arsed wave to the table "—has been kind enough to accept refugees of the House of Snakes and anyone in need onto his family lands, so we may all benefit from the ancient blood wards of Blackbourne Manor for protection.

It shields against the brunt of the Echo Magic and from attacks from creatures and our enemies."

Mumbles of thanks radiated towards Fabian from across the table, which seemed to perk him up a little, as he straightened in his chair.

"Here, we have representatives of families who will maintain order in the camp, and we have some of the finest mages to aid in our task of bringing down the House of Ravens and closing the Echo Dimension gateway."

Azalea couldn't help but be drawn into her grandmother's confident words and aura of power. She had never seen this side of her. The RoRo she knew pottered around in the garden and made wonderful elixirs and balms to sell at the market. She let pride bloom in her chest.

"Let me introduce around the table. From the House of Snakes: Mages Nigel Skeffington, Mage Elaine Stone—" That was the woman still scowling at Danni. The bloke next to Nigel was Russ, and then a few more Azalea didn't catch the names of as she focused on her food.

RoRo continued around the table. "Mage Simon Parry is a weather mage of the House of Eagles. And, over here, my good friend the Shaman Mergen who is in charge of our camp here. He is from the House of Ravens." RoRo glanced at Torin. "He had the unfortunate pleasure of dealing with Korbyn Dumont in Mongolia and here. I assure you; he is on our side."

Azalea felt a cold wash of fear from Torin. Did he know this man?

The shaman stood up and locked eyes with Torin. "Your father killed many of my men, including our greatest shaman, Altan."

Torin lowered his gaze to the table. "I am sorry for your losses. I knew Altan. He taught me a lot when I was a boy."

"Do you know the reason for his death?" the shaman asked with genuine interest.

Torin raised his eyes but didn't make eye contact with the shaman. "Yes. My father killed him for his elemer after he learned of its power to wield magic of both dimensions so easily."

"Yes, this is true." Mergen nodded. It was clear he had been testing Torin.

Torin set down his cutlery. "I found this out the same night we attacked this house. It was only then I saw how heartless he truly was." For anyone who didn't know Torin, it might have sounded cold, but she could feel the emotion simmering so close to his skin.

"I accept you, Torin." The shaman bowed his head slightly and sat back down.

RoRo nodded in approval. "We are fortunate enough to have some among us who escaped the Tower of London during the lockdown: Mage Danni Fletcher of the House of Phoenix, apprentice Evangeline Grey of the House of White Deer, and initiate Jade Pike of the House of Eagles and Winged Bulls." They all waved. Azalea was so glad they were here, too.

RoRo nodded to Azalea's mum. "Many of you know my daughter, Leda, of the House of Bees and Forest Guardian for the Goddess Ninhursag. She is the mother of Azalea Sharp, my granddaughter, of the House of Bees and House of Snakes."

RoRo smiled at Azalea, but her eyes held an apology, a warning. She realized why. "Azalea is Apprentice to Mage Torin Dumont, and she is the daughter of the late Samael Blackbourne."

Shocked gasps filled the room. Azalea's gaze skimmed around. Oh right, no one in the magical community knew that her father had a daughter. *Thanks, Dad.* She knew it was for her protection, but it only added to the feeling that she was the outsider here. On top of that, they could not be pleased she was apprenticed to Torin.

"It cannot be true." Mage Stone's eyes flickered with disgust.

"We would have known if Samael had a daughter. We were all on the House of Snakes council together; he would have told us." Nigel raised his hands, and his House of Snake comrades nodded in agreement.

Fabian leaned forward on the table. "I can assure you it is true. She is my niece; I have known her since she was born."

Azalea placed her hands on her lap. No longer hungry and wanting to reach for Torin's hand under the table.

"And you say this *man*," Nigel sneered, "Torin Dumont, is her apprentice master? How could you allow this, Fabian? He murdered her father, for gods' sake. He blew up our bloody council meeting and tried to kill us all!"

"Now, now. It wasn't as bad as it could have been," the man RoRo introduced as Mage Simon Parry from the House of Eagles did his best to calm the tone. Azalea decided she liked him. He had a round face, a twisty-ended mustache, and a friendly smile.

Azalea held down the strong desire to jump up and defend Torin. But it was the last thing he would want. He could fight his own battles if he wanted to.

"I am aware of who he is," Fabian said through gritted teeth. "And again, I did not allow this."

Azalea could feel the anger bubbling within Torin. Guilt erupted in her. She hadn't known what he would face when she brought him here.

"We don't have time for this squabbling!" RoRo banged the end of her elemer on the table. "We need everyone in this room to work together or we will get nowhere."

"Please, continue." Fabian waved his hand sarcastically, and the skeleton snake wound down his arm. Azalea wasn't sure what to make of it, and no one else seemed to care.

"Thank you, dear Fabian." RoRo ignored his tone. "Most of you are by now aware that Archmage Esther Norwich and the House of Owls are working with Korbyn Dumont. Together, they sought to bring about the destruction of the Echo Magic community by opening the gateway to the Echo Dimension. It is unclear why, but Azalea and Mage Dumont witnessed this firsthand as they attempted to stop her."

Murmurs broke out around the table, and Azalea wanted to sink into her chair like a pile of goo when all eyes turned to them. She did her best to look unaffected by the attention.

"Perhaps Mage Dumont would care to enlighten us with a recollection of the events of last night." Fabian stared at Torin as if daring him to relive the horrible ordeal.

"Certainly." Torin didn't flinch. He remained sitting up straight and spoke with confidence.

Azalea was sure as hell glad it wasn't her having to talk.

He started at the beginning and explained how the Archmage had blackmailed them into finding the relics for her and gave a brief overview of the near-impossible tasks they completed. Torin's tone remained neutral and perfectly humble as he told them about the guardian creatures they encountered; the taniwha, the griffins, the barghests, the Minotaur, and the danger they had been put in to gather the relics.

Azalea couldn't help but feel proud of him and their joint achievements and relish in the reactions as Torin spoke. Old Nigel didn't even try to hide his surprise, and judging from the change in expressions, many of them seemed impressed.

He left out anything about their bond and their mysterious new shared magic, the Shadow Atlas, and her problems with the spirits using her as a doorway.

Torin then relayed the events of the previous night as the entire table remained silent, hanging on his every word. "You need to understand just how dangerous the Archmage is. She sacrificed one of her own. It was Erik Faber of the House of Phoenix, a lad who grew up at the Tower of London, who she knew all her life. She didn't hesitate in killing him. She even called it an honor."

Azalea's breath caught. She had done everything she could to get to Erik, but it wasn't enough. Rage surged through her, and she was shocked at the intensity of it; her gaze flicked to Torin as his speech faltered.

She winced, knowing she had made him stumble. He continued explaining everything about the Echo Dimension gate opening, right up until they got to the Manor last night. Never once did he try to make himself sound like a hero, despite trying to sacrifice himself to save the world.

"And here we are. I believe Rowena had an idea for a solution." Torin nodded toward RoRo and diverted the attention away.

"Yes, as we discussed early this morning. I believe it is possible to enter the Echo Dimension to seek help from the old gods to reseal the gate." RoRo set her elemer on the table, pushing it away a little as if too tempted by it.

"Before we do this, I need to travel to the Desert of Dreams to try to commune with the gods. We need to get more information before making the journey," Torin stated.

"Fat lot of good that will do. No one has spoken to Enki or Enlil in thousands of years. They no longer listen," Fabian argued.

"Then I will speak to any minor god I can find to at least try to get information."

Fabian glared at Torin. "Have you even conducted the ceremony for Azalea to be your apprentice? I don't recall receiving an invitation."

Okay... why the change in subject? Azalea didn't like where this was heading. She could feel Torin's tolerance waning, and they could not afford for him to snap in a room full of mages who hated him this much.

"She passed her test but has not yet consumed the elixir of the gods." Torin folded his hands in front of himself calmly, but Azalea felt his building aggravation.

"And why is that?" Fabian asked.

All eyes were focused on the two men. Azalea wanted nothing more than to conjure a shadow cloak around her to disappear. Instead, she remained still, barely breathing as if that might upset the fragile balance of the room.

"Because she had enough on her plate with everything else and the Archmage's demands."

"Surely you know that taking the elixir will protect her? Help her strengthen her powers. You want her to have protection from the gods, don't you?"

"Of course," Torin said through gritted teeth.

"Very well! We shall do the ceremony as soon as possible. Tomorrow. We can use this opportunity. Azalea can speak with the goddess Ereshkigal about our predicament. Agreed?"

"Wonderful idea, Fabian." Nigel banged his hand on the table.

Azalea's mum frowned but wouldn't argue. Leda wasn't a mage, and Azalea suspected this lot wouldn't listen to her. RoRo didn't seem to object.

"I will go to the Desert of Dreams first. I don't want to put Azalea in further danger. Her magic was nearly drained last night. She needs to recover."

RoRo turned her attention to Torin. "As do you, Mage Dumont. After you have had a proper sleep, you may venture to the Desert of Dreams to seek guidance for us. Azalea will perform the ceremony tomorrow. We cannot put it off if it offers her extra protection and potential answers from the goddess," RoRo said, her voice laced with concern for both of them.

"Very well," Torin said without even glancing at Azalea.

Azalea bit her tongue at the frustration of others making decisions for her. But she knew Torin's fears of her taking the elixir. That Ereshkigal might not let her leave the Desert of Dreams because of the deal with the spirits.

But she didn't share his fears. The great goddess wouldn't keep her there, simply because she hadn't fulfilled her mission and hadn't collected the spirits, and the goddess was waiting for her to fill up her City of Stars.

Perhaps she could negotiate a new deal with the terrifying woman herself.

"I'd be happy to use my ceremony to help get information." Azalea tried to sound as confident as Torin.

"Good," Fabian stated. "In the meantime, we need to plan how to enter the Echo Dimension via the open gateway. I want as many people as we can get researching the safest way to go about this. We want protection spells, potions, wards, or anything that might look like it will give us a leg up."

Azalea cleared her throat, suddenly nervous. "The Archmage and Torin's dad had these staffs. She could still use Echo Magic, so I think they must filter the magic somehow, maybe like our training elemers did. I saw them at Erik's house months ago. His dad, the elemer-smith, was making them." She swallowed hard, trying not to think about Erik's empty shell of a body. She hoped someone had brought him home.

They took her advice, and the mages chatted among themselves, though this quickly turned to arguing. Azalea had said her part. She focused on forcing herself to eat though her stomach was churning with worry.

# Chapter 3

An explosion rattled the house. Azalea flinched at the chandelier above, which shook for several seconds. She grabbed Torin's hand instinctively, and neither of them moved until the shaking subsided.

Torin placed her hand back on her thigh and let his hand linger a second before letting go. "Outside, now," Torin ordered and got up, not waiting for anyone else to react.

Azalea followed suit and motioned for her mum to join them. She caught Danni's eye as they raced past. Van and Jade weren't far behind.

Torin ran down the hall, threw open the front doors, and they spilled out in a rush onto the driveway. Azalea breathed in the chill of the morning air; still without the slightest hint of wind, though the sky above them was in turmoil.

Outside the barrier of the inner estate, vermilion clouds roiled in the sky. Unfamiliar creatures streaked across the stream of magic that flowed like a river between the clouds.

A thunder crack boomed, reverberating right through Azalea's heart. It was not as bad as a spirit going through her, but it felt pretty close. She was glad there were no spirits here. That was one thing she couldn't handle right now.

A second thunder cracked, and everyone ducked as a blast of glaring white light hit the barrier above, sending crackling veins across it.

"Will it hold?" Leda hugged herself, rubbing her arms. RoRo was beside her staring up at the sky, her brow wrinkled in a frown.

"I'm assuming Fabian uses blood magic in the wards." Torin didn't shift his eyes off the barrier above.

"He does." Danni looked over her shoulder as Fabian and the rest of the council of mages joined them.

Azalea stood a few feet away from Torin, not wanting to be too close, but also wanting to keep an eye on him. She half expected him to change his mind and just disappear to solve everything himself.

"That's a nice ring, dear," RoRo commented out of the blue.

Azalea glanced down, the bright green demantoid garnet that Torin had given her when they were pretending to be married in Paphos. "Oh, thank you." She was unable to stop the blush rising in her cheeks. She really should give it back, though Torin insisted it was okay to wear it.

A man came running up the driveway. "A message from the House of Ravens." He went straight to Fabian who opened the letter right away.

Fabian cleared his throat. "It's from Korbyn Dumont and the Archmage. It reads: *Official announcement: The High Council is now under the control of the House of Ravens and House of Owls. Representatives from the House of Snakes Council and their allies are requested to present themselves at the Tower of London within the next ten days to surrender and swear loyalty.*

"*All residents under the protection of the Tower of London are ordered to return immediately.*

*"Failure to comply will result in severe consequences."*

"Oh my." Leda claimed Azalea's hand with hers and squeezed.

"I'm sure it isn't true, Mum. He's bluffing." She patted Leda's hand.

Torin shot her a troubled look. Okay, so maybe he wasn't bluffing.

RoRo moved to the front of the group, next to Fabian and all the other mages.

"What will they do if we don't go back?" Van asked.

"We'll just have to wait and find out." Fabian rolled up his sleeves. "No one is to go back there. That's an order."

Torin tensed and folded his arms. *Please don't turn this into a fight,* Azalea pleaded silently. That was the last thing they needed.

"I better get back to helping down in the healing tent. We had more people come in this morning. Want to come help?" Van very obviously changed the subject.

"Certainly." Azalea linked arms with Van. She needed to get away from all these people and have the space to think since there was nothing she could do here right now. Not until they went to the Desert of Dreams.

She glanced at Torin for permission, and he gave a brief nod.

They walked the short way to the healer's tent tucked amongst the mini-city of tents, containers, and circular Mongolian felt tents known as gers. Van ducked into the patterned orange doorway of one of several gers marked HEAL-ERS, and Azalea followed her into the circular room with lattice walls and six beds tucked around the edges, each with a patient in it and all looking unconscious and well bandaged.

"I admit I had an ulterior motive in asking you to come." Van set about organizing some bandages.

Azalea sat on a stool near the door. "Oh, what is it then?"

Van took a bandage and pulled another stool next to a woman with burns up her arms so horrid you couldn't make out her tattoos.

Azalea looked away, trying not to throw up. Flashes of the first time she saw Erik lying in a hospital bed burned and bleeding everywhere took her by surprise. She squeezed her eyes shut for a second, willing away the tears and the horrible memory. Erik had been a twat, but he didn't deserve to die the way he did. An involuntary sacrifice by the Archmage.

"Can you go find Isaac? I'm worried sick, and there's no phone service." Van raised her elemer over the unconscious woman.

"Yes, of course." Azalea gave a confident nod. Why hadn't she thought of that?

Van smiled, and her shoulders slumped in relief. "Thank you."

Azalea held her breath as Van ran her magic over the burns. "You need to pace yourself, Van. Are there other healers here?"

"I don't think they expected this many people so close to burnout," Van murmured as she pulled away her elemer and began to bandage the arm that was healing before their eyes.

"Just look after yourself. I'll find Isaac, don't you worry." Azalea hugged Van and stepped back out into the cold.

She jogged up the hill and was out of breath by the time she reached the front door. She knew Torin was in the library before she even entered the house.

Shaking off the unease, she followed the maze of hallways until she found him. He was looking at the door before she entered the room. Creepy. They needed to find a way to block the effects of the bond.

He sat alone at a desk tucked into the side of the room between large bookshelves. The eyes of other mages fell on her as she walked past them all working together around the large central table. She ignored them and leaned over Torin's shoulder.

"I need to talk to you," Azalea whispered, fighting the urge to run her hands down his chest.

He turned his head and looked up at her. "What is it?"

Her face was close to his. It would be so easy to kiss him. Just lean down and feel her lips against his like any other couple. But she kept her hands and lips to herself and stepped back. "They're all staring at me."

His gaze was on her mouth. "Just ignore them."

She bit her cheek and sank into the green armchair next to his desk. Time to just bite the bullet and get this over with. "I need to go find Isaac. I know you won't approve, but I need to know he's safe."

Torin sighed. "We need to focus on what's important. We need to get the gateway closed."

"Isaac *is* what's important to me. He's my best friend." She kept her voice low but could tell the group of mages were listening.

He raised his hands behind his head and leaned back in his chair.

Azalea rested her elbow on the armrest. "We can't do anything else right now. Not until after we go to the Desert of Dreams and after the council decides what to do." They didn't need to know she would be going to the Desert of Dreams, too. "In the meantime, I can do something useful and get Isaac instead of thinking about Erik and the Archmage and—" *You*

"—and everything."

He turned sideways in his chair and leaned in close like he was going to kiss her. Her eyes were drawn to his mouth, unable to look away. *Would it be so bad if I kissed him in front of everyone?* A smile crept over his lips, and he pulled away as if he knew what she was thinking.

He shut his book. "Fine. I'm coming with you."

# Chapter 4

Azalea and Torin stepped into an industrial-style kitchen, one of two that sat side by side. This one was empty, and the other, a cozier family-style kitchen, was bustling with voices and clattering pots and emitting wonderful smells. Her stomach growled. She should've eaten more at breakfast but still wasn't sure she could. Every time she thought of Erik being dead, her stomach clenched, and thinking about the Echo gate had her skin buzzing with anxiety.

The swing door between the kitchens remained shut. They crossed the stone floor and slipped outside.

Walking in silence over the neat cobbles, they made their way across a courtyard lined with colorful mosaic pots overflowing with kitchen herbs. They ignored the turbulent red sky above, and Azalea breathed in the still morning air that tasted of smoke and the familiar baked earth smell of the Echo Dimension.

"It's about a ten-minute walk to the front gate." Azalea just wanted to break the silence.

Torin walked so close their arms brushed, and she could feel his warmth or maybe it was his magic. "Better get moving then."

Striding in silence, Azalea wondered if she should say something about last night. Torin was blocking his emotions well this morning, but she was sure she wasn't doing the same.

"About last night." His voice took a serious tone.

A spike of panic shot through her. Maybe she didn't want to hear this.

He glanced at her. "We need to work out what happened with our magic."

*Ah yes, the magic...*

"How can we do that?" She raised her hands looking for sparkles or glowing.

A small grin stole across his lips. "We test it."

"I like the sound of that." She was sure he was going to say they should ignore it and block it out.

"In private, though, and not right now. Today you use the gloves unless I say otherwise." He dug gloves out of his pocket and handed them to her.

"Not a problem." She had no intention of using magic and every intention of making this easy for him, so he wouldn't run off and do something stupid like go to the Echo Dimension by himself.

She slipped on the metal gloves. They were slinky and cold but light, more like wearing thin wool than metal.

They made it to the small side gate without encountering anyone and ducked through it. The blood wards recognized Azalea, which would allow them to get back in as well.

As soon as they were outside the gate, Torin cut a wide arc into the Hollow with his elemer blade. The interdimensional fabric fell away, leaving a dark void edged with frayed shadows. Azalea breathed in the familiar smell of distant snow, though there was nothing to be seen. Just endless blackness.

They didn't stick around.

Torin cut to Isaac's street in London with ease and no sign of weakened magic. Stepping out, smoke hit Azalea's nostrils straight away. She gasped. The street was littered with overturned cars, all smashed in and bent up, and not from driver error—something had moved them all.

"Get down," Torin ordered as the street rattled with an explosion further up. His eyes were solid black from using magic. This was Torin, the combat mage, not the academic. Somehow, he switched flawlessly between the two.

Azalea's heart raced as they ducked behind one of the few upright cars.

"Get inside!" a voice yelled from a window above in the four-story white and gray brick building—John Adams Hall, Isaac's Hall of Residence. Students leaned out the windows, some waving and pointing down to the doors at street level. All of them were yelling, a few pointed at something further up the road.

"Should we go in?" Azalea followed Torin's lead and crouched behind a car.

"I want to see what they're so afraid of."

Azalea wasn't sure she wanted to know, but Torin didn't take his eyes off the road up ahead where the students pointed, and Azalea stayed put. Instead of freaking out, she studied the faces in the windows. She couldn't see Isaac.

A jolt of fear rushed over her from Torin. Her breath caught in her throat as a creature prowled into the center of the street. A cat as large as a tiger stalked toward them. Its sleek black fur shimmered with luminescent blue stripes that lit up with each step, but more noticeable were its wings, not fully unfolded, just hovering above it like it might take flight any second. Azalea couldn't peel her eyes away.

"Azalea! Over here," Isaac yelled from across the road in a doorway, his blond hair bobbing up and down as he waved them over.

Azalea's heart plummeted as the cat's gaze darted to Isaac.

*Shit.* She waved back, gesturing for him to get back inside. He was drawing way too much attention.

"We need to do something," Azalea whispered, clenching the tire in front of her.

"I don't even know what that creature is." Torin crouched, his elemer ready in his hand.

If he didn't know what it was, she was sure nobody else would.

She made a *what the fuck* gesture with her hands to Isaac. Why the hell wouldn't he just get back inside? But he shook his head. She pointed like a crazy woman, and he finally turned to see the cat.

The creature broke into a run, and Isaac didn't have time to make it back in. The cat moved like water, its feet barely touching the ground as it half-flew, half-ran at Isaac.

"No!" Azalea picked up the closest thing to her, a smashed wing mirror, and hurled it at the giant cat.

It clipped its wing and made it look back.

Magic churned in her guts. It wasn't Echo Magic or Shadow Magic that she felt in her skin or her chest. It nestled deep in the pit of her stomach, and it was something else—the new magic she had felt the night before.

Her throw had been too late. The beast struck, swiping its massive paw at Isaac. Isaac dodged, but the blow landed on his shoulder, hurtling him through the air. His limp body landed with a crash on a mangled black fence.

Torin bolted toward them.

Too scared she might use Echo Magic, Azalea kept the gloves on but dashed after Torin. The cat pinned Isaac under its enormous paw; saliva dripped from the beast's maw onto Isaac's face.

Torin threw out spears of shadows, not caring about all the non-magical people watching from above.

Azalea wanted to summon water and hurtle ice at the creature. But she clenched her hands before she did it.

Torin's shadows bounced right off the cat.

"What the fuck?" Torin stopped dead in his tracks as Azalea reached his side.

Sending out shadow ropes, he tried to circle the creature, but they dissolved to nothing as they wound around it. The warmth of the new magic flooded Azalea as Torin pulled her to the side and backed up behind another car.

Azalea surveyed the area. She needed to find something to stop it, preferably a gun, but that wasn't going to happen.

The cat hooked a paw the size of a dinner plate under Isaac and flipped him on his side. He groaned but didn't move.

*Please stay alive, Isaac.* She tried to ignore the magic rising in her guts like she might vomit it up.

Spotting sports gear piled behind a car, she crept around it and grabbed a broken cricket bat.

"What are you going to do with that?"

"Hit it." Azalea stood up.

Torin grabbed her arm and yanked her back. "Not smart."

A pleasant hum of magic vibrated between them; warm and powerful. He froze.

She bounced on her heels. "Let's use our magic." It wanted them to use it.

The cat lowered its head, baring its fangs, then licked Isaac's jacket, and Torin glared up at the many faces looking down on them.

"Them watching hardly matters. You've already done magic." She wrung her hands around the cricket bat's handle. They needed to get to Isaac.

"It's not them I'm worried about. It's the magic. We don't know what it can do, and it's still very much illegal if we get caught."

"No one will catch us here." Her voice grew desperate. "It's up to you. But if it can help Isaac, we should use it." Isaac wasn't moving. She hoped he was playing dead.

"Take off your gloves," Torin ordered.

Isaac howled as the cat flapped its wings, spun around 180 degrees, bit his ankle, and dragged him.

Azalea ripped off her gloves, and Torin took her hand igniting a new warmth pool in her belly. His magic merged with hers, warm, alive, and already so much a part of her.

Their fingers entwined, and they raised their palms at the cat. The energy in Azalea built with a growing heat. She imagined an orb of light as she took in a deep breath. It traveled to her chest and down her arm where it met with Torin's energy and exploded out of their palms.

The force jolted Azalea back, but she ground her foot into the road as the ball of light struck the beast. With a yowl, it collapsed on Isaac's legs. Its eyes closed, and its pink tongue hung from its mouth.

Then calm.

Azalea released Torin's hand and raced to Isaac.

"Isaac. Isaac. Wake the hell up. You can't do this to me."

"It's always about you, isn't it Azalea?" He grinned and took a slow breath.

She sat back on her heels with a breath of relief.

"You're an arse." Then forgetting he might be hurt, she threw herself on him and pressed her face into his neck, her arms wrapped around him, and it was the best feeling in the world when his curled around her back and squeezed.

"Thank you for not being dead," she whispered.

"Thanks for saving me from a giant cat with wings." He started coughing.

Azalea sat up. "Where does it hurt? Are you okay?" She rocked back on her heels and looked him up and down.

"The cat, he's crushing me." He winced and managed a weak laugh.

Torin struggled to move the cat. "A hand here, if you don't mind."

His emotions trickled through the bond. He seemed conflicted about their magic but happy they'd saved Isaac.

"It's still alive. We just knocked it out, I think." Torin risked his hand by waving it in front of the beast's mouth.

Azalea helped him drag the cat's legs off Isaac, glad it wasn't dead. The poor thing was navigating a new world where it didn't belong.

Isaac leaned on his elbows and eyed Torin suspiciously. "Thanks. That bastard was heavy." He tried to move his leg and took in a sharp breath, then closed his eyes.

Torin frowned and pulled up the bottom of Isaac's trousers. His hand came away covered in blood. "We need to get him back."

"You guys are scary; you know that right?" Isaac stared at her face.

She studied Torin and realized their all-black eyes did look rather demonic, though Azalea hardly noticed now. "You've always been scared of me," she joked.

"True that." He grinned. "So you're Torin, Azalea's teacher?" Isaac avoided looking at his leg.

Azalea opened her mouth, then closed it. She hadn't realized the two people closest to her had never met. Isaac had been her go-to person for venting over the last seven months, and a lot of that venting was about Torin.

"That's me. Nice to meet you." Torin held out a hand for Isaac to shake.

Azalea tied her jacket around Isaac's leg to stop the bleeding. Torin was never that polite or keen to meet someone.

"Nice to finally meet you. Azalea's told me a lot about you." Isaac held Torin's stare.

"I can imagine. Don't hold it against me." He smiled and helped Isaac sit up.

What just happened? Was Torin being nice? Azalea wiped her hands on her jeans.

Isaac glanced from Torin to Azalea, then back again. His eyebrows pinched together before he shook his head and focused on Azalea. "You alright?"

"Sorry. Um, yeah, I'm good. I forgot you two had never met," Azalea said, as Torin stood with his arms crossed. She couldn't tell what he was feeling, but she hoped he'd remain nice toward Isaac.

"I suppose you lot had something to do with all this? The gateway thing didn't work out?" Isaac gestured to the sky.

Torin frowned. "You told him?"

"I tell him everything... well, nearly everything." She bit the inside of her cheek. No one knew about their soul bond. She had been very vigilant in keeping that secret to herself. Though she wasn't sure how long it would stay that way; she could hardly keep her hands off Torin.

Isaac narrowed his eyes. He always knew when she was hiding something.

The door burst open behind them, and several students rushed out, saving her from her awkwardness.

"What the fuck is that? Are you a wizard?" a tall bloke with blond hair asked.

"It's a cat, and no." Torin checked the jacket would hold on Isaac's leg.

Isaac patted his friend's arm. "It's fine, Luke, they're the mates I told you about. I'll be 'right."

Torin stared down at the group of terrified students. "You lot, get back inside. Stay in there until the sky turns normal again. Got it?"

"What's happening?" a girl, her eyes red with tears and still dressed in pajamas, asked.

"And what do we do with this fucking tiger?" another asked.

"Why the fuck is the sky red?"

"Why won't my phone work?"

"You can do magic?"

"Where are you taking Isaac?"

The questions escalated as more students stepped onto the footpath.

"Quiet!" Torin yelled.

Azalea squeezed Isaac's hand. He gave a shaky smile, but he was in pain, and there was a lot of blood oozing from his leg.

"The world has been overrun with dangerous magic. You all need to stay inside until authorities tell you it is safe," Torin snapped, then turned around and cut into the Hollow.

Gasps arose from the growing crowd.

"Help me get him up." Torin bent down.

Azalea knelt on one side of Isaac and Torin on the other, they hauled him up onto his good foot as he leaned on their shoulders.

"Shouldn't we help them?" Azalea peeked back.

"I did. I told them to go inside." Torin focused on holding open the cut.

"Bye, guys." Isaac smiled at his friends as they swiveled him around and half fell into the Hollow.

The silence in the Hollow was absolute. Isaac leaned heavily on Azalea's shoulder.

"Um, so I guess we're doing magic in front of non-magic people now?" Azalea asked as Isaac's head lolled to the side. A rush of panic burst through her as she gripped Isaac's arm.

"Secret's out. No point in hiding it." Torin remained calm and checked Isaac's pulse. "He's alive."

# Chapter 5

When they arrived at the estate, the jacket around Isaac's foot was dark with blood. He was alive but not conscious.

"Could we use magic to carry him somehow? Like shadow ropes or something?" Azalea asked.

"I need to conserve my magic so I can get to the Desert of Dreams later. I'll just carry him, it'll be faster."

"You mean *we* go to the Desert of Dreams." Azalea helped keep Isaac upright while Torin maneuvered himself around and hoisted Isaac across his shoulders. He lifted Isaac like he was a sack of potatoes and set off up the driveway.

"No. I mean *me*. You're not coming. You need to conserve your energy for your apprentice ceremony tomorrow."

Azalea bit her tongue to stop herself from arguing and kept an eye on Isaac as they walked, making sure he looked okay, but also that he wasn't listening.

"I know you're worried about it. But it will be fine. I might even be able to help find another option for closing the Echo gate."

"We will have a plan before then. You just need to worry about getting yourself through it."

"Okay." She nodded. He wouldn't be there with her so she could say whatever she wanted to the Goddess when she was there. "Sorry about my uncle. He thinks he's helping."

"Helping, but also trying to piss me off deliberately," Torin said through gritted teeth.

They made it the rest of the way in silence and got Isaac into an empty bed in a healer's ger that had popped up next to the one Azalea had been in this morning with Van. There were no other patients yet.

"What happened?" Van rushed in and set to work, fussing over Isaac and examining his leg at the same time.

"He was bitten by some sort of mythical flying tiger-cat-thing." Azalea stayed out of the way. Van tilted her head for a second, then got on with the job. Torin couldn't seem to handle the waiting around and marched off to the house. Azalea liked to think he was off to get some rest, but it was more likely he would return to the library to continue researching the Echo Dimension.

The overuse of magic and the events of the day before were catching up with her. Her feet felt like they were set in concrete as she stood there waiting for Van to finish.

"Sit down, Azalea." Van guided her into a chair before she knew what was happening. Van was done. "I've healed Isaac. He'll be right as rain when he wakes up." Van beamed, but red veins spreading through the skin around her eyes gave away the effort she'd put in and made her look rather demonic.

"You've still got supplements, right?" Azalea checked. She should have been more vigilant in watching Van. She hadn't needed to fully heal him. What she needed was to keep her magic in reserve, but Azalea wasn't about to suggest that. Not when Van had saved Isaac.

"Uh-huh." Van patted her coat pocket and busied herself writing notes.

Azalea sunk into the chair next to Isaac and held on to his warm hand. She rested her head on the side of his bed—just for a second...

$$\text{) ) ) ● ( ( (}$$

Azalea flinched as a hand pulled away from hers, and she sat bolt upright.

"Isaac?" She must have fallen asleep.

"Did I dream that, or did a flying cat think I was a mouse?" Isaac glanced around, taking in the unfamiliar sight of the circular ger. A few more patients had arrived, but they were all sleeping.

"It tried to eat your foot." Azalea smiled, glad her best friend had survived.

"I feel amazing." Sitting up, he pulled his bare foot onto his lap and started prodding it. "There's only a tiny scar." He ran his fingers over the skin in disbelief.

"You have Van to thank for that."

Van rushed in and nearly bowled Isaac off the narrow bed in an aggressive hug. "Thank the goddess, you're okay."

"Sounds like you're the goddess I should be thanking," Isaac whispered into her neck.

Azalea cringed, wanting to leave the room.

Van, apparently moved by this, kissed Isaac as aggressively as she'd hugged him. "I'm so glad you're safe." Tears escaped the corners of her eyes, which were now less veiny. She kissed his cheek and then went back into healer mode and checked Isaac's foot.

"Evangeline, we need you in healing ger two," a voice shouted from somewhere outside the felt walls.

"Coming!" Van untangled herself from Isaac.

"Can I take Isaac now?" Azalea wanted to find him a room, but more importantly, update him on everything that had happened, and selfishly, she wanted him to be there when she consulted the Shadow Atlas.

"He's good to go." Van kissed him again. "Your grandma should be in the mess hall. Ask her where to put him."

Van left them, and just as she had promised, when Isaac stood up, it was as if there had never been a giant kitty snacking on his leg. They found RoRo in the mess tent which also seemed to be the headquarters for the pop-up village, a big white marquee set up with long wooden tables inside and a sprinkle of fairy lights around the edges. She wasted no time assigning Isaac to a five-bed ger that had no other occupants.

He didn't have anything with him, so they left, and Azalea took him to the house. First stop, her room to consult the Shadow Atlas.

"This is your dad's house?" Isaac took in the collection of family portraits as they went up the main staircase.

"*Was* my dad's house. It's my uncle's now. Apparently, I came here once when I was young. I don't remember it." She'd probably blocked it from her memory knowing her dad was living in this palace and they were in their humble cottage. She knew her mum would never have it any other way. She couldn't be away from the forest. But it still hurt to see the life Azalea had missed out on growing up.

"It'd be a lot of maintenance. Trust me, you don't want a house like this." Isaac ran a finger over a chip of flaking paint.

He noticed things she would never look for. Isaac had always been her neighbor growing up. The difference was he grew up in a house similar to this, not as big, but just as fancy.

"Maybe a dragon destroyed your house?" Azalea said optimistically. It was no secret that Isaac didn't want to inherit his father's estate or the mountain of debt that came with it.

"With my father in it. One can only hope." He chuckled as they turned into Azalea's room. Azalea knew better than to ask about his father because, despite the laugh, he wasn't joking when he said that. His dad was a dick.

She collapsed onto the bed while Isaac sunk into a wing-backed armchair next to the window draped in layers of fabric curtains.

"Good to see Gerald made it." Isaac pointed to the dinosaur toy on the bed by her pillow and smiled.

"Of course, he did, I couldn't leave him behind." She threw the brontosaurus to Isaac, and he rested Gerald on his knee before he turned to the window.

Isaac's face grew serious as he stared at the red sky. "Tell me everything."

"Where do I begin..." She filled him in. Even the part about the Shadow Atlas wanting her to free it. She skimmed over the parts about Erik dying because she couldn't bear to talk about it—it was just too horrible. He listened intently and only interrupted her with a few questions. He'd known about the relic hunt and that they were trying to close the gate, so at least he wasn't shocked by any of that.

When she finished explaining, she felt a little lighter, like the burden had shifted ever so slightly—like it might be doable to fix.

"Torin isn't at all how you described him." Isaac leaned back with his arms crossed, his feet resting on the opposite chair.

She lay on her side, resting on her elbow. "He saved your life. You're blinded by his heroism."

"Have you considered maybe he is a hero? How many times has he saved your arse?"

Hmm... good point. But no. Isaac knew the hell Torin had put her through. "You know he killed my dad, right?" She wasn't even sure why she wanted to make Torin the bad guy again. She just hadn't thought Isaac would be on his side.

"And you forgave him for that. You must have noticed how fit he is? It's rather intimidating for a bloke to stand next to someone like him. Plus, he's a powerful shadow mage."

"So you're scared of him?"

"Of course, I'm bloody well scared of him. He's terrifying. But I saw the way he looked at you, Azalea, and it wasn't very teacherly."

She rolled onto her back and stared at the fancy molding around the central light as a smile twitched at the corner of her mouth. "Things with Torin are... complicated."

"Uncomplicate them then. He's your teacher." He stared down at her like she imagined a big brother might.

"It's not that simple, Isaac. There's more to it."

Isaac leaned against the arm of his chair. "Let me guess, a magic thing?"

"Yes."

"I'm just looking out for you, Zaels. Erik was a dick. Now he's dead. Just be careful. Okay?"

She sat up and crossed her legs. "Okay. But I know what I'm doing."

"Fine. I'll drop it for now." He held up his hands. "Now, what did you want to show me?"

Azalea cringed, knowing he would hate this. She slid her hand under the pillow and pulled out the Shadow Atlas.

Isaac groaned. "This can't be good."

She patted the bed next to her, and he reluctantly walked over, shuffled himself into the mountain of pillows, and leaned back.

"I just need you here in case something goes wrong, or you need to snap me out of it."

Isaac put a pillow in front of him as a shield. "Fine. But you better not summon a demon from the book or anything crazy."

"It doesn't want me to summon a demon. It wants me to release it back to its true form." Azalea reached for her elemer.

"Ah yes, that's so much better."

Azalea hit him with his cushion. "I'm just going to ask it questions. Don't get your knickers in a twist."

"Fine, get on with it then," Isaac said the same way he did when he let her have the last biscuit in the tin.

She got straight to it. Using her elemer to prick her thumb, she dropped a generous amount of blood onto the blank page and closed her eyes. She didn't need to write in it this time; the connection was strong. Meditating on the same questions, she asked it how they could close the Echo gate and what exactly it wanted in return.

*Hello, Mageling.* Deep red ink seeped onto the page.

"That is so creepy." Isaac leaned in closer.

She concentrated on the page.

*Beyond this realm, your answers wait,*
*A way to close the Echo gate.*
*I give to you my one true name,*
*Sitaddaru is yours to claim.*
*A demon in my final form,*
*The Wayfinder in a darkening storm.*
*Bound to you, I will lead your hand,*
*To Kur beyond this mortal land.*
*Across the river where souls are weighed,*
*The cost you'll pay with a silver blade.*
*Your path can lead to many gates,*
*Beyond the mortal realm, fate awaits.*

Azalea nibbled her lip and took a photo of the riddle. Then put down her phone, that still didn't have any service, and rested her hand on the open page of the book. She could feel the creature in there. It desperately wanted to escape, but it also wanted to help. She believed it.

"Thank you. We will get back to you once we have a plan." She shut the book gently.

"It's a demon, and it just gave you its name," Isaac said in disbelief.

Azalea grinned. "I'm sure I can trust it, Isaac. The Shadow Atlas told me there was another way. This is it."

"What did it say?"

"The choice is yours to shut the gate; To sacrifice one more or wait. The future shows another way; A harder path for those who stay." She repeated from memory.

Isaac leaned back into the pillows. "Vague at best. I'm feeling like releasing a demon is an extreme measure."

"And Torin and Uncle Fabian traveling to the Echo Dimension isn't? If they don't die there, they'll probably kill each other." She wasn't exaggerating. The chances of them both making it back alive seemed slim, and it wasn't something she wanted to think about.

Isaac poked her in the arm. "They're both highly trained mages. You're only an apprentice, and I don't know much about that, but this seems a little advanced for your magic level."

Azalea poked him back. "My magic level doesn't matter. The demon is trapped in this form. It needs my help, and I need its help. Simple."

"Okay... assuming that's all good, what does it mean by the cost with the silver blade? I don't like the sound of that," Isaac said to poke holes in her plan.

Fortunately, Azalea had an answer for him. "Not as bad as it sounds. There's this sword in Torin's dad's office. It can be used to collect souls. I'm pretty sure it wants me to collect the souls I agreed to collect and use them as payment to get across some river into the Shadow Dimension."

"Bloody hell, this is getting ridiculous. How many souls exactly, and what river? Mythological rivers in underworlds are notorious for needing payments or judging you or challenging you." Isaac looked worried.

"It's a thousand souls. I don't know anything about rivers."

Isaac sucked in a breath.

She had to give it to the sneaky book. This was the most direct and least cryptic it had ever been.

"I need to do it. I need to go to the Shadow Dimension to get help." She stared at Isaac, who shook his head slowly.

The door flung open, and Torin was there, his eyes wild with the same anger that was radiating off him. "Get away from that book, Azalea."

# Chapter 6

Torin picked up a blanket from the back of a chair and flung it over the book. "What the hell were you thinking?"

"I'm getting answers." Azalea set her jaw.

"You knew I wouldn't approve, but you did it, anyway." Torin ignored Isaac, who was sitting extremely straight on the bed and looking very uncomfortable.

Azalea knew it was the right thing to do. But Torin was terrifying when he was like this, pacing and clenching his fists like he might strangle someone.

She held her ground. "You're wrong about the book."

"You don't know that. It could be a demon. What don't you understand about that?" He continued to pace.

She nibbled her lip. "Oh, it is a demon. It told me."

Torin ran his hand over his head.

"Um, maybe I should leave." Isaac slid off the bed and stood, wringing his hands.

"No. You should stay. Azalea actually listens to you." Torin stopped at the foot of the bed.

Isaac slid into the wing-backed chair. "Actually... she doesn't."

*Traitor.* What's worse was they were teaming up against her.

Torin stared at the blanket hiding the book as if a demon might jump out. "It's a demon, and it told you?"

"Yes, it told me its name is Sitaddaru, and it's a Wayfinder demon. It said there is another way to close the gate, and I believe it."

Torin turned to Isaac who was looking like a deer caught in the headlights. "What did it ask her to do in return?"

"It wants Azalea to free it—Sir," Isaac said obediently.

Azalea narrowed her eyes at him. She stood by her previous thought—*traitor.*

Torin rubbed his hands over his face. She could feel him holding back the rage. He might be on the edge of losing it, but she knew she was on the right track. She wasn't going to do anything stupid. All she needed was to ask the Goddess Ereshkigal at her apprentice ceremony tomorrow before she made any decisions.

"We'll talk about this later. Go spend some time with your family, Azalea. Your mum and grandmother are in the greenhouse and could use some help. I'll find you after dinner." Torin left the room and didn't even slam the door.

☽ ☽ ☽ ● ☾ ☾ ☾

Torin stretched and cracked his knuckles. He'd been sitting there for hours, though he wasn't so keen on leaving the sanctuary of the desk he had claimed in the library. But he'd been summoned, and he didn't want to appear ungrateful or uncooperative, so he made his way to the dining room. He dreaded stepping in there, but it would be rude to turn down his host.

He couldn't stop thinking about Azalea for two very opposite reasons; one, he wanted to kill her for making plans with a demon, and two, he wanted to be near her all the time, the kiss, the magic, her sleeping in his arms. He raised his mental shields as high as they could go.

An explosion above rattled the window. It also felt wrong to be safe in this fortress estate while outside these walls Echo Magic was killing anyone who used it accidentally, and houses and cities were being destroyed by idiots looting and taking advantage of the chaos, not to mention the damage from the creatures rampaging around. Reports were coming in from all over the world, and he and Azalea had witnessed it firsthand.

Torin locked his jaw, took a deep breath, and slowly walked into the dining room past all the staring eyes.

"You're still here." Mage Skeffington scowled.

Torin didn't stop. "How observant, Mage Skeffington."

Azalea caught his eye with a smile, and he was glad to see she'd saved him a seat. He felt bad about the way he had spoken to her before. He felt bad about everything. He was so hot and cold around her; she must have no idea what to make of him. He could hardly stop thinking about how her skin felt beneath his fingers, her lips crashing into his, the memory of waking up next to her. He wanted more, but he was doing his best to rein it in.

He sat down without speaking. They shouldn't be here having dinner. They should all be working on solutions, on getting more people to safety. But he wasn't in a position to make waves.

Plates of food were already on the table, and people were quietly eating their small rations of potatoes, carrots, peas, and chicken.

Azalea sat unusually still. He could feel she wasn't mad at him, just worried and a little scared, which was the last thing he wanted. Hating him would be better than being scared. He had to do better. "How was the greenhouse?"

A burst of relief flowed from her. "It was wonderful. The cucumbers and tomatoes are nearly hitting the roof, and there are pumpkins growing all over the floor. Me and Isaac helped dig up these potatoes." She smiled, but there was exhaustion behind her eyes.

"Good. That sounds good." He swallowed. He wanted to reach over and touch her arm or run his hand along her thigh—something to show he hadn't forgotten last night. But he didn't. He couldn't risk anyone seeing, and he wasn't confident his hand wouldn't glow.

A flutter of warmth flowed into him from her. His mental guards must have fallen for a moment. She gave him a different kind of smile, one she probably shouldn't use at the dinner table as her hand skimmed over his thigh and rested on his leg.

He looked back at his plate quickly, but across the table, he saw Azalea's friend Isaac watching them until Van pulled his attention away.

Fabian marched into the room with a teenager in tow, young, maybe around fourteen, Torin guessed. She was a solemn-looking girl with brown skin, near-black shoulder-length hair, and clever eyes. She studied every face as she entered the room.

"Everyone, this is my ward, Cassie. Sorry we're late." Fabian squeezed her shoulder and left her at the end of the room before taking his seat.

Torin felt a spark of confusion from Azalea, and she pulled her hand away. Clearly, she hadn't known he had a ward either. It wasn't uncommon for heads of Houses to have wards. It was just Fabian didn't exactly seem the type.

Cassie seemed perfectly at home and greeted several of the mages, including Danni, before sitting down next to one of Danni's twins. Mrs. Yates came in with the last two plates and spotted Cassie.

"You're safe my love!" Mrs. Yates set down the plates and squeezed the poor girl half to death.

"Of course, I'm safe, Mum. I did what you said, and Fabian brought me back through the Hollow."

*Mum,* so that made sense. She might be Fabian's ward, but she had a family. That was good.

"Dig in, everyone," Rowena said before she took her seat at the end on the side of Fabian.

Mrs. Yates looked up and mouthed *thank you* across the table to Fabian with her hand on her heart.

Torin ignored the chatter around him and cut his potatoes into neat quarters, wondering how the girl fit into this strange house and where she had come from. Mrs. Yates was too old to be her biological mother, and they didn't look in any way related.

Azalea moved her plate next to his and shoved all her carrots onto his. He didn't think twice about scooping all his peas onto hers. They always did that with the ready-made microwave roasts they had at home. *Home.* He wondered if he would see all his books again.

He went to take a bite of potato but was put off by Van and Isaac staring at him and Azalea. Not just them, but Jade and Fabian, too.

"Your friends and uncle are staring at us," he muttered under his breath.

She glanced up, and they quickly looked away in very obviously different directions. Fabian continued to stare with narrowed eyes.

"You'd think people had better things to do. Just ignore them," she whispered.

"They know something is up with us. They aren't stupid," Torin spoke low so no one could listen in. He especially didn't want Azalea's mum to hear on the other side of her.

"You're paranoid. All I did was give you my carrots. Van knows I hate carrots; so does Isaac."

Torin pushed his carrots around the plate. "And now they know that I know you hate carrots."

She nudged his elbow. "They also know we've lived in your tower together for these past weeks. You're reading into this too much."

Maybe she was right. He was overly paranoid.

Fabian stared at Azalea from his end of the table. "I heard you left the estate today. I thought it would be obvious you are not to leave."

"Yes, and I'm back now. You left, too." She smiled at him which only seemed to piss him off more.

Fabian slammed his hand on the table. "No one is to leave the estate without my permission. Is that clear?"

"Crystal," Azalea said without looking up from her food.

The rest of the meal consisted of Fabian and Danni yelling at each other from opposite ends of the table about the letter from the House of Ravens. Fabian wanted to hand Torin over to them, and Danni wanted to find a way to get everyone out of the Tower of London. At least neither wanted to give in to Torin's father's demands.

Torin remained silent, and no one asked his opinion.

As soon as he had finished eating, he picked up his plate to take to the kitchen and pushed his chair back. The room went silent. He hated that these people watched him like he was about to murder them all.

"Thank you for the meal. I will attempt to visit the Desert of Dreams shortly to get some answers. I will update you on my progress in the morning," he said, feeling overly formal. But keeping things business-like here might be the only way he'd survive this place.

Danni got up as he passed her at the end of the table and hugged him. "Night, Torin. Good luck."

"Thanks, Danni. Maiken will be back before you know it." The twins on either side of her chair grinned at him, and he couldn't help but smile.

"Nighty night, Torin," Zoe and Ava said in unison as Danni sat back down.

"Night, girls." Torin turned but didn't miss the disapproving stares around the table aimed at Danni. Not only from Fabian but from the other council mages.

He left the room quickly, hoping Azalea wouldn't follow him. As a rule, people didn't share dreams, so it would look like she either wanted to do that or sleep with him. Both would send Fabian off the deep end.

No doubt she would appear in his room soon enough, he could feel her scheming.

# Chapter 7

Azalea knocked on the door thirty minutes later, just as Torin got out of the shower. He threw on his jeans and a black t-shirt. He opened the door and glanced down the stairs before pulling her inside before someone noticed. She carried her backpack and wore gray yoga tights and a black t-shirt, which might have been his because it was so baggy on her. Her long brown hair was loose, and he fought the urge to run his fingers through it, unsure where the line between them was anymore.

"You waited for me?" She was nervous and was doing her best to shield her emotions from him, but he could still feel them.

"You're moving in now?" he teased, nodding at her bag.

"I just didn't want to leave my stuff in my room." She remained in front of the closed door.

He took her bag and set it on the chair. "What if someone comes looking for you?"

"I told them I'm going to bed early, that I want to have a good sleep before my apprentice ceremony."

He leaned on the armrest of the chair. "Which is what you should be doing."

"I can't let you go alone. I need to help fix this." She stepped closer to him.

He didn't move. "If it stops all your ideas about releasing demons, then you're more than welcome to come get some real answers."

She twisted her mouth to the side. She was doing a good job of not blurting out what she wanted to say. He could feel her holding it in and could only guess it was along the lines of her being right about the demon—the Shadow Atlas.

"What if someone goes to your room?" he asked.

"I told Jade she could sleep in there and I'd be sleeping in my mum's room. She'll lock the door. Isaac and Van wanted some privacy tonight." She pointed behind her.

Just what he needed, more of her friends close by. "So you assumed it would be okay to sleep here?"

"Yes, it's no different to the other times we've done this." She grinned at him.

He pushed off the chair and stepped toward her. "It's very different because before your family and a council of mages weren't downstairs. It's different because there were lines we didn't cross. This makes it very easy for—"

"Slip-ups?" She stepped even closer to him.

He didn't move. "Yes."

"I'm sure we can both be mature about this and keep our hands to ourselves." She ran a hand through her long hair sending the scent of rose petals into the air.

"Yes, I'm sure we can." Torin swallowed and reached out. Their fingers twined together, pulsing with her rapid heartbeat that he now held in his palm. He didn't react, though the hand of death called to him, he was in control.

He looked down at their hands. They didn't glow, just hummed with pleasant warmth as their magic combined. It felt so natural. "The bond seems stable. Let's not tempt it for now."

Sensing her desire, he closed the gap between them without thinking. Suddenly his hand was on her chin, tilting it toward him. "This is going to be harder than I thought," he mumbled.

"Sorry." She grinned and leaned into his palm, then pulled him down to kiss her. He did so hungrily, knowing they should stop. She pulled away, grinning as she spun around, and stared out the window.

He let out a breath and focused on the sky outside to calm down. The sun had set, but the sky still glowed deep red with streaks of green.

"So, I guess we should go to sleep then." She walked over to the bed and slid into the sheets.

He locked the door and switched off the light, throwing the room into an eerie red glow.

"Sorry, that made the room creepier." He held his hands behind his back.

"It's fine. I'm so tired I could fall asleep in broad daylight right now." She yawned, clearly trying to ease the tension building between them.

Maybe they should focus on their mission right now. "Same here."

He got into bed, keeping a safe distance clear between them. It was the same as the other times they had slept side by side to travel to the Great Desert of Dreams, but it was also so very different.

"Stop worrying so much, Torin. We'll never go to sleep." Azalea threw her hands to her sides.

He exhaled loudly. "I'm finding it very hard to keep my hands to myself. I'm not sure if this was the best idea."

"Same here." She shuffled around again, and his blankets moved.

Torin's breath hitched as her fingers trailed across his chest leaving tiny sparks of magic in their wake. He could feel the warmth of her body as she pressed into his side.

"That isn't helping." He growled and rolled over, so their faces were just inches apart, and somehow his hand found its way to her hip.

"Maybe we just allow ourselves a bit of fun before we go to sleep. It will help," Azalea said as her lips lazily met his.

His hand slipped around her waist and pulled her against him as he kissed her back. "I'm sure it will help us sleep. Just a little fun without going too far. We can do that."

"Exactly my thoughts." She smiled into his lips.

) ) ) ● ( ( (

Desert sands swirled around him, and the heat of two suns beat down, causing his skin to shimmer with a golden tint in this subconscious dream world.

"You should be a god here, Torin. Have I ever told you how hot you are?" Azalea giggled as she swirled around, her silky blue dress flowing around her like mercury.

"Focus, Azalea." He'd have to teach her some lucid dreaming skills at some point so she could filter her thoughts.

Her hands slid around his waist. "Maybe we should continue what we started before we went to sleep." She pulled him into an electrifying kiss.

They moved in synchrony as he was pulled into the intensity of her feelings and the urge for more. Her teeth scraped his bottom lip, and he couldn't have untangled himself even if he'd wanted to.

"This is why I like mortals and their dreams," a voice boomed behind him.

Torin spun around with Azalea clinging to him. Zakar, the god of dreams, stood there with his arms crossed and a wide smile spread across his great, bearded face. Behind him, his sandy dragon eased itself down to sit like a sphinx.

"So much passion." He chuckled.

"We came here to ask for your guidance." Torin untangled himself from Azalea but took her hand when she held it out to him.

"I watch the dreams. I see the turmoil in the mortal realm. Blood red skies, the sorrow of lost mages, creatures of the Echo roaming the lands. A bridge between worlds." Zakar turned serious.

Torin nodded. "Do you know the way to close the bridge?"

"I know many things. This is one, yes."

"Can you tell us please?" Azalea asked.

Torin squeezed her hand. A reminder to think before she spoke. Clearly, both of their judgments were impaired here, and he should know better, but he didn't want her getting on the wrong side of Zakar.

"If you do something for me." The great god folded his arms.

"I will be happy to pay whatever price you ask," Torin said.

"Hypocrite," Azalea whispered under her breath, and Torin clamped his hand over her mouth.

She pulled it away, grinning. "What? You had a go at me for making deals with gods."

Zakar chuckled once more. "She has fire. And she is not wrong. You are right to be wary of making deals with gods. But it is what you will need to do to fulfill your quest. And what I ask is a small price, dreamweaver."

"What is it?"

"I choose to be here in my realm, but I do not see all. Only the unreliable fragments of dreams. I see what is happening in all dimensions, yet I do not see the truth."

"You want to see my memories." A pleasant surprise and an easy price to pay.

Azalea hit his arm. "No! We've had people do that before. You can't do that to him!"

"It's okay, Azalea." Torin ran a hand over her arm.

She stood in front of him protectively.

"Like a tiny dragon protecting her mate." Zakar tilted his head, studying her for a moment, then stepped forward. "You have nothing to fear, little dragon. I will not hurt him."

"It's okay, Azalea. It's different magic than the Archmage's." Torin put his arm around her shoulder and guided her back to his side.

She nibbled her lip. "You're sure about this?"

Torin nodded and faced the god. "You may see my memories."

"Not just your memories today. I will watch your journey. I will see my brothers and sisters in their homes. This is the gift you will give me, and I will call on you in your dreams."

An uneasiness settled over Torin. It was never simple with gods, but this would get them what they needed. A small price to pay.

Torin nodded once more. Without hesitation, Zakar stepped right up to them, his hulking frame towering over them both. He kneeled to the ground at eye level and placed his hands on either side of Torin's head.

Torin tried to keep his breathing calm, but the grip around his head was like a vise. He squeezed his eyes closed and concentrated on the softness of Azalea's palm in his.

"It is done." Zakar rocked back on his heels and stood up to his full height.

Torin hadn't felt a thing or seen a single memory of what the god had taken.

"You saw everything?"

"I saw all that you see." He threw back his head and laughed. "You two are more like dragons than I thought, protective of one another, fighters, willing to take the highest risks. You are right for this task."

"But you saw what's happening in our world? The destruction the Echo gate will cause?" Torin asked.

"I miss the wars of mortals. My time on earth was spent with battles between kings and cities."

This was all a game to the gods. A speck in time to Zakar. Whatever he was doing to help them was for his entertainment, not because he wanted to help.

"How do we close the gate? Is it possible to speak to Enki or Enlil in here?" Torin got straight to the point. He didn't want Zakar to get bored after he already got what he wanted.

He could feel Azalea. She was using all her willpower to restrain herself from talking. Him making that deal had scared her more than she would ever admit.

Zakar ran a hand over his thick beard. "Rowena Sharp was correct. You must travel to the Echo Dimension to speak directly to the great gods. They will not attend my realm, and they are the only ones who have the power to close the gate from their side."

"From their side? Can someone close it from ours?" Azalea asked.

"Yes. It must be sealed from both sides simultaneously."

"And they will know how?" Torin asked.

"They will know how. But they will not share without a price. Some gods do not care for your world."

That much was becoming clear. The gods had forsaken their world long ago.

"What can we offer them?" Torin asked.

"Knowledge."

"I'm pretty sure we don't have any knowledge that the gods don't already have." Azalea snorted, then whispered. "Sorry."

Zakar stared off into the distance. "But I do. They have lost the Scribe. You will tell them you can find him and return him."

"Who is the scribe? Can we actually find him, or is it a trick?" Azalea asked.

"There is no tricking the gods. The Scribe is named Nabu, he is the grandson of Enki, and you will find him in your realm. It is the price."

Torin did not like where this was going. Nabu was a god in his own right, a minor god compared to Enki, and if he was missing, it was because he wanted to be. "Where is he?"

"From what I see in the Scribes' dreams, he has left the land of gods and traveled to the mortal world on the Mushussu dragon."

Just what they needed, an amoral god loose in their world.

"I thought gods were forbidden from leaving their realms?" Azalea asked.

Zakar nodded. "They are. Nabu has broken the creed and offended many by his betrayal."

"A god is in our world." Azalea's hands went to her mouth. "Why is he there?"

Zakar held her gaze with his blazing golden eyes. To Azalea's credit, she didn't look away. "He is the Scribe. The Land of Light has been much unchanged for thousands of years. In his dreams, I see his eyes have been opened to the new world. He is doing what he was made to do: record history."

"So he isn't dangerous?" Azalea asked.

"I did not say that. If you can agree to return Nabu, Enki will agree to close the gate once more."

Torin could feel his magic straining. They had already been in this dream too long. "How do we enter the gate safely?"

"I have taken much of your power. I forget the weakness of mortals. I will be brief. For each person, make an amulet of alexandrite, rosemary, and clay powder. This will balance your magic."

"And when we are inside?"

"You will arrive in the Land of Light and travel to the great sea palace of Enki, the Palace of the Waters."

Relief washed over Torin's dream body. They had a plan. All he had to do was convince a god that he could find a lost god in his world. How hard could that be? He grinned at Azalea, his body heavy with sleep, barely clinging to the dream world.

"Thank you for showing us the way."

"I will send you back now, or you will not retain this information. I will set a clear memory in each of your minds to wake up with." He clapped his hands, and the world went dark.

⟩⟩●⟨⟨

Torin woke with a start. *Amulet of alexandrite, rosemary, and dried clay. Amulet of alexandrite...*

He switched on the lamp and reached for his notebook on the side of the bed. The mattress shifted as Azalea did the same thing on the other side.

He wrote as fast as he could. Then continued to write everything he remembered from the dream, feeling it slip away with every second. He had been trained in memory recall as strongly as his dreamweaving and knew these moments were crucial.

He let out a breath and put down his pen.

Azalea had her knees up with a notebook leaning on them, frowning at the page.

"Did you get it?" she asked.

"I think so. Let's compare notes."

They swapped notepads. He was hyper-aware of Azalea's presence. "We remembered perfectly." He leaned over and, as if he'd been doing it all his life, brushed his lips across hers.

She sighed, then wrapped her arms around him filling every inch of him with warmth. "Thank the gods for that. You did it, Torin. You found a way!"

She released him and fell back on the bed with notable relief.

"You don't need to sound so amazed." He switched off the lamp and grinned to himself in the semi-darkness as he slid back under the covers and she snuggled into his chest. According to his watch, it had just turned midnight.

"You need to get some real sleep if you have any chance of surviving your apprentice ceremony tomorrow. Dreamweaving doesn't count as real sleep."

"I know. At least we have a plan now. Night, Torin," she mumbled already sounding half asleep.

"Night, Azalea." His arm fell over her, and he pulled her in close as if they'd slept this way a thousand times before.

As she drifted off, he got the distinct feeling she was keeping something from him. Whatever it was, she couldn't hide it for long. Not from him.

# Chapter 8

Fabian paced the length of the library. Kat had messaged as soon as phone service was restored. It was well past midnight, and she should have been here by now.

He needed to know what Korbyn Dumont was planning. He'd thought the money troubles were bad, but having the responsibility of this many lives under his roof was much worse. He wasn't his brother; he wasn't made for running the show. He just hoped he wouldn't let them all down. Once this was all over, maybe he would do something good in the world, like getting all these mythical animals somewhere where they could be safe.

The hand-held radio on the table crackled to life. Thank the gods the electronics were functioning again.

"Guest has arrived. Heading to the main house. Over," the volunteer gates-man said.

"Tell her she's late." No response. At least she was here. The uneasy churning in his stomach stopped.

After a great deal more pacing, Kat strode into the library. She was dressed in the usual House of Ravens black tactical uniform, her hair in a tight black braid that bounced off her shoulder, her hand rested on the hilt of the elemer tucked into her belt.

"Kitty Kat, sit down. Tell me it's good news." Fabian gestured to a comfy armchair.

"Of course it isn't." She ignored his gesture. Instead, she worked her way around the large table studying their notes and open research books.

Of course, it wasn't. "Spit it out then."

"You got Korbyn's letter?" Her face was unreadable, as always.

Fabian picked up a book and pretended to study it. "Yes. We will not be responding."

"It's not a joke, Fabian. You need to respond somehow and have a plan. He wants Torin, and he wants the Tower residents to come back. He expects everyone to fold to his new rule over the council."

"He can have Torin." He shut the book again.

Kat's brow furrowed very slightly. "This is serious, Fabian. We both know you need Torin here. He's the one who can fix this mess. You need him on your side."

"I don't." Fabian slammed the book onto the table. He wished the blasted man would just disappear. "After he communes with his god tonight, we will have a plan, and me and you will go to the Echo Dimension. I do not need him."

Kat leaned on the table. "*I* need him. Having him on our side is the entirety of my plan to save the House of Ravens."

Fabian leaned in from the other side of the table. "You're wasting your time; your House can't be saved. Korbyn will kill you when he so much as hears a whisper of your simmering rebellion."

"It's worth the risk. Torin is the key to everything. Why can't you admit that and get over yourself?" Kat threw a hand in the air.

Fabian shook his head. "All you see is Torin as the child he was—your student. But he's a grown man and a murderer who has my niece wrapped around his little finger."

"You're so blinded by hatred that you can't see what's right in front of you." She closed her eyes and shook her head slowly.

"What'd you mean by that?"

"Nothing." She slammed her hands onto the table. "Look, I need to talk to Torin. What time did he go to bed?"

"He left right after dinner." Fabian went back to pacing.

Kat turned toward the door. "Good, he'll be done in the Desert of Dreams. Can you show me where his room is?"

"That's why you came here? You don't have any useful news?"

"Korbyn and the Archmage have taken over the High Council. Some of the members escaped, but the remaining ones would be wise to go along with him if they know what's good for them."

"He's not getting anyone from here. What will he do then?" Fabian gritted his teeth.

She shook her head. "I don't know. He hasn't informed any of us about his plans, but I will keep you updated."

"What about news from outside?"

Kat twisted her mouth. "The world knows about magic for the first time in history. How do you think they're reacting?"

"I assume they've come up with some nice new conspiracy theories."

"Yes, of course they have. But other than that, there's looting in every city, people are going crazy. There are mythical creatures on the loose, towns burned down, there are hundreds of mages dead from burnout around the world." She shook her head.

"We can fix it. The world always bounces back."

"We'll see. Can you take me to Torin, or do I have to wake everyone up finding him myself?"

Fabian scowled, wishing he'd given Torin a room out in the camp, but Rowena wouldn't hear of it. "Fine, come on then."

# Chapter 9

Torin was already awake when the knock sounded at his door. He glanced at Azalea. She was sound asleep, her face resting on her pillow, her hair flowing all around her like a painting.

He shrugged on the dressing gown he'd found in the room, crept toward the door, elemer in hand, and opened it a crack.

"I need to talk to you." Mage Emerson lurked like a wraith on the dimly lit, narrow landing at the top of the stairs as another set of footsteps moved away.

Torin cleared his throat. "Mage Emerson. Is everything okay?"

"It's fine. Call me Kat, Torin, I'm not your trainer anymore."

"Right, sorry—" he glanced over his shoulder "—Kat."

"Can I come in?"

"Um, no." He closed the door behind him, so they were on the landing. He froze as Fabian stepped off the bottom stair and sauntered away. That was lucky.

"And why not?" She used her forceful trainer voice. Memories of early mornings trudging through muddy fields while trying to fend off Kat's Shadow Magic attacks came flooding back. Kat was never unfair to his squad—Kira, Conner, Matt, and Dev—not like his father and other trainers were, but that didn't make her any less terrifying.

He glanced down the stairs. "It would be a lot better for both of us if you didn't know."

"I see." She let a near-silent huff out of her nostrils.

Great, he was back to letting her down. "What did you want to talk to me about?"

"Did you visit the Desert?" Kat asked.

Torin forced himself to stand straight. "Yes."

"Is it feasible to travel to the Echo Dimension? Which gods did you speak with?"

"I spoke with Zakar. He told me how to do it, but I need something from you." As much as he wanted to trust Kat, the reality was he didn't know her anymore. He didn't want to go to the Echo Dimension alone with Fabian, but he needed to ensure she was on his side.

"What is it?" she asked.

"The sword in my father's office." He didn't need it for the trip, but if he didn't make it back, it would protect Azalea from spirits. She could use it to fulfill her quota to Ereshkigal, Goddess of the Shadow Dimension, without dying in the process—he hoped.

But he wasn't about to tell Mage Emerson that this was a test for her.

"What do you need it for? It's silver, not even a functional blade." Her hands rested on her hips.

"Zakar said I needed it."

She nodded along. "I can go tonight. Your father remains at the Tower of London. No one will question me entering the Rook. Kira and I will bring it tomorrow."

"Kira?" A coldness shot through his chest. She was coming here.

"Yes, I've gotten us out of the Tower on patrols for the next few weeks. We will attend Azalea's ceremony. I want people here to know what side we're on before the shit hits the fan."

Torin swallowed. No way he would ever get back to sleep. It had been eight years. Eight years of wondering if Kira was dead or alive. Eight years of dark thoughts, believing he had killed her. Eight years planning what he would say to her if he ever found her. Now his mind was blank.

"Does she hate me?" he asked.

Kat didn't meet his eyes. "It was a long time ago, Torin. Time to put the past to rest."

*She hates me.* Maybe it was better to get it over with. Knowing she hated him might make it easier, make it hurt less.

He nodded.

"I'll return with the sword." She turned and descended the stairs like a cat, silent and deadly.

) ) ) ● ( ( (

After sleeping well past breakfast, Torin marched into the library with all the confidence he could muster. Eyes darted toward him—Fabian, Rowena, Mergen, Mage Skeffington, Danni, and Azalea's mum—all of them gathered on the same side of the large table.

He cleared his throat. "There is a way to go to the Echo Dimension." He stopped on the opposite side of the table. They had been studying some old-looking maps.

Rowena smiled like a proud mother. "I knew you could do it! Well then, what did they say? Who did you speak with?" She looked young enough to be Azalea's mum with the same long brown hair and tall, thin build, though Rowena had a decidedly more positive attitude than Azalea.

Danni smiled. He was glad she had his back. Fabian and Skeffington looked at him with pure hatred while Leda looked conflicted.

Torin stood next to the table. "I spoke with Zakar—"

Fabian cut him off. "I suppose it's as simple as us walking in and telling old Enki or Enlil '*we'll be wanting the gate closed. Thanks, mate.*'"

"He doesn't need your sarcasm on top of everything else," Rowena scolded.

"If you would keep your comments to yourself, I can explain." Torin's blood boiled beneath his skin.

Fabian had the same pissed-off look Azalea often had. At least he didn't have to feel it from Fabian as well.

"Get on with it, then." Fabian took out his anger on a piece of paper, scrunching it up and tossing it violently into the fire.

Torin took the high road and explained what Zakar had told them about the amulets they needed to make, plus the more impossible task of finding Nabu once they'd made a deal with Enki.

"The amulet protects you from Echo Magic? May I see the instructions?" Rowena asked.

Torin handed her the note Azalea wrote after the dream. Her eyebrow raised as she read it, but if she noticed it was Azalea's handwriting, she didn't mention it. She passed the recipe to Leda.

"Yes, we can make this." Leda narrowed her eyes at Torin. She recognized the writing for sure. Maybe it was best to leave before any more questions arose.

"It's all well and good having amulets, but you think the gods are going to agree to this and close the gate?" Fabian asked.

He was sure Fabian was objecting simply because it was Torin who put forward the idea.

"Yes," Torin answered.

Fabian leaned on the table, glaring at Torin. Torin held his gaze and bit his tongue before they got into an argument.

"This isn't helping anyone." Danni clapped her hands in front of them. "Please be civil or you two will never make it back alive, and I promise to kill whichever one of you comes back alone."

"Lovely idea," Rowena said without missing a beat. "I'm sure they will be the best of friends before we know it."

Azalea rushed into the room. Torin felt her restraint not to run over to the table in a panic.

"Sorry to interrupt, but I need Torin... Mage Dumont, to help me prepare for my apprentice ceremony if that's alright."

Rowena's eyes sparkled like she knew something, and he was sure she did. "Certainly, my love. He's just been filling us in on his trip to the Desert of Dreams. I'm sure he'll tell you all about it."

Azalea shuffled her feet. "Um, yes. I'd be interested to hear about it... but we should be off now. You know, lots to prepare for. Torin?"

"I'm free now." Torin stood straight, not sure where to put his hands.

He stood an obvious several feet away from Azalea as they walked out.

"Go practice in the stables," Fabian yelled after them.

⟨moon phases⟩

The fenced area outside the stables was full of mages training in Shadow Magic like hers. Shadows shot past her, crashing into the bail targets as whips, ropes, darts, and solid balls of shadows.

Azalea leaned on the fence, mesmerized by them. "Why didn't my uncle send me to train with these people?" She couldn't help but wonder and felt once again like an outsider.

Torin rested his elbows on the fence next to her, careful not to let their arms touch. "Ouch."

"Sorry... I didn't mean I don't want to train with you." But she saw Torin was smiling and relaxed.

Torin pushed off the fence. "I know what you mean. It was probably because you had plant magic, and he wanted to give you a chance at fitting in with the wider magical community. I suspect your grandmother had something to do with that, too."

Azalea followed him as they headed toward the entrance to the stables. "Or maybe he pissed all of these people off too, and he didn't have any favors left."

"Also possible. You can ask him later." Torin shrugged.

Azalea maintained a respectable distance as they neared the large barn doors. "If you haven't noticed, he isn't exactly on speaking terms with me either."

"Just give him time. For now, let's get started." Torin rubbed his hands together.

"In front of all these people?" Panic shot right through her, tightening her chest. What if they accidentally used their shared magic?

"Calm down." Torin reached for her but must have thought better and pulled back. "We're just practicing meditation. I can't have you using all your strength before the ceremony."

She let out a breath. "Okay, good. Sorry, I'm just a little on edge."

"I know."

She blushed. Of course, he could feel it. She sucked at shielding her emotions.

"I am too," he said kindly. "Come on."

The chill in the air dissipated as they stepped through the open double barn doors.

It smelled of fresh hay and earth with a faint horsey-ness to it, though there were no horses in either row of stables.

She peeked into the first stall to find it clean with a thin layer of straw, Fabian must have at least one horse around somewhere. "How about in here?"

"As good as anywhere." Torin darted off and came back with a thick blanket, maybe from a horse, she wasn't sure, but he set it down over the prickly straw.

Before they started, Torin went over some basics for lucid dreaming. It sounded a little hopeless as the techniques were usually mastered over a long period. Still, it was better to have something. She learned how to ground herself in a dream and to do reality checks while she was awake so she could always discern what was a dream.

Afterward, Azalea fell into a deep meditation, still aware of Torin's presence, but fully focused on her breathing and heartbeat. After the chaos of the days before, it was like taking a mini holiday away from everything.

"Azalea." Torin's whisper broke through her spell.

She opened her eyes and let out a slow breath. Everything felt better already. "How long has it been?"

"Just over an hour." He stretched, looking far more relaxed.

For the first time, she wanted to continue meditating. "An hour. It went too fast."

"See, you can block your emotions when you want to."

"I wasn't blocking them. I just wasn't feeling them. It was nice." She sighed as reality rushed back to her. She hadn't felt anything from Torin that whole time, either. It was refreshing.

"Do you feel ready for the ceremony tonight?" His eyes grew dark and serious.

She nibbled her lip. "I just have to take the elixir?"

He nodded, then unfolded his legs and leaned against the hay bale behind him. "Yes, it will be similar to when you received the mark of the gods. Your tattoo will grow again if you pass the ceremony."

"And if I don't?" She scooted closer to him. His hand fell to her thigh so naturally, and she leaned into his side.

"You will. Just be careful what you say to Ereshkigal. Do not offend her." He nudged her with his shoulder.

She had no plans to. But she would be asking a few questions.

"I can feel you scheming, Azalea. Just tell me what it is before you do anything stupid."

"It's not stupid. I'm just going to ask her about the Echo Dimension gate. She might be able to help us," she said honestly.

"And you're going to ask her about the Shadow Atlas, aren't you?"

Dammit, she really couldn't hide anything from him anymore. Stupid bond. "I'm going to ask her about our bond. I know we already made a deal with Damu to provide all the spirits. But I might as well ask her while I have the chance, cut out the middleman."

Torin rubbed his face, and she felt a spark of frustration. She knew he wanted to go with her, but fortunately for her, it wasn't possible. Ereshkigal was the key to fixing all their problems.

"Stop worrying about me." She tilted her head to the side, listening. "I think we're alone." All the combat noises from outside were gone.

Torin looked a little scared. "It's not good for us to be alone together."

She jumped up with an idea. "Or is it very good? We can test our new magic. You said we need to know what we can do. For you know... safety."

"I said that?" He raised a questioning eyebrow.

"Sure." She wasn't sure he'd said that, but either way, they needed to test the magic before it outed them in public. Using it on the giant flying cat seemed to have gone well enough.

He got up, his footsteps echoing as he walked the length of the stable. She dusted stray hay off her jeans.

"You're right, it's all clear." Torin appeared at the stall entrance.

She bounced on her feet. "So, how do we do it?"

"Come here." He held his hand out.

She nervously stepped forward and took it. He led her into the central aisle and stopped, his magic coursing into her hand so fast she gripped his harder to hold on.

"Like we did with the Archmage and the tiger." His pulse galloped at the same pace as hers, and somehow she could feel both their hearts racing.

They stood side by side and lifted their free hands, facing them toward the back wall of hay bales. Their joined power, stronger than anything she'd felt before, pooled in her stomach eager to be set free.

"It's strong." She gritted her teeth.

He squeezed her hand tighter. "Just try to restrain it. We'll let it out in a quick burst, gentle, though."

"Kay, let's do it. I can't hold on much longer."

"Three, two, one."

The magic surged from her belly in a tsunami that blasted out of her hand as a blazing white light along with Torin's. They hit the stacked hay bales. Straw exploded in all directions, bombarding them with hundreds of tiny pinpricks.

Azalea squealed and closed her eyes as Torin pulled her into his chest. They had done it—well, done something, and it was semi-controlled. She stayed leaning against Torin's chest long after the hay stopped falling around them. His arms wrapped around her in a temporary cocoon of warmth and safety.

She wanted to tell him she didn't want him to leave. But she knew saying it wouldn't help, and they both had to go. She needed to fix things her way—a way he wouldn't approve of.

"What the hell was that?" Jade's distinct New Zealand accent sounded from the barn door.

In full defense mode, Torin whipped around, pulling Azalea with him, nearly ripping her arm out of her socket, and blasted the white light right at Jade. Magic rose in Azalea's belly, but she forced her arm down.

The light bounced off Jade and shot back at Torin. His hand slipped, and Azalea was thrown back into a stall wall, hard enough to crack the old wood as she landed.

Azalea scrambled up. "Jade! Are you okay?" she yelled, then relaxed as Jade gave a thumbs up and hauled herself off the earth floor. But Torin hadn't moved.

He stood like a statue, his eyes blank and unseeing, all white like Jade's sometimes went.

Azalea moved toward him as an icy shiver crawled down her spine. She couldn't feel anything from him. Not a single emotion.

She shook his arm. "Something's wrong."

"He's in a trance." Jade came over, brushing dirt off her sleeves.

Azalea studied him closely. "He looks like you when you have a vision."

"*A great journey led by Sitaddaru for the daughter of the Snake and Bee,*" Torin spoke in a low voice that wasn't his own, hollow and eerie.

Azalea didn't dare touch him as he continued but was glad when Jade caught her hand and gave it a comforting squeeze.

"*Beyond the shadows, she will travel. Three companions. Two of darkness, one of mortal blood. The daughter of the Snake and Bee will return from the shadows.*"

He squeezed his eyes, began blinking rapidly, then collapsed.

Azalea and Jade moved like lightning and caught him before he hit the ground.

"Was that a prophecy?" Jade checked Torin's pulse on his neck.

"I think so?" It most certainly was. And it was about her and better yet, it confirmed she would be going to the Shadow Dimension and would make it back. That took a whole lot of decision-making and worry off her mind. Setting the Shadow Atlas free was the right path forward.

"You know what it means, don't you?" Jade stared at her.

Azalea nodded and chewed her lip. There was no point in lying about it now. Jade had seen everything. "Don't tell Torin what he said."

Jade frowned, but Torin groaned and came to before she could ask anything more.

"What happened?" He rubbed his temples.

"You blasted Jade, but I think it was weak because you tried to stop last minute, and it bounced back and hit you. Oh, and you might have had some sort of prophecy vision or something."

Torin sat down on a nearby crate. "That's not possible."

"It kind of seems possible." Jade glanced at Azalea.

"What did I say?" Torin looked up at them.

"Um, you know. Something vague about traveling beyond this dimension with two companions..." Azalea didn't look him in the eye.

If he noticed Azalea was lying, he didn't show it. In fact, his face lit up.

Jade looked up at the ceiling as if it were the most interesting ceiling in the world, despite it just being old beams and spider webs.

It was a white lie that would help him; therefore it was okay. That's what Azalea told herself, anyway.

"I saw what you were doing when I came in here," Jade said bluntly.

"What, hugging?" Azalea took an extra step away from Torin.

"Yes, and hay raining down like the barn exploded." She picked a large piece from Azalea's hair.

"Yes, about that—" Torin answered a little too slowly.

At this rate, they wouldn't be able to keep their magic and whatever their relationship was a secret for more than one day.

Jade eyed them suspiciously. "I saw the light come out of your hands. *Both* your hands."

"So. The thing is..." Azalea wasn't sure where to go from there.

"We aren't exactly sure ourselves, so we would appreciate it if you didn't say anything to anyone about it," Torin answered, dusting hay off his head.

Jade rested a hand on her hip. "It looked like you were sharing magic. Were you?"

"Technically. Yes." Torin brushed the hay off his shoulders.

Azalea's eyes nearly popped out of her head. He just admitted it. That was the last thing she expected.

"We don't know what we're doing." Azalea picked some hay off Torin's shoulder that he'd missed.

"I can see that, and I don't want to know anymore right now in case anyone asks me. So I'm just going to go..." Jade spun on her heels and dashed off.

"Can we trust her?" Torin crossed his arms.

"I think so." Azalea nibbled her lip, staring out the door after Jade. She hoped so.

# Chapter 10

As the sun set, the sky turned a deeper red, and fewer creatures flew above. Perhaps they had spread across the world. The thought only added to Azalea's guilt. *It's fine, soon everything will be fixed.* She had to keep telling herself that.

She focused on the path ahead as Faraday trailed behind her. Torin walked next to her, so close the back of their hands brushed against each other, sending tiny jolts through her. She didn't attempt to make space between them, and neither did he. Though she did glance down to check their hands weren't glowing. All clear.

They walked down stone stairs surrounded by lines of lit candles. "This is weird," she whispered, wondering how anyone had found the time to decorate for this ceremony on such short notice, but she suspected Van had a hand in it.

"You'll be fine," Torin whispered under his breath.

Her legs shook with each step she took toward the walled garden. Headstones from the neighboring cemetery peeked over the stone wall, backlit by the eerie red sky.

She might have felt like she was going to a funeral if not for her borrowed black, strapless dress. The skirt that flared out made her feel more like a Gothic bride attending her wedding in a graveyard. She fidgeted with the corset top, hoping to make it a little more comfortable and to cover more of the moon tattoo over her left breast, but to no avail. Hopefully, no one would recognize a soul bond mark.

A chilly wind blew, and she was glad she'd thrown a dark gray wool coat over her dress. She would have to show off her tattoos after the ceremony, but at least until then, she would be warm.

She glanced at Torin. The charcoal gray suit he wore could have been tailored just for him. The dark blue tie that she'd found in the attic completed the suit and matched the color of the galaxy tattoo behind the raven on his arm. "You look amazing," she whispered.

His gaze roved over her, and he dropped his mask for an instant. "So do you."

The smell of wood smoke permeated the air as they made their way under the stone arch covered in the skeletons of winter vines. A makeshift stage made of wooden pallets divided the group of witnesses in two. Fire pits and lanterns were scattered around the edge of the crowd and at the corners of the stage, adding to the glow in the darkening night.

Azalea swallowed seeing just how many people were there, it had to be everyone from the camp and the house, though in the shadows of the high garden walls and overhanging oaks it was hard to tell if it was fifty or a hundred people packed into the contained garden.

She smiled and gave a small wave as she passed Danni and the twins, who were standing next to Mrs. and Mr. Yates and the girl, Cassie. In the row behind them were Isaac, Jade, and Van. Isaac gave her a subtle thumbs up, and she returned the gesture, feeling a little better knowing they were all there, though a little weirded out that she would be unconscious while they mingled and drank mulled wine.

As they reached the stage at the end, Azalea stepped up, and Torin remained standing in the front corner where she could still see him. He was doing a better job of blocking his emotions than she was.

She spun around with a swish of her dress to face the crowd.

RoRo and Leda were in the front row. RoRo was beaming with pride, but her mum's smile was false, not reaching her eyes.

Fabian stepped forward, cradling a silver chalice. Jeez, they were putting on a good show for this. A dragon swooped overhead so close it sparked the wards, and everyone ducked at the sound.

"A good omen, I'm sure," Fabian said unconvincingly.

The crowd shared a nervous laugh, and Azalea clutched her elemer handle with both hands in front of her.

"On this night, the sixteenth of February, we gather to witness the apprentice ceremony of Azalea Sharp, Daughter of Samael Blackbourne, previous head of the House of Snakes."

Azalea stood frozen as the crowd clapped. She wanted this over with already.

"I offer Azalea the elixir of the gods. May the shadows protect her always, and may she win the favor of the Goddess. Praise Ereshkigal." Fabian filled the role of ceremony master surprisingly well.

"Praise Ereshkigal." The crowd called back. Some so enthusiastically, she suspected they'd already been into the mulled wine.

Azalea accepted the cup. It was freezing against her ungloved hands, but she focused on remembering what Torin had told her to say. "I accept the elixir of the gods and pledge myself as apprentice to the House of Snakes."

RoRo cheered while her mum celebrated with a more subdued clap. As she brought the cup to her lips, she froze. A wave of fear rushed through her from Torin, and she lowered the cup. Was it poisoned? Should she not drink it?

She looked at him, but it wasn't her he was focused on. His gaze fell on two dark figures at the back who had just arrived. One was Kat, Torin's terrifying teacher, and the other was a gorgeous woman who could only be Kira. Torin's long lost best friend, slash girl-of-his-dreams.

He had his own problems to deal with, and she had hers. She couldn't cope with that right now.

Down the hatch.

She drained the cup, trying not to taste the small amount of dark liquid she'd shot back. Her mouth was burning. Everything went fuzzy.

☽ ☽ ☽ ● ☾ ☾ ☾

Azalea stood in the Desert of Dreams, burning with glorious heat, the same as the night before. But this time she was alone.

Her mouth was dry and her brain foggy as she took in the sights. Usually, she couldn't take her eyes off Torin. This time, it was the immense pyramid that rose out of the marble path. Was it usually that big?

She spun in a circle, trying to gather the warmth of the two suns into her bare arms as if she could take the rays back to winter with her. Her gothic dress was replaced with her silky watery gown that slid through her fingers like it was made of the slipperiest thing on earth—she wasn't sure what that was, and this certainly wasn't Earth.

How long would she have to wait? It wasn't Zakar she was meeting. Ereshkigal had to come from the Shadow Dimension. Or her subconscious did at least. How would she know to come?

Azalea focused on the stream of sand blasting off the sides of the pyramid in perfect lines. Unsure how long she had been there, she had a sudden urge to turn when something in the air shifted.

The dark goddess appeared at the base of the pyramid without announcement.

"You came!" Azalea said with relief and without thinking. She slapped her hand over her mouth. It was so hard to control thoughts in this place.

"I welcome you, daughter of Snakes and Bees. I see you have chosen the correct path." The woman was taller than Azalea remembered, but this time she had glorious ebony wings covered in silken feathers arching over her like the most stunning cosplay outfit ever made. Her deep onyx eyes stared with an intensity that felt like she was drilling into Azalea's soul. Dead-straight hair fell like strands of black, shimmering metal over her striking collarbone, and shadows coiled around her like snakes.

Azalea racked her brain, trying to remember if Torin had told her to say anything particular here. But she was blank, frozen on the spot in either awe or terror, she wasn't sure.

"Speak." Ereshkigal's voice boomed across the desert.

"I wish to become an apprentice," Azalea blurted. But so many questions bubbled up. She wanted answers. But the goddess looked like the type who might smite people for fun. That's what gods did, right, smiting?

Ereshkigal waved her metallic hand, and a small vial appeared in it. "Drink."

This wasn't the sort of place where you checked what was on the label. She threw her head back and downed the liquid that tasted like nothing.

When she finished, Ereshkigal was gone. Azalea spun around to find Isaac standing there.

"Isaac. What are you doing here? How did you get in?" She ran towards him, but he held his hand up, and she skidded to a stop.

"Why do you always lie to me?" he asked, his eyes pleading with her.

Wondering who he was talking to, she turned around. No one else was there. "I don't, Isaac."

His eyes turned dark. "You never tell me everything; you keep me hanging on, waiting for scraps like a dog. I can't do it anymore."

"Don't be like that, Isaac." She reached out but couldn't seem to touch him.

He curled his lip and turned away. "Goodbye, Azalea."

"Wait, Isaac!" she called as he walked away. She tried to run, but her legs wouldn't move. "I'll tell you everything! I promise!" Tears rolled down her cheeks.

She was such a shit friend. Isaac did everything to help her, and what had she done for him? Let a crazy mythical cat loose on his street and only rescued him at the very last minute.

She turned back and nearly crashed into her mum and RoRo. Her head spun, and she wondered if someone had slipped a few extra mushrooms into whatever she'd drunk.

Her mum had the same expression as when Azalea had first left with Fabian—utter disappointment—and it was something Azalea had never wanted to see again. RoRo's thin lips were pursed, and she shook her head while weeping. Azalea had never seen her so much as shed a tear in her whole life.

Leda balled up her apron in her hands. "You have forsaken your true roots."

"You are responsible for taking away our family's magic." RoRo pointed at her.

"You were meant to be the next forest guardian. The forest will be lost."

RoRo stepped closer. "You squandered the gift of plant magic, the true gift of life, and chose death."

"You betrayed your family," her mother cried.

"You're sleeping with the enemy."

"Your soul is tainted."

"You cannot save us."

Azalea fell to her knees, the berating going on and on. And all of it was true. Everything she had done had hurt her family. She'd betrayed her mum and RoRo, every choice pushing her towards Shadow Magic.

"I'm sorry!" she pleaded. "I'll make everything right."

Her beautiful dress was getting covered in tears, and the sand stuck to her face, grinding its tiny grains into her skin.

"It's okay that you chose him, Azalea. It's okay that you didn't save me." Erik stood there, his blue eyes bright and sparkling in the extreme light.

"We tried to save you, Erik. We tried. I didn't choose him." Deep, heavy sobs racked her chest, the very thing she promised herself she wouldn't do in the waking world. She hadn't cried yet and hated herself for giving in.

Why was Erik being so nice? She almost wanted him to yell at her, to punish her for failing.

The sun scorched her arms. "I didn't want you to die, Erik. I didn't want anyone to have to die."

Azalea tried to step closer, but he drifted further away.

"Don't let the Archmage win. Don't let my death be for nothing."

She shook her head as tears clouded her vision. "I won't." Erik scattered into the wind, and her heart was breaking. She couldn't take much more of this.

She collapsed into the pool of her dress, focusing on the solid marble beneath her palm. "I'm done now. Please bring me home!"

"Get up Azalea, you need to pass the ceremony." Torin was there!

"Are you really here?" How could she tell if it was him? He wore the same loin cloth, had the same tattoos as the real Torin.

"I'm here, mageling."

She scrambled to her feet. "I'm up. What do I do now?"

"You are weak. You don't even know what to do to pass." He shook his head and stared down at her.

Her heart plummeted to her bare feet. This wasn't Torin, or she sure as hell hoped it wasn't.

"I will pass. I know you're not real." The problem was everything about this felt real.

He shook his head. "Why can't you try harder? Why don't you listen?"

"I do. Everything I do is because I want you to approve. I want you to be proud, don't you get that? I *am* trying!" She fell to her knees.

"You will never be good enough." He turned away, and her heart shattered.

Sobs wracked her body. He was right. She would never be good enough for him, but the dream didn't need to point that out. She already knew it.

She curled her body over her knees, feeling like she had been drained. She wanted to forget everything those fake people had said to her, no matter how true their words were.

"Please let it be over." She sobbed, picturing the faces of her friends and family. She sat up determined to do better, to be better for them.

"You have a strong will." Ereshkigal appeared, and Azalea's heart nearly exploded out of her chest.

"Is it over?" Azalea wiped her eyes, knowing she couldn't handle anything more.

Ereshkigal bowed her head. "I am honored to receive you as an apprentice to the House of Snakes. You have been resilient and humble in my tests."

"You mean just now? Or with all the spirits and the bond and everything? Because that's been shit." Okay, so all filters were off now. She had zero energy left to care.

"Everything is a test. You wish to ask me questions?"

She sucked back the sobs and forced her chest to stop heaving and her brain to start thinking. "So many questions. My friends are traveling to the Echo Dimension to meet with the gods to try to close the gateway to our world. But I think there is another way I can help them. I believe that path leads to you."

"This is your path. But there is a price." Ereshkigal's wings blocked out the suns as she turned.

There was always a bloody price. "You want me to bring you spirits?"

Ereshkigal paced in front of her. "You are already bringing me spirits. Though I have not seen many of late. You wish to change the deal you made with Damu?"

Azalea stood up and nodded. "Yes. If I bring you the spirits, will you help my friends close the gate?" She was relying on the fact that Mage Emerson would successfully liberate Torin's dad's sword so she could collect the spirits without the side effect of dying.

"The bond I forged between you and the dreamweaver was a gift. You take great risk in rejecting it and offending me." She stopped and glared at Azalea.

Not exactly what she asked, but she'd roll with it. "It wasn't a gift. You made it to give me more power so I wouldn't die gathering your spirits."

Ereshkigal glared at her with eyes as black as an oil spill. "Yet you still have not accepted it."

"We do not wish to accept it. All it's doing is causing us problems. The bond is illegal in our world. Did you know that?" Azalea held her ground.

"Mortal laws do not concern me." Ereshkigal snapped her great black wings shut.

Azalea put her hands on her hips, feeling bolder by the second. "Not to mention we are having a rather shit time trying to keep it secret, what with being able to feel each other's every emotion and all."

"You are holding back. Seal the bond, and no issues will exist. The true power will set in." She turned sharply and paced the width of the marble path.

*Sorry if I don't believe a word that comes out of your mouth, lady.* "Thank you for the generous gift. We will find another way to break the bond. Right now, it is more important to close the gate. Will you help us?"

"I will consider your offer. Bring me the spirits, and come to me in the City of Stars. Prove your loyalty, and you will be rewarded greatly. You have everything you need."

*Come to the City of Stars.* She'd been expecting that, but it didn't stop a torrent of icy fear from washing over her. "Thank you." Azalea put her hands together in prayer at her chest, grateful to be getting somewhere.

"So much confidence for one so young, but so ignorant of what she has before her."

Azalea swallowed, her mouth dry and gritty with dream sand. Probably not the right time to argue, so she remained silent.

"Your time here is up, daughter of Snakes."

"Wait, is there anything else that can help my friends in the Echo Dimension? Anything?" Azalea pleaded.

Ereshkigal snapped her wings open once more and turned away. "I will speak with my sister. She will protect your friends in the Land of Light."

"The Land of Light," Azalea mumbled to herself. She must remember that one. She wondered who Ereshkigal's sister was but decided it might be better not to ask. She could look it up in a book, probably.

Ereshkigal glanced over her shoulder. "They should travel tomorrow before the great feast at the Temple of the Waters. If they arrive before then, they will have a chance. Enki will be in good spirits. I will confer with my sister now."

"Thank you." Azalea bowed low, not sure what else to add. This was more than she had expected.

"I will be there to greet you in the City of Stars. Travel well."

She lunged at Azalea, digging metallic fingernails into the flesh of Azalea's shoulders and back. Blinding pain shot through Azalea, threatening to snap her spine. Then everything went black.

# Chapter 11

Torin stared into the crowd. Kira stood there, like a ghost from his past; beautiful, ethereal, and with a glare that shot daggers right to his heart. Oxygen fled his brain, leaving him dizzy with collisions of guilt and relief.

His head snapped back to Azalea. For a second, he panicked. He couldn't feel her there anymore. It was like her emotions had been switched off.

Fabian's arms shot out as she fell, and Torin was too slow to react, like he was trapped in slow motion. Fabian caught her just in time.

"You were meant to catch her, you fool." Fabian cradled her in his arms.

He rushed over as Fabian lowered her to the ground. "Shit, sorry."

"Fucking useless," Fabian mumbled under his breath.

Torin didn't reply as he looked up, but he'd lost sight of Kira.

"She's out. It could be a while folks," Fabian announced to the crowd. "Eat and drink up, but not too much. Can't have you eating me out of house and home."

A rumble of chuckles followed, and the murmur of voices became background noise.

"You've been hunting that girl for eight years. You might as well go talk to her," Fabian said. The first civil sentence to come out of his mouth toward Torin, but it was not in good faith. Torin was sure he was waiting for him to fail, and he wanted to be there to witness it.

Azalea's grandmother and mum stepped onto the makeshift stage with blankets and a pillow. Torin didn't offer to help. He couldn't risk touching Azalea while she was out; he didn't know how their magic would react. For all he knew, he could be pulled into her ceremony with her.

He watched as they lifted her onto one blanket and tucked another around her. Her loose hair cascaded across the pillow like Snow White in her coffin. He crouched next to her once they were done. He wanted to stroke the hair from her face and kiss her so she would know he was there. Instead of doing something so stupid, he stood up.

"You'll keep an eye on her?" he directed the question at Rowena as Faraday curled up on Azalea's feet.

"Course we will." Fabian nodded toward Kira, who was still at the back with Kat with a wide berth of space around them.

He stepped off the stage and nearly bumped into Danni. They were quickly encircled by the two little girls running circles around them giggling.

"That's her, isn't it?" Danni looked like she might explode with excitement. The opposite of how Torin felt. He wanted to melt into the ground.

Torin rubbed his sweating palms on his trousers. "Yes, and I have no idea what to say to her."

"Just be yourself. She'll see you're still the same boy." Danni ruffled his short spikes of hair.

He batted her hand away. "I don't think I am, and if so, I'm not sure that's a good thing."

Danni caught the two girls with an expert grasp and set Torin free.

Walking down the aisle was nearly as bad as walking up it with Azalea with all those eyes on them. At least this took his mind off worrying about what she might be facing in there. His apprentice trial had been horrible, but it had given him a chance to see his mother one more time. He could still picture her face, sad, disappointed in him. He had promised her he would find her grave, but since he got out of prison, he hadn't even tried.

He silently renewed the vow to find her when he got back.

At the back of the garden next to the skeletons of rose bushes, he stopped in front of the two women in black, his hands sweating like he was about to enter a battle.

"Torin." Kat gave a sharp nod and marched past him, leaving him alone with Kira.

He took in the sight of her—she was alive. She looked the same. The same green eyes he used to see every morning at training, the same black combat outfit with heavy boots, even the same French braids that had fluffy loose parts sticking out. The same scowl as when she was pissed off at him.

"Kira. You look the same." His mouth was dry, his hands were sweating, and just like that, he felt sixteen all over again, but this was much worse. She thought he'd tried to kill her.

"That's all you have to say to me after eight years. After walking out and leaving me for dead." She made no attempt to keep her voice down.

All eyes flicked toward them, and the chatter faded away.

"Let's go somewhere." He eyed the exit to the garden, wanting to escape.

He glanced back to see if Kat might be near for mediating. But she was with Fabian, and all he saw was Fabian's smirk.

He was standing close by with his arms crossed, enjoying this. Wanker.

Torin tried to lead Kira toward the stone arch, but she flicked off his hand and marched ahead of him. Struggling to keep up as she stormed along the wall and down the small path that ran along the side, Torin knew better than to complain. But he didn't like being this far from Azalea. It was strange not to feel her presence, almost like he was empty or missing something.

Kira continued past the end of the wall into a clearing—not a clearing, a cemetery.

She stared out across the shadowy fields. The dots of sheep glowed bright white against the backdrop of night.

He stopped a few gravestones behind her, his elemer not leaving his hand. He wasn't taking any chances.

"I'm sorry I left you, Kira. I didn't have a choice."

She didn't turn around. "You could have stayed." Her voice was stony.

"I murdered a man and nearly killed an entire ballroom full of people—these people." He pointed back at the garden, but she wasn't looking. "I had to turn myself in. I couldn't let him get away with anything like that again."

She swiveled around with silent grace. "We were being trained as assassins. What did you expect? And in case you didn't notice, he got away with it, anyway."

Torin's fist clenched. "But now everyone knows what he is. At least I'm doing something. I told you I was leaving. It can't have been a surprise." He was angrier than he wanted to be. This wasn't how he'd pictured their reunion.

Kira kicked at the base of a grave. "I didn't believe you would do it. Obviously, I realized that too late."

"Yeah. Thanks for all the support," he said sarcastically and immediately regretted it. She was getting under his skin too easily. He had imagined this day for so long. He was supposed to be apologetic and kind and begging for her forgiveness.

Kira twisted around and held her hands up. "You used the hand of death on me, Torin. How am I supposed to feel?"

"Are you just here to make me feel worse? Is that it? I loved you, Kira. I thought I killed you. I had the Paranormal Justice Unit looking for you for eight years. Do you know what that feels like? To think you murdered your best friend?" He focused on the sheep dots in the distance. He couldn't get angry.

She had the decency to look guilty. "I'm sorry Torin. They told me you ran. That you ran, and the PJU caught you, and you gave in to torture right away."

"And you believed that?"

Kira rubbed her eyes. "It was easier to hate you than to know you chose to leave."

He was glad Azalea was unconscious, so she didn't have to feel what he felt right now—like he'd let down the one person he'd promised never to leave. His heart ached for what Kira had gone through and for abandoning her to the mercy of his father.

Memories of that night flooded over him. Kira yelling at him because she didn't want him to leave. Him reaching out to stop her, then it all happened so fast. Feeling the life drain out of her beneath his hand with nothing he could do to stop it. Doing everything in his power to bring her back, but never sure if it worked.

Now he knew. She was alive and real, and that was all that mattered.

There was nothing he could do to make up for his mistakes.

"What are you doing here, Kira? You don't sound like someone rebelling against Korbyn Dumont. You stayed with him all this time."

Kira leaned against an angel statue. "It's not an option to leave, Torin. You're a prime example of that. I'd rather not walk straight into prison, thanks."

"What is it then?" Torin studied her face that had once been so familiar, but he couldn't tell what she was thinking anymore.

"I'm here because Kat believes in you, and I believe in Kat. She watched out for us after you left. I owe her everything. So here." She unsheathed the sword that was somehow attached to her hip. "Cloaking charm."

He blinked, surprised he hadn't noticed. "You got it." Relief flooded him. He could trust Kat, and Azalea would be protected from spirits if he didn't make it back.

"Take it." She shoved the sword toward him.

He accepted it with two hands, feeling its weight. "Did anyone see Mage Emerson take it?"

"Yes, Sampson. But he won't say anything." She stepped back and sat on a slab of stone covering a grave.

Torin nodded. "Good." Sampson was fine. The old butler had promised he would be on Torin's side when he needed it. He hoped that much was still true. The man had a lot of sway in the background at the Rook. He might not be a powerful mage, but he was on the right side of every single person there.

Kira didn't say anything. Usually, he didn't feel the need to fill the silence, but he couldn't handle it.

"The squad?" He rested the sword tip on the ground, gripping the solid handle.

"Still alive," Kira answered.

Relief washed over him. "Where were you? Why couldn't I find any of you?"

"Korbyn sent us to America right after our apprentice ceremonies. This is our first time home. He summoned everyone back."

"They're at the Tower of London?"

"Conner is. Matt and Dev are stationed at Eagle Tower for now."

They were all here and alive. It was strange to think the people he had grown up with were so close and still so distant from him. Would they even want to see him again? "He's taken Eagle Tower?"

"He's taken the High Council. He's 'monitoring' Eagle Tower for their own safety."

"Oh." That couldn't be good.

She checked her watch. "You better get back to your apprentice."

"Yes. I had better." He made no move to close the gap between them. He didn't want to scare her off straight away.

"Are we okay?" he asked.

She gave a small smile. That was the Kira he remembered. "Maybe one day."

"Thanks for the sword."

She nodded and walked away, leaving him standing among the silent gravestones.

Azalea woke up, her face wet with tears and freezing. Torin was right there, leaning over her, fear pouring off him. Her eyes locked with his, and relief flooded through her from both of them.

"It's okay, you made it," he said in a low, soothing voice.

She'd never wanted to kiss anyone as much as she wanted to kiss him at that moment. He knew it, gave a slight shake of his head, and backed away, not even helping her up. He wasn't a coward; he was protecting them. Danni appeared and helped her sit up as Faraday sauntered over and head-butted Azalea's arm.

"Well done, little miss Apprentice." Danni kissed Azalea's cheeks.

Azalea tried to smile, but her arm burned, and so did her side and back. This new tattoo better be worth it. She sucked in a breath as the pain level shot up, and her vision swam. She tried to take off the jacket but was disoriented.

Her eyes fell on the crowd regathering in front of the makeshift stage. RoRo and the other mages were smiling.

"Show us then!" Van cried out with a whoop. "Take it off!"

The burning subsided a little, and Azalea's vision returned to normal. She tried to keep her conversation with Ereshkigal at the forefront of her mind, so she didn't forget.

Van's comment snapped her back to reality.

"Could you help me up?" she whispered to Danni.

Danni grabbed her hands and pulled her to her feet. She was still on the stage with Torin hovering close by.

She mentally crossed her fingers as she peeled away the coat, hoping it was a House of Snakes tattoo and not some weird new magic thing.

The familiar snake on her forearm was the same, though glowing a little brighter than usual as it wound around her forearm and up to her shoulder, its tiny head flicking its tongue at the crescent moon on her inner wrist.

She flipped her arm to reveal a watercolor raven and an emerald-green snake next to each other against a background of dazzling stars. A murmur ran through the crowd as her breath froze in her chest, and she didn't dare make eye contact with Torin. She turned so her back was facing the crowd, but she couldn't see the rest of the tattoo.

A gasp fell across the audience, and she twisted her neck further. All she could see was the edge of a wing with black feathers.

# Chapter 12

"What is it?" Azalea spun around to see her back better. Of course, it didn't work.

"Put your coat back on." Torin shoved it into her hands.

Fabian was beaming. "I am honored to announce that Azalea has passed her apprentice test and has been marked by the Goddess herself." The garden erupted in applause.

Of course, she had been. That's what this whole ceremony was. Why was everyone getting all worked up? The House of Snakes mages and families were cheering and clinking glasses. How long had she been out? This party had certainly kicked up a notch.

"She has been chosen by Ereshkigal!" Fabian held Azalea's hand up like a champion boxer, and everyone cheered again.

"Can someone explain what's going on?" she mumbled under her breath while faking a toothy smile for the crowd.

"The goddess marked you," Fabian repeated as if that explained something.

"I know, I was there." She wanted to see what all the fuss was about.

Torin stepped forward, clearly able to feel her growing panic. "The tattoo is of the goddess."

"You mean she put a picture of herself on me?" Azalea said in disbelief.

"It is the greatest honor." Fabian was actually in a good mood for real. This must be a big deal.

Azalea stepped off the stage and ran out of the garden and toward the house. *A picture of the goddess on her back?* At least that took the focus off the new raven and snake.

Footsteps sounded behind her, but she didn't care who it was. She needed to get this blasted dress off. She raced up the stairs, through the back door of the kitchen, and into the nearest bathroom.

She spun around to look in the mirror and saw huge black wings spread out across her shoulders, the feathers so detailed they could be real. The wings were spread high and curved over her shoulders like real wings, as beautiful and silky as Ereshki-gal's herself.

The top of a multi-layered golden crown peeked from beneath the dress. She needed to see more. Stretching her arms, she grasped for the ties of the corset, but she couldn't reach them. Her chest constricted, and her shallow breaths did little to provide her body with oxygen.

Torin ran through the open bathroom door. "Just breathe, Azalea. Calm down."

"Get it off me." She clawed at her back, knowing she sounded more than a little crazy. She needed to see.

His hands moved across her back with the speed she was after.

"Get away from her!" Fabian yelled.

Azalea spun around, holding the top of the dress to her chest so she didn't flash anyone. "Will someone just open my bloody dress? I don't care who."

Torin raised his hands and stepped out of the crowded bathroom as Faraday jumped up to sit by the sink.

"Danni. Help her, will you?" Fabian ordered.

"No need for everyone to get all worked up. Torin was doing perfectly fine." Danni took Torin's place, her gentle hands carefully untying the laces.

Fabian stepped out with a large scowl on his face.

"Oh, wow," Danni breathed.

"Is it bad?" Azalea asked. If she had a choice of tattoos, getting a huge one of a narcissistic devil-woman was not high on her list.

Azalea spun around and looked in the mirror, careful to keep the front of the dress covering her. But she almost dropped it when she saw the tattoo.

It was stunning.

It certainly wasn't a humble depiction of the goddess, but neither was it vain. The goddess faced straight forward with her black wings raised. In her hands were horizontal golden rods with large rings in a halo around her palms. Her arms were covered in golden bangles and thin strips of gold cloth covered her breasts and crisscrossed down her toned belly, contrasting with her silvery skin. Her skirt was pure shadows that somehow depicted movement in this still portrait. Her feet were bare, with pointed toes like talons.

The look on her face was that of a ruler who commanded respect, but it was a face you couldn't stop looking at—beautiful and terrifying. The whole tattoo shimmered with metallic hues, moving and changing with the shadows as she flexed her back muscles.

"Now that's something." Fabian whistled.

"Oh my goodness," her mum exclaimed and for once, RoRo was speechless.

Azalea let herself relax and felt Torin do the same.

"I need to talk to you all." Azalea needed to recall the dream before she forgot it.

RoRo snapped out of her silence. "Everyone, stop gawking at the poor girl. Let her get dressed so we can hear what she has to say."

What she wanted was to talk to Torin first, but it didn't look like there was much chance of that. Everyone shuffled away, except Danni who retied Azalea into her dress and slipped the coat back over her shoulders.

Azalea stepped onto the black and white marble tiles of the main lobby to find Fabian, Torin, her mum, RoRo, Danni, Isaac, Van, and Jade standing there in front of the wall of obscenely large pots of palm trees all staring at her in awe. Them, she could deal with. At least the whole party hadn't followed her up.

Hugging herself, Azalea rubbed her arms over her coat to get warm again. "Ereshkigal said she will help. She will speak with her sister, who can help you get across the Land of Light. And that you need to get there before the great feast at Enki's palace."

"That's brilliant, Azalea! I knew you could do it!" Fabian wrapped her in a big hug. Wow, he really was happy.

She shared a brief look of concern with Torin.

"When is the feast?" Torin asked.

Azalea swallowed hard. "Tomorrow."

Her heart sank alongside Torin's. Tomorrow was too soon to be saying goodbye.

Azalea slipped away, not able to bring herself to celebrate. She finally felt like she belonged in the House of Snakes, but it was hard when tomorrow felt like the end of everything.

Walking aimlessly to clear her mind, she found herself at the greenhouse. She opened the door to be met with humidity and the smells of earth and tomato plants. It was dark and peaceful after the chaos of being surrounded by people, and the comforting hum of bumblebee dragons buzzed around her—they loved tomato plants.

She trailed her fingers around the leaves of a giant cucumber vine that reached the ceiling. The cool leaves on her skin made her want to reach for Echo Magic. She pulled her hand away and clenched her fist.

The door slammed shut.

"Thought I might find you here." Torin's presence filled the space around her. He was blocking his emotions well, and she tried to do the same, focusing her energy on pulling her aura back in around her as she did with the spirits. She closed her eyes and took a deep breath of plant-filled air.

"I have something for you." His eyes were bright—happy even.

Azalea turned to look at him. He pulled a sword from behind his back.

"Here." He held it out to her with the blade laid across his palms.

She gasped and picked up the hilt, careful not to cut off his hands as she lifted it. "It's so shiny." Her eyes fixed on the rubies and House of Ravens crest on the handle.

His hand lingered. "Yes, those are real."

"Wow." She ran a finger over the cold metal.

"I want you to collect the spirits when I go." He pulled his hand away.

Her heart collapsed into her stomach. He wanted her to break the bond. She swallowed the lump in her throat. Using the sword was exactly what she planned to do but for a different reason now. He didn't need to know she'd changed the deal.

"Okay." She nodded, tears prickling the corners of her eyes. She was doing a horrible job of shielding her emotions, and she hated herself for it. Hated that he could see right through her.

A flash of confusion sparked from Torin. Perhaps he hadn't expected her to agree that easily, but he had no idea she was agreeing to something different. Something that ensured he would make it back alive.

Anyway, she wasn't sure she was ready to break the bond yet. Part of her wanted to know what would happen if they sealed it, what powers they would get, and if their control over their feelings would return. It was tempting. But she wasn't about to say any of that to him.

"You want to break the bond, I understand." She focused hard on the gemstones of the blade, not wanting to look him in the eye.

"If something happens to me over there, you'll be better off if the bond is broken."

"You don't know that. You're talking like you're not coming back."

"Damu said, if one of us died, the other wouldn't want to live. I don't want that for you."

"He also said breaking the bond was just as bad." Or something along those lines, maybe? "You're coming back, Torin." *I'll make sure of it.*

"Just take the sword."

"I'm holding it, aren't I?" Their tension bounced off each other, making this much worse. Azalea grounded herself with her breath and closed her eyes for a second.

When she opened them, Torin was looking at her with pity.

"Stop looking at me like that. We still have one night. Let's not ruin it." Heat filled her face as she thought of all the things they could do with their last night.

Torin stared at her lips. "Stop looking at me like *that*."

"Like what?" The flush spread to her neck.

He rubbed his throat. "Like you're thinking about sealing the bond."

"Is it the worst idea?" She stepped closer. "It could protect us both. The new powers, they'll be stable, and maybe we'll be able to control sharing our emotions. You have to admit that would be a perk."

He didn't move away. "Let me guess, Ereshkigal told you to seal the bond. You know why she wants us to. It means she can get more spirits. The more power you have, the less likely you are to die doing her bidding."

"That doesn't even matter! I have the sword now. She doesn't control us." Though, right now, Azalea very much needed the goddess on her side.

"She's controlling you through that bloody book and through me. She's marked you, for gods' sake. Can't you see what she's doing?"

Azalea bit her tongue. She wasn't going to argue, and she wasn't going to tell him about the deal she made. He would only try to stop her, and she knew it was the right thing to do.

"I'm not going to ruin our last night together. Let's just pretend none of this is happening and we are just two people who like each other and not because of a crazy magical bond. Okay?" she said more forcefully than she meant to.

A smile crept over Torin's face as if he realized the ridiculousness of their situation. He took the sword from her hands and placed it on the bench between the cucumbers. "This is not how I wanted things to be." He pulled her in close.

Without thinking, she wrapped her arms around him and buried her face in his chest. His cheek rested on her head, and his warm breath tickled the hair over her ears.

"Let's just go to bed. I promise I won't try to get you to seal the bond. Okay?" Azalea said, part of her wishing he would just give in.

"As long as we don't have any dreams like the ones last week." He mumbled into her hair. His breath trailed down her neck. He moved lower, landing soft kisses as he did.

The dreams came back to her in a flood of hot memories. She ran her hand up his back as she let out a soft moan, but he pulled away, leaving her with a chaste kiss.

"Sorry. Couldn't help it." He ran his hand through his short spikes of hair.

She realized she wasn't blocking her emotions at all. "Me neither." She grinned sheepishly and stepped back, doing her best to ignore the warmth spreading through her body.

"Oh, I know! RoRo used to make some sort of dreamless sleep tea, maybe that will knock us out, so we actually sleep. I bet we could find the ingredients here."

He folded his hands behind his back as if fighting to keep them to himself. "I think we might need it."

# Chapter 13

Despite the copious amounts of sleep tea, Torin woke up before the sun and left Azalea in bed. The sky was still fiery red and angry. He went downstairs with Faraday and made a cup of tea while no one was in the kitchen, then went to the library to go through the equipment they were bringing.

Faraday sat on the table licking his paws as Torin checked all the items that were laid out—camping gear, ration packs, torches, matches, first aid kits, plus a lot more—at least they were well prepared.

Rowena joined him soon after he arrived. She was not someone he wanted to be alone with. She was too nosy and too clever for her own good. Azalea loved and trusted the woman without question, but he knew she was hiding something and was far more powerful than she ever let on to anyone. She knew everyone in the magic community and in all houses. She'd even been in the same initiate class as the Archmage when they were young. He had done his research, and he was wary of her, though her motives seemed pure enough.

"Morning, Torin. I hope the tea was sufficient, Azalea asked me for the recipe."

"Very. Thank you." He wasn't lying. He'd had a truly dreamless sleep and felt more well-rested than usual.

"Good… good," she mumbled as she set out the amulets she'd prepared the day before.

They worked away quietly for a few minutes, Torin packing his bag with everything they might need, including the relics for the gate that Azalea had taken. Rowena focused intently, reading a map of some sort.

"You know that book Azalea has?" Rowena didn't look up.

A chill shot down Torin's spine. "Which book would that be?"

"You know the one."

"Perhaps," he said noncommittally. She knew about the Shadow Atlas, and he tried not to react.

She handed him the amulets wrapped in paper. "It's dangerous. I knew that when I gave it to her. But she needs it. It's important."

A surge of rage flashed through him. She had given her granddaughter that book purposefully?

"Do you know what it is? What it is capable of?" *What it did to us? People died because of that book.* But he didn't say any of that, and he had a sick feeling that she knew.

"I had an idea." She continued arranging the items on the table.

He stood there holding the amulets. "I don't think you do if you let her have it. You have no idea what it's done to her. It's a demon for fuck's sake, and she's stuck with it now." He stared at her in disbelief.

Guilt flashed across her face, but only for a microsecond, then she was back to serene and smiling. "It is important you let her follow her path with it."

"Give me one good reason why." He set down the amulets so he didn't smash them into the table and clenched his fists at his sides, doing his best to remain calm.

"Because there was a prophecy. Her and the book are part of it."

Great, since when did decision-making come down to prophecy? He'd had enough of prophecies, especially from that bloody book.

"I suppose the book told you that?" He glared at her, but she was unaffected.

"No. The book hasn't presented itself to anyone since her father. A seer predicted it when she was young. I haven't told her, and I will ask you not to mention it to her, but I don't want you stopping her, either." She finished tidying up the leftover paper.

Torin rested his hands on the edge of the table. "What was the prophecy?"

"I'm afraid I can't tell you. It could affect the fates."

He gritted his teeth. "That's not how prophecies work. You know the prophecy yourself, and you're manipulating events to fulfill it. What's the difference in telling me?"

"The difference, Mage Dumont, is that I have to live with that knowledge now. You do not." She put her hands on her hips.

Torin felt a torrent of panic crash over him from Azalea. His sudden anger had probably woken her up. His emotions were slipping more often than not. Faraday was on his feet and pacing in front of Torin like a tiger in a cage.

"Will you excuse me? I need to run upstairs. I'll return shortly."

"What's the rush, dear? I haven't upset you, have I?" she said, a little too sweetly.

"I need to check something in my notes." He marched out of the room.

Faraday nearly tripped him as he dashed up the stairs, but he kept going and followed Faraday into his bedroom.

"What happened?" He was wide-eyed, verging on panic.

"I thought you'd gone. I felt you freaking out." She ran over and threw herself at him.

"I wouldn't leave without telling you." He looked into her eyes which were wide with fear, then kissed her. She relaxed into his chest, still loose with the effects of sleep. He felt her panic instantly wash away. He wished time could stand still in this moment, that he didn't have to leave.

"If I'd known kissing you had this effect, I would have started doing it a long time ago."

She smiled, leaning back onto his lips. "Let's just stay here."

"Hiding out in the attic of your uncle-who-hates-me's house. No thanks." He let out a weak laugh. "We aren't leaving until after lunch, so Mage Emerson—Kat—can get here."

"Is it just Kat and Fabian going with you?" She hadn't asked him about reuniting with Kira. But he was pretty sure that's where this question was aimed.

"Yes. Me, Kat, and Fabian. Dream team," he said sarcastically.

"I wish I could say something to make Fabian behave, but I think it would make it worse for you. He won't try anything while Kat is there. Just watch your back."

"Oh, I plan to. Listen, I need to talk to you about something."

"This sounds bad." Azalea slipped out of his arms and pulled him to the edge of the bed.

"It's your grandmother. She knows about the Shadow Atlas. She asked me about it just now when we were downstairs."

Azalea slipped on a maroon sweater and pulled it down over the top of her black jeans. "She was the one who gave it to me."

"After the gallu told you to find it?" Torin ran his fingers over her arm, the sweater was so soft.

"Yes, but she thought it was my father, too. We didn't know it was the gallu." She sighed.

"What did the book tell you to do?" He needed answers before he left. He wasn't going to leave her with this book and some random prophecy hanging over her head when neither of them knew what it was. He wasn't going to mention it and freak her out either.

She swallowed. "It asked me to free it. I think I should. It can help me, and I just know. It's a feeling I can't explain."

"It's the book's hold on you." He shifted to sit sideways on the bed so he could see her.

She shuffled back and grabbed her socks. "Maybe. But I know what the goddess wants. And it seems smart to do what she wants rather than the opposite."

"I agree."

"Wait, what?" She stopped with a sock halfway on her foot. "You do?"

"Well, no, but I felt how certain you were about doing this a second ago. I'd rather you do it while I'm still here than when I'm too far away to help and worrying about you."

She stared at him and grinned like she'd been given the perfect gift. "So I can free it?"

"Yes. But we need to do it right now." He might regret this later, but he'd take any help they could get.

"Like, right, right now?"

It was now or never. Get it over with. "Yes. Right now. Get the book."

Azalea threw on a mismatched sock and stretched across the bed to reach the book tucked under her pillow.

"Get some salt." He pointed to the cupboard. Houses like this always had salt in the cupboards for protection around windows and doors, it was standard. He rolled up the rug that was half under the bed and pointed to the exposed wood.

Azalea found the salt in the white chest of drawers and poured out a circle big enough for them both to stand in. He stepped into the circle beside her, and she set a protection spell. She was as good as him now that she'd had so much practice.

"It told you how to free it?"

"Not yet."

"Ask it now."

They remained standing in the circle. He took the book from her and held it open in front of him but facing her. His elemer still clasped in his hand beneath the cold leather of the book.

She sliced her thumb with her elemer, and sucking in a breath, she dripped her blood onto the blank pages. Closing her eyes, she focused on her question. *How do I free you?*

Crimson ink seeped onto the page. *To release me from these shadow bonds. Speak my name thrice, and I will be released into my true form.*

Azalea was silent for a while, thinking.

*No. I am not a giant demon who will destroy your ceiling. I assure you I am of normal size.*

She stopped projecting her thoughts. "It seems too easy. It's not a trick, is it?" Azalea asked.

"The trick is we are releasing a demon. It's exactly what it wants, so I'd say it's telling the truth."

Azalea slipped her hands beneath his under the book, the flat blade of her elemer pressing against the back of his hand,

and closed her eyes. His magic flowed straight into her. She was drawing both Shadow Magic and the new magic.

The Shadow Magic trickled out of Torin in chilling streams of blue energy, merging with her purple. Then their light magic blasted through like glorious wildfire, hot and electric as it erupted from their hands and into the book.

"Say it now!" he yelled.

"Sitaddaru, Sitaddaru, Sitaddaru," Azalea spoke.

Torin's eyes flashed open as the weight of the book lifted from his palms. It floated there, glowing as it spun around.

Azalea gripped her elemer tightly, and they stood unmoving, as the book rotated slowly between them. It spun faster and faster, and they were forced to the edge of the circle as shadows formed around the book like a smoggy cloud.

"Should we get out of the circle?" she asked.

"Yes, quickly." He broke the protection spell, hauled her out, then reset it again. And just in time.

The dark cloud grew, spinning faster and faster, then shrank, spiraling in on itself until it condensed with every rotation. Azalea jumped as a crack split the air.

A dense ball of black mass sat on the floor. Then began to uncurl.

First one wing, then another.

"What the hell is that?" Azalea whispered.

He had no idea. "Just watch."

The wings were leathery like a bat with a large hook on the ends. They snapped open to reveal a small body, not unlike a bat, but also something completely different.

"Thank you, Mageling. I always knew you liked me," it said in a formal voice that didn't fit the small body.

It raised its head to reveal enormous round eyes and a small snout with pointed ears that flopped over a little at the top. It had a small mouth with a wicked grin that indicated it was no animal. It had the face of a calculating and smart creature, though its black fur-covered body only came up to knee height at most.

"You're the book?" Azalea's mouth hung open.

"I was the Shadow Atlas. I *am* Sitaddaru, and I present myself at your service." It gave a fluid bow, folding a tiny hand in front of him. It was no bat if it had both hands and wings.

"What do I do?" Azalea whispered.

Torin nudged her forward. "Accept it to your service. That's what you wanted, isn't it?"

"If you'd hurry this along, I would greatly appreciate it. I haven't eaten real food in over a century." Sitaddaru glanced around the room and scrunched up its nose.

Azalea narrowed her eyes at the creature. "You want human food, not blood?"

"I'm not a savage. Of course, I will accept any blood offered to me, but I rather crave a pomegranate." It rubbed its hands together while its wings flapped back and forth slowly, like a newly hatched butterfly.

Torin couldn't stop staring at its tiny black hands with long fingers like a spider monkey. Its feet were similar, with long toes all lined up like they were good for gripping. "I'm sure that can be arranged. Azalea?"

"I'm sure that's fine. Um, I accept you to my service?" She held her hands close to her chest.

"That didn't sound very convincing, but it will do. Now release me." The demon flapped its wings.

Torin folded his arms and stared down at the demon. "You will make an oath to Azalea. I need to know you mean her no harm."

"She is my master now. I cannot do anything to harm her."

"What, like a genie?" She crouched down to look at him.

It scoffed, clearly offended. "I do not grant wishes. But I swear that I mean mage apprentice, Azalea Sharp, no harm and vow to protect and lead her path, always putting her life before my own. Does that suffice?"

Torin interrogated the demon until he ran out of questions. He couldn't trip it up, and it genuinely seemed like its life mission was to protect Azalea. As far as he knew, demons couldn't lie, but he wouldn't put it past the creature to deceive them somehow.

"I trust it, Torin, it's safe." Azalea flopped onto the bed.

"I am a *he*, not an *it*." The demon crossed its arms and frowned like an old man.

"Very well. You are free." Torin removed the spell in the salt circle, scuffed the salt with his foot, and sank into the chair.

The demon flapped his wings and flew to the window. "By the gods above and below, you two really messed up."

"We were trying to follow your ridiculous advice." Azalea leaned up on her elbows.

The demon let out a huff, floated onto the bed, and sat with his legs crossed. "It is rather difficult to only speak in riddles and maps and not actually be able to see what's going on out there, but for a few scribbled words. So excuse me if things are not to your liking, but don't blame it on me."

"Now, what are you going to do?" Torin crossed his arms and looked at Azalea. "How are you going to explain a demon following you around?"

"Can you turn back into a book?" Azalea asked it.

"I'd rather not, but yes. You have the ability to change me at any time. It Is easy to go between forms now that I have done it once."

"Show me."

The demon let out a sigh, but he showed Azalea, anyway.

They stared at the book on the bed.

Torin nodded in approval. "For once, you seem to be right. I think he could be useful, and he clearly has to do what you say."

"Admitting you were wrong? Never thought I'd see the day," Azalea teased.

"Just be careful," he warned.

)))◑(((

Torin got out of the car inside the estate gates and hauled on his overloaded hiking pack. It was faster to drive than walk the extra ten minutes to the gate. Azalea got out behind him but wouldn't look him in the eye. He could feel her tense muscles, her racing heart as if it were his own, and for a second, he imagined staying. An ache grew in his chest at the thought of being so far from her.

She pulled her mum's forest green jacket tight around her, covering up the maroon sweater that he liked so well.

They'd spent the morning getting to know Sitaddaru, and by the end, Torin was convinced he would be an asset to Azalea while he was gone. Even if the demon had some ulterior motives, it was clear he had to do what she ordered. Even Faraday approved. He snuck up on the creature several times to test his reflexes, and Sitaddaru seemed to pass whatever test the cat set.

A second car pulled up, and Fabian and Kat got out with their packs.

Fabian greeted the guards sitting on two plastic chairs then marched up to the gate and out beyond the wards checking it was safe. "Hurry up, you lot."

Kat, dressed in black House of Raven combat gear, followed him, and Torin trudged over with Azalea right behind him.

Fabian faced Azalea and crossed his arms. "Look after the house when I'm gone."

"I will." Azalea ground her foot into the gravel, and Torin felt the slightest hint of guilt from her.

Kat nudged Fabian, and he stepped toward Azalea. "Zaels, I'm sorry I've been an arse. It's not your fault you're stuck with Dumont. I know that, and I promise I will not kill him on this trip."

She stepped closer and pulled him into a hug. "Just keep each other alive, okay?"

He nodded and stepped back.

"Bye Azalea." Kat gave a small wave, whacked Fabian's arm to hurry him along, and led him away from the gate toward the stone bridge over a stream.

"I don't know what to say. Good luck, I guess." Azalea clasped her hands in front of her. He could feel the terror threatening to rip her apart, the same way he felt leaving her. It went against everything his gut was telling him, yet he was more certain than anything that it was the right thing to do.

It suddenly clicked, the thing he needed to know. "What did you agree to? What price did Ereshkigal ask? Was it freeing the demon?" It suddenly seemed too easy. The demon was serving Azalea. How was that helping Ereshkigal?

She paused. No. It wasn't freeing the demon. "It doesn't matter. What matters is you will be safe and make it back."

"Azalea, I can't leave without knowing." What the hell had she agreed to? The goddess didn't make promises with nothing in return.

"Dumont, get your arse over here. I'm not waiting for you," Fabian yelled.

Torin rested his hand on her shoulder. "I'll know if you're lying."

She flinched, knowing he could feel everything without her being able to block it while he touched her. "It was spirits. She wants the spirits I promised."

He stared at her blankly. She was already getting spirits.

"It's not a problem. I can easily get them. I have the sword now, so don't worry about me." She tried to turn away, but he didn't let go.

"Dumont!" Fabian bellowed.

"I'm coming," he yelled back. This was a great way to start the trip. "You need those spirits to break the bond. You need to break the bond in case something happens to me."

"This is more important. I don't want to break it right now. I want to feel it and know you're okay."

"That's the problem. If something happens to me, you *will* feel it. If something bad happens to me—"

"Then I'll feel it. We can deal with the rest later. Just go, before I kiss you in front of Fabian." Azalea clenched her jaw stubbornly.

He closed his eyes in frustration and shook his head, though part of him wanted her to.

"You wanted me to tell you." She shook her head, tears welling in the corners of her eyes. He realized he hadn't seen her cry. Not since they'd gotten back. Not even about Erik. But she clearly wasn't okay.

"Stay safe, okay, promise me that." He resisted the urge to stroke her cheek.

"You know I can't promise that."

There was nothing he could do. He couldn't kiss her or hold her hand or freeze time and never leave. He forced himself to let go of her arm, stepping back.

"This isn't goodbye. I'll see you in my dreams."

"You better be there." She stepped back and wiped her eyes.

It was not the goodbye either of them wanted, but it was all they had. She turned and darted back inside the gate and didn't look back once as she walked to the car. He looked back several times as he walked to the Hollow and watched her as the darkness sealed them in.

"You needn't worry about her. It's us you need to worry about," Fabian said.

If only that were true.

# Chapter 14

Azalea thanked the driver and slammed the car door shut once she arrived at the house. She was fighting tears, but she wouldn't give in to them. It was time to get moving.

She had the sword. All she needed to do was go to Jordan, get the spirits, and her payment would be ready. Then all she'd have to do was follow her book-turned-demon into the underworld and meet with the goddess as she agreed. Simple.

Faraday was just inside the main door. Her boots clomped across the polished tiles of the grand entrance, and she dashed up the stairs. Breathless, she arrived back in Torin's room.

She stood there, blood pounding through her ears as she strained to listen, to feel for Torin. He wasn't blocking his emotions. She smiled to herself. She could still feel him out there. Hopefully, she still would once he went through the gateway. Though it might not be possible once she went to the Shadow Dimension.

He'd once explained how the dimensions were stacked like layers. The Echo Dimension on top, then their world, then the Shadow Dimension at the bottom. The Hollow was a sub-dimension between the mortal world and the Shadow Dimension.

That was a whole lot of space between them if she left, about as far away from another human as you could get. Her stomach roiled at the thought.

Still, she had to do it. Every minute they were in the Echo, they were in danger, and she needed to secure their protection and a way out for them. She grabbed the Shadow Atlas from under her pillow and cut her hand, a little too deep in her haste.

Juggling the book and her bleeding hand, she flicked open a page and caught the stream with the paper. "Sitaddaru. Sitaddaru. Sitaddaru."

She put her palm to her mouth. The tang of metallic blood hit her tongue as the book snapped shut and burst into a cloud of shadows.

A knock sounded at the door.

Shit. Not a good time.

"Hey, Azalea. I know Mage Dumont left, and I saw you come up here. Are you okay?"

*It was Jade. Crap.*

"I'm fine, thank you, Jade. I'll be down shortly." Was that too formal, too weird?

"I got you some tea. I'm coming in." The door creaked open.

Azalea was too far from the door to stop her, and the demon materialized from the shadows and stood in the center of the room with a grin on his weird little face that was rather cute.

"Don't come in!" Azalea called out, but it was too late.

Jade stood in the doorway with her mouth wide open. She was wearing all black as usual but was in practical trousers and a cute lace top that showed off her tiny waist with a leather jacket over top.

"What the fuck is that thing?" To her credit, Jade didn't drop the tray of tea. Just stood frozen in the doorway, with very wide, cats-eye-lined eyes.

"Your blood is delectable." The demon rolled his tongue over the two canines that peeked out of his tiny mouth. "Oh, hello there." He folded his wings back neatly and wiggled his fingers at Jade in greeting.

"Please go and sit on the bed, Sitaddaru. Jade, get in here." Azalea moved quickly, not quite turning her back to the demon as she carefully grasped Jade by the elbow, led her into the room, and shut the door. She steered Jade toward the window and the small table where she helped set the tea tray down and forced Jade into the chair.

"You may call me Sita. It is hard for you humans to re-member names. I know this. It is fine." The demon said as he flapped onto the bed next to Faraday, settled down cross-legged, and patted the cat on the little white diamond shape on his forehead. Faraday lowered his chin and purred; his eyes closed in the most trusting way.

Now that was strange.

"Azalea, what is that thing?" Jade said, surprisingly calm-ly.

"How about that tea?" Azalea set the two cups on the table, sat across from Jade in the other chair, and poured the tea. She handed Jade a cup and set two chocolate digestive biscuits on the saucer in front of Jade.

"I wanted to bring you tea as a thank you for letting me stay in your room. Van told me you were in here. I was not expecting this." Jade held the teacup but didn't bring it to her lips.

"I'm not sure how to best explain this," Azalea pondered.

"I thought you were upset about Mage Dumont leaving, and I come in here to find you not only fine but entertaining some weird creature. Is it from the Echo Dimension?"

"No dear, try the other one," Sita said.

Jade gasped. "What did you do?"

"Just calm down, Jade. Promise me you won't say anything to anyone."

"Tell me what the hell it is first, and I'll decide."

"I'm a him, not an it." Sita crossed his arms and pouted. "And I am a notable demon in the service of the great goddess Ereshkigal, who has assigned me to this young mageling."

"This is all new to me, but as far as I can tell, he will do what I say. I trust him." Azalea nodded to Sita, not wanting to start on his bad side.

"Why do you have a demon? And why are you in Mage Dumont's room?"

Azalea did her best not to blush. "I was going to use his room while he was gone, so you could have mine." *I'm thoughtful like that.* "And I have a small task of my own to get on with helping with the gate. I don't want to rush you along, but drink up your tea because I need to get going. You won't say anything, will you?"

"Not if you let me in on it," Jade said with a scheming look.

"On what?" Azalea put down her teacup.

"Whatever it is you're doing? I can help. Please!" She held her hands together, begging.

"It's going to be dangerous, and it needs to be a secret. It's easier if I go alone."

"I can help. Remember the prophecy Torin somehow stole from me? *Beyond the shadows, she will travel. Three companions. Two of darkness, one of mortal blood. The daughter of the Snake and Bee will return from the shadows.* It must mean I should go with you!"

Azalea paused for a moment. Three companions. Faraday and Sita and Jade.

"You're going to the Shadow Dimension. Aren't you?" Jade said.

Damn her nosiness. "Yes."

"Maybe I'll have a random prophecy that can help. They've helped in the past, remember? And I have Shadow Magic."

"You don't even use your Shadow Magic."

Sita sniffed the air. And both of them turned toward him. "Let the girl come. She could be useful. Her magic is strong. I can smell it."

"You can?" Jade wrinkled her nose.

Azalea couldn't waste time. She needed to get going and couldn't have Jade making a fuss. "Fine, you can come for the first part. But you need to understand fully before you agree, okay?"

"Yay!" Jade clapped her hands together.

Azalea explained the gist of it, gathering spirits, then meeting with Ereshkigal to ensure Torin's, Kat's, and Fabian's safety in the Echo Dimension. She let out a breath. "You still want to come?"

"Hell yes! I'm going nuts here, not being able to help out. I have zero skills for healing and organizing camp crap."

"You made this tea." Azalea took a sip.

Jade raised an eyebrow. "Everyone can make tea. It's hardly a skill. So where are we off to for these spirits?"

"Petra, Jordan." Azalea hopped up. "And we're going to need this." She pulled out the sword and grinned. Maybe it would be fun to have someone along for the ride.

☽☽☽●☾☾☾

An hour later, Azalea had a sword strapped to her back, a backpack over the top that was full of supplies and food, and a duffle bag hung from her front with Sita's floppy triangle ears poking out the top. He refused to be fully zipped in or be turned back into a book.

Faraday trotted at her side as they made their way downstairs.

Jade met her at the bottom of the steps. "A new wave of families and a few near burnouts arrived early today. Everyone will be pretty busy out there."

"Good. Head for the big kitchen."

The house was quiet apart from the sounds of pots banging around in the other kitchen. Mrs. Yates seemed to prefer that one for cooking.

Azalea pushed open the door to the other kitchen and crept in. All clear.

They got halfway across the room when the outside door swung open.

Danni. Her eyes flicked to Azalea's bags. Hopefully, she hadn't noticed the sword.

"Oh no you don't. You better not be following them."

"I promise, I'm not," Azalea said, trying to think fast. Danni didn't have any magic. This was the one time Azalea might be stronger.

"Where are you two off to then?" Danni said with hands on hips.

Jade waved a hand. "We're going to get healer's supplements. Van has nearly run out, and we aren't much use here, so we thought we would help out."

"No one leaves, Fabian's orders. Your use is in staying here and being safe. That's the whole point of this place. Get back upstairs and put your stuff back." Danni pointed to the door.

"We can't do that, Danni." Azalea gripped her elemer.

Danni's eyes narrowed, and her hand went to her elemer that was useless. "I've got enough to worry about without needing to add you two to it. Go upstairs." Her voice was low and commanding. This was agent Fletcher, not friendly Danni.

"I'm sorry Danni." Azalea silently summoned shadows to her knife-tip. She didn't wait. She threw the shadow ropes at Danni before she chickened out. They hit her hard, coiling around her body like a constrictor. All Azalea's panic and urgency forced into the spell, making it stronger.

Danni crashed to the floor, but the ropes covered her mouth so she couldn't yell out.

"Come on." She gestured to Jade before her guilt could get in the way.

"Is she okay?" Jade's voice was laced with concern.

Danni lay writhing on the ground, fighting the shadows. But Azalea didn't loosen them. "They'll wear off once we leave. Go now."

Jade gave Danni an apologetic look as she walked past. Faraday had the nerve to walk over Danni as he followed Jade out the door.

"I'm sorry, Danni. But I have to do this. Tell my mum I'll be back as soon as I can. I left her a note."

Danni thrashed her head to the side, loosening the ropes around her mouth. "Azalea, don't go after him. You'll die."

"Don't worry, I'm not." Azalea grabbed the keys hanging by the door and walked out.

Her heavy boots thudded across the cobbles. She pressed the button on the clicker, and a black car's lights flashed. Jade was already there.

Azalea placed Sita, her bags, and her sword on the back seat. Faraday jumped in and sat in the middle.

"You can't come, Farry, get out. I need to go now." She knew he understood the urgency in her voice, but he didn't move.

Sita poked his head out of the bag. "The shadow cat will join us."

*Shadow cat?* "Why?"

Sita didn't answer. Jade was already in the front and had the engine started. Azalea got in the passenger's seat, and they were off.

Jade turned out of the courtyard and followed the driveway around the house. It was only a few minutes to the gate, but it seemed like forever. Every muscle in Azalea's body was tense, and she half expected someone to run out and stop them.

They made it to the gate without incident. Two of the volunteer guards were sitting on plastic chairs eating sandwiches. They eyed the car suspiciously as Jade parked off to the side.

"Just act normal," Azalea whispered to Jade. She looked over her shoulder. "Get back in the bag, Sita!" The demon was on the seat, patting Faraday.

"Are we going to have to fight the guards?" Jade bubbled with excitement at the idea.

"Let's try not to." Azalea held the empty duffle bag open for Sita to climb back in. She still couldn't reconcile in her mind him being the Shadow Atlas. She got out of the car and gathered up the bags and the sword. Faraday jumped out after them. It seemed she couldn't stop the cat from coming either. At least he could look after himself.

"Hiya!" Jade waved to the guards. "Just wanted to have a look at the gates for ourselves. It's a bit boring up there, you know?"

Azalea took a calming breath and strutted to the gate, as she did she pricked her thumb with her elemer and held it to the freezing metal.

"Oi, don't touch that!" the guard in an oversized oilskin jacket yelled and nearly dropped his sandwich.

"Run!" Azalea called to Jade and swung the gate open. "So sorry, I hope you don't get in trouble over us." Azalea slammed the gate shut after Jade darted through.

"They aren't very competent guards. I suggest you replace them," Sita mumbled from inside the bag.

Azalea shushed him and cut into the Hollow before the guards stopped yelling at each other and got the balls to leave the compound, and before she psyched herself out.

"You're sure you want to come?" she asked Jade, giving her the chance to back out.

She nodded enthusiastically. "I'm all in."

"Oi, get back here!" The guard fumbled with the gate and a blood vial.

The four of them stepped into the Hollow.

# Chapter 15

Fabian stood in the Hollow, tapping his foot. "You know where to cut out, don't you, Dumont?"

"Of course, he does; just shut your trap." Kat whacked him in the arm. A bad habit she'd picked up recently.

He suspected there was going to be a lot of her defending Torin on this trip. Trust her to pick her old student over him. It was never him, but he did his best not to sulk.

Dumont finally got around to cutting out of the Hollow, and a rush of noise cascaded in from outside. Shouting, screaming, cheering, sobbing, loud music—it sounded like a raging music festival.

Kat didn't look surprised. "So, yeah. A lot of nut jobs showed up here to worship the gate. They think it's aliens."

Fabian snorted back a laugh. "Of course they do. Fuck-wits. Let me see."

Dumont held the edge of the cut to stop the doorway from closing, the shadows clawing up his arms as he did.

Fabian peered out. They were on the crest of a hill sur-rounded by scrubby brush, the only reason no one was camped there. Everywhere else was a sea of tents and people. Further into the distance, he saw what they were crowding around.

"Holy fuck."

"Don't usually see you this gobsmacked." Kat shoved him aside.

He graciously let her in front of him.

"Holy fuck, indeed." Kat whistled low.

In the middle of the sea of tents and humans was a column of raging light coming out of a pit surrounded by the fluttering tatters of what might have been a tent once.

"We're going in that? You knew that's what it looked like and didn't tell us." Fabian couldn't help but reconsider this plan.

"Yes," Dumont said bluntly. "Knowing what it looks like doesn't change the fact that we need to go through it."

"I thought we were walking through a gateway, not jumping into a fucking laser cannon."

Kat remained silent, but it was clear she hadn't expected the gateway to be like that either.

Dumont changed the subject. "What's the plan? We can't get out without being seen."

"At this point, I don't think it matters." Kat scanned the area.

"It doesn't matter. But we need to come out closer to the gate. That much is clear," Fabian said.

"It's okay. I've got a plan," Kat said calmly.

Fabian let out a controlled breath. "You knew there would be this many people here?"

"Yes, and I have a plan, so it wasn't important you knew."

Dumont's face crunched into a frown, even more so than before. Good, at least he wasn't the only one in the dark here. "Tell us about this wonderful plan of yours," Fabian said.

This had to be the worst mission he'd ever been on. Everyone had different information, they'd clearly failed to debrief before they left, and none of them trusted each other. They'd be lucky to make it there alive, let alone talk to the gods.

"We'll open the Hollow closer and enter like we're meant to be there. The gate is being guarded by Korbyn's men, and they know who I am."

"And they're going to be happy to see me and Dumont, are they?"

"I suggest you fashion some shadow masks." She molded a web of shadows in the shape of a bird across her face in an instant.

Fabian groaned. "You want us to look like douchey Raven minions?"

"Yes," she said seriously. "Do that now."

Dumont's hand slid from the doorway, and the shadows slipped together as if they had never been there.

"I've never made a douchey shadow mask before," Fabian admitted.

"Just think of what you want it to look like and form a spell cloud in your mind of the image mixed with power symbols you'd usually use for solidifying shadows. Easy," Kat said in full teacher mode.

Fabian turned away and tried it. He turned back, and Kat burst out laughing. Dumont's mouth turned up in a smirk.

"Fuck you two." Fabian rubbed his face to remove the shadows.

Kat chuckled. "You looked like a cute panda cartoon." It was nice to see her laugh for a change, and she had called him cute.

"I was trying to make it a bear." He shot a look at Torin. He was not allowed to find this funny. "I'd like to see you do better, *mate.*"

"Certainly." Dumont closed his eyes and held his elemer close to his face, letting the shadows pour out. They morphed into thin precise lines that wove together to form an intricate raven mask, very damn close to looking like a real bird.

"Oh, fuck you. I've never done this."

"Kat, can you just do it for him so we can go?" Dumont said. "Any wraith or gallu in the Hollow will hear us for miles."

"I can do it. Just give me a sec," Fabian said.

"No, we're wasting time. Hold still." Kat gripped his jaw, her fingers soft but firmly holding him in place.

He kept eye contact with her, leaning into her touch, and smiled as she aimed her elemer at him and sent out a cold trail of shadows that wrapped around his flesh. She tilted his face, admiring her handiwork.

"Do I look amazing? Is it a bear?" Fabian asked.

"Yes, very fierce." Her hand remained resting against his cheek, which he rather liked.

"It's fine. Can we go now?" Dumont had his elemer raised, ready to make the cut.

"Get on with it then, raven-boy."

Dumont cut out of the Hollow. He nodded to Kat, who stepped out without a word.

The chill of the shadow-mask gave little comfort as Fabian stepped into the pit with his enemies. Dumont followed, acting the good little minion with his back straight and one hand on his elemer at his hip, the other rigid against the side of his leg. Fabian copied his stance, keeping his eyes forward and not looking at the insane tube of light streaming from between the two T-shaped monolithic rocks.

He focused his attention on hating Dumont. He was sure that arsehole was as much a raven as these other arseholes. The difference was Dumont was untouchable while everyone need-ed him. Fabian hated that he was the one who had to feed him, agree with him, pretend it was okay that he was Azalea's apprentice master. But that would change one day. One day Dumont would have to start watching his back again.

"It's an honor, Mage Emerson. We weren't expecting you." A man with a demonic shadow mask greeted Kat with a nod of respect.

"We need to perform a test on the gate to measure the rate of output of Echo Magic." Kat glanced at her watch as if he were wasting her time.

Fabian did his best not to move; instead, he noted faces and masks. No sign of old Korbyn Dumont, just the low-level lackeys by the look of it.

The man remained in his position. "They completed the testing schedule yesterday."

"We need to redo a test to confirm the data," Kat said.

"I need to get up on the monolith to measure the stream directly," Dumont added.

"Fine, just get on with it. We've got enough trouble monitoring these conspiracy theorists. We don't need to babysit you as well." The man waved his elemer at Fabian and Torin and nodded to Kat.

"Get on with it then, boys," she barked toward him and Torin. She was a little too good at her role. Though Fabian had to admit he liked her ordering him around.

Kat marched toward the stone monoliths at the center of the pit with confidence. A circular rock wall surrounded the two T-shaped structures. Raven guards were stationed all around the edge and in the entrances to the narrow paths that went off to the sides.

They stopped at the base of the monolith on the left. It had strange animals carved into it, and the gateway of light was above them, not coming out of the ground, but several meters above. It blasted right out from the level top of the stones.

A scaffold platform was already set up against the stones. All they had to do was climb up and jump on in. Bloody hell, this was nuts.

Dumont slowed, his hand resting on the stone as he looked around.

"What's the holdup?" Kat asked Torin.

"I'm just checking he's gone," Torin spoke low.

"Who?" Kat said.

"Erik, or Erik's body. I just wanted to check so I can tell Azalea he's not here still."

Bloody hell, they didn't have time for sentimental bull-shit. Fabian took off his bag and fished out the clipboards Kat had put there. "Look like you belong here at least," Fabian hissed and shoved a clipboard at Dumont.

Fabian pretended to make notes as Torin continued his scan of the area. Three days had passed since the gate was opened, so he doubted they would leave the sacrifice's body just lying around.

"Why does Azalea care? Sounds like that bloke was a trai-tor," Fabian whispered as Torin walked past, pacing between the stone structures.

Dumont stopped. "Believe it or not, she liked him. He wasn't just her classmate, she was—"

Dumont couldn't seem to spit out.

"She was going out with that tosser?" Fabian said louder than he meant to.

"Get on with your job," Kat said loudly.

Torin tensed. "They'd broken up recently."

Was that jealousy he detected? Better not be. Fabian didn't like the vibes he got from Azalea and Dumont. He'd wondered if there was something more between them. Now he found out she had been dating the traitor—she sure knew how to pick men.

"Let's go." Dumont walked to the scaffolding and started up the ladder. "If you'll please follow me, I'll need your help at the top."

Fabian followed him, going against every rational instinct in his body. At the top, the monolith seemed a lot smaller, and the gushing red light from the gateway looked a whole lot bigger.

"This is fucking mad," he mumbled to himself as he stepped beside Dumont.

"Mage Emerson, would you come up here and take a look at this reading?" Fabian yelled loudly. Better get this over with.

Kat scuttled up the ladder before anyone could stop her.

"Oi, no more than two people on the platform!" a guard yelled from below.

Kat squeezed in between them on the wooden boards that lined up with the top of the T-stone. He didn't look down, not wanting to know what they would be stepping into.

"Does anyone else feel underprepared for this?" Fabian clasped the amulet hanging from his neck, praying like hell they worked.

"Yup." Kat and Torin said simultaneously.

"First time we're on the same page. Let's do this." In these situations, it was best not to think. Kat grasped his hand, and he assumed she took Torin's as well.

"Three." Kat guided them off the platform to stand directly on the stone.

"Two." Her palm was sweaty against Fabian's.

"One."

Together, they stepped off the rock and into the gateway below. Fabian squeezed his eyes shut as his stomach plummeted to the earth, and his body was ripped away by the light.

# Chapter 16

Azalea cut out of the Hollow, hoping she'd gotten the right spot. She poked her head out. Yup, this was it, and there was no one around.

"It's all clear." She stepped out, and Faraday and Jade followed.

Jade ran to the edge of the sandstone cliff. "Holy crap, this is epic!"

"Welcome to Petra." Azalea joined her on the flat area right outside the same tomb carved into the cliff where Torin had taken her to watch the spirits. Its smooth columns, decorated carvings, marbled roof, and perfect lines made it look like a palace grown straight out of the rock.

But it was different than the rose-tinted sunset they had watched all those weeks ago. This time it was only mid-afternoon, and the sky was deep red. Shadows stained the rock like old blood coating the walls of the sacred valley. Azalea strained her eyes and was sure she glimpsed the griffin, but she was gone in a flash.

"So, what's the plan? Why are we here with a sword?" Jade asked as she took in the sights.

"Can you see spirits?" Azalea leaned against the rock wall that towered above the valley.

Jade looked over the edge cautiously. "Um, not that I know of. How would I know?"

"Did you ever walk past the chapel by Torin's place?" Azalea scanned the sky, hoping to see the griffin again.

"Yeah..." Jade shuffled back from the edge.

"Did you ever see any weirdos dressed as olden-timey priests, soldiers, or women in Tudor costumes?"

"No. No, I did not." Jade tilted her head in question.

"Then you probably can't see spirits, so this is going to be kind of weird for you because you won't know what's going on. But soon, thousands of spirits are going to pour into this valley, and I'm going to use this sword to send them to the Shadow Dimension. Well... hopefully."

"Okay... Why hopefully?"

"I don't know how the sword works. Maybe I should have tested it somehow." Azalea mused, not that she'd had a chance.

"Maybe a stray spirit will come along to test it on." Jade shrugged. "In the meantime, you need to tell me everything, and I mean everything."

They settled on the edge of the wall with a fifty-meter drop right below. The chill of the wind tickled the stray bit of hair that had escaped Azalea's ponytail, and she felt more alive than ever. She hadn't sensed anything from Torin in a while. She wasn't sure if it was because he was gone or hadn't done anything dangerous yet—like go through an interdimensional gateway. She was on high alert, just waiting for that moment.

"What do you know about soul bonds?" Azalea asked.

Jade patted Faraday as he wound around her leg. "Only that they're illegal and they killed lots of people."

"So here's the thing..." She took a breath and told Jade every-thing. She needed it off her chest, and it was rare she felt so relaxed around anyone. Despite knowing Jade for such a short time, she knew she could trust her.

Jade didn't have over-the-top reactions to everything like Van did and didn't worry like Isaac. She just listened and asked the right questions when she needed to. The sun dropped low on the horizon, tipping the edge of the cliffs on the other side of the valley. The sky turned an even deeper red.

"I can't believe you've been hiding all this from everyone. Although Van told me you had a thing for Torin the day I met her." Jade rubbed her arms. The air was cooling down fast.

"We didn't have a thing! I was with Erik then. Sort of." Her throat tightened at the thought of Erik. She couldn't believe he was gone. She wondered who broke the news to her ex-classmate Livia. She might not like Livia, but this was the last thing she needed after her brother Elam just died.

"Erik wasn't your fault." Jade's arm fell as a comforting weight around her shoulder.

"Thanks. But *all* of this is my fault. Hence the fixing it part."

Sita and Faraday darted past and scrambled over a rock wall, chasing a fire salamander. Azalea swung her legs back over the wall as the lizard with the flaming mohawk scuttled behind some rocks. "Hey leave him alone!" She grabbed Faraday so the lizard could escape. The poor little guy didn't deserve to be a passing snack for her perpetually hungry cat.

"What a cute critter! I want to get a photo so I can draw one." Jade swung her legs over the wall.

"Stop!" Azalea yelled. A man in long sand-colored robes exited the doorway of the sandstone tomb behind them.

"What is it?" Jade froze.

"You can't see that man?" Azalea pulled her aura in close, sure he was a spirit.

"The spirits are coming." The color washed out of Jade's face, and her voice shook. "Sita, get back over here!"

Azalea and Jade backed up, remaining a safe distance away to watch.

"What should we do?" Jade asked.

"Let's test the sword before the procession comes out. Jade, you keep Faraday and Sita here."

Jade didn't hesitate in picking up Sita and placing him on the wall like a small child.

"I will not be manhandled!" he grumbled.

"Oh, shush. Let Azalea do her thing." Jade sat next to Sita, and Faraday perched at her feet to wash his face with his dainty black paws.

Azalea slipped her elemer into her belt and gripped the sword with both hands. The book from Paphos hadn't said anything about how to use it. She certainly didn't want to start stabbing spirits willy-nilly. Maybe just a tap first to see what happened.

*Here goes nothing.*

The next spirit to exit the marbled doorway was an old woman with a gnarled walking stick and a lopsided gait. Azalea stepped up to her, still pulling her aura in close to not draw attention, not yet.

"Excuse me, ma'am." Azalea moved slowly, not wanting to scare her off right away.

The woman didn't even look at her. Her wide eyes locked on the sword. Its silver blade glowed a pale milky blue. Azalea held it out at arm's length—it was bloody heavy—but the woman shuffled near, so Azalea didn't dare move.

The old woman darted forward like a wild cat with a gleam in her eye. She said something in another language, put her hand to her chest, and stepped into the sword's blade.

Azalea gasped. The woman was gone. Azalea lowered the sword and pressed her hand to her chest over her heart. No freezing, no erratic beat—the woman had gone through the sword, not her.

"It worked!" Azalea yelled back.

Sita tilted his head to the side. "Hardly a surprise. Is it not why we came to this land?"

Jade clapped her hands. "I wish I could see it. Do you think I'll be able to see the spirits in the Shadow Dimension?"

"Assuredly. Once one crosses the river, all beings in Kur are visible to mortals." Sita crossed his little arms, and his wings folded behind him neatly.

"Kur?" Azalea asked.

"Ereshkigal's land in the Shadow Dimension," Sita scoffed.

Azalea rested the sword on the ground, it was getting heavy already. "I thought she lived in the City of Stars."

"The City of Stars is in Kur. It is not hard to understand. Though perhaps for mortals it is." Sita sighed and stared off into the valley wistfully.

"Reorrrww." Faraday batted Azalea's leg.

"Shit, incoming spirits." Azalea didn't need to extend her aura out to attract them. As the first ghosts marched out, their gaze went straight to the sword, and she raised it.

This was the royal procession she had witnessed last time. The first men were flag bearers dressed in white, flowing robes. One's eyes filled with fear. He bolted away, racing down the steps into the valley.

Interesting. Some must not be ready. She just hoped enough would choose the sword.

Taking a deep breath, Azalea raised the sword in front of her and braced her feet, just in case. The other flag bearer turned toward her, a look of hope and gratitude in his eyes.

He calmly walked forward and impaled himself. It wasn't gory or dramatic. There was no blood or pain. It was like when the spirits touched her shoulder—they simply disappeared. Although this was far more pleasant, as it didn't stop her heart or knock her unconscious.

More followed: Nabataeans, Romans, Bedouins, people from distant lands, men in gilded capes, children dressed in simple robes and some in elaborate bejeweled designs, women with crowns, beautiful braids, old, young, some pregnant or carrying tiny babies in their arms; most seemed grateful to see her.

She got the feeling they did this procession every night because they always had. It gave them something to keep them grounded. A ceremony. Perhaps this was why they weren't as insane or desperate as the spirits at the Tower—or perhaps they were less tortured. Even so, it was clear they wanted to leave.

Azalea's arms grew heavy as she tried to keep the sword lifted as dozens of spirits surged forward. Their voices grew louder. They had worked out what was going on and yelled back down the procession to spread the news, all formation and formality lost in the excitement.

At first, the line had been slow and cautious, with only a few strays scattering off to return to the valley that was so familiar to them. But as they got more confident, she had to step back and found herself pressed against the stone wall with the drop on the other side. Jade appeared next to her, her hands wrapped around Azalea's, and gave her arms a much-needed rest.

"I wish I could see them. Can you tell me what they look like?" Jade said.

It was the distraction Azalea needed. As the spirits approached, she described them, noting just a few details for each one; a gold bracelet, a kind smile, interesting headwear. It kept her focused and made her remember they were people once, not just spirits she needed as payment.

Dizziness washed over Azalea, and she nearly dropped the sword. Jade took the full weight and steadied her with her other hand. A cloudiness filled Azalea's brain like a sweeping fog. But when she opened her eyes, nothing was wrong, though everything felt a little off. She couldn't put her finger on it.

"You okay?" Jade gave her a reassuring squeeze.

Azalea welcomed the support. "Yeah, just dizzy. I guess the sword must draw some magic to work."

"Move over here." Jade shuffled them all to the side and rested the sword on the stone wall, which was about hip height. She put Azalea's hands on top of the sword and balanced over the cliff-side wall to sit on the other side so they could stabilize it together without having to hold it up.

A strange emptiness overcame Azalea, like a faint ache in her heart. Unexpected panic rose in her chest. "Something's wrong," she said aloud but felt ridiculous. Were the spirits doing something to her?

"Should we stop? How many more do we need to do?" Jade asked.

Azalea hadn't been counting. Faraday jumped on her lap and purred.

"You need another 377 to fulfill the quota," Sita said matter-of-factly. "There's nothing wrong with you, Mageling. Your soulmate has left this realm, that is all."

"That's all." She sucked in a breath. *That's all* felt a lot like someone had died. She hadn't anticipated this feeling and didn't even want to think what it would be like if he died for real.

"Soulmate?" Jade raised an eyebrow.

That knocked Azalea out of her despair. "Yeah, what?"

"Soulmate. You are soul bonded to the raven-mage. Are all mortals this slow?"

"I don't believe in soulmates." Azalea bit the inside of her cheek.

"It isn't a matter of belief; it is a technical term." He folded his arms and tucked his wings in tight. "You may live in ignorance if you choose."

Jade grinned and leaned against the wall, more relaxed now. "That's pretty cool."

Azalea didn't know what to say, but she was too young to have a soulmate. Instead of dwelling on it, she focused on the spirits. It was completely dark by the time the line thinned and the last spirit stepped into the sword.

"It's done." Azalea lowered the sword to the ground with Jade's help. She clenched and unclenched her hand which seemed to have frozen into the shape of the sword's hilt.

"How many was it?" Jade asked Sita.

"1647 souls. The dark goddess will be most pleased." Sita nodded in approval.

"I bloody well hope so." Azalea shook her hand to try to get the feeling back, and Jade did the same. "Thanks for your help, Jade. I needed it."

Jade saluted her. "Consider me the Samwise to your Frodo."

"Oh, don't say that. Their journey was way harder than it should have been." Azalea smiled, feeling lighter already. Step one complete. All they had to do was get to the Shadow Dimension now...

A shadow glided over the stone wall, and Azalea was on her feet. A griffin landed in front of them, followed by the three griffin kittens that tumbled onto the ground with none of the grace their mother possessed.

"Griffin babies!" They ran up to her and started bouncing all around, trying to pull her bootlaces and batting her legs with soft feet with retracted claws.

Faraday hissed and remained on the wall by Sita.

Jade squealed and, after seeing Azalea's reaction, joined her in cuddling the energetic balls of fluff. They were much bigger than the last time she'd seen them just weeks ago.

The mama griffin stared at her, then scratched the ground with her foot. She seemed to be demanding an explanation about the magic destroying the world.

Azalea swallowed. The griffin's beak was very pointy. "I know you trusted us with the relic, but I assure you it is under control. I promise we will fix it." Azalea bowed to the griffin.

Jade had the sense to remain quiet. Azalea cuddled a griffin to her chest, and its soft wing fluttered across her cheek.

The mother griffin snorted and chirped to the babies, who chirped right back and ran to her.

"I'll fix this and see you again soon. I promise." She watched as the griffins flapped around until they got off the ground to follow their mother like strange little ducklings.

"That was weird," Jade said.

"It's going to get a lot weirder, I'm sure." Azalea rolled her shoulders, strangely pumped up from her success with the sprits. "This is your chance. I can take you back now if you want. I can't promise we will make it back."

"I want to come. I know the risks, plus, some giant eagles or perhaps griffins will probably rescue us or something." She shrugged.

"I'm sure they will." *How nice would that be?* "Let's get going then. Sita, lead the way."

"It is about time." Sita's ears pricked up. "Follow me."

# Chapter 17

Wind and light blasted around them. Fabian's fingers slipped away from Kat's, and she was tossed around in the vortex of light. Fabian gripped the amulet around his neck, hoping it worked to protect him.

Then he was thrown out. Sharp grass flattened under him as he lay motionless, gasping for air that smelled of baked earth and sunshine. Sunshine—it was really hot here.

*Kat. He'd let her go.* "Kat!" He forced himself to his feet. He raised a hand to his eyes. A glaring white sun, twice the size of Earth's, doused the patchwork of vibrant green farmland in sparkling light. A rushing river drew his attention. The reeds masking it were tall enough to hide any number of enemies.

"Kat!" He turned to see the gate. It was standing upright on this side, like a doorway; a giant ring at the end of a barren dirt road surrounded by reeds with light being sucked through to their world. Hopefully, it was as easy as stepping through when they wanted to go home.

"Here." A moan sounded from somewhere nearby.

He followed the voice and sunk down next to her. She was lying on a stack of crushed reeds. Her black uniform stood out against the natural landscape. Both he and Dumont were dressed similarly in all black; none of them belonged here.

She sat up and sneezed, cradling her arm. "The Echo Dimension hates me."

"It doesn't hate you, you're just allergic to it." He recalled she was allergic to many plants, and up ahead he could see various plantations spread across the flat river valley.

"Let me look at that arm." He was glad to see the injury was her left, non-dominant hand.

"Where's Torin?" Kat rolled over and groaned.

"I don't know. I was looking for you."

If they lost Dumont now, he wouldn't complain. It would be an easy fix to his problem.

She stood without the use of either arm. "Torin," Kat yelled. "You look closer to the gate. I'll look over here."

Fabian wandered toward the gate, kicking back the tall reeds. "I would have thought there'd be someone to greet us, or guards, or something here."

"Stay alert. I'm sure there will be. I'm surprised there aren't any more creatures going through from this end."

She had a good point. For days there had been new creatures flying above them, plus reports from all over the world of beasts roaming. There had to have been thousands going through here when it opened. Despite the lush farmland, this whole area seemed to be abandoned.

"I found him!"

Fabian sighed and followed Kat's voice into another patch of reeds. Her finger was on Dumont's neck. "He's alive."

"Wonderful," Fabian said.

"I don't need your sarcasm, Fabian. We need Torin, so stop wishing he was dead."

Damn, she knew him too well. "For you, Kitty Kat, I will protect him with my life."

"Just stop being a dick and help me."

Fabian slapped him hard on the face. Not for fun, but for medical reasons...

Kat shot him a death stare, but Dumont squinted up at them and blinked.

"What happened?" Dumont pushed back the reeds poking him in the face.

"We all made it." Kat helped him sit up. The relief clear in her voice.

Dumont blinked and looked around. "Good. Have you tested your magic?"

"Not yet." Kat shook her head.

"Stick to the plan," Dumont ordered.

"No one put you in charge, mate. Kat is in charge, and she wanted to find you first, so calm your tits."

Dumont clenched his jaw.

"I am in charge, and I order you both to act like a team. Test your magic now." She reached for her elemer on her belt. "Like bloody children," she mumbled.

Fabian cut into the Shadow Dimension. It was far harder than back home but possible. He tried to pull through some Shadow Magic, but it was weak and required too much effort for the thin sliver of shadow that wisped out of his elemer's tip.

On top of that, the Echo Magic around him vibrated so loudly that he felt it through his whole body, calling for him to use it. He hardly ever used Echo Magic, but here it felt like it wanted to burn him up.

"We can't use magic here." Dumont pointed out the obvious.

"This isn't going to work." Kat dug into her pocket. "Gloves on."

That he agreed with. He slipped on the thin, magic-blocking gloves and felt instant relief from the pull of Echo Magic. All he had now were the daggers Kat had strapped all over him, but unlike Kat, he wasn't trained in how to use them.

A thundering arose in the distance. Dots appeared miles away at the edge of the farmlands.

"Looks like we've got company." Fabian squinted into the distance.

"Hopefully it's a welcome party," Dumont said, but the look in his eyes indicated he didn't believe that for a minute.

"Just let me do the talking. You two shut it." Kat had a dagger in each hand, as did Torin.

It took about ten minutes of high-intensity standing still before their new friends got close enough to ID. Fabian suddenly wished they had brought larger weapons. The newcomers came into vague focus, thundering up the dirt road in a cloud of dust.

They were massive with bodies of giant scorpions and the upper half of armored men. Fabian did his best not to crap himself. If they weren't friendly, this would be over quickly. "What the fuck are those?"

"Scorpion people," Kat replied, without a tremor or any sign of fear in her voice.

Dumont frowned. "Aqrabuamelu."

Fabian glared at him. "Is that supposed to mean something to me?"

"They are called Aqrabuamelu. There are records from Mesopotamian and Babylonian mythology. They guarded Utu, the sun god's—"

"I don't give a shit about that. Give us something useful." Fabian focused on details as the group of twenty or so thundered closer: eight powerful legs that looked like pistons of solid copper, a huge stinger curled at the rear. The top half was fully plated copper armor. Half carried bows; half carried curved blades the size of a man. Most disturbing was the clicking scuttling sounds of their legs as they ate up ground faster than a car.

"Venomous stings, godlike powers, arrows that hit with fatal accuracy. I expect they speak Archaic Sumerian like the gods—" Dumont said.

Fabian clapped to get his attention. "Weaknesses, Dumont. Give us something."

"I don't know," Dumont snapped back.

"Fat lot of good a historian is in the field." Fabian shook his head. The one time when history might be useful.

"Surrender weapons," the voice of the scorpion man in front boomed out. He stopped about a bus distance away, blocking the sun with his massive figure.

"English," Fabian whispered toward Dumont under his breath. If this was the end, at least he got the last word in.

"Greetings. We wish to travel to Enki's Palace of the Waters," Kat said confidently.

"No mortals in the Land of Light," the front one bellowed. He seemed to be the chap in charge.

Fabian stood his ground. At least he would look the part if this was the end. He refused to show any weakness in front of Dumont or Kat.

"We wish to speak with Enki and Enlil." Kat locked eyes with the leader.

"No mortals in the Land of Light, no mortals in the Land of Light, no mortals in the Land of Light." The other scorpion people joined in, their voices out of time and getting louder.

"I don't think they understand." Kat glanced between them.

Dumont yelled something in whatever he thought their ancient language was, but his voice was drowned out by their repetitive bellows. They made no move closer, though.

"You got any grenades?" Fabian asked.

Kat patted her bag. "A few, but it's not the right message if we want to make friends here. I don't think Enki or Enlil would appreciate us blowing up their guards."

"I'm not sure making friends is an option at this point." Fabian kept one eye on the guards.

"They are guardians appointed by the gods. Maybe it's a test?" Dumont said.

"Do you have any flash grenades?" Fabian ignored Dumont. Test or not, they couldn't take the risk.

"I've got a few." Kat already had them out of her pack.

The scorpion people stopped chanting.

"Give one here, you count down, we'll throw it in three, and we'll run back to the gate," Fabian said as Kat handed him the grenade.

"Three, two, one." Kat counted, and he pulled the pin and hurled it over the first row of scorpion people, then sprinted toward the gate.

A blast of light and what sounded like a small gun fight shattered the air behind them. He didn't turn around. Dumont ran beside him with Kat slightly ahead. But she skidded to a halt when a figure appeared from the sky above the gateway.

Fabian had always believed in the gods. That was where his magic came from after all, but until that moment, he hadn't thought angels existed. The woman with shimmering white wings that were tipped in gold, though, seemed to be just that. She landed right in front of Kat, and he felt his jaw drop. The pearlescent sheen of her skin, her black hair, her star-tipped crown, and her come-hither smile nearly brought him to his knees. The only thing that stopped him from prostrating before her was when he noticed the pure white dragon touch down beside the gate, crushing the reeds flat as if they were soft grass. Thin and slinky, like a wingless Chinese dragon, it circled several times, wound into a ball, and closed its eyes. The reeds folded up around it like a basket.

Kat glanced back as Fabian and Torin caught up and stood on either side of her. They all remained silent as the woman stepped toward them, her silky white dress with golden braids around the top half billowed around her, clinging enticingly to her form.

"You can stop drooling now," Kat hissed.

Was that a hint of jealousy? He hoped so. He was sure he wasn't drooling, but he snapped his mouth shut and made a note not to stare at the angel-woman's fine breasts, even though he could see her nipples quite clearly through the thin fabric.

"I've been expecting you." The woman's voice dripped with honey.

"And you are?" Kat asked.

She put her hands to her chest and giggled. "I apologize. My name is Inanna." She bowed. "It is a pleasure to meet mortals in this land. It has been several millennia since we have had the honor."

"It's very nice to meet you too. But would you mind mentioning that to your goons back there?" Fabian pointed back with his thumb. "They seem rather set on killing us."

She let out a shrill whistle, and the scorpion men retreated. Fabian smiled but didn't relax.

"They are Enki's men, stationed here to guard the gate. It was hard for me to arrive in time, so they had not been warned."

"Thank you for coming so fast." Dumont appeared a little starstruck. "You are *The* Inanna?"

"She's the goddess of love and war if you didn't know," Kat whispered to Fabian.

Of course, he knew who she was.

Inanna clapped her hands together. "I am still remembered!"

Maybe it was best not to tell her that Sumer was long ago, and most people had forgotten the gods.

"I'm also the goddess of sex and fertility." She stepped closer and ran a finger down Torin's chest, seductively.

Fabian opened his mouth. But Kat elbowed him in the ribs. "Don't," she hissed.

"You don't even know what I was going to say," Fabian whispered. If she was going to seduce anyone around here, it should be him, though that might affect his chances with Kat somewhat negatively.

"Thank you for coming to meet us," Dumont stuttered and took a step back. "If it isn't too much trouble, could you please direct us to Enki's palace? We've been sent to close the gate to our world. We believe he and Enlil might be able to help. There isn't much time."

Inanna pouted and put a finger to her lip. "I can take you there, but you should not speak of such serious matters before feasting."

"No, we should not," Fabian cut in. He would not get on the wrong side of this goddess because Dumont wouldn't man up. "We would be honored if you would take us."

Inanna's attention turned to Fabian, and she looked him up and down. "Splendid. We can still make it in time for the feast."

"Thank you. We are grateful for your assistance." Kat stepped slightly in front of Fabian, shielding him from the goddess's view.

"I promised my sister I would aid you on your quest. But I will give you one warning." She folded her wings in and motioned them to move closer to her.

She was only slightly taller than Fabian and Torin but held an unmistakable air of power. "You must not speak to Enlil."

"Why not?" Fabian had to ask.

"Like many of the gods here, Enlil has no love for mortals. He sent a great flood to destroy humanity once before. He will not hesitate to do so again if he hears of recent events."

# Chapter 18

"Cut into the Hollow," Sita ordered.

"Where exactly is the gate to the Shadow Dimension?" Azalea sliced through the air almost effortlessly.

"I am the gate," Sita said smugly.

Jade followed them in, and the darkness sealed them inside. It was a pleasant relief to be away from the constant pressure of Echo Magic in the air.

"What's that supposed to mean?" Jade asked.

"No more talk. I will show you." Sita used his claw to slice into the air. The air pressure changed, and a stream of Shadow Magic blasted into the void laced with the distinct smell of the Shadow Dimension, electrical energy and a sky heavy with waiting storms.

"That's the Shadow Dimension?" Azalea crouched to peer through the gap.

Sita nodded proudly. "Indeed."

"We won't fit through that gap though," Jade pointed out.

Sita flew up to eye level. "I will extend it for your abnormal human tallness."

"It can't be that simple. We searched the entire planet for relics to open the Echo gate, and you can just open this in a second?" Azalea didn't know what to trust anymore.

Sita opened the doorway further as Jade held him up. "The Echo Dimension gods are dramatic and showy. Their gateway needn't have been so elaborate and obvious. The Dark Goddess is wise and knows the value of subtlety and secrecy."

"It'll be fine Azalea. The prophecy said we would make it back. Have a little faith." Jade nudged Azalea.

Sita's black claw sliced a streak right down to the spongy blue ground and he flapped through without another word. Faraday followed without looking back.

"We have to go now. We can't let Faraday go without us." Jade was fearless.

Azalea wished she could be more like her. She had to do this, for Torin, for everyone.

Jade ducked out of the slit in the darkness, and Azalea followed.

The hairs on Azalea's arms rose as soon as she stepped out. They were in a dark tunnel, a cave that extended as far as she could see. Flickering flames rose from iron sconces bolted to the walls, and Shadow Magic surrounded her, buzzing like static electricity, screaming out for her to use it.

"Gloves on now." Azalea reached for her bag.

Jade moved fast, and they both slipped on the iron gloves that were as light as cashmere. The prickling in her hands stopped, but it was clear they couldn't risk even a drop of magic here or they would burn up.

Azalea looked up from the bag and jumped, reaching for her elemer. A tall man greeted them with a solemn bow, his skin a deep red like dark iron-rich earth, his crimson hair spiking up at all angles.

"Sitaddaru, it has been too long. I did not expect to see you upon these shores again." The man stared at Sita with glowing red eyes.

Sita crossed his arms. "And here you are, same job, same absurd hairstyle. Some things never change, ay, Neti?"

"At least I've been here, fulfilling my duty, not trapped as a book." Neti glared at Sita, then began to chuckle as Sita flapped onto his shoulder and ruffled Neti's hair with his tiny hand.

Still smiling, Neti turned his gaze to Azalea and Jade, then eyed Faraday with suspicion.

"I do not meet many mortals who remain in their flesh," Neti said in a gruff voice.

"We would like to remain in our flesh if that's okay with you," Azalea said, wishing she hadn't read any mythology and didn't know what happened to the goddess Inanna when she came here.

Neti bowed his head, and Sita flew to the ground by Faraday. "You will remain unharmed, as long as the Dark Goddess wishes."

Azalea had to trust he was telling the truth but couldn't help wishing Torin was there beside her. He felt even further away now. Just a faint sense of something she couldn't put her finger on told her he was still out there somewhere.

Her head felt clearer than it had in weeks without his emotions clouding her. She felt like herself again, but also like something important was missing.

"You will pass through each of the seven gates to reach the banks of the Eridan." Neti gestured to the first gate, a mass of metal that blocked the mouth of the tunnel with a perfect circle cut from the middle with rays of iron spread out from it like a sun.

"At this, the sun gate known as Shamash, you will surrender your conduits of magic and defense."

Azalea and Jade exchanged confused glances.

"Your elemers and the sword," Sita translated.

"Will we get them back?" Azalea asked.

"It is at the will of the goddess."

Jade slipped hers out of her belt and held it in her palm for a moment before handing it to Neti without question. He bowed, took the elemer with both hands, and placed it in a reed basket.

Azalea sucked in a breath and held hers out. It felt like giving part of herself away. She hadn't been without an elemer since she arrived at the Tower seven months ago. She handed over the sword as well.

"Proceed to the next gate."

Azalea and Jade walked side by side through the tunnel. It was almost completely soundless. Her ears pulsed with the pressure of Shadow Magic around them, but she got used to the strange fizzing in the air and listened as each booted footstep hit the stone floor.

They walked for about five minutes. Faraday and Sita trailed them, but Neti had remained behind. The next gate appeared out of nowhere. They stopped abruptly as a gate of bright metal emerged along with Neti.

"At the gate of the moon, known as Sin, you will surrender all nourishment."

"Food in your bags," Sita nodded to her pack.

Azalea swallowed. She didn't like where this was heading. She took the ration packs, the apples, a block of cheese, a stick of salami, and the pack of chocolate digestives she brought as a treat and placed them in the basket. Jade did the same, staring at the block of chocolate she had to leave.

The next three gates were the same deal. A walk, a sudden appearance from Neti, and he took more of their stuff. At the Mercury gate, Gugdud, he took their phones, watches, and ear pods. The Venus gate, Dlibat, they lost their toiletries and medicines. At Mars, Mastabarru gate, he took their spare clothes.

"My bag's almost empty now." Jade stared into it.

"It'll be okay. We might get it back," Azalea said, but the same concerns plagued her thoughts. The walk between each gate became torture, each longer than the last. They were all on edge, unable to anticipate when the next gate would appear.

"Fucking hell! A bit of warning would be nice," Azalea yelled the next time Neti appeared with a gate of shimmering copper.

Neti stared ahead. She suspected he enjoyed this. "At this, the Jupiter gate, Umunpaddu, you will offer your bags and foot coverings to the Dark Goddess."

"We're not going to have anything left by the end of this." Jade unlaced her boots and slipped her socks inside.

"I think that's the point." Azalea had a good idea what they would be losing at the next gate. Her feet met the cold stone, and she placed her boots in the basket alongside her bag.

"At least we aren't walking on hot coals, or glass or something," Jade said.

Azalea had to smile. "I am so glad you're here with me. I am going to owe you forever."

"I signed up for this, too. Sam and Frodo all the way."

Azalea's heart raced as they padded toward the next gate, her soft untrained feet feeling every tiny pebble and crack.

She tried to listen, this time for a sign that Neti would appear. The sound of water crept closer. They turned a corner, the first in the tunnel so far, and there was the opening. The wide mouth of the cave with a rushing river just outside, lit up only by a night sky of sparkling stars. The water raced past the white marble jetty that shone bright with starlight, making the small boat, with carved ends tied to it, bob about in the current. Then with a crack, a golden gate appeared.

"Maybe this one is heaven?" Jade smiled.

"Only one way to find out. Hi, Neti." Azalea tried to get a rise out of the stoic guardian who appeared before them.

Faraday wound around Neti's legs. Traitorous cat, he should be on her side.

"At this, the Saturn gate, known as Kaimanu, you will shed your mortal vestments and enter the lands of Kur in your purest form."

"Is he serious?" Jade's hands were on her hips.

Neti stared straight ahead, holding out his basket.

"I think so." Azalea chewed the inside of her cheek.

"Sita, is this really necessary?" Jade asked the demon who had quietly been following behind this whole time.

"It is. I cannot interfere. It has always been this way."

"Better get it over with then." Azalea peeled off her mum's green jacket, feeling bad for parting with it. It wasn't too cold at least, and the hum of magic in the air almost worked like a heater, like it was keeping her skin buzzing which in its own way kept her warm.

She took off her jeans, suddenly awkward that she was undressing in front of her friend.

Azalea glanced at Jade to check she was okay. "Oh my gods, you're naked already."

Jade shrugged, standing there completely nude except for the thin metal gloves. "You said get on with it, no point in faffing around."

Seeing Jade so chill about the whole thing, Azalea stopped worrying, peeled off her maroon sweater and t-shirt, and slipped out of her bra and knickers.

They placed their clothes in the basket. Azalea did not make eye contact with Neti. Though he didn't seem interested in their nakedness; he just stood there like a red, earthy statue.

"Your tattoos are amazing." Azalea wanted to see more but didn't want Jade to think she was checking her out. She wondered how long Neti would make them wait. He made no move to open the gate.

"Thanks." Jade held her arms out so Azalea could see. Her tattoos on both arms matched perfectly, unlike Azalea's which were very different for each house.

Azalea held both arms out for Jade to see hers. They spent so much time rugged up in warm clothes, they had never had a chance to see each other's tattoos.

Jade's were classic black tattoos that went perfectly with her goth vibes. The ones on her right arm were silhouettes of winged bulls in various poses. Some were flying, some lying down, some meeting other bulls. It was like a mini story painted across her arm. Scattered behind them were bright red, tiny poppies falling from her shoulder to her wrist.

Her left arm was a classic eagle spread across her biceps and on her forearm a similar scene to the winged bulls, but it was eagles in various flying positions circling one point. It was striking and had the same poppies tumbling through the sky.

"They're amazing," Azalea breathed, noting the symmetry in both arms and how well they matched and harmonized with Jade's personality. She appeared to have good balance all around.

"Holy shit, yours are amazing!" Jade's wide eyes scanned Azalea's body slowly.

Azalea's cheeks heated. Her left arm only had the simple watercolor azalea flowers with bumble bees hovering over it. Her right arm shocked her once more. It had grown again. She rolled half the metal glove back. The snake that used to sit with its head at her wrist had coiled around to the top of her hand. Its cute little head now sat perfectly centered on her hand, poking its tiny tongue toward the glowing crescent moon that curved over her knuckles and behind her arm were the new raven and snake designs that she rather liked.

"It wasn't like that before." Azalea looked down at her chest. The tattoo that was a mirror image of Torin's glowed but wasn't any different. She craned her neck to try to look over her shoulder but couldn't see if the one on her back had changed.

Jade gasped.

"What!" Azalea spun around like an idiot, trying to see.

"It's her. Ereshkigal." Jade stared past her.

"Yes, it is. But you already saw that one." Azalea furrowed her brow and turned back to Jade. But Jade wasn't looking at her, she was pointing across the river.

Azalea gulped. Ereshkigal herself stood on the opposite bank of the river between two hanging lanterns. In the distance, a mountain range pierced the sky, one peak higher than the rest and belched black smoke in an ominous backdrop that sent a shiver crawling down Azalea's spine.

"You must discard the gloves and adornments to cross," Neti said.

Azalea gripped her necklace, the locket Torin had given her. She unclasped it and handed it to Neti along with the demantoid garnet fake wedding ring she'd grown so attached to. She made a promise to herself that she would make it out and get them back.

# Chapter 19

"How did you get her to help us?" Fabian asked as they passed yet another plantation of date palms on one side and fields of barley on the other. The same as the last two hours of scenery, albeit with more settlements and many more people, all of whom prostrated themselves in the dirt when Inanna floated past. Most of which she didn't even acknowledge.

Torin hesitated, suspicious any time Fabian opened his mouth. "Actually, it was Azalea. Ereshkigal is Inanna's sister. Azalea spoke to her during her ceremony."

"Told you the ceremony was a good idea." Fabian tapped his chin.

Torin gritted his teeth. *Be diplomatic.* "There was a reason I was waiting for her ceremony. She's a target for Ereshkigal now."

"She was chosen by her. It's an honor." Fabian kicked a rock into a channel off the side of the road. Inanna, who floated gracefully in front of them, looked back and frowned.

"And did you think what she might have to agree to in return?" Torin snapped and forced himself not to tell Fabian to stop acting like a child.

"What?" Fabian stopped in his tracks.

Torin paused. He couldn't get into this with Fabian, he was just digging himself a hole. "It doesn't matter. It isn't set in stone yet."

"Stop walking," Fabian growled. "Tell me."

Inanna dove from the sky and hovered in front of them with slow flaps of her wings. "My dear sister asked me to help you."

"Out of the goodness of her heart?" Fabian crossed his arms.

Torin cringed at the way he spoke to the goddess. He cleared his throat. "Why would she do that? Didn't she, um..." Torin didn't know how to put it.

"Hang me from a hook and leave my rotting corpse exposed for all to see? Yes," Inanna answered.

Kat's hand went to her mouth. They all knew the mythology, the story of Inanna's descent to the underworld. Well, maybe Fabian didn't, but Torin hadn't wanted to bring it up.

"I admit, I had ulterior motives when I visited for her husband's funeral rites," she said with a sly smile.

"What are you getting in return?" Fabian asked.

Torin noticed Kat tense up at the same time as him. This was risky being so direct.

"The price for my returned life when I was in the underworld was my husband's. He remains in the Shadow Dimension for half the year, his sister volunteered to remain the other six months so Dumuzi did not have to remain full time. I believe it is time he returned to his place at my side."

Fabian nodded as if he understood. "I'm sure he will be glad of the opportunity to return to your side."

"Indeed, my hope is that he will help me rule. I have not been able to maintain full control. Enki and Enlil continue to meddle, as always. Enlil maintains his palace in the mountains but still interferes. But I could use my husband now. I believe he has matured enough to take the position seriously."

"How long has he been gone?" Kat asked.

"I gave up counting long ago. I believe it has been several millennia." She smiled and floated above them and swirled around. "There is the city. Can you see it in the distance?"

The grids of barley stopped at the edge of the ocean on the hazy horizon next to the outline of a city.

Their conversation stopped as they made their way closer. The structures slowly revealed themselves and the scale of the city. A stepped pyramid, a ziggurat, towered over the walled city next to what must be Enki's palace, a fortress that rose above the low-level city in a mix of mud-brick towers and the rich blue sheen of lapis lazuli stone.

"Now that's a palace," Fabian exclaimed.

Torin had to agree with him there.

"It is not as fine as my city of Erech but closer to the gate," Inanna said as her dragon flitted off and circled the towers before disappearing inside somewhere. They passed a collection of mud cottages beyond the city walls. One had a nursery of baby goats outside, all bouncing around and headbutting each other to see who could get on top of an overturned trough.

Azalea would love them.

Torin couldn't help but wonder what she was doing. It was unnerving not feeling her presence. As much as he didn't want to when she was around, he had to admit he missed her.

At the edge of the city, the walls revealed just how tall they were, at least the height of a five-story building. But that was quickly forgotten when two giant lions hurtled toward them from the gate. Inanna stepped forward when the great beasts were nearly on them, twice the size of a normal lion and with dark manes that curled under their bellies.

She crouched down, and they leaped on her like kittens, bowling her over, but she wrestled them to the ground in a tumbling, playful embrace that would have been certain death for anyone else.

Torin heard Fabian let out a shaky breath, and he couldn't blame him. He realized he hadn't been breathing that whole time and did the same.

Inanna stood and dusted herself off as the lions bounded ahead. "They will not hurt you." She laughed, seeing all their faces.

Inanna and the lions led them through the great archway of lapis lazuli that marked the entrance to the inner city. Crowds parted as she walked them through the compacted earth streets. Torin had no preconception of what the Echo Dimension would be like, but it certainly wasn't a bustling city.

"Who are all these people?" Surely, they couldn't all be gods. They manned a variety of marketplace stalls. Torin stayed close behind Kat and Fabian as they walked by a shop with bright pyramids of spices that scented the air. Women and men in a variety of fashions stood by their products: fresh dates, bright red pomegranate seeds, tiny squares of perfectly arranged dessert morsels that had Torin's mouth-watering, and colorful felts, and textiles.

"Most are spirits chosen for their skill and ability. Over the years, they have been brought to this land from the Shadow Dimension. Some are commoners, deities, and other beings: minotaurs, shifters, elves, demons." She scrunched up her nose. "The inner ring are the nobles, the ancient kings, and demi-gods. But we will go beyond to the palace."

As expected, gods were snobs. They reached a set of vibrant blue steps that, up close, shimmered with tiny sparkles of gold, and followed them to the grand doors of the palace.

"Greetings." A two-faced man spread his hands to welcome them. He had to be Enki's messenger, Isimud. It was hard not to stare at his two faces; they were on opposite sides of his head, and one seemed a lot happier than the other.

Isimud snapped something at the servants, who promptly came back with a chilled mint tea that Torin was grateful for. They had been walking for hours.

Inanna insisted on escorting them to their appointed rooms alongside Isimud. It was disconcerting following a man whose face was backward all the time, staring at them as they walked.

They went up two flights of expansive stairs and trailed off down a smaller hallway that was open on one side, letting in the warm sea air that smelled of salt and summer.

Torin's heart clenched. He tried not to panic or stop walking but was forced to press his hand to his chest to ease the pain.

Inanna turned to him with a knowing smile. "It is your bond. It grows more distant."

Torin moved his hand away quickly but noticed Kat watching him.

"Bond?" Fabian slowly turned.

Torin shot a look at Inanna, hoping she would get the message. She tilted her head and narrowed her eyes but didn't say anything more.

"It's nothing." Torin caught his breath. It felt like Azalea was even further away than before.

"What did you mean, Goddess? Is there a bond to our world? Is it dangerous to stay here?" Fabian asked.

"It is only your raven-mage. He has a unique bond. But does not wish to discuss it. You are all safe in your mortal forms here."

"Good. It better not affect this mission, Dumont."

Torin didn't say anything. Fabian wasn't stupid, he would catch on eventually, but Torin would do everything he could to put off that day.

Isimud stopped abruptly. His head swiveled around. "Your rooms in the east wing. Enki will be pleased to welcome you as guests at the grand feast tonight. Appropriate attire is within. Please make use of it."

Fabian and Kat took the first two rooms, and Torin walked into the third.

"I will help you dress." Inanna followed him without asking, and Torin's skin prickled with unease.

The room was over the top. The colorful mosaic floors had a scattering of natural woven rugs. The bed was the size of two beds and was framed in gold with a canopy of white flowing curtains waving lazily in the breeze. The room had huge arched windows with no glass. A wide doorway opened onto a balcony that had a white day bed surrounded by live palm trees in bulky pots.

"This is very nice of Enki." To be in the presence of a goddess—a goddess he had read about since he was a child—was overwhelming and he couldn't think what to say. She was even more stunning in real life than in the stories. But why was she here talking to him?

"I see what is in your heart. I see the bond. Why do you deny it?" Inanna went to the closet and pulled out what looked like a dress.

"Because it was not a choice." Torin set his bag down on the bed, not wanting to place it on any of the gold furniture in case he scratched it.

"A bond such as this should be celebrated. It is a splendid gift. Great power for a mortal." She shook her head and put the dress back, then pulled out a red one with shimmering gold beads.

He took a breath. It was important not to offend her.

"I understand, but this type of magic is illegal in our world, and the bond is with my apprentice, Fabian's niece. He would not approve."

"Oh, I had suspected a love triangle." She sounded disappointed. "Never mind. What is the problem? You fear he will challenge your honor?"

"He already has enough reasons to want to kill me. I'm not looking to give him another one."

"I see the pain in your heart. You want him to accept you, but do not believe there is a path to this road."

He wasn't sure that was entirely accurate. He had never considered it an option to make amends with Fabian. "There is not. He will never forgive me for what I have done."

"It is not forgiveness from this man that you seek, it is forgiveness from yourself. Only then can you embrace life and the gifts you have been given."

"Thanks. I'll keep that in mind." Torin shifted between his feet.

"I can stay if that is what you wish. I can make you forget." She moved closer.

Torin took a step back. "Um, thank you for the offer. But no." He was sweating and couldn't believe he was turning her down, but she wasn't the one he wanted.

A flash of anger burned across her eyes. Then her face went serene.

He didn't dare breathe. This was the goddess who sent the murderous Bull of Heaven to rampage on earth after the great hero Gilgamesh rejected her. She wasn't accustomed to rejection then and probably wasn't now either.

"You take the bond seriously. Good. There is still hope for you." She trailed her fingers over his cheek.

A shiver ran down his back, but he remained still. This was his chance. "Would you pass on a message to Enki for us?"

"Perhaps." She studied his face.

Torin kept his voice steady. "Please tell him we know the scribe Nabu is missing. If we were to find Nabu and return him, would Enki agree to close the Echo gate?"

She smiled to herself, thinking it over for a moment. "I will do my best to pass this message on. See you at dinner." She pressed her lips to his, and then she was gone.

Torin swallowed. That was a road he didn't want to go down. One step at a time, all he had to do was survive dinner. He looked at the outfit Inanna left on the bed, and he let out a groan.

# Chapter 20

Azalea stepped onto the boat; the stern curled over in the shape of a snake that stared at them. The prow was the body of a man that seemed to grow out of the boat from the waist up. He stared straight forward and held a punting pole.

"This is so weird," Jade whispered as she slid onto the wide central bench.

"It's going to be fine." Azalea sat down and hugged herself to cover her chest. Faraday bounded in after them and sat between Azalea's feet.

Sita was in the boat in two flaps of his bat-like wings and took the seat at the front, behind the man.

Neti untied the boat from the wharf and bowed as it drifted into the river. "May the goddess bless you."

"Thanks, Neti, look after our stuff." Jade waved like she was off on a log flume ride, not floating across a river to meet a notoriously temperamental goddess.

Azalea hugged herself tighter. There was no breeze to speak of, but a shiver ran through her. The Eridan river was wide and inky black beneath the starlight, and it seemed to take forever for the boat man to punt their way across with his long stick.

A small jetty of white marble got closer, and before she knew it, the boat tapped against the side, and two servants rushed to secure the ropes like their lives depended on it. Could spirits in the Shadow Dimension even die? She had no idea how it worked and noted to ask later.

"Exit the vessel and bow to the Great Goddess Ereshkigal, Queen of the Underworld, Ruler of the Shadow Dimension," one servant said in heavily accented English. Azalea was thankful it was in English.

Azalea and Jade scrambled out of the boat and did as the man said. There was nowhere to hide, no clothes to feel safe behind—she suspected this was the point of giving up everything along the way—so they arrived vulnerable.

"I welcome you to the Underworld." Ereshkigal towered over them by at least a foot, and nothing in her voice indicated a warm welcome. She wore flowing silver robes and a multi-layered golden crown that contrasted with her silver metallic hand, with which she reached out to pat Faraday.

Faraday went right up to her, head-butted her leg, and sat there staring up at her, accepting her gentle strokes of his head. Sita stood in front of his mistress and bowed.

"Welcome home, my pets. You have earned your place once more, Sitaddaru," she crooned.

"It is an honor to finally return." Sita ducked his head in a bow, and the goddess handed him an amulet in the shape of a multi-pointed star, which he placed over his head, so the trinket rested on his furry chest.

Azalea's heart plummeted to her stomach. Pets? As in plural. But Faraday was hers, she had found him all wet and bedraggled outside her cottage. She had fed him, loved him, given him her bed to share.

Tears prickled at the corners of her eyes. Was everything a mind game? Was everything in her life a manipulation out of her control?

She bit the inside of her cheek, refusing to let the goddess see her pain. Once again, she crossed her arms over her chest.

"You have treated my pets well. You will be rewarded."

"I don't need a reward; I just need you to live up to our deal." Azalea swallowed back the building panic. "And Faraday is my cat. He'll be coming back with me."

Ereshkigal reached down to pat Faraday. "I am glad you have grown attached to him, but he is no normal cat. I'm sure you noticed."

It was hard not to notice the way he appeared at just the right time, but it didn't matter. "He knows he is special, but I'd love him even if he was just a plain old black cat. I want him to return with me."

"He is a shadow cat with the ability to travel beyond the confines of mortal space; he may go with whom and where he pleases."

Faraday trotted to Azalea and wound around her legs. She hoped that meant he was picking sides. But Ereshkigal didn't seem to notice.

"Now we begin." Ereshkigal nodded to her two attendants, who scuttled back several paces and sunk to the ground, eyes down, falling prostrate on the dusty earth.

Azalea swallowed. She thought they'd already begun. All she wanted was some clothes and to confirm that the goddess would help them. Now, clearly, was not the time to ask.

"Few mortals have crossed these waters willingly. Now, void of your possessions, you have nothing to offer." Her voice boomed as shadows streamed from her hands, forming shapes all along the riverbank. "Feel the bare earth beneath your feet, the force of Shadow Magic around. See my power and know you are alone."

Azalea did her best not to flinch and forced herself to remain standing as her knees turned to jelly. She squeezed her legs together, wishing she at least had some pants to pee in. The shadow shapes along the water's edge morphed into rows of bodies, all hung from giant hooks gouged into their backs.

Jade let out a whimper, then clamped her mouth with her hand. Her eyes darted to Azalea, who was certain she looked the same. Freaked out.

Ereshkigal grew, the air around her vibrated with magic, her crown glowed, her cloak spread around her with invisible wind, and her wings snapped open with a crack that made Azalea jump. They were just like the wings in Azalea's tattoo, glorious black, feathered, and terrifying, so large they blocked out the entire night sky behind her.

"You are nothing. You will remember this feeling." The goddess's voice reverberated right through Azalea's heart, so all-encompassing she was sure Torin would feel it however far away he was.

*You are nothing.* Exactly how she felt, as small as a cockroach ready to be stepped on by a goddess who could change her mind on a whim. *Please don't let that be the case.* As long as Torin, Fabian, and Kat made it across the Echo Dimension and back, it would all be worth it.

Jade stood with her hands clutched together in front of her with only a slight shake. Azalea was glad she was the one there with her. If she could hold it together, then so could Azalea.

"You have seen what I do to people who betray me. You are warned. You have earned the right to enter the City of Stars." Ereshkigal gestured to the path where the two servants stood. "Accept these garments and amulets."

Azalea forced her legs into action and wobbled her way over to the man closest to her. He handed her a simple off-white tunic-style dress, which she took gratefully, and pulled the rough fabric over her head. She tied herself into the soft leather sandals and slipped on the amulet, a leather strap necklace with a silver circle. Inside was a black elongated crystal and a smooth black stone.

"It is a tourmaline. It will balance your magic in this realm, and obsidian to bind you to the palace," the servant whispered.

"What do you mean, bind?" she hissed under her breath.

"My words are wrong. I mean belong. It shows you belong at the palace. People will respect you. It is an honor."

She almost snorted aloud. That was not what it sounded like. He was backtracking. He bowed and walked backward, continuing to bow. She exchanged a worried glance with Jade.

A road appeared like a mirage coming into focus. It was smooth black, like any road at home, but without the lines. A carriage pulled by two enormous jet-black serpents glided toward them so smoothly they could have been moving across water.

Ereshkigal's eyes ran over the amulet, pleased. "I will leave you to explore the city. The carriage will take you to the palace when you are ready."

Azalea glanced at the bodies on hooks along the river and swallowed. "Can I talk to you about our deal? I sent the spirits you asked for. Will you help my friends? They've already left for the Echo Dimension."

"I always keep my word. Do not question me." Ereshkigal took off with two great flaps of her wings and flew into the night. A sleek black dragon appeared in the sky, taking Azalea's breath away as it joined Ereshkigal, swooping and diving like it was dancing among the stars.

The carriage got closer. It was shiny black and looked like a modern version of one of the Queen's carriages, designed with angled edges and no ornamentation.

"It is customary to tour the city before any formal meetings," the servant who had given Azalea the clothes said, apparently more talkative when his boss wasn't around.

"When will there be a formal meeting?" Azalea asked. Jade stood next to her.

He bowed his head. "It is the will of the Great Goddess."

"Meaning?" Jade's gaze locked on the formidable serpents as they approached.

"She will summon you when the time is right." He dipped into a short bow and gestured to the carriage that clattered to a stop.

"Your friend will give you a tour of the city, then return you for a meal."

Azalea and Jade exchanged a look. *Friend?* Azalea tried not to get her hopes up, but it could be Elam or Erik. Though Erik hadn't gone through her as a spirit. What if it was her father?

Her palms grew sweaty, and she wiped them on her tunic.

A raven landed on the top of the carriage, and the door swung open.

"Hello, Azalea."

Azalea froze on the spot, and Faraday stepped in front of her and hissed. "Oh, fuck," she squeaked.

It was Ambrose. Yup. Same red hair, still tall, and with a sour lemon look on his face.

"You know him?" Jade glanced at her, then set her suspicious gaze on Ambrose.

He was the last person she expected to see, her ex-classmate who had tried to stab her in the elemental battle in class and probably blamed her for his death.

"Yes, she knows me." Ambrose strode over and crossed his arms as if going against his will to keep them to himself.

This could not be happening. Panic spiked in her chest. There was nowhere she could go. Could you be killed in the Shadow Dimension?

"This is Ambrose. He was in my class," Azalea said through gritted teeth.

Ambrose's hands curled into fists. "And she got me killed."

"You got yourself killed." Rage flared through her. This was one death she refused to feel guilty about. "You were stalking me, digging into my brain every day, and trying to kill me in front of our class. This isn't on me."

"Oh, that Ambrose," Jade whispered to herself.

"I didn't have a choice. My father joined the House of Ravens. They were counting on me." Ambrose leaned against the carriage.

"Well, you failed, and thanks to Erik, I'm still alive." Azalea set her jaw. She would not be bullied by him.

Ambrose smirked. "You do know you're in the Shadow Dimension, the Underworld, right?"

"Erik's dead," Azalea said bluntly. "You know, your former best friend who you stabbed?"

Ambrose's tough-guy facade dropped. "I killed him? But he isn't here."

Azalea's throat grew tight. *Erik wasn't here.* "You didn't kill him, the Archmage did." *But I could have saved him.* There was the guilt again, and if Erik wasn't here, that meant she could never tell him how sorry she was.

"That bitch. She handed me over to the Ravens knowing what would happen."

*So that's how he died.* Azalea didn't want to know the details.

"I'm sorry, Ambrose. A lot has changed since you left." She wasn't sure what she was apologizing for, but she needed to say it to someone.

Ambrose turned away and held the door open. "We need to get going. Get in the carriage."

"You okay Azalea?" Jade touched her arm. "That guy seems like a douche, but we should probably go with him."

Azalea glanced around. They were in the middle of nowhere in a strange world. She nodded and let Jade lead her to the carriage.

"Where are we going, anyway?" Jade ran her hand over the plush velvet seat once inside, and Sita stood on the seat next to her by the window.

Ambrose slammed the door shut and tapped the roof. "We're going to see Elam."

Azalea inhaled sharply but tried to hide the shock from Ambrose by picking up Faraday and pulling him close to her chest. *Elam was here.*

# Chapter 21

Azalea stared out the large glass window of the carriage. "Is it always this dark?"

"No, it's just nighttime." Ambrose cracked his knuckles, then must have noticed her glare. "The days are short here. Only a few hours because of the angle of the sun at this time of year, and it's a red sun, so yeah, it's usually quite dark."

"Thank you. That wasn't so hard, was it?" Azalea continued to stare out the window so she wouldn't get psyched out by Ambrose. At least he wasn't trying to read her mind, probably couldn't here.

They arrived at an immense wall of smooth stone and drove straight through the open iron gates.

Jade sat across from Azalea, their knees just touching, her hands pressed up to the window next to Azalea's. Ambrose shuffled to the other side. "This was not what I was expecting," Jade whispered.

"Me neither." Azalea took in the city as Faraday curled onto her lap. Sita stood at the other window, peering outside on tiptoes.

It might be dark above, but within the walls, there were lights everywhere and people. Colorful lanterns hung from shop fronts, and restaurants with tables out front were busy with patrons. They turned down what seemed to be a food street; market stalls had sizzling things on sticks, brightly colored sweets were stacked in delectable towers, and giant woks were filled with noodles being tossed in the air effortlessly. People still ate here, good to know.

Their carriage slowed as they made their way through the traffic of a mix of pedestrians, camels, carts, bicycles, chariots, and donkeys. People moved when they saw the giant serpents slithering up the road, and Azalea couldn't blame them. One lady fell off her bike, trying to get out of the way.

"Where are we going?" Azalea couldn't see much past whatever was directly out her window. There were no cars, but the buildings seemed to have electricity. Most were two stories and a mix of mismatched architecture for every era and continent on earth; mud-brick structures with flat roofs with wood beams coming out were next to something that looked like it came from an old Japanese village, which was next to a modern-looking brick building with a barber's shop which was next to a Victorian pharmacy. So weird.

Ambrose sat with his arms crossed, staring at the back of the carriage. "You'll see when we get there."

"Sita?" Azalea glanced at the demon.

Sita looked out with his little hands resting on the window frame. "The city is much changed since I left. I do not recognize it."

"But you're a Wayfinder demon," she teased.

Ambrose tensed up, and Azalea ignored him.

"I always know where I am. I can always find anything and anyone I am looking for," he said with a huff. "I am simply not familiar with these merchants."

After a traffic jam involving several camels, they stopped in front of an unassuming, hole-in-the-wall type place with a neon sign that read 'Pub'.

Nerves shot to Azalea's belly. She was going to see Elam! Her mouth went dry. What do you say to someone who's just died? Would he hate her? Would he blame her?

"Let's get on with it." Jade gave her a kind nudge.

They left the carriage and entered the pub. Azalea's eyes fought to adjust to the darkness. There were only a few candles set in rough sconces that were covered in wax and unevenly set in the walls. The place was pretty empty. She scanned the room, hoping to catch a glimpse of Elam. But he wasn't there.

"Are we late?" Azalea whispered. It didn't feel right to talk loud in there.

"We're right on time," Ambrose murmured.

Azalea gripped Jade's arm. She'd seen that look in Ambrose's eyes before, right before he tried to drive a knife into her guts. "We need to leave."

She pulled Jade toward the door, but a man stepped in front of them, and he was holding a knife.

"We have unfinished business, little snake." Ambrose's lips curled into a disgusting smile.

But why had Ereshkigal set this up? Did she want Azalea dead? Did she know who Ambrose was and didn't care?

"Good luck." Sita darted under the man's legs and dashed out the door.

"Oh crap," Azalea muttered under her breath.

Jade bounced on her heels. "We can take them." Though there was nothing to indicate that was true. Azalea wasn't trained in any form of fighting, and she was pretty sure Jade wasn't either. They stuck close and backed up until they hit the bar.

Two more men came out of the shadows.

"Just go for the balls," Jade whispered.

Azalea had planned to do just that.

"Ambrose, don't do this. It's your own stupid fault you're here." The edge of the bar dug into Azalea's back.

"Good diplomacy," Jade said sarcastically.

"It's your fault I'm here, and I'm going to have a little fun." He chuckled. "No Erik to protect you this time."

"Erik's dead, remember," Azalea blurted out. Hoping it would throw him off.

It did. He froze, and it was just enough time for Azalea to grab a bottle off the bar. She hurled it straight at his head. The crash was shocking. She'd intended it to hit him, but until this point, she wasn't sure if the spirits here were solid or not. The answer was yes.

The bottle struck him in the temple and shattered. Blood gushed from his head. His mates just stared at him as if it happened in slow motion.

Jade grabbed her hand, and before she knew it, she was being swept out the door. She smashed into someone as soon as they hit the street and skidded across the footpath on her bum.

"Get up! Let's go." Jade tugged her up and toward the carriage.

A hand landed on her shoulder, and Azalea's body tensed until she heard her name.

She spun around. Sita was back, but it wasn't him who called to her. Jade clung to her arm, trying to get her to move, but Azalea froze.

The door of the pub flew open, and Ambrose swayed with blood pissing out of his head. His friends all wielded knives.

"Get back here bitch so I can finish what I started!" Ambrose leaned against the wall, leaving a bloody handprint smeared down the dirty brick.

Azalea and Jade backed against the carriage. The towering man she'd run into moved in front of her and Jade. Sita hovered next to him, quietly flapping up and down.

"Go back inside, son." His voice was gruff but familiar.

Confusion settled over Azalea, or perhaps it was shock from throwing the bottle at Ambrose's head.

Ambrose stumbled toward them, a knife clenched in his blood-covered fist. His buddies circled the stranger.

"Do you want to end up down below or properly dead?" The man stepped toward Ambrose, an elemer in his hand streaming shadows.

"He can do magic down here." Jade looked at her hands. "We should try to get our elemers back."

She was right, they should, but she was too focused on what was happening to answer.

Ambrose shot forward and did his best to dodge past the man. He was bloody fast—Azalea recalled he had been a rugby player—but he wasn't fast enough.

The man didn't even move, just flicked his elemer. Ambrose tripped over some shadows, and before she could blink, he was spun into a tight cocoon of writhing darkness.

The other blokes ran at the man, but with a flick of his elemer, the man launched short strands of shadows that were barely visible until they were around the men's throats choking them. Struggling to breathe, the men scrambled inside gasping for air and clawing at their necks.

The man defending them turned around, and Azalea's breath caught.

"It's okay, Petal. It's me." He smiled nervously. The same smile she saw in the photos that sat on the mantle at her mum's cottage. The same eyes as Fabian and the same look Fabian always had in awkward situations.

Her breathing turned quick and shallow; her hands trembled as she tried to process her spiraling thoughts.

"Dad?" Azalea clutched Jade's arm, depending on Jade to keep her upright.

"It's me, Pumpkin."

This couldn't be real. She'd looked for him for so long. She'd put so much effort into bringing him back only to have the world come crashing down around her. A deep ache clawed through her heart. *Was she strong enough for this? Was this her chance to get answers?* She found her mind suddenly blank.

Her mouth was dry. "Is it really you?" The last time she'd seen him he was part of the gallu. Had he survived that? Was this another of Ereshkigal's tricks?

"I understand if you don't want to talk to me, if you blame me for the gallu. You've been through hell." He ran a hand through his dark hair that hung loose over his shoulders. His eyes were brown, and he was tall, taller than she imagined.

She looked up, meeting his gaze. "I tried to get you back..." She shook her head slowly. "I screwed everything up. I'm sorry."

He took a step forward, and she tensed. He folded his hands in front of him as Jade gave her arm a comforting squeeze, and Sita flew over and stood next to them.

Her father held his hands together on his chest, his eyes glossy with tears. "I have you to thank for setting me free. I can never repay you for what you did for me, and I'll never forgive myself for leaving you. I'm sorry, Azalea."

Her throat grew thick with guilt. "You were murdered. You weren't given a choice in all this either." How could she tell him about Torin? How could she tell her father that every inch of her life was entwined with that of his murderer?

He shook his head slowly. "There is so much I regret. Maybe we can talk?"

She nodded in agreement and looked down as hot tears welled in the corners of her eyes. She squeezed them away, not wanting to show him she was just a weak little girl after all.

She forced a smile. "For the record, I'm sorry you got eaten by a gallu. But I'm glad you made it back here."

He chuckled, a rich warm laugh that she felt like she remembered or wanted to remember at least. "I'm one lucky man."

She wasn't sure about that, he seemed rather unlucky if you asked her. "Do you remember being in the gallu?" She tried to subtly change the conversation away from his murder.

"No. It's all a blur. Thank the gods. I don't want to know what that thing did while I was part of it."

So maybe he didn't remember Torin with the gallu. One less thing to worry about. She wanted to ask him why he left her and her mother, why she never grew up knowing about Shadow Magic. But she couldn't bring herself to do it.

The sound of hoofbeats plodding past filled the gap of silence.

"Hi, sir. I'm Jade. Azalea's friend from the Tower of London. We're not dead by the way, just visiting." Jade held out her hand, and he shook it.

Azalea mentally thanked Jade as her brain tried to catch up.

His hand went to his heart. "Thank the gods. I didn't want to ask. You are too young. How exactly is it you find yourselves here?"

"It's a long story—" Jade started.

Azalea cut her off but patted her arm in apology. "We are here at Ereshkigal's request." She studied her father's reaction to see what he would make of it. She didn't want him to know about Fabian and Torin in the Echo Dimension just yet, not until they knew he could be trusted.

"I hope you are not in any danger." He frowned at Sita who glared back at him.

"We know what we are doing." Azalea squared her shoulders, feeling more in control of herself now, though she partly felt like she was in the Desert of Dreams at the strangeness of this situation.

"Would you like to come to my flat for tea?" he asked.

Azalea froze at the thought of it. This was all happening so fast.

"I think we better be getting to the palace. Ereshkigal will be expecting us." Jade came to the rescue.

Azalea nodded. "Yes. Maybe we can come another day?" She wasn't sure how long they'd be sticking around, but she needed time to think and prepare herself before they had this talk. Part of her wanted to hate him for leaving her, the other half wanted him to be proud. It was very confusing.

"Sounds good, Pumpkin. Sita can find me, and if you need me, I live in the Archivists Sector."

She nodded and turned toward the carriage. The serpents who had been curled up unfurled to their full length. The raven was there again, she noticed it only had one eye.

"Goodbye, Azalea." Her father waved.

She paused, gripping the metal bar on the side of the carriage. "Bye, Dad." That felt weird saying aloud. She hauled herself inside.

Sita sat right in the middle and Jade flopped onto the seat across from him as Azalea slid in next to her.

"You okay?" Jade picked up Faraday and placed him next to Azalea.

"I have no idea." Azalea buried her face in her hands as the carriage lurched forward, unsure if she wanted to laugh or cry.

Jade nudged her shoulder. "I take back what I said about wanting an adventure. It's been fun, but I'd love a cup of tea now and some of those digestive biscuits."

"Me too. I'm not sure we'll find biscuits here." Azalea took a calming breath and didn't look out the window as the carriage turned a corner, away from her father.

She didn't take anything in as they wound through the streets, climbing higher into the city. She could hardly see the palace as they drove through the gates to the innermost barrier. Its walls of black obsidian rose straight up all around them, culminating in sharply spiked towers she could barely make out against the night sky.

They were hustled out of the carriage, through a side door that didn't seem very grand, and through a maze of hallways clearly used by servants, then handed off to another lot who took them in a sleek elevator twenty floors up.

Before they could protest, Azalea and Jade were guided to separate rooms across from each other.

Azalea was left blinking and wondering what the hell had just happened. Fortunately, Faraday had slunk in with her somehow.

"Oh, Farry." She picked him up and cuddled him as she took in the room. It was massive and looked more like a sleek, modern hotel than a room in the underworld. Most surfaces were polished concrete so shiny she could almost see herself. This included the bed, which was a huge base of concrete with a mattress draped in a perfectly fluffed white duvet covered with animal furs, which she hoped were fake, though she suspected not.

There were concrete shelves filled with leather books across one wall, and the other had a built-in desk complete with modern lighting and notepaper. Opposite the bed was a fireplace set into the wall with a fire already roaring.

Faraday hopped out of her arms to sniff everything in the room.

"Do you get the feeling this is just a luxury prison?" she said to the cat, who continued his investigations.

Suddenly feeling claustrophobic, she ran to the door. It was locked. She banged on it with her palm.

"Jade. Jade! Can you hear me?" Her heart pounded in her chest. She continued banging until her palm was red and hot.

She paced the room before sitting on the edge of the bed, where a piece of paper caught her eye.

The front of the folded parchment read: *Loyal servant Mage-Apprentice Azalea Sharp.*

Not a fan of the loyal servant part. She opened the note.

*Forgive my deceit. I wished to witness the manner in which you faced an enemy. Tomorrow we will speak.*

*— Queen of the Underworld, your devoted Goddess, Ereshkigal.*

Azalea was a captive, and that had been a test... great.

# Chapter 22

Fabian sat down next to Kat at a giant table covered in more food than he had ever seen in his life: seared lamb, goats' heads with their eyes still in, platters of dates arranged in artistic formations, flatbreads coated in amazing-smelling herbs with olive oil beside them, plus fruits dipped in spices he didn't recognize, all spread out for them.

"You look beautiful, Kat." Fabian was drawn away from the food to admire how amazing she looked in the stunning gown of crimson silk that flowed around her like she belonged in this world of gods. A belt of multicolored beads drew his eyes to her waist, and her neck was adorned with a collar of muted gold.

"Thank you. You look... interesting." She smiled a full smile that went right to her eyes, a rare thing.

He flashed her a grin. She was impressed by his costume. Fabian rather liked the outfit he'd found amongst the assortment of unfamiliar garments in his room, a white tunic with a crimson sash. He'd added a belt with feathers that hung down from his waist. He'd have to ask where to get the fancy gold headdresses some gods were wearing. Then he'd really fit in.

"Is it safe to eat all this? It won't trap us here or something?" He eyed a plate of mystery meat nearby that was steaming rather invitingly.

"No idea, but you might be thinking of the Fae, not gods." Kat took a sip of golden liquid in a crystal glass and nodded in quiet approval.

Fabian scoffed. "Fae aren't real."

"Just don't get drunk." Torin joined them, ever the wet blanket, taking a seat on the other side of Kat and looking very uncomfortable and formal in a long red robe with beads and feathers at the bottom and on his cuffs.

They ate in silence, taking in the strange assortment of gods and creatures chatting away. The main gods were seated at the head of the room where Enki was right at the center. He was an imposing fellow, taking up a fair amount of space, and seemed to think it necessary to wear his full collection of gold armor to dinner. Beside him was a woman, presumably his latest great-granddaughter he was shagging. Fabian knew his Sumerian mythology as well as any mage, whatever Dumont wanted to think, and Fabian was well aware of Enki's incestuous family tree. Not something he planned on asking about.

After all his observations, it was clear none of these gods were the top dog, Enlil.

Before long, Inanna left her golden throne and appeared at their table, drawing up a chair to sit opposite the three of them. Mischief danced in her eyes.

She reached out a graceful hand and placed it on Dumont's.

Dumont didn't pull away. What the hell was this? How had he been the one she took a fancy to?

"I forgive you for not accepting my advances. I see your heart belongs to another." She looked Torin in the eye and put his fingers in her mouth, sucking them slowly. Torin looked horrified.

Fabian nudged Kat. "What's going on here?" he whispered.

"No idea, but it can't be good," she whispered so close to his ear that her breath tickled his neck.

*Come on mate, take one for the team.* They couldn't afford to offend a goddess, especially this one.

"I apologize if I gave you the wrong impression. I do not wish to offend," Dumont said dryly. To his credit, he didn't take his hand away.

"No offense is taken, my dear." She released his hand with a sly smile and plucked some grapes off his plate. "A soul bond is such a rare thing. I have not witnessed a fresh one in a century. It is thrilling."

"Soul bond?" Fabian leaned in. Surely it would be common knowledge if true. That sort of magic wasn't something that could easily be hidden.

Torin went rigid and actively avoided looking at Fabian. Why didn't he just deny it? Clearly, this woman was playing games.

Fabian tried to get Kat's attention, but she looked down at her plate.

"What the hell is going on?" Fabian asked. "Dumont, do you have a clue what she's talking about?"

Dumont stared right at Inanna as if pleading with her silently. "It's a long story, one I'd rather not go into." He said without looking away.

"Look mate, if you're secretly soul-bound to someone, I'm all for it. You're a rebel—I get it. We can use that extra power, no judging. Just don't lie about it."

Inanna reached over and took Fabian's hand in her silky soft palms and stared right into his soul. "Lies and hatred run deep within your hearts, burrowing like maggots, turning your souls black as pitch. There is no place for secrets here."

Fabian's heart seized in his chest. Now wasn't the time for secrets to be coming out. He snapped out of it quickly. "Look, Goddess, your majesty. We need to work together here. Bringing up the past isn't going to help either of us. Right now, our state of denial is working."

It was clear she wanted them to talk about the whole Torin murdering his brother thing. Probably for the entertainment of the court, and it was not something he was going to encourage. His state of denial was working perfectly fine, but it was a thin line he was balancing on that kept him from killing the bloke.

She looked back at Torin like she wanted to devour him, that or get him back for rejecting her. Stupid man, why the hell would he say no to such a woman, soul bond or no?

"I do not care for pettiness and lies. Therefore, I will make things easier for you both," Inanna said loud enough for every-one to hear.

"Please don't." Dumont gripped the table, begging like a man pleading for his last meal. "We can work something else out."

Why was he so freaked out? Was he about to prostitute him-self out to the goddess? That would be some good entertain-ment.

Inanna gave them both a look that chilled Fabian's soul. She turned around to face the room. "Gods and goddesses, demi-gods, great kings, and nobles, hear me." The chatter of the room died down.

Beads of sweat formed on Dumont's brow. He whispered something to Kat that Fabian couldn't hear.

Okay, now he had a really bad feeling about this. "What did he say to you?" Fabian nudged Kat.

"Shush." Kat slapped his arm. "Just do your best not to react, okay?"

He frowned at her. Why was it him she was worried about?

Inanna waited for complete silence. "I am pleased to announce this man, Mage Torin Dumont of the House of Ravens, a mortal, has entered into a soul bond with his apprentice."

*His apprentice.* The words rang in Fabian's ears. He was going to throw up.

The goddess continued, "Few mortals risk their lives to attain such power. He is honored with this gift by my sister. Celebrate with us."

A roar from the crowd of gods thundered through the room along with clinking mugs and sloshing wine.

Fabian's brain took a second to catch up and overcome the disgust. His blood boiled, pounding in his ears with a new level of hatred.

He lunged for Dumont, but Kat blocked him.

"You bastard! You tricked her. What did you do to her?" Fabian fought against Kat, but she had his arms behind him in a second, locked so he couldn't move.

"I didn't do anything, just listen." Dumont glared at him in challenge, his muscles tensed in a practiced defensive posture. Fabian didn't care, he could take him.

"You fucker." He charged forward, hoping to get close enough to head butt the man. But Kat was there.

A cheer went up from the room. Clearly, these bloodthirsty gods wanted a fight. But it was muffled by the rage pounding through Fabian's head. He would kill Dumont for this. Screw the quest. That murderous predator had gone too far.

"It isn't what it seems, Fabian. Just let me explain." Dumont's calm repetitiveness drilled into Fabian's skull, clearly trying to be rational, but Fabian could see what was building behind his eyes. He wanted to fight as much as Fabian did. It was better they just got it over with.

Damn Kat for being so strong. He fought to get out of her grasp without hurting her but was not successful. This couldn't be happening. A soul bond. Azalea being his apprentice was bad enough, but this went way over the line.

"There is nothing to explain. You've ruined her life." Fabian choked out the words. Poor Azalea, this was his fault. He should have protected her instead of leading her into the clutches of their enemy.

Dumont's eyes flashed with rage. "We didn't choose this."

"You ever touch her again, and I swear I will kill you," Fabian said as calmly as he could. He wanted it to be clear that he meant it.

Inanna grinned and stood by the table again like an MC at a wedding waiting to make an announcement.

"This is not the only quarrel between these two men. I have seen into their hearts. Both have the hearts of warriors. They deserve the honor of eating in our halls!" Inanna called, ringing in more cheers.

"What battles have they fought in?" A drunk bird-headed god yelled from the other side of the room.

"Both have defeated the gallu of the underworld in many battles." Her voice boomed across the room. "But this mage, Fabian of the House of Snakes, seeks retribution for the murder of his brother at the hand of this man, mage Torin of the House of Ravens. The death was honorable, the soul taken with the divine gift—the hand of death."

A gasp filled the room, followed by more drunken encouragement. Great, now they were praising Dumont for being a murderer, just what he needed.

Inanna called for more drinks while everyone debated which of them would win in a fight. Kat still had a firm grip on Fabian's arms. If she hadn't, he would have proven some of those animal-headed fuckers wrong.

Enki stood up, and the room went silent.

"I like to see passion in my men. But this is not the place. Tomorrow, you will overcome your differences in the arena for all to witness." His face was serious, and he rapped his knuckles on his armor twice before sitting down. The crowd responded with the same two taps on their chest, then sat down and went back to whatever court gossip they were rambling about.

Kat forced Fabian back into his chair. He was so angry, the sides of his vision clouded with darkness, his hands burning to draw forth Shadow Magic and slice Dumont to pieces with it.

If he was being offered a chance to take down Dumont, he was bloody well going to take it and make the most of it. All he knew about soul bonds was that they were illegal. He shook his head and stared down at his food, unable to focus on eating. The things that man had put Azalea through were unacceptable, now this.

Tomorrow he would finish this. Azalea could hate him all she wanted for it, but she would be better off without this raven bastard ruining her life any further.

He made a silent vow to himself that he would do better with his ward, Cassie, than he had with Azalea. He had let her down. He wouldn't do the same again.

A small rumbling filled the room. Torin gripped the table and looked at Kat, but no one else reacted to the small earthquake, just held onto their cups and kept talking.

After sitting silently, not even listening to what Dumont and Kat were mumbling between them, or what the gods and old kings were arguing about, he realized a servant was asking him to stand up. They must have overstayed their dinner welcome.

Fabian kept his eyes down and his hatred locked inside to save for tomorrow. As they reached the gold-plated door, Enki's voice boomed out. "If you prove yourselves worthy, I will help in your plight, mortals."

# Chapter 23

Torin locked his door and collapsed into bed. He needed to talk to Azalea. Sleep was slow, but eventually, he found himself standing in the living room of his tower at the Tower of London.

It was nighttime, the fire was burning low, and the coffee table had a plate of chocolate digestive biscuits, a pot of tea, and two teacups.

Now all he had to do was stay asleep long enough to hope Azalea turned up. He had no idea what time it was back home, or if time even passed in the same way here.

Unsure how long he waited, the conversation went over and over in his mind about how he would tell her that Fabian knew about their soul bond.

He blinked, and she was there.

"You're okay!" She ran over and threw herself at him. The warmth of her magic sunk into his as he curled his arms around her and pulled her in close to kiss her. She leaned back, grinning. "Hi."

"Hi, yourself." Even in the dream their magic wanted to merge.

She rolled off him, fell back onto the couch, and closed her eyes. He felt her relief and how much she was relishing the moment. She opened her eyes, and a sinking feeling hit his gut.

"No," he groaned. "What did you do?" He felt her guilt piling on... she was hiding something big.

"Don't be mad at me." She sat cross-legged facing him. "I did what Ereshkigal told me to do. I just wanted to make sure you're okay. Is her sister helping you?"

He arranged the cushion behind his back. "Yes, we're all fine. Inanna found us in time."

"Good." Azalea rubbed her face, the relief pouring off her like crazy. He hadn't even considered how worried about them she might be.

She was nibbling her lip.

"Just spit it out, what did you do? You can tell me."

"I got the spirits. I went to Jordan with Jade, and the sword worked perfectly."

"Good, I'm glad." He poured tea for both of them. She clearly wasn't telling the whole truth and was much better at controlling herself in dreams than before.

"Tell me about the Echo Dimension." She stared longingly at the biscuits on the table.

He would play along, for now. "Enki won't talk to us yet, but I believe he will help. We just have to do it on his terms. Which fortunately seems to mean waiting."

She nodded along, only half listening.

"Are you sure you're okay?" he asked.

Her face pinched with concern. "Yeah."

The dream flashed for a second—like a glitch. A room with black walls and sleek concrete floors appeared, then vanished. He jumped up. "What the hell was that?"

"Is this proper tea? Can I have tea in a dream? I need tea." She leaned forward and took a cup with shaking hands.

"Where are you, Azalea? That wasn't part of my dream-scape."

"Now, this is going to sound bad. But I promise you it's not." She took a sip of tea then put down the cup, and Torin reached for her hands before she could pull away. The magic flowed between them, building to a soft white light over their skin.

*Oh gods, not again.* Why had he left her alone?

She kept her eyes down; she was scared of him, and he hated that feeling.

"I'm in the Shadow Dimension, Torin." She looked down at their hands, gripping his far too tightly.

"You can't be." He couldn't move, couldn't react. "I'd know." He choked out the words.

"I'm not dead, but I wasn't even sure I'd find you in my dreams, it's hard to hold on."

"No." He folded his fingers into hers trying to strengthen the connection. Her magic sank into him, warming him.

She pulled her hands free and clung to him. "I'm sorry, I had to do it to make sure you were safe."

"It's okay, we can fix this." He rocked her back and looked her in the eyes. "I'll come find you. I'll get Inanna to take me to you."

Azalea shook her head. "You can't. You need to get the gate closed, and from this end, I can make sure Ereshkigal keeps her word. I did this for a good reason, Torin. I can't go back now."

Frustration built under his skin. "I hate being this far from you; it's too much. You should have used the sword to get the spirits to break the bond."

An ache spiked though his heart, and it was coming from Azalea.

"This was more important than our bond. I used the sword and exchanged the spirits to get Ereshkigal to help you. If you still want to break the bond later, I'm sure we can work out how. Let's just deal with one problem at a time."

"What was the deal you made? Tell me exactly."

"I haven't spoken with Ereshkigal yet, but in the apprentice ceremony she said that she would consider my offer and to bring her the spirits and go to her in the City of Stars. She said you would be safe."

Torin's chest tightened. No wonder she felt so far away. "You conveniently left that out before."

"She said she would speak to her sister, and her sister would protect you in the Land of Light and that you had to get to the great feast at the Palace of the Waters. Did you make it in time?"

"Yes, we made it, and Inanna helped us, so she held up that end of your deal. But you can't trust her."

"I know that. She set me up when I arrived; Ambrose was waiting."

He ran a hand over his head.

"I think it was a test, but me and Jade got away, and then my dad showed up, which was super weird." She seemed a little more relaxed now that was off her chest.

"Bloody hell. Jade is there? Your dad?"

"I smashed a bottle on Ambrose's head." She giggled.

"How the hell did we get in these situations? Tell me every detail, you need to be ready to face anything tomorrow."

Azalea told him everything that had happened to her, including having to enter through the seven gates of the underworld and facing Ambrose and her father. He wished he was there with her. He told her everything he'd seen in the Echo Dimension which sounded as much a farfetched tale as hers when he said it aloud. Then he got to the bit about the feast and stalled.

"So what was the food like?" she asked, snuggling into his side.

"The food was fine. But the thing is—" he considered not telling her, adding to her worries for when they got back—if they got back—wasn't the best idea, but he had told her to be honest, so he had to do the same "—Fabian knows about our soul bond, Inanna told him."

"She what!" Azalea sat up. "Oh, crap."

"I know. We are going to have some big problems when we get back."

"It's fine, we can work it out." She pressed her hands to her temples. "Just stay as far away from him as you can and keep Kat near you."

"Yes, about that. Enki has ordered us to do some sort of battle in an arena tomorrow to work out our issues. We seem to be the new entertainment for the gods." Torin poured more tea.

"You can't do that!"

Torin took a sip, glad teapots could refill themselves in dreams. "I'm going to try to get out of it, but I don't exactly have a choice."

"Just don't hurt him, okay?" She nibbled at a digestive biscuit nervously.

*She was worried about Fabian? What about him?* "I don't plan to. But he's seriously pissed off."

She dusted the crumbs off her hands. "Just make it look good. It's a show they are after by the sound of it. I just need you to come back to me in one piece. Him, too, I guess."

He set down the teacup. "*You* need to find a way to come back to *me* so I don't come looking for you."

Azalea looked up and kissed him without warning. He leaned into the kiss, her lips warm and very real feeling.

"I miss you. I wish we could just stay here." Her breath moved across his lips.

"Me too."

Torin's concentration flickered. Someone was shaking him, trying to wake him. No. Now was not the time.

"I have to go. Just find a way out, make that your priority." He kissed her hard as if that could make up for their distance and lack of time.

"Don't go." Her arms wrapped around him so tight he was sure she would be there next to him when he woke up.

He opened his eyes and groaned.

Kat sat on the edge of his bed with her back perfectly straight and a scowl on her face. "We need to talk. You need to let Fabian win."

# Chapter 24

Azalea banged on the door, her fists red and tender, but again, no one came. The day crept by, though it was hard to tell it was day at all. She never saw the sun, but the sky warmed to a deep red for a few hours, then darkened once more.

She opened the window to fight the trapped feeling. Below her, the city sprawled out like a fan in rings of walls that seemed to divide up the areas. Closest to the palace were houses that looked like smaller palaces. It was hard to tell the scale, and it had gone by in a blur when they drove through.

Beyond that wall were large manor houses, some with central courtyards, all on wide, tree-lined roads, though all the trees had leaves of deep reds and purples—very alien.

Then there was the greater city, where she was last night, where the fan spread into mazes of smaller streets and alleys. The buildings were no more than three stories high, and even from this far, she could see all the colorful signs and lanterns.

Azalea sat down at the end of her bed, holding back tears as the unfamiliar moon rose, glowing a dull pink. She hugged Faraday to her chest, feeling helpless. Hours of banging and yelling at the door had gotten her nowhere. She hadn't heard from Jade or Sita.

A tapping sounded at the window, and she jumped when she saw the raven. It had to be the same one from the carriage. It tilted its head to the side and let out a croak.

Wait, she knew this raven. She stepped closer, curiosity taking over caution.

It had one eye.

She went to the plate of food she'd only nibbled at, took a strip of dried meat, and tossed it at the raven. It caught it, held it with its foot, and tore it in half, swallowing it, then ate the other half and let out a croak for more.

"Are you Licorice? Torin told me all about you," she said to the bird as she handed over more bribes of meat, which the bird ate greedily.

Suddenly, the door flung open, and Azalea jumped as the raven flew off.

"You're extremely impatient," Sita grumbled.

Azalea marched over to him in the doorway. "Where have you been?"

"Busy. I'm afraid the divine do not work on the same time frames as mortals, nor do they care an inkling about your needs." He flapped into the air at eye level.

"I did everything she asked." She reached for her elemer before remembering it wasn't there.

"Just continue to do things the way she wants, and all will be well. Trust me. Now follow me." He turned and flitted out the gilded door frame.

Azalea dashed after him. "Wait, is Jade coming? Is she okay?"

"Jade is looked after, I assure you." Sita continued down the obsidian hall.

Azalea was not assured, but it was better she saw Ereshkigal alone so as to not put Jade in any more danger. She promised herself she would come back to Jade with good news.

They wound through hallways of shimmering stone guarded by armored creatures and copper-plated warriors.

Azalea stuck close to Sita as they entered a cathedral-like room with sleek black walls lined with stained-glass windows depicting scenes of battle in reds, deep blues, and purples. Above them, chandeliers with flickering candles hung on long chains from the high ceiling.

Her footsteps echoed as they made their way to the black throne at the end of the long room. Two massive marble pillars framed a throne on a podium, and on either side of that were tall candles next to vases of brown wilted flowers—their petals looked sad on the cold marble floor.

"Welcome, daughter of the Snake. You have passed many trials to prove your worth." Ereshkigal sat straight with her hands folded serenely in front of her. Her gold crown glowed against her jet-black hair.

Azalea wasn't sure she was worthy but decided polite was the way to go. She tried to appear calm, but her stomach was tying itself in knots, and she desperately needed to pee.

"Thank you for seeing me. I'm sure you must be very busy." Azalea kept her hands tightly clasped in front of her. Faraday sat on her feet.

"I am always busy. After our discussion in the dreamscape, I spoke with my sister. I have honored our bargain, and she will continue to aid your companions in the Echo Dimension."

"Thank you." Azalea bowed her head. It seemed appropriate. "Will she help them shut the gate?"

"She is Queen of the Echo Dimension and is in the ear of Enki, but it will all depend on Enki's will."

That had to be good. Her plan had worked so far. "Will you be the one to shut the gate from the other side?" Azalea asked cautiously.

"It is what I hope. It has been many thousand years since I stepped foot on the fertile soils of the mortal world. I should like that, but I require Enki's permission."

"Why would you need permission? And why do you want to go back?" Azalea asked, hoping that wasn't too bold. Surely a great goddess could do whatever she wanted.

Ereshkigal tilted her head as if amused. "A curious mind you have. All gods are banned from your world with the exception of Geshtinanna. It was agreed in the treaty when we returned to our realms." She summoned Faraday, who jumped onto her knee and sat down.

Azalea did her best not to scowl at the traitorous cat as Ereshkigal continued, "As for the reason of my return, I should like to find out why the soul reapers no longer send me spirits."

"Oh," Azalea said. That made sense. She'd like to know that too, not that she'd heard of them before, but it was their fault she was in that mess.

"Why did Inanna agree to help you?" Azalea asked. That was the part that didn't make sense. She knew the stories about Inanna's descent to the underworld. Had they made up since then?

"That is where you come in, my dear girl. That is why you are here." A thin smile crept to her lips, and her dark eyes crinkled with crow's feet.

Azalea swallowed.

"I made a deal with my sister. She wants her husband returned, so I offered her an exchange." Ereshkigal's metallic hand glided over Faraday's sleek fur.

"I am the exchange." Azalea's heart sank.

"You are. Dumuzi will return to his wife, and you will take his place to maintain the balance of seasons in the mortal world. Six months of the year, you will remain here. Six months of the year you will return to your home and deliver me new spirits."

Azalea's heart squeezed in her chest. "Why would I agree to that? I don't want to send spirits anymore. I sent you over a thousand!" She did her best to keep breathing and hide the panic. At least Torin wasn't here to feel her freaking out.

"You misunderstand me. This is an honor. I will grant you powers over spirits. You will be a demi-goddess, worshiped here and in your own world."

Azalea didn't know what to say. Her hand went to her neck instinctively reaching for the locket Torin gave her but only found Ereshkigal's amulet.

Ereshkigal stilled, her metal hand resting on Faraday like a statue. "I acknowledge you have already brought me spirits. You are the first mortal to pass and make it this far. You released my gallu and brought in many spirits to begin repopulating my city. For this I thank you."

"You're welcome," she said, not sure why.

"Bring forth the treaty, Sitaddaru."

This was happening fast. Azalea felt like she was being backed into a corner. Her neck prickled, and she shot a sideways look at Sita. This was his fault, the Shadow Atlas's fault, Ereshkigal's pet, a pet that knew everything about her. She needed to know more before she signed her life away—literally—this was a deal with the devil herself, and she needed more time.

Sita puffed out his chest, and a cloud of shadows appeared in front of him, along with a scroll in his hands. Servants appeared with a table and placed it in front of the steps up to Ereshkigal's throne.

Azalea cautiously stepped forward as the goddess stood and snapped her wings to their full width, taking Azalea's breath away. They made their way to the table where the scroll was rolled out and written in the familiar, red, elegant handwriting of the Shadow Atlas. It was still hard to associate Sita with the old book sometimes, but the writing was clear.

"I have taken the liberty of drafting the agreement for both parties to look over, so there is no confusion." Sita gestured to the document.

Azalea nibbled her lip until she tasted blood in her mouth.

"Under this treaty, Azalea will agree to stay in the Shadow Dimension six months of the year. The other six months she will provide spirits to Ereshkigal, five thousand per cycle—"

"No, I don't want to provide spirits. It's killing me every time, and I can't stay here. I won't be a prisoner!" Azalea said through choked breaths, unable to keep her fears inside anymore.

Ereshkigal placed her hands on the table. "It will not be the same as before, child. That was a test. With my divine powers and blessing bestowed upon you, you will feel no pain and no harm will come to you."

"This is a great honor you are offering me." How to put this without getting thrown into a dungeon? "But I am still young. I don't think I'm ready to be away from my family for that long every year."

"You mean the one in which you share the soul bond? This is not an issue. You may break the bond, or, as I suggest you do, seal the bond and you will be as one. This will allow him to travel alongside you."

She really didn't seem to be getting the point. "I'm not sure he would want that, and I cannot speak for him. I just want him to return safely." Azalea bit her lip, hoping this wouldn't offend the goddess.

Ereshkigal's eyes narrowed. "You would be a fool to turn down such power offered to you both. The bond will no longer be needed to sustain your power. You will have the ability to sever the bond yourself if you choose to."

"Thank you." Azalea's heart clenched. She wasn't sure what to make of this news. In a twisted way, she was being offered everything she wanted. But giving up their new magic felt like she'd be ripping out a part of herself, but sharing emotions with Torin forever was also not an option.

"Do not thank me. I take no pleasure in my gifts being rejected. With your shared abilities, you could destroy your enemies and be the most powerful beings on earth. You are foolish."

Sita's claws made scuttling sounds on the stone as he shifted from foot to foot impatiently. He clearly wasn't impressed with the way she was handling this.

"Why do you need more spirits?" Azalea asked. She needed to understand the point of all this.

Ereshkigal spoke patiently. "The gallu uprising took a great number of our citizens. I sent as many gallu as I could to your world to be killed and our army tried to banish their horde beyond Kur, over the great mountains, but too many soldiers were taken. After this, many of our citizens chose to leave the City of Stars. We lost many of the old kings, a tragedy for our city."

"Where did they go?"

"To the beyond. It is unknown, but after time, all spirits choose this path and leave our world for the unknown. It is the cycle, but losses in great numbers harm our city. In addition to this, Enki sends messengers to hand-select spirits to take to the Echo Dimension when he has need of them. He has taken many."

"I'm still not sure why I should agree to this. It does not seem fair to me. Why do you need me to stay?" Azalea asked.

Ereshkigal stood up, her wings stretched high, blocking out the light. "It is more than fair, child. You will be a demi-goddess here, not a prisoner. You may go anywhere you like, you will be given the best rooms, the best servants; you will be revered. It is not an offer to be turned down now, or ever offered again."

Azalea tried not to shrink away from the goddess's power.

Ereshkigal continued, "There must always be a balance. When my sister, Inanna's life was returned, another had to take her place. She sent her husband, Dumuzi, but he was not content to remain here and took advantage of his sister's love for him."

"What did he do?" Azalea wasn't sure why this was relevant.

"He convinced his sister, Geshtinanna, the goddess of agriculture to take his place for six months of the year."

Azalea nodded as the heaviness of understanding settled over her. "Her absence and return control the seasons in my world."

"Indeed. The mortal world would wither without her. The cycle must continue."

"I see... but what will I do in the Shadow Dimension?"

"You will assist me in maintaining order, and I will teach you to use my magic." Ereshkigal's tone grew sharp. "If you want me to close the gate to the Echo Dimension and ensure your friends make it back to their home safely, I suggest you agree to this."

Azalea swallowed hard. It was clear she had no choice.

Sita cleared his throat. "I will continue. The other six months Azalea will provide five thousand spirits to the Shadow Dimension."

*Five thousand?* She supposed that was doable. All she'd have to do was hit up a few big cemeteries. Sita continued, "In return, Ereshkigal will commune with the Echo Dimension gods and, when given permission, will travel to the mortal realm where she will not influence the free will of any mortals. When summoned, she will close the Echo Dimension gate as is her duty."

"What are the terms for a broken treaty?" Ereshkigal asked, clearly already knowing the answer.

"If the contract is broken by Ereshkigal, Azalea is freed of her obligations to collect spirits in the mortal world but remains bound to spend six months in the Shadow Dimension every year until a replacement is available. If the contract is broken by Azalea, she will remain in service to Ereshkigal until her natural death."

Azalea sucked in a breath. That was steep. She had no plans of breaking the contract. Six months she could manage—until her death—that was something she was not willing to commit to.

"It all appears to be in order. I agree with the terms." Ereshkigal swiped the quill from Sita's claws and jammed it into the heel of her palm.

Azalea couldn't help but gasp, but Ereshkigal wasn't fazed. The shaft of the quill sticking into her skin turned red. She casually removed it and signed the bottom of the page in one graceful swishing motion.

Sweat beaded on Azalea's palms.

"There isn't time. If you wish for me to help, you will sign this now so I can return Inanna's husband to her and set events in motion. It is crucial."

Azalea wished someone was here with her, anyone to talk this over with. But all she had was Sita, the untrustworthy book who had screwed her over so many times. But he had gotten her this far...

"Sita, should I sign this? Is it the right thing to do?"

"It is, Mageling." His sharp teeth poked from his muzzle as he spoke. "This contract is fair. It is what is best."

"Enough with this drivel. I grow weary of your indecisiveness. This is what you wanted, is it not?"

Azalea nodded. It was. "Yes. Thank you for this opportunity."

Azalea took the quill from Sita, unable to hide the shake in her hand. His little black fingers wrapped around her thumb.

"Do you want me to do it?" Sita asked.

"Yes please." She nodded. Quietly freaking out about how her life was about to change, she squeezed her eyes shut as Sita jabbed the sharp spike into her skin. She didn't make a noise, and when she opened her eyes, the pain was gone.

She took the quill and quickly scribbled a shaky signature on the parchment beside the goddess's. A wet warmth spread over her hand, and she glanced down. Sita was licking her palm.

"Sita!" She swiped him away and curled her hand into her chest in shock.

He winced but didn't look overly apologetic. "Sorry, force of habit."

"It is done." Ereshkigal stepped toward Azalea and gripped her wrist.

A surge of power rushed into Azalea's arm, right into the bones. Ereshkigal grabbed her shoulder, forcing her to stay there and accept the blast of power searing through her veins.

The magic spread through her, her blood felt like it was boiling, and her eyeballs wanted to pop out of her skull with the pressure.

Then it changed.

It felt like the magic was soaking into her, dancing through her blood and filling her with brilliant colors and lights.

Suddenly it was over, and Azalea stepped back. She stared at her arm, branded with a gilded circle around her wrist. Then looked up.

The dark world was vivid with color. The goddess was outlined in a blaze of shimmering black and purple. The petals on the floor were the brightest red she had ever seen. So bright it could be a new color, and she almost wept at the sight of it. How could something be so beautiful? She picked up a petal, staring at it, then saw everything beyond was just as bright.

Ereshkigal smiled. "It is done."

# Chapter 25

The crowd roared in Torin's ears. How the hell had they gotten into this? The white sun was high in the sky and had him dripping in sweat already. The ridiculous "battle outfits" they were wearing didn't help—no shirts and thick wool-like skirts that were scratchy but easy enough to move in.

He gripped his elemer and tried to block out the massive amphitheater and the crowd that rose all around them.

Fabian paced in front of him like an impatient lion, his eyes locked on Torin. That arrogant arsehole had brought this on them both. He couldn't have just kept his mouth shut so they could work all this out when they got back.

"You don't look ready, Dumont," Fabian barked.

"I don't want to do this. This isn't why we are here." He'd had a long talk with Kat before this and had promised he would try to get out of it or let Fabian win. Apparently, she knew Fabian quite well, and he wasn't going to back down, so it was up to Torin. He didn't inquire how well they knew each other, and he really didn't want to know. But one thing that was clear from their little chat was that Kat was not happy with either of them. It made Torin feel like a student all over again.

Fabian raised his fists, bouncing from foot to foot. "Man the fuck up. Own up and face your problems. No more cowering behind Danni and Kat. It ends here."

Magic churned in Torin's blood, but he couldn't get angry now. It wouldn't help either of them. He'd explained his whole situation with Azalea to Kat, but she didn't seem to believe him, and it was clear she was team Fabian. Gods knew why.

"I won't do it." Torin gritted his teeth as he faced Isimud, Enki's two-faced messenger.

Isimud's head swiveled round, revealing the other side, the angry face. "I know you are an ignorant mortal, but it is not an option to turn back now. The gods are waiting. Get into place," he ordered.

Torin glanced at Kat, who shook her head slowly, telling him not to back down. His options were not good: back out like a coward and piss off the gods, or fight Fabian and risk killing him with the hand of death if it got too serious. He felt like Kat might be wrong in this instance.

"The winner will knock out their opponent!" Isimud announced, his voice booming across the arena.

Knock him out. Maybe he could manage that. He just had to stay defensive and keep his emotions under control.

The earth shook. Isimud froze as the rumble continued around them, longer than the last time, and louder. Inanna stood with her lions at her side, unmoved. But others in the crowd darted looks around. Then it stopped.

Isimud continued as if it never happened. "The use of magic and elemers is allowed if the mortals can handle it." Isimud's other head had spun around and chuckled.

Their magic wasn't to be counted on here, so Torin planned to take Fabian down in hand-to-hand combat after they'd put on enough of a show. Shouldn't take long. Fabian was much older than Torin, and he was a gallu tracker, not a fighter.

"Contestants, take your places," Isimud's voice bellowed.

Torin crouched, ready to react, his elemer buzzing in his hand. He'd tested his magic the night before. The amulet dulled Echo Magic so much he couldn't do anything useful, and the Shadow Dimension was so far away it was too slow to draw enough magic to react quickly.

"I've been waiting a long time for this." Fabian had a manic grin on his face, making Torin wonder if he was drunk.

Torin kept his mouth shut, knowing anything he said would only piss Fabian off.

"Commence the battle!" Isimud yelled.

Fabian rushed at Torin, eyes blazing. Torin darted to the side, almost reacting too slowly. He was out of practice. The point of this was a show for the gods, so it couldn't be over too quickly, and he needed Fabian to feel like he had gotten his anger out, at least for now.

"You are never going near her again. I'm going to make sure of it." Fabian lunged.

This time Torin was prepared. He sidestepped and cut into the Shadow Dimension. It was more like a stab with all his weight behind it as he sliced through two-dimensional barriers and summoned through the weakest shadows he had ever seen. He focused the shadow into a tight rope and whipped it across the sandy ground to catch Fabian's ankle and slam him flat on his back.

A cloud of dust rose with the impact. The crowd roared, but he blocked it out.

Fabian stabbed his elemer into the empty air and conjured a thick stream of shadow, enough to slide under the shadow wrapped around his feet and free him.

"You fucker." Fabian, still lying down, sent tiny darts of shadows at Torin, far more solid than the shadow Torin had managed.

Torin didn't have enough Shadow Magic to make a shield. He had no choice but to duck. He avoided a dart hitting his face but felt the wind across his cheek. Fabian was back on his feet.

"My brother deserved better than the shitty death you gave him," Fabian growled and sent another wave of darts.

Torin summoned a shadow shield, but it was flimsy. They continued back and forth, throwing weakening shadows at each other, but blocking just as efficiently.

"Is that all you got, old man?" Torin baited him, hoping it would speed things up to get this over with. If Fabian had one thing, it was overconfidence.

Fabian threw down his elemer, and Torin's jaw cracked with a punch he hadn't seen coming. His teeth rattled, and the metallic tang of blood burst into his mouth. Stunned, he cradled his jaw and didn't have time to block as Fabian slammed an elbow into Torin's ribs.

Torin doubled over but threw up an arm to block any further blows. Fabian darted back, panting hard, but the blood lust was clear on his face. He would not back down.

He shot forward, but Torin was ready. Throwing down his elemer, he dodged Fabian's next blow.

His hand hummed with the old familiar magic he worked so hard to suppress, the want to kill consumed his blood and overpowered all his other magic, fighting to take over. He wouldn't let it. A jolt of fear and panic shot through him—Azalea. He was surprised she could feel him this far away. He had to ignore her.

With clenched fists, he forced the magic away and ran at Fabian. The crowd was screaming around him. This is what they had come for.

He hit Fabian in a high tackle and slammed him into the ground. The breath left Fabian's lungs with a loud huff followed by a groan, then gasping breaths.

"You had enough yet?" Torin asked as he towered over Fabian.

"Not a chance." Fabian twisted in the sand and went for Torin's ankles, trying to topple him.

Torin shifted quickly, but Fabian caught one of his legs and yanked. Torin didn't let it throw him. He swiveled the foot in Fabian's grasp and balanced on it, landing a perfect kick into Fabian's ribs. He could have kept kicking, but he didn't want to do too much damage.

Fabian let go and rolled away. But somehow got up. His face was covered in sand mixed with sweat and blood. He spat on the ground and wiped his mouth, the grin long gone.

"You've ruined her life." Fabian stalked forward like a panther sizing up its prey.

"I know. It was not my intention."

Fabian sneered. "Yeah... right. Still following daddy's orders."

"That isn't true." Torin gritted his teeth. There was no point in explaining. Fabian was not ready to listen.

"You've corrupted her. Poisoned her mind. You're controlling her."

"That isn't how it works. You know better than anyone she doesn't do anything she doesn't want to. She doesn't listen to me."

"You don't know her," Fabian spat.

"I know her better than anyone," Torin yelled. Immediately regretting raising his voice. He mustn't let Fabian get to him.

Fabian's look turned to disgust. He whipped his hand through the air, and somehow he was holding his elemer.

Torin had no time to move as Fabian summoned shadows and sent them flying. Torin spun around so his shoulder caught most of the rain of shadow shards. He didn't even see what they were, but they felt like razor blades slicing through his arms and the back of his head.

Rage filled him, and he ran at Fabian. "You're the one hurting her!" Torin yelled and punched Fabian in the face. It didn't knock him out but sent blood flying.

"What?" Fabian asked, confused. He paused, catching his breath.

Maybe Torin had hit him harder than he thought. "You didn't even tell her about your ward."

"Why should that matter?" Fabian said.

"And she feels everything through the bond." He suspected Fabian was stalling for time.

They circled each other, bouncing on their feet, but Fabian didn't strike. Had he really not known? It didn't matter.

Torin took advantage of the moment, his old training overriding everything. He had to take Fabian down before he used magic again. Torin was at too much of a disadvantage, and his elemer was too far away to get to. That was what he got for trying to play fair. No more.

He launched himself at Fabian. The old snake, *the cobra*, was too slow, and Torin put all his strength behind it and landed a blow to the side of Fabian's face. Fabian swayed for a moment before crashing to the ground.

Adrenaline rushed through Torin's veins, replacing the need to kill. He'd missed that high. The sweetness of the win. He beamed at the crowds of cheering gods, and for once, he felt like he was on top of the world.

))⟩●⟨⟨(

Azalea gripped her pillow in panic. She hadn't felt much from Torin in the past few days, but right now, he seemed to be riding a rollercoaster. One minute he was gripped with fear, then he wanted to kill someone, followed by the most intense joy she had ever felt from him.

She just had to hope no one was dead.

The feelings subsided, and she leaned back in the bed, running her hand over the new bands of tattoos that circled her wrist. Hopefully, Torin would get over his triumph soon and go to bed. She needed to talk to him, and he was not going to be pleased.

# Chapter 26

Even in her dreams, everything seemed brighter. Azalea paced the train station platform, taking in the vibrancy of a woman's red coat as she passed by. She wasn't sure why she was at a train station; she didn't even recognize it. It seemed like something out of a movie. People rushed back and forth around her wheeling suitcases and yelling into their phones, all ignoring her. She stopped below a gigantic clock that read 5 pm.

She wished she had some sort of control over her dreams like Torin did or that she would have picked a more relaxing meeting point. Every time she made a move for a seat, she was either cut off, bumped into, or the seat disappeared entirely.

Her arm caught her eye, though she didn't want to look at it anymore. Gold bands encircled her wrist with the snake tattoo gliding over the top. An honor, according to Ereshkigal, but she felt more like a captive than ever. The bands were metallic like real gold, as if they had been pressed into her skin, melded into her, and infused with magic.

She walked to the end of the platform, and he appeared.

He was wearing a smart suit and carrying a cane similar to his father's. He grinned, and she ran towards him, throwing herself in his arms. Hugging her tightly, he kissed the top of her head.

"This is what you want me to wear?" he teased, frowning down at this suit, and tossed away the cane like it was a snake.

"I have no idea. Maybe I saw this in a movie? You'll have to teach me more about controlling dreams because this isn't what I would have asked for." She stepped back and looked down to see she was wearing the same red coat she'd seen on the woman before. She wished she knew how to do that.

"Where do you want to go?"

"That hotel in Cyprus. I wish we could have stayed there longer." It was the first place that came to her head. They had been happy there, fake married, and on a relic hunt. She wished they could just go back to then and not find the relics.

He smiled. "A hotel room might not be the best idea. We need to talk, not get distracted."

He was right. She desperately wanted a distraction, but she had so much to tell him, and it was impossible to tell how much time she had left. She might have been asleep for a while already.

"How about that beach in New Zealand?"

"Trust me and close your eyes." He took her hands, and their magic softly combined.

A wave crashed in front of her, and Azalea's dream eyes flicked open. Salty air filled her nostrils, and she took in the scintillating sparkle of the blue expanse before her, more vibrant and electric than she had ever seen in real life. She couldn't help but strain her eyes looking for the taniwha they'd watched disappear into this very water—even if this was a dream—Torin's dream now.

His hand wrapped around hers and guided her up the beach. They sank into the grainy sand and leaned back on their elbows, staring out across the water. Far more relaxing than the chaotic train station.

"Are you okay? I felt some crazy stuff from you before I went to sleep. Your fight with Fabian, I take it. You won?" she asked, not quite ready to throw bad news at Torin.

"I knocked him out. But he legitimately tried to kill me, so I don't think we're going to be friends any time soon."

"He's an arse." Azalea tilted her head to the side, appreciating the warmth of the sun on her cheek. She was probably not concerned enough that her uncle had tried to kill Torin. "I'm glad you're both okay. You are okay, aren't you? I felt how scared you were at one point." She knew he could change himself in dreams and could be hiding it from her.

"I'm fine. Just a bit bruised. He got me in the jaw, so I'm not sure how easy eating will be when I'm awake." He nudged her shoulder. "You know, you're taking this very well. I thought you'd be pissed off about it."

She took a breath. "So the thing is…"

He sat up, dusting his hands on the suit trousers he was still wearing, and gave her that look that said he knew what was coming. "Just tell me."

"Actually, it's good news." She remained reclined in her red coat, trying to look casual and hoping he couldn't feel her slightly deceptive inclination.

"I would love to believe that," Torin said.

"Well, you should. Ereshkigal is sending Inanna's husband Dumuzi back as we speak, so she should be happy. It should help with you and Enki coming to an arrangement. I'm assuming he was pleased with your display of manly fighting?"

"That *is* good news, and yes, the gods took great joy in the ridiculousness of us mortals. I think we're good with that."

"Good. That's good." She nibbled her lip and stared intently at the ocean, hoping to catch a glimpse of the taniwha.

"What else did Ereshkigal want, other than the spirits?"

Azalea trickled sand through her fingers. "What makes you think she wanted something else?"

"I'm assuming she didn't do it out of the goodness of her heart."

"No. But it's good news depending on what way you want to look at it." Azalea didn't look up.

Torin sat up. "Just spit it out."

"I did what she wanted, and you'll be pleased to know she fixed my problem with spirits, and I can break the soul bond—that is, if you want to." Azalea looked up and met his eyes, trying to read him, but he kept his emotions concealed.

"What's the bad news, then?"

Had he even heard her? She said she could break the bond. Shouldn't he be thrilled? She swallowed and rolled up her coat sleeve to reveal the gold bands.

"She made me a demi-goddess of spirits. The new powers protect me from the spirits." She took a breath and continued before she saw Torin's reaction and chickened out. "But I also have to collect more spirits for her. They need them down here, and I can do it. I just have to spend six months of the year here in place of Inanna's husband."

She glanced up, expecting to see the familiar disappointed, angry look on Torin's face she knew all too well. But it was the opposite. His face fell. He shook his head slowly but didn't look at her.

"You shouldn't have had to do this. This was my fault, and you're the one paying the price."

Azalea pushed herself off her elbows and sat up, dusting the sand from her hands. "It wasn't anyone's fault." This was worse than anger. He was blaming himself again.

"What will your family say? How can I face them? I can't tell Fabian."

"Maybe he'll say *omg I'm so proud, Azalea the screw-up is now a demi-goddess and has saved the world. She is so amazing,* or something like that," she said in her best Fabian voice.

"You shouldn't joke about this, Azalea, it's serious."

"You're too serious." She said it a lot more aggressively than she meant to. "This is a dream, Torin. We're stuck where we are, but we can make the most of our time here. Yolo and all that." She shuffled closer to him in the sand and rested her hand on his cheek, turning his head to face her.

"I'll find a way to get you back."

"Just kiss me. I'll find my way back. Don't you worry about that." She kissed him hard, hoping it would distract him enough to forget everything.

His hand slid around her and shifted her without warning. Lowering her onto the sand, he held himself above her. Her skin buzzed as he dipped down to kiss her, and she wove her hands around his waist, pulling him down.

"What about the soul bond?" he asked.

She frowned. She thought they were done with talking. "It's a dream. It doesn't count."

"I mean, you said you could break it."

"Is that what you want?" Her heart thundered in her chest, unsure what answer she wanted to hear the most. Breaking it would free them both, but sealing it would lead them into the unknown—the most powerful mages in the world, but tethered to one another forever.

"I don't know anymore." Torin's deep brown eyes stared into her soul as if searching for the answer.

A wave of heat rushed through her. What if they didn't break it? Yes, they would be stuck with each other, but was that so bad? After they closed the gate, maybe they could help set the world in balance again, maybe they could take down Torin's father once and for all.

"I don't know either." She bit her lip, their eyes locked in the most intense stare of her life. Could they be on the same page? She couldn't take the tension and pulled him into a kiss.

His lips were hot and hungry against hers. Torin shifted, kicking sand over both of them, and Azalea burst out laughing. Torin rolled off her and flicked all the sand off his head.

"Maybe we should have gone to the hotel room after all." He smiled, dusting off Azalea's coat as she sat up.

"There's still time." She grinned and caught a glimpse of the shimmering body of the taniwha dance over the swell of a wave far out at sea.

# Chapter 27

Torin followed Kat and a nervous fox-faced man through the open-air hallways lined with blue and white mosaics, all framed with gold, and down a set of winding stairs to a courtyard of fountains and citrus trees. He was glad to be back in his normal clothes, though even the light fabric of modern wool weighed on his bruised ribs. They had all their gear with them in case this meeting went well.

"Please wait here, sir." The fox-man scampered off.

Kat sat on a bench under an olive tree looking back to her normal self, dressed in combat clothes. "You let him land a blow. You're out of practice."

"Lucky shot," Torin said, trying not to open his mouth too much because it bloody well hurt.

She snorted most unsympathetically. Torin crossed his arms and watched Fabian descend the stairs, still with that arrogant swagger that gave no indication he was the loser in their little fight.

"You woke up," Torin said.

"I'm not that easy to get rid of." Fabian sneered. A purple bruise rose over his cheekbone, but he gave no hint he was in pain. But Torin knew exactly where he'd hit him in the ribs, and he would sure as hell be feeling it today as well. He hid it well though.

"Can you two just pretend to act civilized for this meeting? Everything depends on it," Kat barked.

"I'm well aware," Torin said, his jaw aching and his head groggy from dreamweaving. He hadn't planned on staying in there so long, but after he and Azalea had caught up properly, Zakar had decided to appear and demand an update on everyone's progress in far too much detail.

This meeting needed to go smoothly so they could get the hell out of there.

The fox-faced man darted back and gestured for them to follow him. They were led through several walled garden courtyards, each with a different set of statues, fountains, or meticulously pruned trees until they exited into a large orchard outside the inner-city wall.

Out of the dusty earth grew rows of pomegranates and around them were lush date palms. A woman with flowing green hair and skin the color of the barley fields walked up to them and handed them each an open pomegranate.

"Eat, please," she said in a cool, soothing voice, the sort you could listen to all day.

Torin dropped a few ruby-red pomegranate seeds in his mouth, letting the tart sweetness slide around on his tongue, trying to work out if this goddess was who he thought she was.

"Thank you," Kat replied and introduced each of them. Torin was more than happy for her to take command.

"I am Ninhursag, goddess of plants and the earth, creator of humans alongside my former husband, Enki. I wish to offer protection for my children of the mortal realm."

Torin nearly choked on the seeds.

"Thank you. We will accept any help we can get." Kat stared at the woman with childlike wonder. Something Torin had never witnessed in his former teacher.

Torin stood rooted on the spot, forgetting how to speak coherently. "You created humans."

"Yes, Enki and I toiled for many moons on that project." A genuine smile touched the goddess's lips. "Others did not believe it to be successful, but to this day we remain in faith of our creations. Though your world faces many new perils since our time."

Fabian looked at Torin. "There are a lot of arseholes down there, that's for sure."

Ninhursag raised an eyebrow.

"Humanity is worth saving. I assure you," Torin spoke quickly. Trust Fabian to let their grudge destroy the world.

Ninhursag handed Kat a leather pouch. "These seeds, when planted, will absorb the surplus of Echo Magic in the air and set your world to the correct balance."

"Thank you. How do we plant them?" Kat asked.

The goddess put her palms together at her chest serenely. "Go to my children of the House of Bees. They will know the forest guardians who will understand the task at hand. They will plant the seeds across your world."

Kat opened the pouch and looked in. "I don't want to seem rude, but is this enough?"

"One on every landmass will be sufficient. The trees will grow in all provinces and in all soils. Once the gate is closed, the rebalance will be swift."

Fabian folded his arms across his chest. "So Enki is going to agree to close the gate, you know this?"

"I believe he intends to, or he would not have called me here," Ninhursag said. "But you must act swiftly, there is not much time."

Torin looked around. "Not much time before what?"

A trumpet sounded, and a procession of guards with flags marched in time into the orchard.

"Enki has come, and we do not do well in the same space. I take my leave of you and wish you well on your quest."

Torin bobbed his head in a bow. "Thank you. We are honored to have met you."

A gold chariot rolled up in front of them in a cloud of dust as golden wings sprouted from Ninhursag's back, and she shot into the sky.

Enki's voice bellowed across the courtyard. "I bring good news, mortals. I will close the gateway for you."

Torin followed Kat's lead and bowed as Enki stepped down from his chariot. He was huge, like the god Zakar, and made Torin feel like a beetle that could easily be crushed underfoot. There was no smile beneath his great crinkled beard, and his dark skin gleamed in the sunlight like he'd been overly oiled. He wore a simple tunic over which rested a copper breastplate, engraved with fish and patterns of water. The rest of him was all muscle.

"What do we need to do in return?" Kat asked.

Enki's gaze drifted over their heads as if he refused to look down to their level. "I will accept your offer to return the scribe Nabu to this land."

Torin let out a silent breath of relief. "Thank you."

Inanna ran into the orchard with streams of white silk floating behind her in the wind. "Good news! My husband has been returned to me, and to show my appreciation for this sacrifice, I bring news of your homeland."

"What sacrifice?" Kat asked.

That was probably referring to Azalea's deal, but Torin wasn't going to be the one to break it to Fabian. He'd put that off as long as he could.

"Good news, I hope," Fabian mumbled. Clearly, he wasn't thrilled with the idea of finding the lost god either.

"Oh, my apologies. It is not good news. I was just pleased about my husband. I came to inform Mage Blackbourne that the House of Ravens has captured your ward, young Cassie Yates."

Torin's heart fell. That poor girl, he'd only met her a few times at the house, but she seemed like a bright young thing. He wouldn't wish this on anyone, not even Fabian.

"Fuck." Fabian rubbed his temples. "She cannot be near him. I need to get back there."

Inanna looked straight at Torin, and he quirked his head, confused. "I am very sorry. She is your kin, is she not, Torin?"

"No. I don't know her." Torin turned to Fabian. "I promise I will help you get her back, though."

"This is really bad," Fabian said and started pacing. "Korbyn was not meant to know about her."

Kat grabbed his arm to stop him and gave his shoulder a friendly squeeze. "We'll get her back, Fabian. She is a child. He won't hurt her."

*You sure about that?* Torin kept that to himself. Kat was in denial if she believed that. "Why did Korbyn take her? Why shouldn't he know about her?"

"It's a long story. Stupid girl, she would have snuck out to pick those blasted mushrooms or to go to that cottage on the edge of the woods. She never bloody listens."

Kat remained close to Fabian. "She didn't know the danger or that Korbyn has men patrolling Blackbourne's perimeters."

Fabian threw his hands in the air. "I should have told her or locked her inside or something."

"You know very well that's ridiculous." Kat nudged Fabian with her elbow. "Kira probably knows where she is. We'll get her back."

"Why didn't the blood wards stop her?" Torin asked.

Fabian looked toward the gate. "She has a bloodstone with my blood in it. It was so she could always get back in if she was in danger."

Maybe Fabian did have a fatherly side.

Kat adjusted her bag; it was clear they would be leaving. "It's not your fault, Fabian. You did nothing wrong."

Enki clapped as loud as thunder, nearly knocking them all over in fright. "Enough of this. You will leave now. Inanna will accompany you, and when you return with my grandson, Nabu, I will close the gate from this side, and Ereshkigal will close it on the other side. Our worlds will be in balance once more."

"You are giving my sister permission to enter the mortal world?" Inanna clasped her hands together as if praying to Enki.

Enki gave a slow nod. "Yes, she has requested it and will be allowed this privilege as long as she takes no mortal lives."

Inanna frowned. "So be it."

"Let's get on with it, then." Fabian marched off without waiting.

# Chapter 28

"I already told you she went this way. Stop asking." Sita steered them around a sharp corner and onto a curved staircase.

Azalea was still getting used to seeing magic around her. Sita was surrounded by a deep violet glow that kept catching her eye. So was Faraday who trotted along in front.

"Why didn't Jade come and get me?" Azalea tried to keep up with Sita as he tilted his wings and swerved upward.

"She's been very busy while you spent a great deal of time sleeping," Sita yelled back.

"It wasn't normal sleeping, I had to speak with Torin and Zakar."

"Let's just say what it is. You were meeting up with your lover, but if that's the story you want to go with, then very well."

Azalea was already puffing from the stairs. "That's not fair, and you know it. He informed me that things are going well in the Echo Dimension, and hopefully, they will be leaving soon."

Sita spun around, flying backward for a second. "And how did he take the news that you are staying here?"

"He didn't seem to believe it. But that isn't a problem right now. Right now, I just need to find Jade so we can get her home at least."

Sita turned back and kept flying. "She's well ahead of you on that."

"How?" Azalea did her best to keep up.

"You'll see." Sita spun around with a sly look on his face.

As if on cue, footsteps thundered on the stairs toward them, and Jade hurtled around the corner followed by Elam.

"Elam!" Azalea said as Elam crashed into her, and she grasped him by the shoulders. She could feel him. She pulled him into a hug, and he squeezed her back quickly before pushing her away and shooing her down the stairs.

"No time. Just run." Jade grabbed her hand and pulled her away from Elam and into a run, dragging her down the stairs. Silvery magic surrounded Jade, but Elam only had a faint glow of gold, barely visible, and a strange shimmer about him.

"Elam, you're here!" Azalea looked back. Jade let go of her hand and kept running.

"Just keep running," Elam said with a grin.

Gods, it felt good to see him. That image of him sprawled in the alleyway was never far from her mind when she closed her eyes. This new image of Elam, full of life and color, was a gift.

Jade, on the other hand, appeared sharper and more in focus, and her hands were wrapped around a bulging bag that glowed bright silver.

"I'm so sorry you died, Elam. I didn't mean for any of this to happen." She hadn't even thought about why they were running. Seeing him made everything so much better.

Elam kept running. "It's fine, Azalea. I count myself lucky you were there with me at the end, or I wouldn't have got to come here. The other options aren't so great, from what I hear."

This wasn't right. He shouldn't be grateful to her. He should hate her.

"Why are we running?" Azalea's breath grew heavier. It had been a few weeks since she'd been for a decent run. Unless you counted running from that minotaur man. It seemed like a lifetime ago, but it was just a week.

"We stole a dragon's egg," Elam called back over his shoulder.

"What!" The Elam she knew wouldn't be stealing things. But she supposed death could give one a new lease on life, so to speak.

"Sita told us to. We can use it to get back." Jade continued to pull her along as they ran cradling the bag like a lady with a pregnant belly.

"That's the egg?"

"Yes."

"Now what?"

"We need somewhere to hide," Elam said. "Ambrose has been following me, waiting for me to find you and lead you off somewhere, no doubt. We can't go to my place."

Where did he even live? What did people do in this city? Her mind flickered to the pub when they first arrived. "I know where we can go. Sita!" she called to the demon flying behind her. "Can you find my father?"

"What an absurd question." He scoffed. "Follow me." He flew over their heads, and Elam ducked but kept running, and they left the narrow tower and turned a corner onto a long hallway lit by the red glow from stained glass windows.

"This is the last stairwell," Sita said as they hurtled through a narrow arch, the flicker of flames sent shadows scurrying across the walls all around them.

"Who are we running from, anyway?" Azalea asked, trying not to trip over Faraday.

"Not who," Elam called.

Jade shuddered. "Giant snake statues—they weren't just statues."

"But they were slow getting out of the wall." Elam was panting hard. "It's bought us a bit of time."

"Once we are outside the palace gates, Azalea can stop them from tracking us," Sita said.

"I can?"

They dashed down until they hit a long, straight tunnel. At the end, Azalea tried not to panic as they skidded to a stop at a black iron gate.

"It's got a spell on it," Azalea's hands curled around the cold metal.

Jade's eyebrows pinched together. "How do you know that?"

"That hazy purpleness glowing all over is a bit of a giveaway." Azalea pointed at it, and they stared at her like she was crazy.

"The gate isn't glowing," Jade said.

"No, it really isn't." Elam gave her a sideways look.

Azalea paused and stared at the gate. "You guys need to get your eyes checked. Shouldn't you have ghost vision or something, Elam?" It was definitely glowing.

"I might be a ghost, but ghost bodies here are pretty much the same as humans. Just get on with it."

Jade pulled the egg out of the bag and cradled it in her arms. "It's getting heavy."

The egg had azure blue scales that shimmered with tiny rainbows and a faint glow of purple the same as the gate. "It's beautiful," Azalea said.

"There is no time." Sita snapped her out of her daze with the mesmerizing egg. "Mageling, put your hand on the gate and order it to let us through."

Azalea cringed at the nickname, and Jade giggled. Azalea put her hand on the gate and closed her eyes. The statue guards must be getting close.

The hum of the gates resonated through her, not connecting with her magic like Torin's did, but more recognizing it and reacting. In her mind, she saw the gates opening for her, and her hand stretched away. Her eyes flashed open, and the gate pulled her along as it silently swung away.

She stumbled forward. "Holy crap, it worked."

"Move along now." Sita flapped behind Elam and Jade, hitting them with his wings to hustle them along, not that they needed any extra motivation. They were outside the gate in an instant. Still in the tunnel, but not far from the end, where Azalea could hear rushing water.

"Now seal it once more," Sita ordered.

Azalea did as he said. It was too easy. "How did I do that?"

"The powers Ereshkigal bestowed on you connect you to the palace as one of its residents now. I wasn't sure it would work, but she appears to have given you high-level clearance."

"What's all this about new powers? You haven't got enough weird magic stored up?" Jade smiled, probably on a high from escaping danger. They seemed to be getting lucky lately.

"I have a lot to fill you in on. But first, how do we stop them from tracking us?" Azalea asked Sita.

"Hand her the dragon egg," Sita ordered Jade.

"Okey dokey. Just don't drop it, it's bloody heavy." Jade kept the egg close and handed it to Azalea so it was right against her body.

As she stepped away, Azalea felt the true weight. "How the hell were you running with this thing?"

Jade shrugged. "I'm just awesome, I guess." She was so tiny but must have arm muscles hidden away in there.

Azalea focused on not dropping it. Hot, turbulent magic buzzed in her hands.

"Focus, Mageling." Sita flapped up and snapped his claws in front of her face.

"Tell me what to do."

"Close your eyes and speak to the dragon within. Show it your intentions and why your quest is important. If it deems you worthy, it will stop emitting the tracking energy that the serpents pick up on."

"Is it okay if I sit down?"

"Yes, just do it quickly."

Azalea carefully dropped to the cold flagstones that lined the tunnel floor, sat cross-legged, and closed her eyes. She knew how smart dragons were, even baby ones. She could not mess this up. Faraday rested his head on her knee.

"I can hear them coming," Elam said.

"Be quiet," Sita ordered.

Azalea went straight into meditation mode, her breathing and heart slowed, and she focused on the egg. All she could hear was her breath and the buzzing magic from the egg. They were the only things in the world at that moment.

"It's not working," she said, pushing down the rising panic.

"Give it here." Jade scooted in close, pulled the dragon egg onto her lap, and closed her eyes.

Azalea watched as Jade's silvery magic merged with the egg.

A roar thundered in the tunnel. Two stone serpents raced towards the gate but suddenly stopped.

Jade's eyes flashed open. "I think it's working."

"Cutting it a bit close." Elam sounded like the careful boy she remembered.

Azalea let out a relieved breath, glad the snakes were on the other side of the gate. The giant serpents with three horns on their heads slithered like real snakes. Their stone bodies, the size of Great Danes, clattered against the floor as they turned away, no longer interested in her party.

Azalea shook Jade. Maybe a little too over-excited. "You did it!"

"Thank fuck for that. Where are we off to now?" Jade asked.

Sita flew off without looking back. "To my old master's house. Follow me."

"You don't think Ambrose will find you, Elam? Wasn't he following you?" Azalea slipped the dragon egg back into the bag Jade handed her, and Jade pulled it over her head once more.

"He was lurking at the back gates of the palace expecting me to go out the way I came in. He won't find us," Elam said.

"Good, let's go then." Azalea jumped up, and they jogged after Sita.

They walked for what seemed like an hour. Sita led them down backstreets and alleyways until they were out of the inner circle of town. It was difficult to tell what direction they were going in, but Azalea occasionally caught glimpses of the black spires of the palace behind them and the mountain bellowing smoke behind that.

Azalea couldn't take her eyes off Elam. Just knowing he was here "alive" in some form made her feel lighter inside.

Sita stopped. "He is here."

Azalea craned her neck up to the brick apartment building as tiny flakes of ash rained down from the sky, falling like snow onto the black smudged street. She pulled open the door and stepped into the narrow lobby with cubes of mailboxes down one side.

Sita flitted past her and stopped at an elevator that had an out-of-order sign on it that looked like it might have been there a while. They took the stairs, passing apartments as they went up with bikes and shoes all stored outside their entrances.

They stopped at a door that looked like all the others with chipped paint, but only one pair of shoes outside. Azalea took a deep breath and knocked.

Once again, she had no idea what she would say to her dad, but hopefully, he was willing to help.

The door swung open. Her father stood there with his eyes shining as they locked on Azalea. "You came back."

Azalea shuffled between her feet as Faraday raced inside. "Um, yes, we need your help."

"Of course. Welcome, come in, come in." He guided her in with a gentle hand on her shoulder. "Hello Elam, good to see you again."

Azalea turned around. "Wait, you know Elam?"

"He's how I knew you were at the palace," Elam said. "I came looking for you, but they took me to Jade, and from there, we worked out we both knew you. But I met your dad when I first came here. We arrived at the same time, and he recognized me from... you know." He winced.

Azalea's hands went to her mouth. Jade and Sita slipped past her to get inside, but Azalea couldn't make herself move.

"You said you didn't remember, but you do. You remember being in the gallu. You remember killing Elam." Azalea faced her dad, a new wave of horror settling over her. He must remember Torin.

"That's rough." Jade sunk into a tatty armchair by an old radiator and a wooden coffee table, the dragon's egg in her lap and sweat beading on her forehead. She was tough for that petite frame.

Azalea forced herself inside. She took off her shoes and walked across the chipped tile floor. Though she wasn't sure she wanted to hear any of this.

Her dad gestured for her to take a seat at the patio table. "I remember some things, just snippets. Elam's face was fresh in my mind, so I remembered him."

*This was not good.* Azalea shuffled in the rickety metal chair.

Her father continued. "I sought out Elam and explained about the gallu and apologized. That's how we both worked out we were talking about the same Azalea." He smiled as if he were proud of her.

Azalea nibbled at her lip, and Faraday jumped on her lap. Did he remember fighting her at the end? Did he remember Torin was there?

Elam leaned on the back of a gray sofa. "It's fine. I know it wasn't your dad's fault, the same as it wasn't yours, Azalea, and it wasn't Erik's or Livia's. It was the gallu's fault and mine for being so stupid to go after it."

"I was that stupid, too. I went after it, and I wouldn't be alive if Faraday and T—" She was going to say Torin. But she wasn't sure how her dad would react to her teaming up with the man who murdered him. "—my teacher... turned up."

Elam looked confused. He hadn't known Torin was her teacher, so he probably assumed she meant Mage Shepard, which seemed a very unlikely scenario. Fortunately, he didn't say anything.

The guilt piled back on. She would have to tell her dad about Torin soon because she had to update Jade on the progress of the mission and how the others were doing in the Echo Dimension. It was hard to keep Torin out of it.

"I only have a vague memory of the gallu's end, but you freed me and so many others. I am forever in your debt, Azalea. I'm here to help, whatever you need."

She wasn't sure if *vague* meant he did remember Torin was there and was going to avoid the subject, or that he actually didn't remember. Either way, she could work with that. "We have a dragon's egg. Can you hide it for us until Jade can use it to get home?"

"A dragon's egg?" His gaze shot to the bag on Jade's lap.

Jade patted it softly. "It's okay, I took the tracking off it. No one followed us."

"I see. How about I make tea, and you can all tell me how I can help and then fill me in on everything?" Her dad filled an old-fashioned kettle to put on the stove.

Words caught in Azalea's throat, and she couldn't think of what to say, overwhelmed that he would just accept that she needed help and agree so easily. He reminded her so much of Fabian, but only in appearance, not in the way he spoke or his mannerisms. He had a strong confidence about him like Fabian, but without the arrogance and defensiveness Fabian always had. They had the same long dark hair, but Fabian mostly kept his tied up. This man had his down. He appeared younger than Fabian, though she knew he was older. His eyes looked tired, and his expression was severe, like he wasn't capable of having fun. She couldn't quite wrap her head around the fact that she was talking to her dad.

She still had many unanswered questions about her child-hood that she wasn't sure she was ready to have answered, so she watched him make tea. He did it the same as any human alive would, but the difference was he was still dead. This was his life in this crappy flat, doing whatever he did day-to-day. She didn't fit into this world and didn't want to.

Elam dragged over another metal chair to sit on, Sita perched next to Jade on the dusty windowsill above the radiator, and Azalea's dad leaned against the kitchen bench as they sipped at the weak tea. She already missed biscuits from home.

"I don't know where to begin," she said honestly.

"How about you tell me why you are here." Her father set down his tea.

Jade adjusted the egg in her lap. "Do you want me to explain?"

"No, it's okay." Azalea turned to her dad. "I don't want you to hate me, and you probably will if I tell you everything."

"There is nothing you can tell me that would make me hate you. I've been a terrible father, Azalea. I was never there, even when I was alive. Just give me a chance to help you now."

He had a point. She had spent a lot of time hating him, not only for dying but for not being there when he was alive. She drew on that old hatred to try to mask the guilt.

"I wanted to learn Shadow Magic so desperately. You probably know that, but when I found my teacher, you have to believe me when I say I didn't know who he was. He was the one who saved me when I tried to bring you back when I released the gallu."

Elam let out a small gasp. This was probably news to both him and Jade.

"I have a vivid memory of your body lying there. I was helpless," her father's voice trailed off.

Azalea cleared her throat. "Well, obviously I didn't die. It was my teacher who brought me back with necromancy, along with some intervention from the gods."

"It wasn't Fabian?" her father asked.

Azalea shook her head. "No. If I had known who he was when we first met, I never would have asked him to teach me. But it was too late. The gods, Damu and Ereshkigal, bound us together so I could be a portal for the spirits to the Shadow Dimension."

Her father's eyes grew dark. "A portal for spirits? You are bound to this man?"

"Yes, but I'm on top of it, and I have a way to undo it if we want to."

"You were bound to someone against your will. Of course, you will undo it."

Azalea swallowed, looked down at Faraday, and patted him forcefully.

"Unless you are in love with him? Are you?"

Unexpected anger burst into her chest, this was none of his business, he had no right to judge her. She forced her jaw to unclench. "It's complicated right now. Anyway, the point is, he is with Fabian and Kat in the Echo Dimension, and they have a plan to close the Echo Dimension gateway."

She turned to Jade, so she didn't have to look at her dad. "They're on their way back soon, I think."

"How do you know this?" Elam asked.

Azalea twisted her mouth. "Um, dream magic."

"House of Raven's magic?" her father growled.

Jade set down her cup loudly. "Azalea, just spit it out. There's no point in beating around the bush."

"So the thing is…" She swallowed. This was probably the end of their short-lived friendly relationship. "The man I'm soul bound to is Torin Dumont."

Her father's face drained of color, and his teacup dropped to the bench with a clatter.

# Chapter 29

"You sided with the House of Ravens!" her father's voice boomed.

Faraday shot off Azalea's lap.

Sita launched into the air and flapped in front of her father. "Do not raise your voice to her like that."

"It's okay Sita, cool it," Azalea said. Sita's eyes glowed red, and he lowered himself onto the coffee table and sat with crossed arms in front of Jade. "And no, we have not sided with the House of Ravens. We are doing everything we can to bring them down."

Her father slammed his fist onto the table. "Yet you're in bed with Korbyn Dumont's son? You are bound to him. You're sharing his magic. How is that not being on their side?"

"Because he isn't one of them!" Azalea yelled, then told herself to stay calm. "He turned his back on his father once he realized what he had done. He didn't know the truth, and he regrets what he did every day of his life. He's trying to fix it all, and he's killing himself doing it."

Her father shook his head slowly, his lips curled into an unlaughing smirk. "He knew what he did when he murdered me. I saw the coldness in his eyes."

"He thought you killed his mother," Azalea spat back. Her magic threatened to boil over as she leaned back in her chair and crossed her arms.

He looked at her, and for a moment, she swore she saw guilt. "Fabian wouldn't allow this."

"Fabian is not okay with it. He tried to stop Torin from teaching me, but he never bothered to tell me why. I didn't know, but we can't change it now, and I don't want to."

She realized in that moment she meant it—she didn't want to change anything, not with Torin, not with having her chance to learn Shadow Magic.

Jade suddenly sat up dead straight, and Elam darted over and caught the egg before it rolled off her lap as her eyes went all white.

"She's having a vision." Azalea rushed to her side.

Jade's voice changed to one that wasn't her own, an eerie whisper. "Many will fall at the hands of the dark goddess. A city to fill. A gate to close. Lives to extinguish."

Jade blinked and scratched her chin. "That was weird."

Azalea took her hand and checked her pulse to make sure she was okay. "You had a vision."

"Yeah, I know. I actually remember it this time. I saw Ereshkigal on a killing spree on Earth." Jade narrowed her eyes as if she was seeing it before her.

Azalea gripped Jade's hand. "What! She can't do that."

"I'm sure she can." Elam leaned toward them, concern plastered across his face.

Azalea let go of Jade's hand and stood up. "But the contract. It said she couldn't interfere with humans."

"It did indeed," said Sita, grinning ear to ear. "And do you know what happens if she breaks the agreement?"

Azalea glanced down at her wrists. "I'd be free of the contract; we can go back to help."

"Yes, but only temporarily." Sita sat there smugly as if he had known all along. "Your prolonged absence will affect the balance of magic and the seasons on your world. You will eventually have to return."

Azalea knew this, though she didn't want to accept it. "When can we leave?"

Sita's ears flopped forward. "Your gold bands remain. It has not come to pass yet."

"But a bunch of people dying isn't what I want. Can we stop her? She can't have left yet." Azalea went back to her chair at the table to stop herself from pacing the small room.

Sita rubbed his hands together. "I put that clause in the contract for a reason. She was always going to do this. It is her way, and being among mortals is too tempting."

Azalea slumped back in the chair. "You could have warned me."

"It would not have made a difference," Sita said. "You would just feel guilty. My way was better."

Azalea tapped her hand on the table, unable to sit still. "How about Jade goes back with the dragon's egg and I'll go ask Ereshkigal if I can go with her? She's leaving soon. There's still time."

Sita shook his head. "She won't let you go with her. It will upset the balance."

"I can try." Azalea set her jaw stubbornly.

Elam waved his hand in the air like he was in class. "Or you could just go with Jade and use the dragon's egg now and try to stop her."

"How exactly are we supposed to stop her when we need her to close the gate?" Azalea asked. "And I can't leave until the contract breaks, and by then it'll be too late."

Azalea's father took a seat next to her at the table. "If I could take your place, I would."

He looked like he wanted to take her hand, so she pulled it away and rested it on her lap. She wasn't ready for that yet. "Thanks, but that doesn't help us."

Her father got the message.

"I'm going to find her before she leaves. I have to at least try to stop her somehow." Azalea knew it sounded mad, but she had to do it.

Sita's hands wrapped around the amulet on his chest. "There is no point."

Azalea was already up and ready to leave. "Why not?"

"The great goddess has left. Can you not feel it?" Sita nodded to her amulet.

Azalea held the obsidian stone the same way Sita did. He was right, something felt different. Azalea slumped back into the chair. *Now what?*

"You and your friends can hide out here until you can leave," her dad said.

"I work at the library here," Elam said. "I can grab some books, and we can go through the old texts to find out more about the dragon's egg. We'll be ready to use it when you need to leave."

If she trusted anyone to do research, it was Elam, and Jade was already making a nest for the dragon in an old blanket tucked up in her chair next to the radiator.

Jade patted the egg. "Nice and snug. Let's do that, research tonight while we wait until Ereshkigal breaks your contract, then we can cross the river again once you're free of it."

Azalea rushed over and hugged Jade. "I promise you will get home, whatever happens." A night of researching and planning sounded like just what she needed to take her mind off Ereshkigal and her contract—not to mention worrying about Torin.

# Chapter 30

Within the hour, they'd gathered up their bags, and Torin and Kat trailed Fabian, who marched at full speed behind the squad of scorpion guards escorting them. The clickity-clack of scorpion feet on the dry earth was rhythmic, almost relaxing as they trekked up the dusty road. Inanna was on her white dragon, flying above them. Enki hadn't been kind enough to let them borrow a gold chariot. He seemed to relish in mortals doing things the hard way, and Inanna just didn't seem to notice or care.

Fabian walked so fast he might break into a run at any second. Torin couldn't quite piece together how Cassie fit into Fabian's life. She was his ward, yet Azalea hadn't known about the girl. She was off at boarding school, almost like she was being hidden. Probably for her own protection, the same way Azalea's father tried to protect her from the magical world and dirty politics.

"Fabian, is Cassie your daughter?" Torin asked. The man hated him already. It didn't matter if a few questions pissed him off. It would be worth it to solve the mystery.

Fabian didn't reply. Just kept marching.

"I kind of want to know too." Kat nudged Torin.

Kat jogged to catch up with Fabian, and Torin slid up next to her, hoping she could do better at getting answers.

Kat nudged Fabian's arm as she sidled up to him. "Fabian, it's important for me to know all the facts if we're going to help her. Tell me anything you can."

"She isn't my daughter, okay," he snapped, but there was clear worry behind his voice.

"Who is she then?" Kat said, straight to the point. "Mr. and Mrs. Yates seem a bit old to be her biological parents."

Fabian's hands clenched into fists at his side. "She's adopted. Can you just leave it at that?"

Kat kept up with his increasing pace. "No. We can't leave it. If Korbyn can use her against you, we need to know. You know how he works."

"I do know. That's why we need to get to her." Fabian stopped abruptly. His eyes were wild, almost panicked. "I made a promise to my brother I would look after her if something happened to him. And guess what? It did. Now she's gone." He held his hands up in the air and laughed. "I should not be in charge of other people's children."

"So she's your brother's daughter? She's Azalea's sister?" Torin said with a sinking feeling in his stomach.

Fabian stared at him with a serious expression. "No, you fuckwit. She's *your* sister."

"What?" Torin tried to work out if he was serious or just being a dick.

Kat was ahead of him. "Fabian, don't be an arse. Just tell us."

"I am serious. She is Torin's sister. You wanted more info. You want to know why I'm so worried. That's why." Fabian threw his hands up.

Torin studied his face. "You're not kidding, are you?"

"She is Korbyn's daughter, and he has no idea," Fabian said. "He can't find out. She deserves so much more."

Torin stood there, numb. Trying to process that information. "I have a sister?"

Fabian shoved him in the chest. Hard. "Get a grip. She doesn't know about you. She's better off without you, and you know it. I don't need your help."

Torin's magic flared in his chest, but he clenched his fists, fighting the tingle in his hands urging him to reach out and use it on Fabian.

"That isn't fair, Fabian. Don't use this against Torin. Just calm down, take a minute to explain this, and we can come up with a rational plan to get her out."

Fabian ran a hand over his head, then tightened his greasy ponytail. "Fine. From what I know, when Yelena, Torin's mother, came to my brother seeking refuge, she was pregnant."

"She wanted to save her child," Kat said.

*And abandoned the other one. What did she think I was, a lost cause at ten years old? Why hadn't she taken me too?*

"She wanted to escape Korbyn and his raven cult and knew Samael would help her. He always was a bleeding heart." Fabian snorted and shook his head as if that were a bad thing.

Torin swallowed the bitter feelings. He had a sister. A sister. Whether she knew she had a brother or not, he would do everything he could to protect her from his father, *their* father.

"So you brought her up?" Torin asked.

"No. Clearly, I shouldn't be looking after other humans. I did my best to keep her hidden. I sent her to school, I pay for everything, but Colin and Mary brought her up." Fabian stared off into the reeds.

Torin stepped in front of him, so he was forced to look at him. "You hate my family. You hate the House of Ravens. Why did you do it?"

Fabian let out a huff of air. "Because she was an innocent baby with an unfortunate father. You, on the other hand, were old enough to know better, and you're a murderer. I don't like you and never will. It's not rocket surgery, mate."

"I never asked you to like me, and I am sorry for everything I did. You have to know that by now." Torin actually felt sorry for the bloke. "We will get her back."

Fabian stormed off. "No. *I* will get her back."

"I have a sister." Torin turned to Kat and smiled. An unexpected spark of hope ignited in him. He had family.

"Apparently," she said with a sad smile.

He didn't need her feeling sorry for him. There was no way he was going to let Korbyn get his claws in her. No good could come of it.

"Let's get moving." She squeezed his arm, and they followed Fabian.

A bolt of lightning split the sky with a blinding silver flash. Inanna's dragon swooped down in a tight turn and flew close to the road ahead of them.

"That was right over the gate," Torin said.

Fabian broke into a run. Torin and Kat followed suit as the sky boomed with thunder. It reverberated through Torin's chest like an extra beating heart. The pebbles on the road rattled, and a perfect streak of vertical lightning hit the earth in front of them. The scorpion guards came to an abrupt stop.

"No! Don't stop now. We need to get to the gate." Fabian yelled and darted toward the wall of scorpion legs.

"Fuck!" Kat grabbed Fabian and pulled him to the ground as a heavy gray cloud descended over their path, blocking out the sun to leave them in a dull grayscale setting. Kat's hand stayed wrapped around Fabian's arm, holding him down. Torin crouched next to her, mostly blocked by the scorpion people, but able to make out the road through the gaps between their many legs.

"Oh, crap. Anyone got Enki on speed dial?" Fabian said under his breath.

"We might need more than Enki," Kat whispered.

A dark patch of cloud descended onto the path, but it wasn't the cloud they were looking at. It was the giant man riding atop it. He wore shining silver armor and had a full white beard that was very square with a streak of black running through the middle. His eyes were deep gray and outlined in black. In his hand, he held a staff that blazed with pure silver energy—same as the lightning.

"I hear that mortals walk these lands. I did not give permission for this." His voice shook the land.

The scorpion people fell to their front knees in a unified clatter of armor.

Torin held his breath. The temporary prison Enki and Ninhursag made was clearly not strong enough. If this was Enlil, this might be the last thing they ever saw because he was famous for hating humans. He had sent the great flood to earth the first time, and from the look in his eyes, he appeared to be more than happy to do it again.

Inanna's dragon circled in front of the scorpion guards. She stepped from its back mid-flight and with two flaps of her wings, she gracefully descended onto the road.

"Good day, Enlil. So lovely to see you out and about," Inanna said cheerily.

# Chapter 31

Azalea couldn't stop rubbing her wrist and checking it, just to be sure. The tattoo of the gold band had broken in the night. It was still there, but under her wrist it had split, leaving a gap that showed her skin once more. Azalea wasn't sure if she wanted to know what Ereshkigal had done to break the contract.

"Good morning, Petal. I'm glad you stayed. Tea?" her father asked as she stumbled from the pillow pile in the corner where she had slept and eased herself onto the metal chair at the table.

She wasn't sure how she was supposed to act around him. "Good morning," she said, overly formally. "Yes, tea would be lovely, thanks."

Her friends and their research remained sprawled across the small living area. Jade tucked up in the fetal position on a tiny sofa, spooning the dragon's egg, a pile of books at her feet. Elam slept on the threadbare rug with a cushion under his head, an open book laid across his chest, and many more scattered around him.

How many people had Ereshkigal killed while she was sleeping?

As her dad made tea, she tiptoed over to Elam and carefully plucked the book from his chest.

*The Undomesticated Power of Dragons,* the title of the heavy tome read. It made her miss the Shadow Atlas in its old form. Sita was great, but she had become so accustomed to having the book around it felt like something was missing all the time. Something other than Torin. That was another feeling she couldn't shake, but if all went well today, she might be seeing him again very soon.

She talked in hushed whispers with her father, only superficial things, as she wasn't ready for the hard stuff yet.

"Maybe we should wake them." Azalea sat at the table and flicked through the chapter Elam had been reading. It was exactly what they needed. It claimed that unhatched dragons could travel between dimensions. It just required a lot of focus, a worthy intention, and clear direction. Sita had been right to tell them to get the egg.

The sooner they could leave, the better.

"I wanted you to come live with me, you know." Her dad topped up her tea from a chipped white pot and sat down. "Both you and your mother."

Oh, they were going to have this conversation now. Azalea looked up from the book. "Then why didn't we?"

"We agreed that it was safer for you at the cottage. Away from any danger." He sipped his tea.

Slow anger spiraled in her stomach. "You mean mum decided that?"

"She did, but we agreed upon it together." He rubbed his beard and looked into his cup. "I was going to teach you Shadow Magic when you got older."

"I wish you'd been there to teach me. Then I might not be in this mess." Azalea took a sip of tea. It was nothing like the tea at home.

"I asked Fabian to look out for you if something happened to me. I should have known he would be useless."

"He isn't useless." She set down the cup loudly. Fabian was the closest thing she felt she had to a father, and he'd done his best.

"He should have taught you," he spoke through gritted teeth.

Azalea glared at him. He was in no position to judge. "My mum wouldn't let him. He only intervened when it was too late, as you know. But you can't blame him."

"I was under the impression you did not get on with him."

"Right now I don't, because of the way he treats Torin."

He nodded. "Understandable. I would probably do the same."

Her neck bristled, and the rage sent magic to her hands. She clenched her fists, unsure what type of magic might even come out these days.

"We better get going." She stood up, leaving her unfinished tea, and woke the others.

Bleary-eyed, they got up, and over more tea, they discussed how the dragon egg worked and how to get across the river.

When it was time to leave, they all stood around awkwardly.

"Maybe it's best if you and Elam stay here," Azalea said to her dad. "We wouldn't want you to get into any trouble by association with us."

Her father crossed his arms; clearly, he was as stubborn in his ways as Fabian. "If you say so, love. I better get to work, anyway."

She didn't make a move to hug him and didn't particularly want to. He hadn't seemed to want to fight for her when she was younger and didn't seem motivated now, either. "Hopefully it works, or we'll be back here pretty soon."

"You'll fix the gate, I know it." Her dad pulled her into a last-minute hug.

She froze for a second, then melted into his warmth. This was what she had wanted all these years. At least now she knew he was fine, and she was okay without him.

"You will." Elam threw himself on her in a hug. "It's been lovely to see you. Please stop feeling bad about my death. And can you give Livia a message for me?"

"I'm not sure she'll listen if it comes from me, but I'll try," Azalea promised.

Elam sniffled. "Tell her I love her and that she needs to let me go. Ducky would want it. Would you tell her that?"

"Of course, assuming she knows what that means." She squeezed Elam back and nodded to Jade who was already waiting at the door, the dragon egg tied tightly to her chest like a baby with some cloth her dad must have found.

Azalea waved goodbye, and they slipped outside, Faraday and Sita leading the way.

They got into the taxi carriage her father had ordered and it didn't take long to get to the river.

Lines of confused people waited on the other side of the riverbank, all naked and waiting for something to happen.

"Are they all new spirits?" Jade stared at them as she stepped out of the carriage.

"Yes." Azalea's throat grew tight. Ereshkigal had been busy while she slept.

"Will the boat take us to the other side?" Azalea asked Sita, hoping they wouldn't have to swim in the inky black water.

"I shall ask the boatman." Sita flew ahead of them.

They walked over, and Sita spoke to the man attached to the prow of the boat. He was wooden, and when his head moved, it sounded like creaking tree branches in the forest. He and Sita spoke in the old language. Sita flapped back in a hurry.

"Get in now." He waved his hands.

Azalea and Jade didn't question him, though the boatman had a distinct frown on his overly lined face.

"This is highly unusual," he mumbled in English.

Without another word, he ferried them across. Right toward the crowd of waiting spirits.

Once on the other side, Jade clutched the egg as Azalea helped her disembark and Sita kept the crowd at bay. None of the spirits had seen a demon before, but Azalea couldn't stop to be nice or to explain. They would all find out where they were soon enough, and they were already filing onto the Maglium Boat, which expanded before their eyes to fit the number of spirits.

Azalea spotted Neti at the last gate and ran straight to him.

"I cannot let you pass back through." He stood with his hands folded in front of him.

"We know, it's fine. We just came for our stuff. Do you still have it?" Jade said, carefully keeping the egg hidden under her arms.

Neti chuckled. "Won't do you much good here."

"We just want to eat some of the biscuits we bought and see our things. We're missing home and thought it might help." Jade pouted.

Neti turned to Azalea. "I heard what Ereshkigal did. You are a demi-goddess now, and I am pleased to serve you." He gave a short bow.

Their items materialized at his feet.

Azalea grabbed her basket. "Thank you, Neti. We won't forget this."

"Enjoy your biscuits." He chuckled.

They got their bags, the sword, and baskets of clothes and dug out the digestive biscuits, making a show of enjoying them, which wasn't hard because Azalea hadn't had a biscuit in days. She slipped on the ring Torin had given her, and the locket with the little watch inside. Her fingers found the cool handle of her elemer, and she felt like herself once more.

They moved a bit further away from Neti and sat down like they were having a picnic by the river.

Azalea stuffed all their items into her bag, except the sword which she laid across her lap.

Sita fluttered over, leaving Faraday on guard duty. "Are we ready to go?"

"Yes." Jade nodded and rubbed the dragon egg. "Azalea and I will keep a hand on the dragon's egg and focus our intent into it. Sita, you guide it with your Wayfinder magic, or whatever it is. It should be that simple."

"I'm ready. Faraday, come here now." Azalea waved to the cat.

Faraday darted over to sit on Azalea's lap, and Azalea moved closer to Jade. Their knees touched, and she reached for the dragon's egg nestled in Jade's lap. They slid off their amulets and placed them on the compacted dirt.

"Everyone, close your eyes," Jade whispered.

# Chapter 32

"What are our options here?" Fabian whispered to Kat as Enlil's cloud lowered him to road level. Inanna stood her ground with her wings unfurled to their full glorious width. The guards in front of them were still kneeling, useless bastards. As more clouds rolled in from all directions, the sky darkened, the clouds swirling unnaturally making the air thick and humid.

"Be quiet," Kat hissed back.

Dumont crouched low. "Maybe we can reason with him."

"Go on then." Fabian nodded toward the god of gods on the other side of the barricade of scorpion guards. If Enlil was going to smite anyone, it might as well be Dumont.

"Just stay hidden and let Inanna do the talking." Kat hit Fabian's arm.

Enlil sent a bolt of lightning from his staff that crackled its way across the sky right above them—he was the boss.

"You dare try to imprison me!" Enlil said, his eyes blazing with silvery fire and staring straight at Inanna.

Innana wasn't fazed. "My lord, it was for your safety. You do not need to concern yourself. We know how you like things to be, and we wished to restore the balance before it became a problem for the realm."

"It is already a problem; one I will now fix. Find the humans and kill them." Enlil boomed orders at the scorpion guards.

A clatter of armor sounded as the troop stood up. Fortunately, they didn't turn around, not yet at least. Somehow Enlil didn't know they were there. Perhaps he thought humans were larger, or he hadn't thought to look for himself.

"Calm down, lads. I thought you took orders from your queen," Fabian whispered to the guards at the back.

"Shut it," Kat hissed.

"Stand down. There is no need to seek the humans," Inanna ordered the guards, then casually strutted to her dragon, who silently landed in the reeds just off the road. She stroked its head and whispered to it before it took off into the sky, and she sauntered back over.

Enlil's cloud went from gray to blueish-black, and he glared at Inanna. But she paid no attention. Instead, she paced slowly in front of the line of guards.

"You may be queen, but I am more powerful, and I let your experiments go on far too long. This ends here."

"You got a plan for getting to the gate?" Fabian whispered.

Kat pointed up to the sky. "We wait."

Dragons descended from above, with Inanna's white dragon leading the way. There were five of them, their thin bodies undulating through the air like sea serpents in water, and they were huge. Enki rode upon the back of a blue one that had scales like metal plates and long tentacle things trailing from its jowls.

Dumont strained his neck to look above the guards. "How far is the gate?"

"It's still a mile away," Fabian said.

"Can you run that far?" Dumont asked.

"Course I can. I'm just a little concerned about the angry god who wants to kill us." Fabian shielded his eyes against the glare of the clouds as the dragons got closer. The third one was green with gold speckles, the goddess Ninhursag on its back, her streams of green hair trailing behind her like a cape.

Behind her, a man covered in dark armor rode the fourth dragon. It was shimmering black with no identifiable features. The fifth was a fiery dragon that crackled with flames and had a heat shimmer rising from its back; it was the only dragon with wings, and they were massive and aflame—you'd see it coming a mile away. The man upon the dragon was apparently fireproof. He had dark skin, a shiny bald head, and wore no armor; instead, he wore leather—this had to be Utu, god of fire and patron of the House of Phoenix.

"I think we got the A team." Fabian let out a breath. Even he had to admit this was rather epic. At this rate, he might get back to save Cassie after all.

Dumont stared like a pathetic fanboy with his mouth hanging open as the dragons circled to land in the reeds beside the road.

"Get ready." Kat scanned the road on either side.

Fabian was happy to follow whatever direction she went. She had good instincts.

"They're all here. It's like the Avengers," Dumont said, probably not realizing he even said it out loud.

"Shut up so we can hear," Fabian said as the last dragon folded itself into the reeds, the flames singeing a charred circle around it.

The gods snapped out their wings and flew from their dragons to stand beside Inanna without so much as a hint they even saw the humans or scorpion guards.

"Why do they even have dragons if they can fly?" Fabian asked, finding it very hard to stay still and wait.

"Same reason we have cars when we can walk," Kat said.

Fair call. If he had a dragon, he would make good use of it as well.

Dumont butted in. "The dragons can fly a lot further, and they use them to communicate between other dragons across great distances."

Fabian didn't answer. Bloody know-it-all.

"We only seek to set the balance once more and shut the gate. We only ask for time," Enki said, his copper armor easy to spot through the gaps in the guards.

Enlil sent a crack of lightning straight into the road in front of the gods causing everyone to jump. "I have warned you many times about your human creations. They are abominations, and it is time someone ended them."

"We do not have the right," Inanna said. "When we left earth, we left the planet in their hands. It is up to them to fix their issues and be caretakers for their own world."

Enlil didn't seem to give a shit; it was clear he was growing impatient. "Not when their issues trickle into our world and threaten the balance of magic. They have gone too far. I will destroy them and close the gate."

Kat motioned for them to follow and crept toward the edge of the road, shielded by the giant bodies of the gods and scorpions. Here they got a better view of the dragons and a clear line of sight up the road to the gate in the distance.

Ninhursag spread her wings wide. "I will not let you destroy our children."

"We only seek to close the gate," Inanna added.

"Once my grandson, Nabu, is returned," Enki's voice boomed.

Fabian walked as silently as possible. Each footstep on the compacted earth road had him holding his breath. They reached the reeds and crouched down, watching and waiting for a signal from Kat.

"I have been lenient far too long." Enlil turned and stepped back onto his cloud.

"We must stop him," Utu, the fire god's voice rumbled.

"What are we waiting for?" the harsh voice of the god in full armor said.

Inanna grabbed his arm. "No, my husband."

He slapped her hand away. "I do not take orders from you, woman."

Through the gap between scorpion men, Fabian tried not to stare. The gods having a domestic spat was the last thing they needed. He couldn't help but wonder how she had gotten her husband back after all this time. If it were him, he'd be pissed off at her too after being left in the underworld for so long.

"You ought to, or I'll send you right back to the Shadow Dimension," she snapped back. "Just wait."

Enlil was on his cloud, floating toward the gate. Fabian wanted to scream at them to do something but was certain that would not end well for him.

"What's the orders?" Fabian asked Kat, the sooner he could get this over with, the sooner he could get to Cassie.

"We get closer to the gate and hope like hell they stop him in time." Kat stood and began walking up the side of the road, not looking back.

"Enki, Utu, delay him," Inanna ordered.

The two gods didn't argue. Inanna wove her way through the scorpion men to stand in front of the three humans.

"Quickly, with me," she said to Dumont.

Dumont stood up. "What's the plan?"

"We're going to get you as close to the gate as we can. Dumuzi, Ninhursag, take these two mortals by dragon-back. I have this one."

Inanna led Torin toward her dragon, and his face fell. "We're riding dragons?"

"You with me," Inanna's husband in the dark armor, Dumuzi, was his name, barked at Fabian.

"Yes, sir." Fabian wasn't going to argue with this bloke. He exchanged a look with Kat, and she nodded to him as she went off with Ninhursag toward the green dragon.

As they got closer to the dragon, he realized just how big it was. In the sky, it had looked lithe and feather-light. Up close, it was a solid mass of muscle and scales. But its face was covered in a fuzz of fur, and it had a short mane that looked silky soft. The dragon turned to them and snorted, sending a wave of hot air over Fabian that smelled like a smoldering fire.

"Hello there, big fella." Fabian bobbed his head in greeting.

The dragon let out a sharp snort and turned away.

"Hold on," Dumuzi said as he lifted Fabian without permission and put him on the back of the dragon as if he were a child.

The mass of muscle moved beneath Fabian's thighs as he adjusted himself between two rigid spines. Okay, so he was riding a dragon. He gripped the spine in front of him, hoping it would be enough. His feet had no real grip, and the scales were slick like metal and very warm—almost too hot.

Before he could figure out the best seating posture, Dumuzi vaulted on in front of him and, without a word, the dragon took off.

Fabian's heart dropped to his stomach as they shot into the air. He was no stranger to heights or speed, but this had his toes tingling as the ground fell away beneath him.

"You humans are more trouble than you are worth," Dumuzi said, his deep voice rushing over Fabian as they gained speed.

"Why are you helping us, then?" Fabian yelled, the adrenaline rush giving him unneeded extra confidence. He knew what Kat would be saying. *Keep your bloody mouth shut.*

"Because I was ordered to. I will get you to the gate, mortal. Have no fear."

Fabian held back a snort. *Have no fear.* If he survived this, he vowed he would help protect the dragons and other weird creatures now in his world. As long as this dragon didn't throw him off.

They flew in a wide arc away from the fight erupting near the gate. Utu and Enki had somehow gotten between Enlil and the gate and were driving him back with fire and water. A fireball shot through the cloud, sending it off to the side.

Fabian didn't see what happened next. He gripped the dragon as it banked and shot straight up. Linking his arms around the spine, he held his breath and locked his muscles in place. Holy crap, they were high up.

They leveled out, and he let out his breath. He suspected Dumuzi was waiting for the right moment to get to the gate with a clear shot. On the other side of the portal, he spotted the green dragon with Kat doing slow figure eights in a holding pattern above the river. Dumont was above them, Inanna's dragon a glimmer of perfect white against the darkening clouds.

Enki drove Enlil back further with a massive gush of water that roared from his staff, blasting Enlil straight in the chest.

Apparently, that was their cue. The dragon twisted into a sharp dive and shot toward the ground. The wind rushed past so fast Fabian couldn't even catch a breath. His lungs tightened, protesting as they continued down, his eyes streaming, unable to see where the hell they were going.

"Jump on my command," Dumuzi's voice roared in his ears.

Great, he was going to die.

Fabian's arms were locked around the dragon's spine, and every instinct told him not to let go, but hey, when a god tells you to do something, it's probably best to listen.

Suddenly, the dragon leveled out, and Fabian opened his eyes. The gate was about a football pitch length away from them, and the two other dragons were moving in.

This might just work.

A roar sounded to his right, followed by a wave of intense heat. He ducked his head behind the dragon's spine, letting it shield him from what felt like the blasting exhaust of a rocket.

He glanced up to see Enlil tumble from his cloud as it dissolved into steamy mist. Enlil hit the ground with a battle roll and was upright, aiming his staff at Utu. A streak of lightning hit the fire god right in his wing. He twisted midair, spiraling toward the ground. His dragon was there in seconds, its flaming wings lighting up the mist that was spreading across the land in an eerie blanket. The dragon slid under Utu right before he hit the ground, catching him in a fiery wing and rolling him onto its back.

Fabian let out a breath as they sped toward the gate. There was little time to think.

"Be prepared to jump," Dumuzi bellowed.

Fabian loosened his grip on the dragon's spine and wondered how the hell he was supposed to get his leg over and jump off at this speed.

The two dragons up ahead streaked toward them, nearly at the gate.

Fuck it, it was going to hurt either way. Fabian gripped the spine behind him with one hand and swung his leg over so he was sitting side saddle. The green dragon got to the gate first, and he held his breath as Kat launched herself gracefully from the dragon with a kick off its side, propelling her straight through the blazing light of the gate.

She disappeared. He had an overwhelmingly strong urge to make sure she was okay, and suddenly jumping through the gate seemed like a great idea.

Dumont's dragon was up next. A blast of lightning shot the base of the gate, sending a surge of electricity through the red and green light pouring through it. Inanna's white dragon remained on course. Dumont launched himself into the portal of light, and the dragon slowed only slightly as it passed by.

"Stop them!" Enlil screamed at the scorpion guards scattered around the gate, unsure who to take orders from. Fabian suspected they weren't the smartest bunch, but at least they weren't going after him.

The black dragon neared the gate. Fabian lined himself up with the circular portal. Apparently, his dragon wasn't going to slow down. He loosened his grip on the spine and tensed his muscles, ready to push off.

For a second, it was like time stopped. His heart pounded in his ears. The gate was right there.

"Now!" Dumuzi yelled back.

He heard a scream—one of the gods—and it sounded like pure, agonizing pain, but he didn't have time to see who had been hit.

"Thanks for the ride, mate," Fabian yelled as he pushed off the dragon straight into the blasting light that may as well have been a black hole to nowhere.

His ears filled with the roar of the gateway; his eyes squeezed closed as he gave in and let himself be tossed around, feeling like an old rag in the wash.

He was weightless for a second, suspended in the air, then he shot out and his stomach plummeted. He was falling and falling fast. He squeezed his eyes shut tighter, waiting for the pain. A second later, it came. His shoulder hit the earth, sending dust around him as the air was forced from his lungs.

He wheezed, unable to catch his breath. The bruised ribs from his fight with Dumont weren't helping.

"Fabian, get up fast." It was Kat, and it was possible they were both dead.

He opened his eyes to see her dirt-streaked face above him, a tight smile on her lips. Was that relief on her face?

Kat's arms were under him before he could react, pulling him up.

He forced his legs to help out and tried to gasp in breaths of air, feeling like a fish on the riverbank. In a moment, he saw why she was rushing him.

They weren't dead in the Shadow Dimension. They were back at the ruins where the gate was. Back on earth. And thank the gods.

No time to relish in the relief. They were surrounded by House of Raven guards, and they looked pissed off.

"Move now," Dumont yelled.

Fabian surprised himself with a laugh, he was actually relieved to see Dumont had made it. Shaking his head to forget the thought, he leaned heavily on Kat as she pulled him in another direction. That's when he spotted the opening to the Hollow. Thank fuck for that. She pretty much pushed him into it, and he collapsed onto the spongy blue floor.

# Chapter 33

Everything went quiet. Azalea held her breath and kept her eyes squeezed shut as she gripped the dragon's egg and Jade's hand. Faraday's claws were like tiny needles in her legs, and she crouched over him to make sure he stayed there. There was no feeling of movement, no wind, no light, no sound.

Suddenly her bum was cold. She opened her eyes at the unexpectedness of it.

"Holy crap. That was it?" Jade looked around.

Azalea took her hands back, her knuckles frozen in place from how tight she had been clutching the egg. She was sitting in the entry hall at Blackbourne Manor on the black and white tiles.

"You did it!" Azalea leaned over Faraday and the egg and hugged Jade tightly.

Their entrance must have made some sort of noise because she looked up to see Mrs. Yates staring down at them with wide eyes and a smashed teacup on the floor.

"Where did you lot come from? Were you at the Tower?" Mrs. Yates asked, her eyes darting around the room as if looking for someone.

Azalea carefully set the sword on the floor and stood up, suddenly conscious of the strange clothes she was wearing, the off-white tunic with a belt of colored beads around her middle. "No. Sorry."

Tears brimmed in Mrs. Yates' eyes. "You haven't seen our Cassie? She isn't with you?"

Azalea and Jade exchanged a confused look as Jade clutched the egg close to her chest. She, too, was wearing a tunic.

"No. I'm sorry. What happened to her?" Jade asked.

Mrs. Yates burst into tears, and Azalea froze, unsure what to make of the situation.

"Mary, where are you? What's all this racket?" Mr. Yates bellowed down the hallway. He entered the space, and Mrs. Yates collapsed into his arms. "There, there, my love. We will get her back. Don't you worry about that."

"Who's there?" Nigel Skeffington's voice echoed up the hall.

"Azalea and Jade are back, and they have a creature with them!" Mr. Yates yelled back, keeping a wary eye on Sita.

Multiple footsteps thundered up the hall.

"Azalea! Thank the gods you're okay!" RoRo burst into the foyer first. "I swore I heard your name from all the way in the dining room and here you are, in the flesh." She wrapped Azalea in a hug as soon as she was on her feet.

RoRo froze mid-hug. "Gods! Is that a demon? Azalea, did you bring this demon into the house?"

Azalea moved closer to Sita. "Oh, um yes. Everyone, this is Sita. He has been most helpful, so please be polite."

Sita puffed out his chest and folded his arms, staring at each person who entered the room.

"Contain that creature," Mage Skeffington ordered. Two younger mages stepped forward but didn't go for Sita, perhaps unsure how to contain him.

The council members RoRo must have been meeting with were there, and none looked pleased. Everyone seemed to be there: Mage Stone, her eyes narrowed in on Azalea; Mage Parry, who smiled at Azalea; Mergen the shaman, and, of course, Skeffington closely followed by his sidekick Russ. Plus a few young House of Snake and Eagle mages, by the look of their arm tattoos.

"Do not touch me." Sita waggled a finger at the two men, and he ducked behind Azalea, a hand safely on her leg, and she was more than happy to shield him.

Danni ran into the room with Zoe and Ava trailing behind. "Where have you been!" Danni hit Azalea on the arm.

Azalea grinned. She'd never been so glad to see everyone in her life. "Ow, it's a very long story."

"Is that thing safe? You swear by it?" Danni pointed at Sita.

"Yes, he's fine. He's the last thing we need to worry about," Azalea said.

"How did you get in here? The wards should not allow for this," Skeffington said, apparently not happy at being ignored.

Azalea and Jade glanced at the dragon's egg, and Jade hugged it closer to her. "Like she said, it's a long story."

"Everyone into the library now," Skeffington ordered.

Azalea clasped her hands in front of her as they grew damp with sweat. How was she going to tell them what she knew without giving anything about her and Torin away?

They were bustled into the library. It must have been late evening because the fire was roaring, and the sky outside was growing dark, though was still tinged with the unnatural red and green hues. Their trip back must have been longer than the one second it felt like.

Azalea and Jade sat on the same sofa. Jade set the egg in her lap, guarding it like a good dragon guardian. Everyone else settled around the large table and in various chairs around the room.

"Please do not tell me that is what I think it is?" Skeffington asked from his seat at the large table.

"Do you think it's a dragon's egg?" Jade said. Her face dead straight.

Azalea tried not to giggle. It was clear the disrupted sleep she'd had over the past days was not enough. She might be starting to crack up. She'd hoped she'd feel at least a little closer to Torin now that she was back, but their connection felt further away than ever. He should be back by now.

"Where did you get this?" the weather mage, Mage Parry, asked kindly from his lounge chair.

RoRo didn't sit but stood with her hands on her hips. "More importantly, were you gifted it, or did you take it?"

"We were not exactly gifted it. But it was necessary to get back. We have information, and it's time-critical. We couldn't wait." Azalea crossed her arms over her chest and glared around the room.

"From where exactly have you come?" Skeffington asked as if wanting to catch them out.

Azalea and Jade looked at each other, suddenly wishing they'd arrived somewhere else, so they had time to regroup and plan their story better.

"We assumed you'd followed the others to the Echo Dimension. Did you not find them?" RoRo said.

Azalea didn't look her grandmother in the eyes. "Not exactly."

"But they're on their way back now. They have a way to close the gate," Jade added.

"That is wonderful news indeed," RoRo said. The bags under her eyes didn't escape Azalea's notice, and for the first time, she saw that she had aged.

Mage Stone banged her hand on the table and went back to standing with her arms crossed, glaring daggers at Azalea and Jade. "And how do you know this if you were not with them?"

Azalea held her gaze. "Jade's premonitions. She's from the House of the Winged Bull. She had prophecies."

It was Skeffington's turn to glare at them. "I will ask again, and please do not lie. How did you acquire this dragon's egg, and where have you been?"

Azalea sighed. "We have been in the Shadow Dimension. I made a deal with the goddess Ereshkigal to help us close the gate and protect the others in the Echo Dimension."

"Good gods! You stole this dragon's egg from the Shadow Dimension?" Mage Parry's face grew redder, and he looked like he might faint. Skeffington just scowled.

"No, we just borrowed it. We *could* bring it back." Azalea supposed that was true.

Jade shot her a horrified look. It was clear she was already attached to it.

"And what happens when they find out you took it?" the old mage demanded.

That was the least of their problems. What happened when Ereshkigal found out Azalea left? Could she track her somehow? Azalea rubbed her wrist.

"She will forgive Azalea." Sita perched on the back of the couch behind Azalea.

Mage Skeffington narrowed his eyes at Sita. "Why does it say this?"

"It is a he, and he is Ereshkigal's demon." Azalea didn't appreciate his tone.

Sita stretched his wings out. "And Azalea is now a demi-goddess of the Shadow Dimension. They had an agreement. She will be protected."

Azalea winced. She wasn't sure that was true and really hadn't wanted to bring that up right now. She twisted the demantoid garnet ring, sending a silent prayer to Torin to make it back soon. "Yes, well. She broke the agreement, and here we are."

"Oh, Azalea. What happened? What did you agree to?" Leda's hand went to her heart.

She tried to give her mum a comforting smile. "It doesn't matter right now. The point is Torin, Fabian, and Kat are on their way this very minute. But we can't close the gate until we find the scribe, the god Nabu who escaped the Echo Dimension." Azalea said, hoping that was very clear. "Sita here is a Wayfinder demon, he can help us."

Sita flapped down to the armrest by Azalea and puffed out his chest. "A simple task."

"And we can close the gate once Nabu is returned. Inanna and Ereshkigal agreed to close it from either side," Jade added.

"Will she still do so knowing you have betrayed her and returned?" Mage Skeffington said bluntly.

Jade let out an obvious sigh. "That is why we need to hurry."

"This is dangerous. We should send her back," Mage Stone barked and banged a fist into the desk.

This woman had some unresolved anger issues, but Azalea wasn't about to bring that up.

Mage Parry twisted his mustache and tilted his head. "Something doesn't add up. I've never heard of a prophecy being so specific in instructions. How can you be sure of this?"

"We just can," Azalea said, getting impatient. A sharp burst of magic shot right through her, taking her breath away, and she doubled over. She gulped to catch her breath at the shock of it. But she knew instantly what it meant—Torin had returned.

"What's wrong, petal?" RoRo darted over and rubbed Azalea's back, just as she had whenever Azalea was sick as a child. Azalea straightened up once the feeling passed. It wasn't exactly pain, but it was certainly intense.

"Fabian and Torin are back," Azalea said without thinking as she rose from the couch.

"And how exactly do you know this? More prophecies, I suppose," Mage Stone said sarcastically.

"Um, blood wards," she said, hoping that was a thing they did. "I've got to go."

Mage Skeffington stood up. "Hold your horses, young lady. We aren't letting you out of our sight."

Azalea realized she was in trouble. She could feel Torin's panic as he got closer. After being separated for so long, it already felt like he was right there beside her. His magic screamed out to her, and she was starting to worry about what might happen when he got here in front of all these people. Maybe she should leave. But it was too late now. He was right outside.

# Chapter 34

"I am never riding a dragon again," Torin said as they walked up to the main door. He'd said it several times up the driveway as well, and now he was just trying to distract himself from what was inside. Azalea. Azalea and a strong feeling that they might both lose control of their powers when they reunited.

But also overwhelming relief that made him not want to care. She'd made it back.

Mrs. Yates was there at the front door before they could open it. Fabian led the way in, and everyone had already gathered in the entry hall.

"Tell me what the hell happened with Cassie!" Fabian yelled as he marched in, and the room went silent. Azalea stopped herself as soon as she saw Torin, and it was good she did because he was verging on losing control of their shared magic as it screamed out to her.

Torin didn't hear the rest. People squeezed into the room, but all his focus was on Azalea as she slipped around the group and stood on the stairs out of the way while he remained close to the door.

The relief he felt from her was immense and the same as his own. They stared at each other, grinning for what was probably a little too long. He only looked away when Danni nearly bowled him over in a hug.

"Gods, am I glad to see you." She stood on tiptoes and ruffled his hair.

"Same here." He stepped back from her and couldn't help but catch her infectious smile. It felt damn good to be back. The smell of damp evening air and wood smoke almost made this place feel like home.

He felt Azalea's gaze on him, her critical eyes running over his face, taking in his bruised jaw and the cut in his eyebrow. Fortunately, she couldn't see his bruised ribs, or cuts, or bumps from the blows he'd taken from Fabian. He hadn't told her how bad the fight really was. Danni released him and without realizing he had moved, he found himself at the bottom of the stairs, staring up at Azalea's very real, very alive, beautiful face.

"Are you okay? Did you get attacked on the way?" Azalea stepped down a few stairs before stopping, her magic pulsing toward him and digging under his skin, calling. Jade sat a few steps up from Azalea with Sita and Faraday. So everyone knew about the demon, at least.

Torin moved to the side of the stairs so the rail was between them. The sounds of Mrs. Yates sobbing and Fabian yelling were a distant buzz, and there was only her.

"You made it back," Torin breathed. He could tell she wanted to ask questions, and he probably had just as many for her; like how the hell she escaped, or what would happen if Ereshkigal found out? But now wasn't the time. He wanted to lean over the rail, pull her down to him, and kiss her, or even just touch her skin and know that she was real.

He could feel her restraining herself, holding back in front of all the people just the same as he was.

"No greeting for me?" Fabian said with a sneer as he sidled up beside Torin with a less-than-friendly slap on the back and shot Azalea a stinging death look. Kat appeared on his other side; she'd be glad to be rid of both of them and her mediator duties once this was all over, no doubt.

"Welcome home," Azalea said dryly, then turned to Kat and smiled. "It's nice to have you back."

More people came in from outside, including Azalea's friends Van and Isaac; someone must have messaged them. As soon as they spotted Jade and Azalea, they rushed up the stairs, Van gushing over them and checking them over for cuts and scrapes and ordering them all to the healer's gers right that minute. But it would have to wait.

Fabian remained there with his arms folded.

Rowena clapped her hands to get everyone's attention, and a few more mages slipped into the room. The large entrance to the house was now feeling very small, with people squishing into every corner of it even between the large palms in oversized pots.

"Well, tell us then, were you successful?" RoRo asked impatiently.

Torin didn't see Azalea but felt as she walked down the stairs and moved in beside him trying to hide in the crowd. Her magic screamed out to him, but he pretended everything was fine, that the buzzing under his skin wasn't clawing at him, that he didn't want to push her against the wall and kiss her like no one was there.

"Everything went very well, thanks to Enki and Inanna. We really got them on our side," Fabian announced.

"And Ereshkigal," Jade added.

Fabian made his way to the center and shot a quizzical look back at Jade.

Torin wanted to reach out for Azalea's hand. Squeeze it to know things would be okay, even if they wouldn't be. Because Torin knew what was coming, and Fabian was about to find out a whole lot more things he wasn't going to like.

"I arranged for Ereshkigal to get Inanna's help, and she promised to close the gate from this side," Azalea said quietly to her uncle.

"If she's still willing to do that," Rowena grumbled.

"You what?" Fabian snapped at Azalea.

She wanted to duck behind that giant palm frond.

Torin gripped his elemer as her anxiety flashed straight into him like she wasn't shielding at all. This was far worse than before they left. He wasn't sure he was doing much to shield his emotions right now, either.

"Not to worry, apprentice Azalea is under house arrest right now until we work out how much trouble she's gotten into." Mage Skeffington grumbled.

Torin glanced at her, and his heart skipped a beat. Azalea's hands were glowing. She looked at him, startled, and he gave a subtle nod toward her hands. She stuffed them in her jacket. He looked at his and saw the same. He slid his elemer into his belt and shoved his hands into his pockets.

Fabian's eyes narrowed in on Azalea. He'd seen it, too. Torin felt Azalea's heart plummet, but Torin didn't need to say anything, Fabian flicked his head to the side telling Azalea to leave. She saw and turned to the stairs as Torin, surprised at Fabian's helpfulness, turned in the opposite direction.

But Mage Skeffington grabbed her arm. "Don't you move a muscle."

"Don't touch her!" Torin reacted without thinking and sent a shadow rope around Mage Skeffington's arm and yanked it away from her.

Azalea's hand radiated light, too bright to hide, and Torin was at her side in an instant as Mage Skeffington went bright red with anger. Fabian appeared in front of them, backing Skeffington to the other side of the room. The old man seemed almost too shocked at the disrespect to react. Torin might have laughed if it wasn't so serious. Azalea had her eyes closed, and her hands clenched at her sides.

"Just breathe." Torin didn't know what to do, he couldn't touch her, or she would lose it, and he was in a very similar boat. He gripped his elemer and moved in front of Azalea, his hands glowing just as brightly as hers.

"Someone detain that girl!" Skeffington yelled.

"No need for that, mate. Calm it down," Fabian said.

But two mages closed in on Azalea.

"Don't touch her!" Torin glared at them.

Azalea's eyes shot open and locked with Torin's. Her control slipped, and he grabbed her hands just in time. Their magic collided and flowed between them like water over a dry creek bed. It was wonderful and mortifying. The light poured from their hands, then flashed bright, sending the two men flying across the room into the crowd.

The ball of light lit up the entire room, so bright it forced everyone to shield their eyes. The magic from the two mages surged back, and Azalea plunged the room into darkness as tendrils of shadows spewed from their combined hands.

Torin couldn't stop it. All he could think to do was wrap his arms around her, folding her into him and absorbing the magic, willing it, and her, to calm down.

He wasn't sure how long they stood there, but when Torin opened his eyes, the shadows were clearing thanks to Fabian, and everyone was staring at them. Azalea was limp, drained of energy, and leaning heavily on his chest.

"Everyone, calm down," Danni ordered, stopping the worried voices around the room.

Torin, still with Azalea in his arms, moved so their backs were against the stairs, and the light filtered back to normal.

"Show me your hands." Mage Skeffington marched over and ordered.

Azalea nodded to Torin, and he let her slip from his arms so they stood side by side. Fabian crossed his arms and glared at Mage Skeffington.

Torin held up his hands as the man asked. They were glowing more faintly than before but looked exactly the same as Azalea's.

"Well, I never," Mage Parry muttered as he peered over Skeffington's shoulder.

Torin pulled his hands away, and Sita slapped Skeffington's hands when he reached for Azalea's. The man pulled them back abruptly.

RoRo remained still, a knowing look spreading across her face. For some reason, the plant mage looked very pleased.

Azalea's mum found her way across the room and stood beside Azalea with an arm around her shoulder. "What is it, Petal?"

"I'm okay, mum, it's not bad. You don't need to worry." Azalea wrapped an arm around her mum's waist, and Torin folded his across his chest.

"A dragon's egg and now this... it is clear these two are a danger," Mage Skeffington said to the room, not Azalea or Torin.

"Azalea is a demi-goddess, and you should address her with more respect!" Sita flapped in front of Skeffington's face.

"This isn't dangerous," Azalea said quietly. "We can use it."

"That's what they always said, but history tells another story. There are laws for a reason." Skeffington held his hands in front of him as if he were giving a sermon.

"Agreed," Russ backed him up. *Russ, what a waste of space.*

"Lock them both up," Mage Skeffington ordered without explanation.

"No, you will not! Will someone tell me what is going on?" Leda demanded, gripping Azalea tightly.

Skeffington nodded to his sidekick to do something, but Mage Stone, the evil witch, was already there in the wings waiting. "It appears your daughter has entered into an illegal soul bond with this man."

"Just wait a minute," Leda said, more forcefully than he had ever seen the calm, passive woman. "They have done nothing wrong."

Mage Skeffington raised his voice. "Their bond is illegal. There is no telling how dangerous their magic might be. You just witnessed it firsthand. They need to be separated."

Torin shuffled closer to Azalea, worried she would retaliate on purpose this time. He planned to cooperate, then work the rest out later.

Azalea stomped her foot. "We can help! This magic is what we need to find Nabu and close the gate."

Mage Skeffington yelled, "Someone, take her upstairs. Everyone else, leave. We will speak with Mage Blackbourne, Mage Emerson, and Mage Dumont alone, then decide what is to be done about this soul bond."

Fabian stepped in. "I invited you into my home to keep you safe, and this is how you treat my family? I won't have it!"

Mage Skeffington blinked. "I am a far more powerful mage than you, Blackbourne. Don't test me."

"This is my house!" Fabian held his hands up. "We need to find Cassie and this Nabu bloke. We don't have time for this!"

Mage Skeffington ignored Fabian, and for once, Torin actually felt sorry for him.

"I can help." Azalea pleaded.

*Calm down and let Fabian handle this.* Torin called inside his head, hoping she would get the message. She must have felt his urgency because she stood still.

Fabian turned to Azalea, and Torin and leaned in close. "Just play along with it, I'll fix this," he whispered.

Torin's heart thundered in his chest as he let them put handcuffs on him behind his back and did nothing as he watched Azalea's mum lead her up the stairs when all he wanted to do was call for her to come back. At least she was alive and safe. The rest they could work out.

Torin followed the procession of mages into the dining room and was forced into a chair. He fought to keep his panic under control. The last thing he wanted was to be a prisoner again. But Danni was there, Kat was there, and it seemed Fabian might have had a recent change of heart toward him.

The "debrief" was more like an interrogation and not just aimed at him. Kat received the same treatment, being from the House of Ravens. She remained calm and rational, despite the Snake council members getting worked up over every little detail as they tried to explain what had happened in the Echo Dimension. The only one they seemed to want to listen to was Fabian, and it was clear they didn't trust him either. All Fabian wanted to do was go after Cassie, so his irrational behavior wasn't helping any of them.

After explaining several times that they needed to find Nabu, it felt like the message was falling on deaf ears.

Torin let out a frustrated breath. "Look, I know you don't want to hear it. But our best bet is to let Sita find him, and for me and Azalea to go after him. We can both travel in the Hollow and our new magic can be of use."

"I doubt that from what we just witnessed," the old man said.

Torin wished his hands were free so he could knock Skeffington's head onto the table. "That wasn't Azalea's fault. If the magic is focused and channeled in the right way, we can use it."

"You've used it before then?" Danni asked, looking betrayed by the idea.

He felt guilty for not telling her, but she had to understand why. "Yes, we took down the Archmage and my father after the gate was opened. That's how we escaped."

"But you didn't kill them?" Mage Skeffington looked unimpressed.

"We weren't trying to kill them." Torin did his best to remain calm. They were wasting valuable time here. The faster they could leave, the faster Cassie could be saved, and the gate could be shut.

Torin took a calming breath. "Look, the best chance we have for Cassie is for Kat to go back to the Tower and talk to Kira to find out as much as she can. Without that intel, we have no hope. In the meantime, I will find Nabu and get the gate closed."

"Yes! Please just listen to him," Fabian said, but his disheveled, crazy hair and desperation weren't winning him any votes.

Mage Skeffington shook his head. "The House of Ravens is preparing to attack here in two days. We need to focus on strengthening our wards and preparing to fight. The gate can wait."

"The gate can't wait." Torin clenched his hands into fists. "The gods must have contained Enlil for now because he hasn't destroyed the world. But they can't hold him forever. We need to get it closed. Fabian can stay here and prepare for the attack."

"You are the one in handcuffs here. You are not calling the shots," Skeffington said with a smug smile.

Rowena rapped her knuckles on the table. "I agree with Torin. Fabian needs to be here. Mage Emerson will get word from the House of Ravens to find out about Cassie," Rowena ordered. "But I am sorry Torin, we cannot let you go after the god Nabu. It is too much of a risk."

The other mages all agreed.

Torin bit his tongue, holding back every rude thing he wanted to say to these smug lounge-chair mages. It was clear he would have to find his own way to get out and fix this mess.

"Lock him up in the basement," Mage Skeffington ordered.

Fabian gave him a nod and a knowing look as they hauled Torin away. Hopefully, he had a plan.

# Chapter 35

Azalea sat on the bed in her room at Blackbourne manor, and as sheets of rain blasted her window, she found herself missing her room at the Tower of London. She missed her plants, the cozy fireplace, and her favorite patchwork quilt. It was silly, she knew, but she wanted to go back to before this happened, when it was just her and Torin drinking tea in his office with the fire roaring off to the side, planning their relic hunts. She wished she had known then that those were the good times.

Her thoughts were interrupted by a knock on the door.

"Come in." She hugged a pillow to her chest.

Jade walked in with a dragon egg-sized lump under her hoodie.

"The guard let you in just like that?" Azalea moved over so Jade could sit next to her.

Jade shrugged. "I gave him a cup of tea, and he let me in."

She smiled and shook her head. "And he didn't think you might help me escape with the dragon's egg?"

"Turns out most people don't know much about drag-ons." Jade shuffled onto the bed next to Azalea and pulled the dragon egg from under her shirt and into her lap. "She needs to stay warm, so I'm carrying her everywhere."

"She?" Azalea admired the egg's iridescent sheens of blues and greens.

Jade stoked the egg. "I'm pretty sure. I think we used a lot of her power getting here. Poor little gal." Jade glanced at the door like she was waiting for something.

"And you know this how?"

"This might sound weird, but I think she knows me. She can understand me, and somehow she told me." Jade put her ear to the egg and grinned.

"That's not the weirdest thing I've ever heard." Azalea flopped back on the bed. "Do you happen to know where Torin is? I've been listening, and they didn't take him to his room."

Jade leaned back. "I saw them take him down to the basement. And if you're thinking of trying to break him out, I'm sure he'll be guarded."

"There'll be a way around them. We just have to get creative." *Or test out my new powers.*

Jade stood up abruptly. "Well, I better be going. Just stay here for now. And don't do anything stupid."

"Why do people always say that? I've been actively trying not to do stupid things." Azalea sighed.

"Help is coming, trust me." She winked as she headed for the door.

Azalea fell back on the bed. She felt drained from being in the Shadow Dimension, like the gravity here was suddenly too high, and every part of her screamed for sleep. But sleeping without Torin was something she couldn't face, not when he was so near. She had to tell him again that she could break the bond. Though a small voice in the back of her head screamed, *Don't!*

The buzz of Torin's magic seeped through the walls, calling to her like a siren song. It was strangely comforting, and she realized how much she'd missed his presence when she was in the Shadow Dimension.

He was awake now. She was certain of it. Perhaps if they both went to sleep, they could speak in a dream and make a plan.

She rolled over, crawled across the bed, and burrowed into the blankets still clothed and with all the lights on. Faraday tucked in at her side, and she closed her eyes, willing her brain to stop thinking and go to sleep.

But the more she thought about trying to sleep, the more awake and the more exhausted and frustrated she got. She lay there listening for his heartbeat, hoping to hear it through the layers of ancient stone, but all she heard was the heavy patter of rain on the roof.

Just as she was slipping into sleep. A knock sounded at her door.

She sat up, and Fabian was there. "Get dressed. I'm breaking you out."

☽☽☽●☾☾☾

Torin leaned against the cold stone wall and slid onto the only wooden crate that wasn't broken or full of crap. The room was small and had clearly been designed as a prison, but now it seemed to be a storeroom for old rubbish that people had forgotten over the years. There were crates of dusty bottles, bikes missing handlebars, a block of a TV that looked like it was from the eighties, and everything smelled musty and damp.

He supposed he should be grateful he wasn't outside in the rain. He could hear the gush of water down a drainpipe coming from somewhere above him and the slow drip of a leak in the stone-floored hallway beyond his cell.

His head fell back against the wall, and he closed his eyes. Every fiber in his being told him to break down this place and go to Azalea. Even with their unsealed bond and unpredictable magic, they had an advantage. They could use it to get the god Nabu to return to the Echo Dimension. They could take out anyone who stood in their way and use force to make sure the gate was closed.

But that approach would not make them any friends; it would get them locked up for life. On the other hand, maybe it would be worth it to do one good thing in his life. Then there was Cassie. A sister he hadn't even known about and felt an obligation to. He had to get her away from his father. Perhaps he could turn himself in, make an exchange for himself. But then the gate wouldn't get closed. He couldn't be everywhere at once.

The guilt kept piling on, and he was getting sick of it. Being trapped in this cell could be his tipping point. He could feel the instability beneath his skin, something dark just waiting to burst out. His magic and the hand of death combined with whatever their new magic was. If he was locked up for much longer, it wouldn't end well.

*Stop feeling sorry for yourself.* He couldn't sit here wallowing. He kicked a metal bucket out of the cluttered path and went to the door. It was solid metal with hinges on the outside. The wall was stone, and there was no external window.

He listened for several minutes. There was only one person out there. He felt a sudden wave of panic from Azalea, and he froze. She was somewhere above him, probably in her room, but he wasn't exactly sure where he was. They'd blind-folded him to come down here, and this wasn't in the floor plans he had studied as a boy; those were scratched in his brain, never to be washed clean.

Why hadn't Danni been down to see him? Was she that mad at him for lying about the soul bond? Had she turned on him too? He understood why Kat wasn't here. She would hopefully be meeting with Kira to find out more about Cassie. Though that wouldn't be easy for her either since she blew her cover with the House of Ravens when they went through the gate. He had to hope Kira truly was on their side.

He remained still and closed his eyes, seeking something from Azalea. He felt nothing. Had she escaped? Fallen asleep? Been knocked out? He had to get to her before she tried to get to him.

"Hey, mate. I know you're out there. Can I get a glass of water or something? I'm parched." Torin banged on the door.

"Sorry. I'm not supposed to open the door." The voice sounded young. Must be one of the House of Snake mages; and by his observations, none had any solider training, only magic.

"Look. I've got a killer headache. Just chuck me a bottle of water or something." Torin did his best to sound non-threatening.

Several minutes passed. Torin made a few mild groaning sounds that he believed were quite convincing. It wasn't entirely a lie. His head was pounding, and he was trying to ignore the rest of the protests from his bruised body.

A thud sounded on the other side of the door, and Torin crouched, ready to attack as the door creaked open.

"Poor lad, he's actually a good bloke," Fabian said from the doorway. "Are you coming or not?"

Torin straightened up. "This isn't a trick is it?"

"Why would I bother with that? I'd just leave you in here to rot."

He had a point. Torin walked past Fabian out the door and glanced down at the young mage whom Fabian had knocked out somehow.

"Azalea is waiting upstairs. I suggest you two get away from here as quickly as possible."

Torin studied Fabian's face, he seemed to be serious. "You're letting me leave with Azalea?"

"Don't make me change my mind. I've already sent that demon fellow off to find Nabu. You two are our best shot at setting things right. Now give us a hand." Fabian nodded to the guard, and Torin grabbed the boy's legs, and they shuffled him into the storeroom.

"What are you going to do?" Torin asked.

They set the boy down and left the room. "I'm going to wait for Kat to find out where Cassie is and go get her." Fabian shut the door behind them.

"Sounds like a plan. I don't suppose you can tell me where we might be able to go nearby until our magic recovers?" Torin asked, hoping he wouldn't push it.

Fabian nodded. "There's a cottage not far from here..."

# Chapter 36

Torin crept up the stairs with silent footsteps, already sensing her. Pushing the trapdoor above him open, he peered out, and there she was, standing there just as Fabian had said.

"Azalea," he whispered, and she nearly jumped out of her skin as she spun around.

Her eyes lit up when she spotted him. He climbed out carefully, and she ran to him.

He caught her mid-jump, and she wrapped around him like a monkey. "I missed you." He breathed into her hair.

Azalea kissed him. "I can't believe you're here." She lowered her feet back to the floor and pressed her head into his chest. "We should get the hell out of here before someone finds us."

She pulled away and stared up at him with a smile that melted his heart. They fell into the kiss at the same time. Her lips were on his, soft and warm, better than he remembered. He breathed in the scent of soap and the familiar smell of her magic he suspected only he would recognize.

He lost all concept of time in the kiss, but reality trickled back, and logic took over. "Okay, we really need to get going." Both of their hands were glowing.

Footsteps sounded on the ladder, and they broke apart.

"I see you two wasted no time in catching up." Fabian nodded at their lit-up hands, not looking overly thrilled.

"Thank you, Uncle Fabian!" Azalea threw himself on him. "For everything."

"I promised not to kill him, there'll be time for that later," Fabian joked, or Torin hoped he was joking.

Azalea stepped back, beaming, and adjusted her backpack. Torin stayed a safe distance away so as to not risk Fabian changing his mind about helping them.

"You two better get going. I'll be sounding an alarm in about twenty minutes, so get the hell away from here."

"Thank you, Fabian." Torin inhaled, and deciding to take a risk, he reached out a hand.

Fabian stared at it for a long moment, then clasped it in a firm shake. "Good luck you two. Don't fuck it up this time."

# Chapter 37

"Over here!" Azalea ran through the gap in the trees, finally spotting the cottage through the sheets of rain as she hugged herself, unable to stop shivering.

An owl hooted above them. "About bloody time." Torin followed her up the muddy track.

She shot him a look. It had been Torin's idea to find the abandoned cottage, which turned out to be over a mile's walk along the edge of the woods. Apparently, this was one of Cassie's favorite places to go, something Torin had learned from Fabian.

She moved faster when she spotted the front door. It had been easy to escape the Blackbourne manor grounds, all they'd had to do was climb a tree and drop from an overhanging branch on the other side of the fence.

The door to the cottage opened easily, and Azalea fought off the shiver in her spine. "I wish we had some air magic or a fire to get dry." She grumbled, rubbing her hands together as she looked around the spartan cottage. There wasn't much to it: a few old rugs, a wooden table and chairs, and a stone fireplace she wished was lit.

Torin searched the cupboards and came back with some wool blankets in various tartan patterns. "These look clean." He held them to his nose. "Well, they don't smell."

"Just what a gal wants to hear." Azalea took a blanket gladly and stripped off her coat, then stood there feeling self-conscious.

"I'll look away if you want to take off your wet clothes." Torin pulled out the mismatched dining chairs so they could hang their garments.

She peeled off her shirt, and by the time she'd stripped off her wet jeans leaving on her underwear and wrapped herself in the nice dry blanket, Torin had done the same. She needed to dry off before she dug out any clean clothes.

They stood there facing each other, finally alone and looking like drowned rats wrapped in tartan. "We're a pathetic sight." She accidentally snorted, then burst out laughing. Torin shook his head, then joined in. It was nice to see him happy for a change.

Still grinning, Torin grabbed another blanket, spread it across the floor in front of the cold fireplace, then sat down, leaning against the threadbare sofa. He patted the ground next to him. "In all seriousness, we need to talk, and we need a plan."

Azalea sunk down next to him and leaned her head on his shoulder. "Can't we just be happy for a second? We made it back; we found each other again."

"I wasn't sure we would." Torin rested his head against hers.

She pulled her blanket tight around her. "Torin, before I was angry at you for trying to close the gate, but I see why you did it now. You were trying to save everyone, but I was only thinking of myself. I didn't want to lose you." She knew it was out of the blue, but she'd wanted to say that for a while.

He brushed a strand of hair over her ear. "I know. I could feel it."

She stared into the empty fireplace. "Remember before, in the dream, I said I could break the bond. Ereshkigal gave me the power to do it."

Everything stilled around them. He clearly hadn't been expecting that.

He sat up straighter and shuffled against the couch. "And you, that's what you want to do? You want to break it?"

A spike of uncertainty coursed through her from his direction. That was what he wanted all along, wasn't it? She would have to go back to the Shadow Dimension soon to maintain the balance, it would be better for both of them if they broke it. She was giving him a way out if he wanted it. Even if it wasn't what she wanted.

Seconds passed between them where all she could hear were their heartbeats. She bit her lip, trying not to cry. He was taking too long.

She couldn't take the silence. "It's what you wanted, isn't it? It was the whole point of working together so we could break this curse."

"Azalea—"

Her heart was breaking. He was going to say he didn't want it, that he didn't want her. She had done exactly what they had planned. She had done the impossible and found a way to break an unbreakable bond. But as one half of a broken soul, she was devastated and suddenly wished he would get this over with.

Torin couldn't even look at her. "—Azalea. If this is what you want."

*He thought this was what she wanted.* Hope fluttered through her chest and sparked a warmth of magic in her hands. She hit him on the arm. "Of course, it isn't, you dimwit! Why would you think that?" She spun around to face him.

He sat there, stunned. "You said you found a way to break the bond. It's what you wanted. Why would you tell me otherwise?"

She shook her head. "Because I'm trying to be honest with you. It doesn't mean I want to do it! I thought it was what *you* wanted."

"Oh." He narrowed his eyes, clearly confused. "Oh. You mean—?"

That glimmer of hope ignited sky-high in her chest. "Yes, you idiot. I love you. I was waiting for you to say you don't want to break the bond."

"You could have just said that." A smile crept to his lips, and she felt relief bleed off him.

"Well?" She looked at him, her heart open and laid bare for him to see and feel everything.

He twisted around so their knees touched and wrapped both her hands in his. "I'll make this as clear as possible. I don't want to break the bond either, I love you too."

She grinned and rocked forward to meet his lips. His eyes darkened as something fiery built between them. Bursts of light pulsed from their skin as their magic curled together, and his hands buried in her hair.

Torin pulled away from the kiss, his dumbstruck look a mirror of her own.

"You're sure this is what you want?" he asked.

Azalea folded her hands in her lap, so as not to get too carried away. "Yes. Like Ereshkigal says, it's a gift so we might as well use it."

"I couldn't care less about what Ereshkigal thinks right now. I've got other things on my mind." He reached out and tipped her chin up.

She leaned forward and ran her hand the length of his thigh. "I have some idea of what those things might be."

He kissed her briefly. "We don't have to rush things, Azalea." But he didn't pull his hand away and neither did she.

Azalea bit her lip and crawled onto his lap, suddenly feeling bold. "Ereshkigal said if we seal the bond, we'll be in control of our emotions again." She brushed her lips against his cheek. "And we should have control over our new powers."

His hands moved to her hips under the blanket and slid up to her waist. "So you're just using me for my magic." He kissed her again pulling her closer.

She smiled onto his lips. "I think you'd know if I was. I'm an open book, after all."

"An open book that's bloody hard to read." He ran a hand over the soft dip in her back.

"Shut up and kiss me." She smiled as he did just that until he pulled away again.

"Azalea, I know this isn't the most romantic setting—"

"Don't you say we can wait. You know very well we can't, and I really don't want to. I even brought protection, just in case." She reached over for her jacket, glad of her wishful thinking when she was packing.

"Just checking." He grinned.

Their conversation was lost when Torin's lips met hers once more. He deepened the kiss sending shivers of pleasure all the way through her, and before she knew it, he rolled them both to the floor with his weight on top of her.

She pulled him toward her, wanting him closer, the blankets warming them were long gone, and she quickly removed her underwear not wanting any more barriers between them.

This was what she had been waiting for, what her dreams denied her, and in real life, it was so much more. *Why had they waited to do this?*

She arched into him, the magic between them flickering and burning, wanting more. They came together so naturally like they'd done this a thousand times, sensing what each other wanted without words, moving in perfect unison.

Rain continued to beat down on the roof, but it became distant as something awoke deep within them. Light streamed from their combined bodies. The earth beneath them trembled, but they were consumed with each other, and time lost all meaning as they joined completely—magic, body, and soul.

A final shiver ran the length of Azalea's body, and the warmth of Torin was suddenly gone as he collapsed onto the blanket beside her. Her heart didn't stop racing as her wet hair soaked into the tartan patterns, and they both caught their breath.

"That was... magical?" Azalea said, unable to find the words to describe whatever just happened. Epic was one that came to mind.

"I hope you mean good magical?" Torin teased.

"You know I do." She turned her head lazily toward Torin and grinned as her body relaxed completely, enjoying the total surrender. She took in a deep, satisfying breath. Her magic was no longer turbulent and screaming to get out but was in harmony within her and with everything around her, especially Torin.

He leaned on his elbow, and with his other hand, he laced his fingers with hers on her bare stomach. There was no rush of magic, no push and pull like before. Instead, it was like the gentle trickle of a stream sending a faint and pleasant warmth through her fingertips. Enough magic to balance them as if they shared one deep pool of power. She recognized the smile of relief on Torin's face, then blinked in confusion.

"I don't feel any of your feelings! At all." She shook his hand excitedly.

He grinned back. "Same here. Thank the gods."

"Hey!" She pushed him with their joined hands, but he pulled her at the same time, so she rolled into him, half resting on his chest.

Azalea released his hand and nestled into his side. His arm wrapped around her, holding her close, and with the other, he pulled a blanket over them. "Let's test it. What do you feel now?" he asked.

Azalea felt a wave of desire roll over her, spreading through her entire body with a heat that pooled in her belly. She let out an involuntary gasp.

Torin's chest rose and fell beneath her flushed cheek with a chuckle.

"Yup. I felt that." She let out a shaky breath.

Torin kissed her hair. "It seems we can shield our emotions now and let them through when we want. As a choice."

She believed him but didn't test it. She wasn't sure what her magic could do anymore and didn't want to risk hurting him while she was low on energy and control.

"That's good," she mumbled as tiredness settled over her. "I wish we could just sleep here."

With one hand, he toyed with the demantoid garnet on her finger, twisting it perhaps without realizing he was doing it. "I know. We can rest for a while, but first, you need to fill me in on everything that happened in the Shadow Dimension, without leaving out any details."

Azalea groaned, not wanting to ruin their good times, but knew he was right.

"Where do I even start?" She filled him in on everything she could think of, and he asked a million questions in return. Then he recounted his adventures in the Echo Dimension, though she suspected he filtered it a lot for her benefit. He was covered in bruises.

"Was my mother there?" Torin asked after a long silence as his fingers twirled around her hair.

She shook her head, tracing the shape of the moon tattoo on his chest with her finger. It was no longer a crescent moon, but a full moon with a border of intertwined knots with no beginning and no end. "I didn't see her, but it's so big. I'm sure she could have been. I could ask my dad next time."

"Next time... I hate that you have to go back."

"It won't be so bad. Maybe you can come with me." She tried to make it sound like a trip to Cyprus rather than the underworld.

"I did see Licorice though!" She suddenly remembered. "I think it was her, anyway. She must have sensed our bond. I fed her some of my food, which she seemed happy about."

"Sounds like Licorice." Torin chuckled. "That's amazing. I'm glad she found you."

"Me too," Azalea said, knowing how much that bird meant to him.

Torin's fingers trailed over the chain of the locket on her chest. "Oh, and I forgot to tell you. I have a sister."

"What!" Azalea sat up. "How? Who?"

"Cassie. Fabian's ward. Turns out she's my sister."

"How is that possible?" Thoughts whirled in her head, trying to piece together a timeline of how that worked.

The door flew open, and a gush of freezing air rushed in. Azalea pulled the blanket around her, and Torin stood up, not even bothering to cover up.

"Oh, gods. Please put that away." Kira stepped into the faint light.

Azalea's heart was racing. For a second, she thought it was the Archmage or Torin's father. Although Torin's ex-best friend/possible first love also wasn't so great at this moment.

"Kira! What the hell are you doing?" Torin realized he was naked, grabbed another blanket, and wrapped it around his waist, leaving his very toned abs exposed.

"Get dressed." Kira nodded to their drying clothes.

Azalea agreed with her on that. Fortunately, she had dry clothes packed. She threw the shirt, socks, and trousers to Torin, and they changed while Kira turned her back.

"What are you doing here?" Torin asked.

Azalea stuffed the wet clothes into her bag and put on her fleece. It was damp but warmed her quickly as she slung her bag on her back.

Kira glared at him. "I've come to take you in."

"In where?" Torin asked.

Kira stepped closer. She was wearing full House of Ravens combat gear. Her eyes were lined in black, and her hair was in a braid down her back. She was stunning. Azalea swallowed. She could never compete with a woman like that.

"To the Tower of London." Kira threw a handful of powder at Torin.

He clearly hadn't been expecting it. His eyes were wide and confused as Azalea reached out for him.

"Leave him," Kira ordered.

Azalea twisted her ring, then froze. But before Azalea could run, Kira tossed the same dust in her eyes, and the world swam.

She felt herself hit the floor like it was an out-of-body experience. Sounds muffled, but she distinctly heard Kira's voice. "Sorry, it had to be this way, Tor."

# Chapter 38

F abian rolled over in bed, sensing something was wrong. His eyes shot open.

"Why hello, Kat, this is a pleasant surprise." Her alluring silhouette was backlit by the red glow of the sky visible through the large windows. He was glad he never bothered to close the curtains.

"You did say I was always welcome in your bedroom." Her arms were folded, and she looked like she'd stepped right out of a black-and-white movie.

"And I stand by that." He patted the bed for her to sit down, but she remained standing. "Where did you sleep last night, anyway?"

"In the camp."

"And you'd rather sleep down there, than here in my rather inviting bed?"

"Yes." She picked up the book he had been reading, then put it back down.

Okay, so maybe she hadn't changed her mind about him. He hadn't given up hope he would win her over yet. She was in his bedroom, after all.

"And why is that?" he asked.

She stared out the window. "Because I can't trust you."

He sat up and leaned against the grand headboard without making a sound, not wanting to scare her off. "Come on, Kitty Kat. I am highly trustworthy. You may have noticed I haven't been shagging anyone since you came back into my life, and I've followed every order you've given me. How good was I in the Echo Dimension?"

"You can't make up for everything in a few short weeks. Do you not remember why we broke up? You basically blamed me for your brother's murder and told me you never wanted to see me again."

Ah yes. He did recall saying that. But she also used the term *broke up*, which meant she admitted that they had been together. A good sign.

"I said I was sorry."

"That doesn't magically wipe it from my memory." She turned to face him.

"Very well. Why are you here then if you didn't come to your senses about being in love with me?"

She ignored his comment but sat down on the bed.

"Cassie is fine. I talked to Kira. She's been checking in on her. Korbyn doesn't know she is his daughter."

"You told Kira who she was?" He clenched the blanket in his palm.

"I had to. She needed to understand the details so she could best protect Cassie." Kat had no remorse, and there wasn't the slightest hint of an apology.

"Fine, whatever." He clenched his jaw. Before this week, the only people who knew Cassie's true identity were him, Colin, and Mary. Now it seemed like everyone knew. He had tried to protect Cassie for so long; it wasn't fair her innocent life had to be ruined by all these politics.

He switched on the light. "You didn't tell her where Torin and Azalea went though, right?"

Kat blinked at the sudden brightness. She'd never been in his room. When they had been together, he avoided this place at all costs and never would have risked bringing Kat here. They'd always spent time at his flat in London when he worked for the Paranormal Justice Unit. It all seemed so long ago now.

"Yeah, I did actually," she said.

He threw the blankets off and stood up. "I need to warn them. I need to tell them to leave." He marched right past Kat and around the bed to his walk-in wardrobe.

"Gods Fabian, some warning please." Kat looked away. "You don't need to worry about them."

"Nothing you haven't seen before, love," he yelled back, certain she enjoyed the show. "And I *do* need to worry. I don't know anything about this Kira so it's better to be safe than sorry." Fabian dressed quickly, grabbed his phone, and called Azalea. No answer.

"You got Torin's number?" Fabian asked.

Kat called him. "No answer."

"Crap. I'm sending someone to look for them."

# Chapter 39

A zalea sat up in her old bed, in her old room at the Tower of London, and glanced around sleepily.

*Wait? The Tower of London?* She threw off the blanket as the events of last night rushed back at her: escaping Blackbourne manor, sleeping with Torin, sealing the bond, then Kira turning up—the last part was not how things were supposed to go.

Where the hell was Torin? If it wasn't for the stinging in her nose, the taste of blood in her mouth, and the warm hum of magic coursing through her veins, she might have thought Kira's arrival had been a dream. But she pressed her finger into her hand and saw that this was very real.

She wiped her nose with the back of her hand. It came away with fresh blood. Whatever that powder was that Kira had thrown on them, it had knocked her out and messed up her sinuses. She spotted a bottle of water and drank half, then wet a towel to dab at her tender nose.

It was just getting light outside. She ran her hand over the dried-out bamboo on her windowsill, wishing she could use Echo Magic to revive her poor plants. The morning sunlight filtered through their crispy leaves, throwing soft patches on the rug beside her bed.

As much as she wanted to stay, she needed to get out and get to Torin. Good memories of the night before washed over her, and she smiled to herself. It had been so much better than she'd imagined, so much better than her dreams.

She tried the door, but as expected it was locked from the outside, and probably with magic. She banged on the wall, hoping Torin might be on the other side. There was no response, and she didn't sense him.

Faraday crawled out from under the bed, stretched, and gave her a foul look for waking him up.

"Good hiding, Farry!" She swung him up into a big hug, so glad to see him. He blinked slowly, then wriggled out of her grip and went back under the bed. "Don't worry. I'm going to find a way out."

"Torin!" she yelled one last time, banging on their shared wall. She'd always hated him being that close. Now it was the opposite; now she wished he was on the other side.

"*Azalea?*"

She spun around. She'd heard his voice as clear as day.

"Torin?"

"*Where are you?*"

"Where are *you*? I can hear you, but I can't see you."

"*I'm locked in the cells under the Barracks.*"

"I'm in my room in your tower. How are we talking?" She spun around again, looking for the source of his voice.

"*It's in your head. Our connection is strong enough for telepathy.*"

Oooo, this was new and so much better than sharing emotions. Azalea closed her eyes and concentrated. "*Can you hear me?*"

"*Yes. Are you okay? Did they hurt you?*"

"*It worked! I didn't say any of that aloud. I'm fine. No thanks to your mate, Kira.*"

*"I'm as surprised as you are."*

Azalea wouldn't say she was exactly surprised, but she pushed that thought to the back of her mind so it wouldn't pop up and changed the subject.

*"We didn't get to test our new magic together."*

A flush of heat ran through her with a very strong visual image of their time in the cottage. *Stop getting distracted.* What they really needed was to test it together to make sure it was safe and see what they were capable of, though it looked like she'd have to resort to winging it.

*"It's risky to use it without testing it. Just hold off and be careful, okay?"* Torin said.

*"We could take down anyone. I can feel it."* Azalea felt in control of the power as it circulated her body. The powers she shared with Torin mixed with whatever Ereshkigal gave her, plus the underlying coldness of the Shadow Magic dwelling in her chest felt in perfect balance. For the first time in her life, her body felt right. She also recognized how dangerous that could be.

*"Exercise control, no matter what the situation,"* Torin said.

*"What's your big idea then?"* She knew he was right and took it seriously, but since they were here, they also had a chance to help Cassie and Maiken get out.

*"I'm going to offer to cooperate with them if they return Cassie."*

*"That doesn't sound like a good plan. We can find a way out and get Cassie and Maiken too."*

Then the voice in her head was gone. No way she was going to sit around waiting.

A swirl of shadows clouded the air.

"What the hell is this?" Azalea waved her hand and stared. She would never get the image in front of her out of her head.

Sita, the bat-winged demon, was perched on Faraday's back.

"Good morrow, Mageling. My affections with your Shadow Cat have paid off. He has retrieved me in my time of need. I could not get through the wards here." Sita dismounted and unfolded his wings.

"Um, that's great, Sita. I didn't know you could do that, Farry." She crouched down and rubbed under his chin until he let out a rumbling purr. "You really are a good boy." That explained a lot about how he got around.

Time to see what she had to work with. She checked her bag and found everything was still in it, including her elemer and phone. She tried to call Fabian, but there was no signal. They must still have a blocker on.

Sita flapped over to the door, and his tiny hands wrapped around the handle and shook it violently, but it didn't open for him either.

"It is charmed," he muttered.

"Where have you been, Sita?" She checked her closet for anything that could be a weapon.

"Unlike you, I have not been napping and sitting around." He flew over to the window and settled amongst the bamboo, scanning the grounds outside.

"In case you hadn't noticed, I have been taken captive once again, and it wasn't exactly a voluntary nap."

"I don't need to hear your excuses. I have been tracking the scribe. We must go at once before he moves again. Get prepared to leave now."

"Okay.... But do you have a plan to get out of here?"

"Yes, we will use your powers. I sense they are stable now. You sealed the bond." He spun around with a sly smile.

"Yes, not that it's any of your business."

"Ereshkigal will be most pleased." He smirked.

*Damn, he was right.* She would be pleased. It might be handy to have one good thing up her sleeve when she was being dragged back to the Shadow Dimension. Though she wasn't sure how getting out of here might go if it was up to her magic.

She changed into clean clothes and tied her hair into a messy ponytail. She didn't want to waste time dealing with brushing and knots; it wouldn't help her escape. She emptied her bag and repacked it with clean clothes. She put on deodorant, took two painkillers for her headache, and threw the rest in her bag that was still wet from the night before.

She stood with her hands on her hips. "I'm ready. But Torin isn't going to want to leave without his sister."

"We will attempt to retrieve her, but leave her if we must," Sita grumbled as he flapped out of the plants, sending dead leaves fluttering to the floor. "Now sit down."

Azalea sank onto the floor. "What exactly are we doing?"

"We are accessing your powers, as you clearly haven't done so already." Sita flapped his wings with an angry crack.

"But you said my power was balanced. I feel great."

"Yet you do not *see.*"

"I can see." She frowned.

He narrowed his eyes at her. "You are not *looking.*"

She rolled her eyes. Sita was behaving very much like his Shadow Atlas form right now. "Can you just spell it out for me?"

He let out a huff. "Remember how you could see in the Shadow Dimension. Draw that same power."

She remembered the vivid colors of the Shadow Dimension, the sharpness of lines, the vibrancy when she first saw that red petal.

"Stupid human. Be still." He snapped his fingers. "Close your eyes."

Closing her eyes, she let her breath guide her, sinking into a pleasant place of calm.

"Call to the Shadow Dimension."

Her eyes flashed open. "My elemer."

"You do not need it. Do not rip and tear like an elemer, call like a whisper on a breeze, let the magic soak into your flesh."

Azalea relaxed at the sound of his voice. He could be a meditation instructor if he wasn't so impatient. She remembered how the power felt when Ereshkigal gifted it to her. Alive and colorful, dancing inside her. The opposite of what you'd think of the Shadow Dimension.

Filling her lungs, she pulled in a deep breath, letting her body relax, starting from her head, softening her cheeks and jaw. The energy moved through her neck and back, across her collarbone, and down her arms until her fingers felt weightless with soft tingles. Her belly expanded with each inhalation, and with the exhalation, the energy flowed through her abdomen and all the way down her legs.

She wasn't sure how long she sat there breathing, but it was a welcome holiday from all the chaos.

When she was ready, she opened her eyes and saw her room filled with the soft glow of magic. Mostly her own purple and green magic, leaving its mark on her private space—it was strangely comforting.

Her feet were freezing, and her knees creaked when she stood up. The morning sun was much higher in the sky. She went to the window and saw the casemates along the north wall glowed with golden magic. She could actually see the protective wards.

"You *see* it now. Do you not?" Sita asked. Faraday slipped out from under the bed and slid his way around her legs.

"It's beautiful. I didn't think it would work in this world." Tears threatened the corners of her eyes.

"We have no time to waste. What color is the door?" Sita snapped.

"It's glowing kind of bluish black around the handle." She went to touch it, and the colors expanded like an old bruise stuck on the door.

"Just the handle?"

"Yes." She nodded.

"Good. Find something to wedge up the hinges and pop the door off. And hurry." Sita flapped impatiently.

She had to admit it was a brilliant idea. Though it also seemed too easy. After a lot of sweating and swearing, she used her elemer to wedge the door off, and it crashed into the landing at the top of the stairs.

Azalea grabbed her backpack and stepped over the door. She paused briefly at Torin's room. The place seemed so empty without him.

As soon as she was downstairs, she shielded herself with a shadow cloak and slipped outside. She breathed in the fresh morning air. She always loved that smell after rain—wet roads mixing with the oversaturated earth ready to become mud as soon as you stepped on it. She paused at the top of the stairs, checking the courtyard for any stray spirits or House of Ravens or Phoenix guards, but it seemed they weren't bothering with this area.

"You go get the girl first," Sita said.

"But I need to get Torin out."

"No, the girl first. Your mage has too many people watching. He must be last."

*Her mage.* She kind of liked that. Sticking close to the walls, she made her way toward the Barracks on the large open walkways that were usually packed with tourists that seemed far too empty. The white tower loomed in the center of the grounds, its grand boxy facade casting a long shadow that stretched to the buildings behind it.

Her shadow cloak felt stronger than usual like no one could see through it.

"Which entrance? Do you know where the guards are?" Azalea whispered.

"The shadow cat will take you. Meet me in the archives of the British Museum. I will monitor Nabu and follow him if he moves." Sita turned away.

"The museum? How do I know where to go?"

Sita flew off without saying goodbye. Oh dear, she knew the museum was huge, and she suspected the archives below were just as large. She sighed. New plan: find Torin, rescue Cassie, go to the British Museum to find the fugitive god, close the Echo gate. Too easy.

Better get on with it. Faraday trotted ahead and seemed to know where he was going, so under a shadow cloak, she followed him past the Barracks and toward the main door to the hospital building on the other side of the White Tower.

It was strangely quiet inside. They headed for the stairwell rather than risking the elevator and getting caught. But Azalea froze halfway down the stairs. Livia was walking right towards her and apparently couldn't see her. Her face was sallow, her blonde hair limp and oily, like she couldn't be bothered washing it anymore.

Azalea thought of Elam and how terrible she felt for Livia, despite her being a bitch. This was her chance to make things right.

"Livia," Azalea whispered just after Livia had passed.

Livia twisted around, her eyes wide with fear.

Azalea dropped her shadow cloak. "Sorry to scare you. Please don't yell."

Azalea prayed to the gods Livia would be rational, just for a moment at least.

"Give me one good reason not to turn you in right now," Livia said, holding her elemer out in front of her, despite not being able to use her Echo Magic. Though Azalea suspected she wouldn't be opposed to burning herself out if she got to take Azalea down with her.

"Please just listen to me," Azalea said.

"This is all your fault," Livia hissed, her face turning red.

"You know that isn't true, Livia. It's your grandmother and Korbyn Dumont doing all this. I'm here trying to find a girl to get her to safety. Can you help me?" She kept her voice soft and calm, hoping to keep Livia listening long enough to think about it. "She might be hurt. I think Maiken would know where she is, can you take me to her? Please, Livia?"

Livia swallowed. Her hand was shaking as if she could hardly keep it up. Azalea saw the conflict behind her eyes.

"We can stop all this. We've found a way to fix it. You can have your magic back. Just like before."

"They want to make the world better." Livia's voice cracked. "They want a world where we don't have to hide. Where we can all be free."

"Does it really look like that's what they're trying to do? You can't use Echo Magic properly anymore. What sort of world is that?"

"I know what you're doing. You're trying to trick me. The same way you tricked all of us before to help you, and now Elam is dead. He is dead because of you."

Her words hung in the silent stairwell.

"I'm sorry Livia. I know you're hurting. But I saw Elam. I went to the Shadow Dimension."

Her face twisted. "What a horrible thing to say. Everything you say is a lie. My grandmother told us you weren't to be trusted."

"I'm not lying. I saw him, and he told me to tell you he loves you, and that you need to stop hating yourself. He said Ducky would want it."

Livia remained frozen on the stairs, her face contorted into a twist of raw pain. "Ducky? He told you that?" She bit her lip, clearly holding back tears.

"You know what that means, right? Because I don't."

"Ducky was our imaginary pet duck when we were kids. We weren't allowed pets," she said nostalgically, like she forgot it was Azalea she was talking to. "He truly said that?"

Azalea nodded. "I'll see him again soon if you want me to tell him anything."

"You can tell him I love him too." She wiped a hand across her cheek and turned away. "You can find Mage Fletcher in the end office down on the ward."

"Thank you, Livia," Azalea said and continued down the stairs.

# Chapter 40

Sitting on a stone bench in the cold cell at the Tower of London, Torin had nothing to do but focus on the various pains welling up over his body and reflect on the past day that now seemed like a dream.

Faced with losing everything—with losing Azalea—he realized how little everything else mattered. He shouldn't have cared about feeling guilty all these years for things his father did. He didn't need Fabian's forgiveness. He never did anything for himself, it was always others or a great goal. Getting revenge for his father, trying to make his father proud, trying to take down his father, trying to live up to the expectations of the Archmage and the Paranormal Justice Unit. Always trying to impress, to work for others.

He finally knew what he wanted—he wanted *her*. Azalea.

All he had to do was forgive himself so he could be with her. All the guilt and shame were eating him alive, and she was the light at the end of the tunnel; she was the light on the other side of the Hollow. He saw that now, and after opening himself up to her, after risking it all, he knew she was his path, she was his future—she was the reason he was alive now and the reason he had to keep living. She loved him.

The cell door swung open, breaking him from his new appreciation for life, and Kira glided in and shut the door behind her. Torin sat up straighter on the wooden bench.

"Sorry, I had to do that. Now that Kat is gone, your father is suspicious of me. I had to do this to prove myself, to show your father I'm on his side." Kira leaned against the door.

Torin kept a cautious eye on her. "You could have explained that."

"It needed to be real for when you got here. I needed you to believe I'd betrayed you to put on a show for your father."

"Well, you got that." He'd been wild when he arrived and was sure the guards reported that to his father. He just couldn't believe this was the same Kira. She certainly had the confidence of the Kira he knew, but she seemed so cold, so distant.

"Have you come to break me out?" Torin asked.

"No. I just came for a chat. You need to wait." She crossed her arms.

Torin tried to read her, to work out if she really hated him. "I have somewhere rather important to be."

"I just wanted to pass on a hello from the boys." She looked at the ground.

Was this her reaching out? Maybe she didn't hate him. "As in…"

"Conner, Dev, and Matt. They're all here now, not at the Tower, but they're around."

He saw through her confident shield. She was as nervous as he was. He had to trust that she had a plan and forced his shoulders to relax. "And how's the old squad doing?"

"Good. Really good. We were all posted together, and now we're back here."

An awkward silence filled the air. They were talking like this was a school reunion, stepping around the fact that she had poisoned him to get him here and was holding him captive.

"Look, Tor. We all want you to come back. You need to be the one to take over when he's gone," she snapped.

That was the last thing he expected her to say and didn't really match up with not wanting to help him escape.

"I'm all for taking my father down. But I can't do that from in here." He kept his eyes locked on her, waiting for any sign of deceit.

She nibbled her fingernail, something she used to do when she was nervous. "We need to wait for the shift change to get you out. And after your father speaks with you. He needs to feel like he is in control."

"What is his plan? Why is he doing all this?" Torin asked.

"You think he'd tell me?" Kira scoffed. "All I know is him and the Archmage have taken over the High Council. He's spending a lot of time at Eagle Tower. They're cooperating over there, but that's because they killed several of the High Council members."

"This won't last. My father and the Archmage both want control. They'll turn on each other at some point."

"I agree, but not until they establish mutual power. All they need is to get rid of the House of Snakes, and everyone else will fall into line. There won't be anyone to oppose them." Kira paced in front of the door.

Torin leaned back on the bench feeling every single bruise on his body. It was clear Kira wasn't going to hurt him, and he wasn't going to risk hurting her to escape. "He always wanted to control everything and everyone, but this is going too far."

Kira stopped and held a hand against the door. "He wants the world to be afraid of him."

"Yes. I'm still surprised that the Archmage is going along with his plans. Opening the Echo Gate set her at a disadvantage."

"She has a way around it. They say she can still use Echo Magic," Kira answered straight away.

Torin rubbed his face and winced, forgetting the bruising on his jaw. "Azalea mentioned some staffs Mage Faber, the elemer-smith, was making. He must have perfected them. I'd just like to know what they have planned."

Kira moved to sit next to him on the bench. "I talked to Kat, and she believes his plan all along was to infiltrate the mainstream government. He wanted magic to be exposed, and then he is going to target parliament."

Torin tensed, aware of her closeness. "We'll stop him before it comes to that."

A thud sounded from outside, and the door swung open.

"Oh, Mage Reid. I didn't know you were in here." Azalea's classmate Livia stood at the door looking very guilty. "Um, this guard just fainted, it seems, and the Archmage and Mage Dumont said they would like you to see them in the Archmage's office."

"They did not say that." Kira stood resting her hand on her hip. "Did you just knock out that guard with the sleep powder?"

Livia cringed. "Would you believe me if I said no?"

Torin groaned. "Did you see Azalea by chance?"

"Um, yes. So..." Livia rubbed her neck and looked at the ceiling.

"This is going to ruin everything." Kira shot a death glare at Torin. "I take it you didn't actually train Azalea. You've just been shagging her, right?"

Anger flared through Torin, but he didn't react. He suspected there would be a lot of similar comments in the future.

Livia's hand went to her mouth, her eyes wide. "That little slut. I knew it."

"Watch it," Torin growled and shot Livia an unimpressed look. She took a sharp breath and backed against the wall.

He calmly turned to Kira. "Give it a rest, Kira. It's not like that."

"From what I've seen, it is."

"You have no idea what's going on with us," he said, his voice growing louder.

She glared at him. "Oh, so you don't have a soul bond with her, then?"

Torin was dumbstruck. Did everyone already know?

"You what!" Livia burst out. "Oh my gods."

Torin flashed her another look that said shut it.

"Kat told me," Kira said.

*Course she did.* That's probably how she knew they'd be in the cottage too. "Livia, would you please tell me where I can find Azalea? It seems I will be leaving now."

"I'll take you there," Livia said, suspiciously cooperative. From what Azalea told him, they did not get on.

Torin didn't need her as an extra complication. "No, just tell me. You're safer staying as far away from us as you can. For now, you're protected by your family."

"But Azalea is going to see Elam again. I want to go with her," Livia whined.

Ah, there was the truth of it. "That isn't how it works. You can't pick and choose to go to the Shadow Dimension."

"But she's going back there." Livia pouted.

Kira didn't even hide her surprise at the news. Apparently, Kat hadn't told her everything.

"It's not a holiday, Livia. It is a world of dead people, and I'm not exactly looking forward to the prospect of Azalea going back there. Just stay in the world of the living, and let us fix things."

Livia sniffed. "Fine. She's in the hospital ward. I told her where to find Maiken in the office at the end."

Kira dragged the guard into the cell and told Livia to get away from there so she couldn't be connected to this. Kira gave Torin his elemer that she'd taken from the cottage, and Torin set a shadow cloak over himself, then followed Kira's purposeful strides down the concrete basement hallway and up a set of stairs that led to the caf.

Kira positioned herself so Torin could walk right next to her, close to the wall, as if in her shadow, her body shielding any movement he might make. His magic was a new level of effortless; it was as easy as walking or floating in water.

An invisible compass pointed him toward Azalea, but it wasn't a forceful pull like before. It was like her magic linked to his in a meandering stream, connecting them, but with no screaming emotions or forceful magic.

He couldn't help but stare at Kira. He didn't want to take his eyes off her in case she wasn't real. He'd hardly had time to believe she was here, like this was just another dream, and she would be dead again when he woke up. Those dreams had plagued him for years. He pushed his finger into his palm and saw that it was solid and real. This was no dream.

He smiled, even as they walked by the House of Ravens and House of Phoenix guards mingling with Tower of London residents. It wasn't so different from before, though there was a subtle tension lingering in the air. Like a balloon might burst at any moment.

They made it to the hospital without incident. Kira was on good terms with all the guards and lightheartedly talked her way into the hospital as if it were nothing. Torin slipped in the doors close behind her, his footsteps never making a sound.

They got to the end of the long hallway, and Kira opened the door without knocking as Torin removed his shadow cloak. Maiken stood up dead straight behind her desk, looking terrified. "Torin!" she exclaimed.

"It's good to see you, Maiken. Was Azalea here?" Torin said.

Maiken glanced toward Kira, and her eyes narrowed. Torin shut the door behind them. "It's okay Maiken. Kira is with us."

"You sure about that?" Maiken looked Kira up and down.

Torin gave a sharp nod. "I'd bet my life on it." That wasn't a lie. He didn't blame Kira for her actions and sure as hell owed her for his.

"In that case, it's good to see you, Torin," Maiken darted around the desk and threw her arms around him. She sagged against Torin with relief as he hugged her. She was thinner than before and had never been one for public displays of affection. He hated to think what she had been through here.

"Danni and the girls are just fine. It's you they've been worried about," he said.

"I know. Azalea just filled me in." Maiken released him, and Azalea appeared in the corner.

He shook his head but couldn't help smiling. "This is you staying put?" He took two steps, and she was there to meet him. His arms wrapped around her, and she snuggled into his chest. His cheek rested on the top of her head.

Azalea pulled away, and he was pleased to see neither of them were glowing, nor could he feel her emotions.

"Sita found Nabu, and we've also found Cassie," Azalea said. "She's asleep just down the hall. We can all get out."

*Thank the gods.* He had wondered where the small demon got to. This might actually work if they could drop Maiken and Cassie off at the gates of Blackbourne Manor.

Livia appeared in the doorway. "I want to come too."

"You again," Kira snapped.

"No. Not happening. We don't need to give them any more reasons to attack," Torin answered without even needing to think about it.

"But Azalea saw Elam. He's in the Shadow Dimension," Livia repeated.

Torin took in a sharp breath; they didn't have time for this. "We know. You can't just go there. Azalea has been given certain... permissions."

Azalea gave him a weak smile.

Livia stamped her foot. "Why should she get special treatment? I just want to see my brother."

"This isn't the time, Livia," Azalea snapped.

"Come on. I'll take you to Cassie. Does she know you?" Maiken asked.

Azalea shot a look at Torin. He wasn't going to be the one to tell people they were related. He would take the high road and leave that up to Fabian if he wanted to.

"We met her briefly. She should recognize us. Let Azalea talk to her first," Torin said. He wasn't sure what rubbish Fabian had told her about him, but it was safe to say it wouldn't have been positive.

Maiken went to the cupboard. "She is able to leave, but she'll need these crutches. She broke her ankle after falling out of a tree when the House of Ravens idiots tried to catch her. We haven't been able to spare healers for non-life-threatening injuries, sorry."

A rush of anger washed over Torin on her behalf. She was too young to be caught up in all this.

Azalea went into the room with the crutches and, after about ten minutes, came back to the office with Cassie clicking behind with overconfident swings of her legs and a big grin on her face.

Her hair was dark brown, nearly black, the same shade as his, and was tied in tight braids close to her head, the same way Zoe and Ava often had theirs—Maiken's specialty. He was glad she had been well looked after here.

It was hard to take his eyes off her. He couldn't help but search for details in her face from his mother or father. Thankfully, she took after their mother, and he now knew why she seemed so familiar when he first saw her. She had the same wide smile as his mother and the same cheeks. She was slimmer and shorter than his mother had been, more wiry like their father.

Azalea grinned beside her but didn't give anything away.

"Do you want to come with us Maiken?" Torin checked.

She nodded. The exhaustion in her body was clear. "My patients are all stable. But the tunnel is heavily guarded now. I'm not sure how we can get out."

"Azalea and I can take care of that," Torin said.

"We can?" Azalea asked.

*"Time to test out our new powers."* He spoke to her in his mind.

*"Yes!"* Azalea's eyes lit up.

"Sorry about this, Livia, but it's for your own good." Kira's hand slipped into her pocket, and she artfully tossed sleep powder into Livia's face. Torin caught Livia as she went down, and Azalea helped him carry her into Cassie's room.

"What about you?" Torin asked Kira.

"I need to stay here to coordinate from this end."

"You mean plan for the attack on the House of Snakes?"

"Yes, unfortunately, it's inevitable now. Kat knows everything I do. It's up to the Snakes to protect themselves." Kira glanced out the door.

"We'll try to get back there in time. We can close the gate and still make it," Torin said.

"Good luck, Torin." Kira walked over and kissed him on the cheek.

A flush ran up his neck along with a thrill of hope. Was this her forgiving him? "You too." There was so much he wanted to say to her, but nothing seemed right. He let her walk out of the room. He couldn't help but notice Azalea frowning after her. Was that jealousy he detected? He couldn't help but smile to himself.

"We're going to need to move fast." He turned back to Cassie, remembering they needed to go.

"I'll grab a wheelchair." Maiken left the room.

Cassie glared at Torin. "I'm capable of walking."

"I'm sure you are, but we need speed. You're taking the wheelchair, no argument," Torin said firmly.

"Gods, you sound just like Fabian." Cassie snorted.

Azalea giggled. "You kind of did."

He just shook his head but smiled, glad Azalea was putting Cassie at ease.

Maiken came back in and got Cassie into the wheelchair, and they made their way down the hospital ward. Only the eerie groans of patients followed them to the elevator.

*"I can't believe you have a sister,"* Azalea said in his head.

*"Me neither. Let's try to keep her alive."*

The elevator doors opened, and as soon as they stepped out, they were surrounded by House of Raven and House of Phoenix guards. The Phoenix guards, now missing their Echo Magic, were armed with SA80s.

"State your purpose," a raven guard said.

"We are leaving," Torin didn't need to look at Azalea. In unison, they raised their arms and shot a blast of white light from their hands. The guards tumbled like dominoes. Torin held his ground as the magic reverberated from the tunnel and back on them.

All forms of Shadow Magic pulsed through his veins; power symbols for magic he didn't even know appeared in his mind.

He used the new symbols to merge Shadow Magic and the new magic, and without speaking to Azalea—even in their minds—they coordinated raising all the guards up and pushing them together to tie up with white magic and shadows that wove into ropes entwined with delicate enchanted fibers.

"That was insane!" Cassie yelled, practically bouncing in her wheelchair.

Maiken did not look pleased. In fact, she looked like she might turn on them.

"We can explain later, Maiken. Just trust me," Torin said.

Maiken pushed Cassie past the group of unconscious guards. "What the hell was that?"

"It's a really long story," Azalea said. "But we found a way to close the Echo Dimension gate, so we're going to drop you off very quickly."

"Why quickly?" Cassie asked.

Torin didn't want to go into the details of the possibility of Enlil coming through the gate and destroying everyone if they didn't find Nabu in time. "Because we need to get the gate shut so the magic can rebalance."

They continued down the dripping tunnel to get as close to the end as they could to open the Hollow.

"There's something you're not telling me. What's going on with you and Azalea and this magic?" Maiken stopped, pulling the wheelchair to a halt.

Azalea bit her lip and looked at Torin. "There is," Torin replied. "But this magic is the key to us shutting the gate and fixing everything. Please don't stop us, Maiken."

"Despite your past, Torin, I always saw you as very sensible. I'm starting to doubt that now." Maiken glanced between them as if trying to solve a puzzle.

Azalea wrung her hands. "Don't blame Torin, it's all my fault we got into this mess. But I promise we can fix it."

"I just hope you know what you're doing," Maiken said.

"We do," Torin promised. "And we will be there for the battle to help."

A chill settled over the tunnel, and Torin turned just in time to block a wall of shadow daggers tearing toward them. His shadow wall held strong. Without thinking, he took Azalea's hand, and together they shot a single beam of light and blasted down the attackers. Again, the power echoed back on them with a surge.

*I think we're absorbing their powers,* Torin realized. That would explain why it knocked them out and all the new power symbols gathered in his head. The light must drain them of their magical energy.

"I think you're right," Azalea said aloud. She didn't let go of his hand, gripping it tight as if he might disappear any second. He wasn't about to do that but gave her hand a squeeze in recognition.

With his other hand, he used his elemer to cut into the Hollow.

He had to let go of her to help Cassie into the dark void. Maiken followed her, then Azalea.

"Wow, there are so many colors in here," Azalea said as the void closed behind them.

He studied her face, trying to work out if she was hallucinating or something. "There aren't any colors, Azalea. It's all blue and darkness, like always."

She glanced at him like he was the crazy one.

He cut out of the Hollow, and Maiken stepped out first. He helped Cassie down, and she stood confidently on her crutches.

"It's them, it's them! Hold it there!" the guard shouted from the other side of the gate.

"We better be going," Azalea said quickly, holding the edge of the Hollow open.

"Oi! Grab them. Don't let them get away," the guard yelled at Maiken as he went about unlocking the blood wards of the gate with a small vial around his neck.

"Back in the Hollow," he ordered Azalea.

He turned to Cassie. "Cassie, I just want you to know I'm nothing like my father, okay?"

"Um, okay. Sure. Thanks for the rescue." She gave him a weird look and focused on hobbling toward the gate.

"I'll take your word for it for now, but I want an explanation when this is over," Maiken called after them, and Torin stepped back through the Hollow.

# Chapter 41

The Hollow closed, but instead of being left in the usual glow of blue light, Azalea spun around, taking in the network of colors pulsing around her like roots of trees all wound together.

"What is it?" Torin looked at her panicked.

She watched a pulse of blue light travel through the air around her and absorb into the spongy floor. "It's beautiful."

Torin's hands were on her shoulders, shaking her. "Azalea, focus."

"The Hollow is alive; I can see it. It's how it takes us where we want to go. It can see, and it is everywhere." She snapped out of it as her hand found the warmth of Torin's, and she smiled. "Sorry. I got Ereshkigal's powers back, and I can see magic everywhere. It's very distracting."

"As wonderful as that might be, we need to get moving. Where did Sita go?" He held her hand, patting the top of it to get her attention.

"He said we were to meet him in the archives at the British Museum." She tried to focus.

"Good. They don't have any wards," Torin said.

"That's right, you stole books from there, didn't you?" Azalea nudged him in the side with her elbow.

He winced.

"Eeek, sorry," she said. She'd forgotten about his bruised ribs.

"I borrowed them with every intention of bringing them back."

"Well, did you?" She raised an eyebrow.

He let go of her hand and held up his elemer. "No, I'm still using them."

She held up her hands. "Hey, no judgment here." She was doing her best to keep her hands off him so they wouldn't get distracted, but it was hard. At least she couldn't feel his emotions anymore. That certainly wouldn't have helped their situation.

He cut into the Hollow. The edge of the cut sparkled blue, and she could see the tiny magical fibers trying to knit back together as soon as he opened it. Fascinating.

He stepped out first and held a hand out to help her down, which she didn't need but took anyway since he was being all gentlemanly.

"Why would he be in here?" Azalea whispered. The room was huge, with rows and rows of gray shelves on tracks with little steering wheels on the sides for moving them about.

"He's a scribe. He's probably looking for records," Torin said as if it was obvious. "Can you summon the demon?"

Azalea shrugged. "He usually just comes when I need him." She didn't want to yell. This place was far too quiet. "Sita," she hissed, poking her head around some shelves.

The familiar flapping of Sita's bat wings got closer and stopped when his black figure perched on a shelf above them.

"It is about time. Nabu remains here, but you must make haste, as he grows impatient with his findings."

Sita flew away, and Azalea took off at a run to keep up. Torin's footsteps were right behind her as they descended a flight of stairs, ran down a long hallway, and into another records room just like the one above. Only this one had an enormous colorful dragon curled up at the end. It was breathing deep heavy breaths that sent a pleasant smoky fog across the room. Its iridescent wings were folded back, and its pointed muzzle had whiskers so long they coiled around its legs, vibrating with every breath it exhaled.

"Oh, wow." Azalea bounced on her heels. Torin had gotten to ride a dragon, an experience that was now high on her bucket list.

"That is Enlil's dragon. The one Nabu stole." Torin's voice was low, his eyes unmoving from the creature.

A young man popped out from behind a shelf. Azalea would have mistaken him for a uni student who got lost on his way to a party if it hadn't been for the golden magic around him, so bright it was almost blinding. His blond hair rested in a controlled sweep across his forehead, and he wore an ankle-length skirt covered in large feathers with a strip of light material that wrapped over one shoulder, giving a clear view of incredible abs and toned pecs.

He marched over to them. "Are you the keepers of these histories? I seek information on the true gods." The man asked politely and without a second glance at the dragon right behind him.

"Certainly. What is it you seek?" Torin asked, not missing a beat. Sita hopped across the shelves above them, and Faraday stuck close to Azalea's legs, so close she nearly tripped on him twice.

This wasn't how she'd pictured the scribe god. She had been imagining an old, bearded man like a wizard or something. This guy had to be her age.

"These artifacts are from the first cities, but all I see are meaningless merchant receipts." His voice rose, and he smashed the small clay tablet he'd been holding to the ground. "Where are the real records?"

Torin reached out as if he could have caught it. Azalea noticed the flash of pain across his face at the artifact's destruction and how he stared at the pile of clay shards on the ground.

Azalea held her breath. Nabu certainly had the temper of a god.

He stopped and looked at them. His eyes were a piercing green, and it seemed he was looking into Azalea's soul.

"Oh, I see. You are not attendants here." He glanced up at Sita, then glared at Faraday. "You are servants of the Shadow Dimension. You have come for me."

"Yes. Enki and Inanna wish for you to return," Torin said. "And we wish to close the gate."

Nabu narrowed his unnaturally emerald eyes. "You do not look like great warriors."

"You don't look like a god." Azalea narrowed her eyes in return.

A sly grin crept across his face, and his gaze flicked to her wrist tattoo. "You do not belong here any more than I do, little girl."

Azalea fought the urge to hide behind Torin. She didn't need to be reminded of that fact. Nabu looked like he was the sort of boy who would have tortured animals as a child, if he ever had been a child. Instead, she stood her ground and looked him in the eye. "I am aware of that, but we are here to ensure you get back home nice and safe."

He dropped the rest of the clay tablets on the floor and leaned against the shelf. "I do not like what I've seen of this world. It is as I feared. The gods have been forgotten."

"There are some of us who still remember," Torin said. "Those with magic recognize the old gods."

"How many Houses of magic remain?"

"There are eight now," Torin answered.

"So few..." Nabu looked down at the pile of tablets, but there was no regret in his eyes.

"Yes, but the gods are still remembered, they took on other names throughout history as humanity spread," Torin said.

Nabu tilted his head, his eyes fixed on Torin in interest, like a snake about to strike.

Torin continued. "For example, Inanna is also known as Ishtar, Isis, Venus—"

"What of Enlil? Does his name live on?"

"Well... yes, in a way—" Torin stuttered.

"Enlil wishes to destroy your world. I seek reason for him not to. If there is any hope of convincing him not to, I must find record of him."

Oh, that wasn't what she expected.

Torin crossed his arms, clearly getting impatient. "Records of Enlil exist, but in different forms, he is best known in Greek mythology."

"You lie. I found many religions in this realm, but they do not mention Enlil."

"He was also known by the names Zeus or Jupiter. There are many tales depicting his strength and power. He was ruler of the gods and was also a powerful weather mage known for his lightning bolts."

*Also known for being a petty, power-hungry rapist, as were many of the gods.* Probably better if Torin didn't mention that. But from what he told her about Enlil, she wouldn't be surprised if those myths were based on fact.

"You will show me these records." Nabu banged his hand on the metal shelf, making it ring through the long room.

"We could give you books to return with," Azalea suggested.

Torin gave a curt nod in agreement. Beads of sweat appeared on his forehead. "Yes, and a device that contains all our knowledge. Someone in the Echo Dimension should know how to work it."

"Or you could get Ereshkigal to send you a recent spirit who knows how to work it to help you."

"Yes, this would please me. I would also ask a favor of you if I am to return so willingly."

"Name the favor," Torin said.

Azalea froze. From what she had seen, bargaining with gods was a tricky business, and she didn't want them in more hot water.

"I will leave you a chronicle of the gods. With it, you will spread word to the mortals of this world of their creators."

"*We can do that. It's not so bad,*" Azalea said to Torin in his mind.

"*No academics would ever believe me if I pulled something like that out of thin air.*"

"*Come on. You can't say no. Just think about all those juicy records and you get to be the first in history to read them.*" She knew Torin would never pass up the idea of gaining new knowledge, especially something so historically significant.

"*This is true. It's too good to pass up, and we don't exactly have a choice.*"

"*Maybe I can help you start a Vlog. We could call it 'The Prophet Torin.' It has a nice ring to it.*" She swore she felt him send an eye roll in her direction.

Torin cleared his throat. "I promise we will spread the word."

Nabu smiled to himself. "I flew to many places. Civilization has expanded far beyond Enki and Ninhursag's dreams. You have grown beyond the magic of the gods. I will be glad to share this news with my kin."

"I'm sure they will enjoy it," Torin said.

*"They could do with some new stories,"* he said in Azalea's head. Azalea smiled and nodded.

"Very well. We will exchange records, and I will accompany you to the gate for my return."

Torin and Azalea found as many relevant history and mythology books as they could carry on trolleys, plus an old laptop and a hard drive filled with documentaries and records from the digital archives, and wheeled them back down to the sleeping dragon. The museum seemed lax on security, though she suspected Nabu might have something to do with that.

Nabu placed the books and computer into a seemingly bottomless leather bag, strapped it to the sleeping dragon, and handed Torin a tanned leather book.

"I bestow this chronicle of the gods to you, Mage Torin Dumont of the House of Ravens. As keeper of this tome, do you swear to spread the truth of the true gods, the Anunnaki, to the people of your land?" Nabu said.

"I swear it, and I thank you for trusting me with this honor."

"Very good," Nabu clapped his hands together, in a much better mood. "We will travel by dragon-back."

"Really!" Azalea bounced on her heels.

Torin's face dropped. "It's fine, we can travel by Hollow."

"Nonsense. It would be our honor." Nabu seemed excited by the fact, too. The dragon let out a long yawn and sneezed.

Torin had no choice but to follow Azalea over to the dragon. She was not passing up this opportunity. The dragon blinked slowly and stretched out its front legs, its long body uncoiled, and it straightened out, carefully walking its feet backward, to not knock anything over.

She opened her backpack for Faraday to climb into, and she put it on her front to keep an eye on him.

Nabu helped her onto the dragon, and Torin settled behind her, wrapping his arms around her. She leaned into his chest, and he kissed the top of her head. She knew how nervous he was, but he didn't show it, and she couldn't feel a hint of it.

Sita opted to sit in front of her and grip the same giant back spine.

"We are ready Mushussu," Nabu spoke to the dragon, and it crouched on its back legs like a spring, staring up at the ceiling that now seemed very close.

Azalea held her breath, and with a snap, they disappeared.

# Chapter 42

Azalea let out a whoop as the dragon appeared high in the sky and took a dive through a cloud that looked fluffy but was very wet. They raced toward the ground. Torin's grip on her waist was so tight she could hardly breathe, but she didn't try to move him.

She glanced back to see his eyes were squeezed shut, and every muscle was tense. A shame because he couldn't see the beauty of the rocky landscape below as they dove closer to the ground. The beam of red and green light in the distance shone like a beacon spiking high into the sky.

Nabu sat close to the head of the dragon, his legs gripping the rainbow scales and his hands relaxed on the white mane that circled the dragon's neck silently guiding the dragon toward the light.

Their flight path flattened out closer to the ground, and Torin's grip on her eased. A camp city was set up all around the gate. Tiny people down below pointed to them in the sky, and Azalea waved at them as they flew past. Might as well make a grand entrance. After all, how often did one get to ride in on a rainbow dragon?

It was over all too soon. The Mushussu dragon flew straight toward the light beam and circled the space around the mono-liths of the gate making the area seem a whole lot smaller and a little too close to the beam of magic for Azalea's liking, but they glided to a stop, and the dragon's legs folded underneath it, so its belly rested in the sand.

"Thank fuck for that," Torin mumbled.

"Come on, that was amazing!" Azalea said as Nabu jumped off in front of them.

Azalea lowered her bag to the ground. Faraday jumped out, and Sita flew off the dragon, a little more crooked in his flight than usual.

"I should have liked to stay and see more of what this world has become." Nabu sulked, hopefully not regretting his decision enough to stay.

House of Raven guards filed into the circular space surrounding the two T-shaped monoliths that the blazing light drove skyward from. The guards were armed with elemers and shields made of living shadows.

Azalea grabbed Torin's hand without question and raised it toward the largest grouping of guards near the stone-walled entrance to the gate area. The light pooled in Azalea's stomach, and without any effort, it joined with Torin's and exploded out in a convergence of magic. She was prepared for the recoil this time and braced herself as the return of magic surged into her and recharged her. Now that she knew what it was, she could handle it. Though she was confident she could do this magic alone now, it was enhanced and more controlled when combined with Torin's.

*"Nice one,"* he said in her mind.

*"Worth sealing the bond? No regrets?"*

*"No regrets."* He spun them around and blasted light at the guards coming from the other side of the circular space. The guards fell instantly, and their magic rushed into Azalea and

Torin. Her head swirled with new power symbols, stolen from the heads of the mages who now lay scattered across the sand. She didn't think they were dead, just drained of magic. Hopefully.

She let go of Torin's hand and hit him on the arm. "Good. It's too late for regrets."

He laughed and put his arm around her as the other guards scattered down the stone hallways that branched off the sides.

"Aren't you two just full of surprises? I didn't even have to lift a finger." Nabu leaned on the dragon lazily. It was clear he wouldn't have lifted a finger even if they had needed it.

"Are you able to communicate with Ereshkigal and Inanna via the dragon?" Torin asked.

Nabu studied his fingernails. "I am."

"Will you please request that they come to the gate to close it?" Torin gritted his teeth.

"Certainly."

They all stood there. Nabu didn't move. Azalea shuffled between her feet, impatient for something to happen and uneasy with the roar of the gate continuing above them. She stayed away from the stone platform beneath the gate. All she saw when she looked at it was the memory of Erik's body lying there, so still.

"*Do you think he did it?*" she spoke in her mind to Torin.

"*Be patient,*" he said, but he looked just as tense as her.

"*I certainly prefer this to feeling each other's emotions.*" She tried to lighten the mood. Her mind was less cloudy, more focused.

"*Same here.*" Torin turned to look at her, and they stared at each other like weirdos as they mind-spoke.

*"We shouldn't have waited,"* Azalea admitted, feeling a glow rise on her face.

Torin ran his thumb over her cheek. *"You were worth the wait."*

*"So cheesy."* She shook her head.

The light was blocked out for a moment as a dark shadow descended from the sky. The blur materialized into a black dragon, and from the dragon dropped Ereshkigal, her wings spread wide, black as the Eridan river. The dragon and the woman landed at the same time on the other side of the Echo Dimension gate. The dragon padded around on its scaled legs until it was face-to-face with the Mushussu dragon. They greeted each other with friendly snuffles, no doubt speaking mind-to-mind, and the black dragon gave the rainbow one a lick with its long tongue, then rested in front of it with its face on its paws.

They were adorable. Azalea couldn't help but be jealous of Jade for a moment with her dragon egg.

"You dared to leave the Shadow Dimension without my permission?" Ereshkigal's voice boomed over the sound of the gate.

Azalea swallowed but held up her wrist to show the break in the gold band tattoo. "You were the one who broke our agreement."

She felt Torin tense beside her.

"How did you get out?" the goddess asked with genuine curiosity on her face.

"We borrowed a dragon's egg," Azalea said terrified.

Instead of yelling, Ereshkigal just shook her head. "To think I could trust mortals, to gift you my powers, and this is how I am repaid. It seems I have no need to close the gateway."

"Wait!" Azalea called.

Ereshkigal strode toward her dragon, but Nabu caught her arm.

"No greeting for me, sweet Ereshkigal?" Nabu crooned.

She straightened and brushed off his hand. "Nabu. I did not expect to see you here. This is not your dragon."

"It is not. But I am aiding these strange humans in their quest. I will return home, and you will close the gate. That is what was agreed."

"It seems agreements mean nothing to these mortals."

"From what I understand, it was you who broke the contract, and might I add that if we do not close the gateway, Enlil will find a way to destroy this world."

"He is contained. Inanna ensured it."

"For now. But he will escape, and when he does, and this world ends, those spirits will not go to the Shadow Dimension. Most will disappear out of your grasp forever, and then there will be no more."

"I do not forget betrayal." Ereshkigal shot a death look at Azalea and made one sweep of her wings to propel herself back onto the dragon.

"Please wait. I'll fulfill my end of the deal; I'll get the spirits and go back with you." Azalea's heart thundered in her chest.

"*No!*" Torin's voice echoed in her mind.

"*The gods only granted her leave in the mortal world if she closed the gate. She has to do it, or she won't get any more spirits. We both have to do this,*" Azalea said to Torin.

He shook his head. "*Just be careful.*"

Azalea took two steps toward Ereshkigal and the black dragon. "We accepted your soul bond and wanted to thank you."

Ereshkigal turned back and studied them. "You did, I see."

Azalea pressed her fists into her sides.

"Please, we need to close the gate!" Azalea yelled over the howling magic.

Ereshkigal sat astride her dragon, her back straight, her wings still spread wide. "You will return the dragon's egg."

"I don't have it here." Azalea held her hands out.

"I will close the gate; we will retrieve the dragon's egg."

Azalea swallowed. She had to be careful here. "No. You broke our agreement because you are killing people to get spirits. That is exactly what I didn't want to happen."

"It is the fastest way."

"No, it isn't. You have me now. After you close the gate, let me stay a little longer, and I will collect more spirits, then I will go willingly with you."

Ereshkigal continued to glare at her. It was impossible to tell what she was thinking.

Torin spun Azalea around to face him. "No Azalea. Think about what you are agreeing to. You can still get out of this deal. This is your chance."

"Not if we want the gate closed, it isn't. You know as well as I do this is the only way. I'm not going to be blamed for upsetting the balance of magic again." She reached up on her toes and kissed him softly. His eyes were filled with fear, and she was glad she couldn't feel it.

Azalea turned back. Ereshkigal's eyes narrowed, and a thin smile tightened her lips as if she had already won.

"I will close the gate, and you will return to the Shadow Dimension with me after one cycle of the moon," Ereshkigal said. "You will accompany me to gather spirits."

Azalea's heart raced. This was probably as good as it was going to get. She hated that she would have to take the dragon's egg from Jade but had expected this from the moment they took it.

She also didn't mention that she and Torin were facing incarceration for their soul bond. Perhaps the goddess could help them out of that bind if she needed her assistance so desperately.

"Demon, write down the new terms." Coils of Shadow Magic reached from Ereshkigal's fingers into the leather bag strapped to her dragon and recoiled with parchment and a quill to deposit in Sita's tiny hands.

Azalea trusted Sita but knew he wouldn't be able to get out of this a second time.

"Azalea, think this through. We can find another way," Torin said.

Ereshkigal loomed over them. "There is no other way. She is lucky I need her. Otherwise, she would be dead and in the Shadow Dimension already. You should be more grateful, Raven Mage."

Torin's arm fell protectively around Azalea's shoulders. "Your *gift* has cursed us both. Her time in this world will be spent locked up because of you, as will mine."

"I expect with those sorts of powers no prison will hold you, unless you wish it to."

"I don't wish to be fighting and running my whole life and missing Azalea for half of it."

"We all make our own futures, Raven Mage." Ereshkigal closed her eyes for a brief moment. "Inanna is on the other side."

"Is that a hint for me to leave?" Nabu said.

"It is an order to leave. I suggest you follow it. Demon, bring the contract to sign."

Nabu didn't move from his spot, but Sita rushed over with the contract. Ereshkigal signed it with the blood quill straight away. Azalea did her best to skim-read it, and it seemed fine. She ignored Torin's protests and sucked in a breath as the quill took her blood, and she signed her life away. Torin dug into Azalea's bag and handed over the relics to Ereshkigal to close the gate, and without ceremony, she used shadows to slot them into their depressions in the giant stones.

Azalea's chest was tight, but she knew it was the right thing. Her wrist stung, and the tattoo instantly bound together in a solid gold band once more.

She sucked in a deep breath and turned toward Torin, hoping he would understand. But what she saw made her heart plummet. The thundering gateway of magic had masked the footsteps of the army surrounding them. Rows of soldiers dressed in army uniforms appeared on top of the surrounding circular wall and at every exit to the sandy arena.

Azalea froze as guns pointed at them from every possible direction. A low growl came from one of the dragons, and Ereshkigal rose into flight, looking down on the army.

"You dare attack your goddess!" Her voice boomed louder than a megaphone across the ruins.

To the soldiers' credit, they stood their ground while probably pissing themselves. None of them spoke.

"Return through the Hollow now, and I will show mercy," Ereshkigal said.

"FIRE!" a soldier yelled.

The air exploded in a cascade of bullets and raining shells. Azalea ducked, and Torin's arms fell over her protectively. But they weren't aiming at them. Ereshkigal let out a scream that sliced through the air like a knife.

Azalea looked up. "No!" she cried as bullets struck the goddess from every direction, tearing through her body and leathery wings.

Azalea stood up, rage consuming her as she blasted white light at any soldier she could see. Because they weren't using magic, none came back on her, but the light was enough to blast them off the wall. Torin did the same beside her.

Nabu roared in anger, his golden hair glowing, but it seemed he had no power here. He launched rocks with super speed at the soldiers. The dragons seemed stunned at first, but silently rose and sent bursts of fire from their mouths at the soldiers on ground level as they tried to scramble back through the narrow stone corridors.

It was all over in seconds, though it felt much longer. Ereshkigal gave an laborious flap of her wings, then tumbled to the sand below. Azalea rushed over to her.

Deep vermilion blood seeped from the bullet holes littering her body. Nabu kicked aside several dead men, and Torin propped the goddess up against the wall. Azalea held back the need to vomit at the sight of blood and bodies all crispy and strewn across the ground.

Nabu adjusted Ereshkigal's crown and ran his hand over her cheek. "Ereshkigal, speak to me. You will not let these humans have the satisfaction of harming you. Look, we have killed them all. These two servants are loyal to you."

"Go now, Nabu; there is no time. I will shut the gate before my body fails. It is too weak in this realm to heal," Ereshkigal said, her voice faint.

"Very well." He stood up. "I will hold conference with Zakar for updates on your progress, Mage Torin Dumont. Do not let me down. The world must know of the gods once more."

"I will not let you down." Torin nodded, his face streaked with sweat and sand.

Without a word of goodbye, Nabu mounted the rainbow dragon and flew high into the sky, then dove back down and disappeared through the gate of light.

Azalea's hands were sticky with blood, immortal goddess blood, though she didn't seem so immortal right now. Her pale skin had paled even further. She gripped Azalea with her metal hand. It was cold but surprisingly soft.

"We must do this now," Ereshkigal wheezed.

Power rushed through Azalea. A blinding flash behind her eyes forced her to squeeze them shut. Azalea doubled over as pain flooded her body. It felt like gravity had been turned up and she was being pulled into the ground like an extreme electromagnet.

The gravity switched off, but it felt like her head was spinning in a particle accelerator. She tasted blood as she bit her lip or her tongue as her jaw clenched down and every muscle in her body was electric with energy and pain.

Warmth flooded her, and she flopped over, falling onto a warm body. She felt his magic soothing her and knew it was Torin.

"Azalea, open your eyes." Was she back at the Tower? Because that was Torin's teacher's voice. Why did he love ordering her about so much?

She groaned and opened her eyes. There was silence. She sucked in a deep breath of air that smelled of dust and electricity. But there was no light anymore, no gateway to another dimension, just two giant T-shaped standing stones in a pit of old stone walls.

"She did it," Azalea breathed. She sat bolt upright, gripping Torin's arms that were supporting her. Ereshkigal lay unmoving on the stone between the monoliths, exactly where Erik had died. Around her lay the jade relics that had fallen from their place in the gate.

Torin helped her up, and they rushed over to the goddess. On the other side, her dragon padded over and licked her face.

"She's still breathing. I think she used us to ground the gate back to this world." Torin lifted his hand from her neck.

Azalea knew the goddess was still alive because the glow of purple magic still surrounded her, but it was no longer a vibrant cloud of power, just a faint film that barely covered her.

"Let's get her on the dragon," Azalea said.

"No." Sita appeared from wherever he had been hiding. "The dragon can carry her with its feet. It will be safer."

Torin didn't argue, but grabbed all the relics and shoved them in Azalea's bag. They moved the goddess in front of the dragon, and he licked her and made a purring sound over her.

"You okay?" Torin said as Azalea stepped back.

"I'm great." She grinned at him. "Look Torin, we did it. The gate is closed. We actually did it."

Torin stood there stunned for a second, as if he hadn't realized either.

"We did it!" He picked her up and spun her around. Her lips fell to his so naturally, and he kissed her with an almost giddiness.

He put her down, both equally reluctant, it seemed, but they had a goddess to save.

"Let's take her to Maiken," Azalea said.

# Chapter 43

Fabian swung open the front doors and barreled out onto the driveway. The old Land Rover crawled up the gravel. Too slow.

He took in a shaky breath, waiting for the vehicle to stop. He spotted her bright eyes through the back window and threw the door open.

"Oh, Cassie." He pulled her into a hug before she could even get out. "I'm so sorry." He didn't want to let her go. It was a miracle she'd made it back to him at all, not that he wanted to share those fears with anyone. But in the hands of Korbyn, he was ashamed to say he had expected it.

"All right, sir, give her some space. Let the poor thing out. Mary will want to be seeing her, no doubt." Colin grinned and pried Fabian off Cassie.

Cassie smiled, not looking too traumatized by her ordeal. "I'm glad you missed me."

"Course I did." Fabian stepped back from the car.

"Righto, easy now, love," Colin said as he lifted his daughter out, and Fabian saw her leg in a cast.

"What did they do to you?" Fabian growled.

"Oh, this? I fell out of the tree when I was trying to escape them. But Mage Hawkins has been looking after me very well.

You needn't have worried." Cassie tried to wave a hand from her crutch.

The door slammed on the other side, and Maiken walked around the back of the car.

"Hello Fabian." She smiled, but her eyes lacked their usual fierceness, and she walked with an aura of exhaustion around her.

"Maiken, you're a sight for sore eyes." He kissed her on the cheek and pulled her into a hug. Something about being away had made him a lot more inclined to hugging. "Gods, Danni and the girls are going to be so happy to see you."

Maiken's eyes lit up. "Speaking of which, where might I find them?"

"I'll send someone to get them, but first let's get you out of this damp and next to a fire. I'm afraid time is of the essence, and I need you both the tell me everything you can about the Tower of London and what's been going on."

"Of course," Maiken said.

Colin beamed as Cassie swung her way inside, a little too quickly, on the crutches. She was always overzealous with everything she did. But seemed in good spirits and more than happy to be home. Hopefully, that meant Korbyn hadn't found out about her. It seemed like now might be the time to tell her the truth.

Mary met them on the way in the door, screeched with glee when she saw Cassie, and bundled her into a protective hug.

"I'm fine, mum. It's just a broken leg."

"Oh, my poor angel! My sweet lamb. We'll make sure that horrible man never finds you again," Mary said with tears streaming down her cheeks.

Colin put an arm around his wife and Cassie. Fabian's chest grew tight seeing them together.

"How in heavens did you get back, my love?" Mary stroked Cassie's cheeks, and she batted her mother's hands away.

"Stop fussing, mum. It was Azalea and Torin, they rescued us! It was amazing. They took down all the guards by themselves and took us in the Hollow and dropped us off here."

"Did they now?" Fabian smiled to himself. Once Azalea finished her training, she would be a force to be reckoned with, the type of mage the House of Snakes desperately needed, and his heart swelled, knowing he'd helped set her on that path.

Once in the drawing room, they situated themselves on the three large couches that faced the fire in a U-shape. Maiken stared at the doorway, her hands wringing in her lap. Without seeing them, Fabian knew the moment Danni and the girls arrived. The lines of stress on Maiken's forehead smoothed out, and an enormous smile lit up her face.

"Mum!" the girls squealed in unison as they ran into the room and jumped onto the couch.

Maiken pulled them into a hug, but her eyes tracked a slightly more composed Danni hustling toward her. "Gods, Maiken, I was so worried about you."

"I'm alright." Surrounded by her family, Maiken looked more like herself. "They needed me there, but I'm glad to be back with you."

Danni sat next to her with her arm over Maiken's shoulders. "So what's Korbyn up to?"

Between Maiken and Cassie, they got snippets of information about what was going on inside the Tower, but not nearly enough to be useful.

None of it mattered, though. Maiken didn't have any new information to share, and as glad as he was that they'd made it out safely, Korbyn would be pissed off enough to attack them. Soon. All Fabian could do was hope he'd be ready.

Cassie slumped against the couch. She shook her head every time her eyelids drooped, and Maiken didn't look much better with her head resting on Danni's shoulders.

Fabian clapped his hands together. "We're not going to solve the world's problems today. Why don't you two get some rest?" He rubbed his jaw. "Danni, would you mind getting Rowena for me?"

Fabian stared at the flames dancing in the fireplace. He'd seen firsthand what lengths Korbyn would go to, and he didn't want any of the people sheltering here to be subjected to his wrath, but with so many of his prisoners having escaped, Fabian knew Korbyn would be out for blood. He wouldn't stop, and Fabian wasn't sure if he could win a battle between the two of them.

A pat on his shoulder snapped him out of his daze. He turned to find Rowena studying him. "You need to get some rest."

"I can't. Hell is about to rain down on us." He waved his arm toward the couches and Rowena sat across from him. "Azalea and Torin escaped."

Her lips twitched, settling in a smug grin, almost like she knew he'd helped them.

"Then they were captured by Kira." He'd seen Kat play the part of double-agent so well through the years. He hoped they could trust Kira, that she'd captured them to help free Cassie, but how could he know for sure? "But they escaped with Maiken and Cassie."

"Where are they now?" Rowena tapped a finger to her lips.

He shrugged. "Only the gods know."

"They'll do what's right." She nodded. "Don't you worry that pretty head of yours."

Fabian shook his head at the absurdity of a Dumont doing what was right. He just hoped Azalea would be okay.

"Well." Rowena stood. "I guess we best prepare for war."

After a meeting with his most trusted mages and the makeshift warriors, he sent people to the camp to warn everyone and to evacuate anyone not prepared to fight into the cellar rooms under the manor.

He paced the floor, hoping it would be enough, hoping these people would survive this. The room felt like it was closing in on him. He needed fresh air, and the healers needed to be prepared for more casualties.

The cool air cleared his head as he strode into the healer's ger. "Maiken, what are you doing here? I sent you to get some rest."

"They need me." She stood by a stretcher, looking down at the man on it.

Fabian clenched his fists. Would no one do what he said? "Van has this under control." Saying the words out loud, he realized how unbelievable they were. Van's eyes had been red for days with veins spider-webbing around them. "You should be—"

"The sky! Look at the sky!"

Fabian raced out, followed by Van, Maiken, and for some reason Azalea's friend Isaac, who was not a healer and had no magic to speak of.

"They did it!" Van squealed and threw herself on Isaac.

"They did!" Isaac kissed her, and they jumped around in circles, holding hands like little kids.

Maiken was beaming. "Can you believe it, Fabian?"

"No, I cannot." He looked up, and a glimmer of hope burned in his chest. *They had done it.*

He wiped his eye as Danni sprinted down the hill toward the camp, pointing at the sky. "Did you see it?!" She threw herself on Maiken. "Can I use my magic again?"

"No!" Maiken pulled back, horrified. "There are still high levels of Echo Magic in the air, until it can be cleared somehow, it won't be safe."

"Oh, but the tree. I thought—"

"We still have to grow it," Fabian said, unable to pull his eyes away from the clearing sky.

"No, I saw it. Rowena and Leda planted it out back beside the cemetery. It's as tall as a hundred-year-old oak," Danni said as if they should already know that.

"What tree?" Maiken asked, looking at them as if they were all crazy.

"The one from the seeds Fabian, Kat, and Torin bought back from the Echo Dimension. It absorbs and rebalances Echo Magic."

They all continued to look up at the sky in awe. White and gray clouds amassed like they had always been there, no sign of the red or green eerie light, though a few dark silhouettes still cut through the clouds.

"Yes, we were gifted it by the goddess Ninhursag." Fabian shrugged and let the corner of a smile creep to his lip. "You know, because I'm that good."

Danni snorted with a half laugh.

"You actually went to the Echo Dimension and made it back!" Maiken looked appropriately impressed.

He put an arm around her shoulder. "Oh, the tales I have to tell you." He couldn't help but grin. Things were looking like they were working.

"Azalea and Torin must have found Nabu. You should call off the trackers Fabian. We need everyone back here." Danni squeezed him out and put her arm around Maiken's waist.

"Very well." He raised his eyebrows and took his phone out. The truth was, he'd called the trackers back not long after he'd sent them out for show.

"It's even more certain Korbyn and the Archmage are going to come after us now, you realize. They've lost their prisoners and the upper hand with the gate." Danni slid into her PJU persona effortlessly.

"I am well aware," Fabian answered.

Rowena power-marched down the hill, puffing as she stopped in front of them, hands on hips. "I take it you noticed the sky? I checked, and it's safe to use Echo Magic here."

"Really!" Danni didn't even wait. She whipped out her elemer and summoned a fireball into her hand.

Everyone else ducked, probably expecting it to blow up or for her to burn out.

Rowena frowned. "Yes, well, that looks safe. I was going to add that it will take a while to spread beyond these grounds, so for now, we can only use Echo Magic here."

"Spread the word we can use Echo Magic but only within the grounds," Fabian said into his walkie-talkie.

"Things are looking up." Rowena looked very pleased to have her elemer back in hand.

Fabian stared into the distance. "Yes, but I have a bad feeling about what's coming."

"Oh, stop being a party pooper." Danni ruffled his hair, and he smoothed it back again.

"Just trying to be realistic, love." He turned and glared at a guard, looking a little too relaxed. "Back to work people!" he yelled and felt better.

)))●((( 

An hour later, people were still running around like headless chooks. He was back up at the house when the alarm at the front gate sounded.

A spear of ice shot through Fabian's heart. This wasn't enough time. They weren't prepared.

The radio at his hip blared to life. "Gatehouse to Blackbourne. Enemy in sight." A pause with a heavy breath, then more static. "Mate, it's the army. They've got fucking tanks and everything." The man's voice trembled.

"Shit." Fabian ran a hand over his slicked-back hair. This was it. "Copy that."

He grabbed the binoculars and raced upstairs to Danni's bedroom which overlooked the front of the estate. The guard was right. It was the actual fucking army—as in the British Army, not Korbyn's.

He got on the radio again. "Make sure everyone is evacuated underground."

They must have been brainwashed by House of Owls magic.

He just had to pray the wards held. In here, they were safe.

An explosion rattled the windows as a cannon fired. Fabian gripped his chest. He would feel every hit the wards took.

# Chapter 44

It was black for a moment, then Ereshkigal's dragon which they sat upon appeared in the sky amid drizzling rain. Azalea covered her eyes and clutched the jet-black spine in front of her. Faraday and Sita were tucked safely in her bag, and Torin's arms wrapped around her, also gripping the spine. She felt secure in her seat, and as they dove, she screamed in delight.

Torin's forehead pressed into her shoulder. "Gods help us," he muttered.

Azalea glanced over the side of the dragon, trying to see where they were. She caught a glimpse of a white turret of Blackbourne Manor, then got her bearings and saw the gers spread in perfect rows across the lawn.

"Down where those gers are if it's okay!" she yelled to the dragon, hoping it understood her. They descended slowly, as if the dragon was checking it was safe.

BOOM! An explosion came from directly below them. The dome of the shield over the estate flared with light. At the point of impact, fractures of silver sparked and spread across the dome like shattering glass.

Azalea jerked her head to the other side of the dragon to see chaos at the gates. A tank fired at the house. Another explosion and the shield crackled with fractures again. This time, some of them stayed visible.

Not good.

"What was that?" Torin squeezed Azalea's middle.

"It looks like an army at the gates. They've got tanks and trucks and everything." Azalea could hardly believe it herself. If that was Korbyn, he had gained a lot of supporters very quickly.

Torin, apparently forgetting his fear for the moment, looked over the side of the dragon as they effortlessly slipped through the blood wards of the shield and headed for the tents.

They flew between the rows of gers on the makeshift boardwalk and hovered as the dragon gently lowered Ereshkigal onto the wet ground, then flew over her and landed so Azalea and Torin could get off.

"Thank you." Azalea kissed the dragon on its black furry cheek, and it let out a huff of smoke, curled up around the edge of a ger with its head on the path, and began purring again. It seemed dragons tired easily, or this one just trusted them to help its master.

"Maiken!" Torin bellowed.

Maiken was already out the door, followed by Van and Isaac. Ereshkigal lay on the ground with her wings spread wide, her black dress twisted around her with a serene expression on her face that made her look like a dark angel that had collapsed from the sky.

"Oh my word," Maiken exclaimed but kneeled immediately to feel the goddess's pulse. "She's alive. Help me get her inside."

Isaac and Van rushed over and hugged Azalea at the same time.

"Is that a goddess?" Van asked, pulling away, her eyes wide with awe.

"Yes. It's Ereshkigal. We need to warn Jade in case she wakes up. She wants to take the dragon egg. Where is Jade?" Azalea looked around. The camp was empty.

"Jade's gone under the house with everyone else who evacuated. If you haven't noticed, we are under attack." Isaac looked torn between terrified and excited.

"Why aren't you two down there?" Azalea asked.

"We volunteered to be medics," Isaac said.

"What can I do?"

"You can go join your mother and the others under the house, young lady." RoRo marched toward them on the board walk.

"RoRo!" She ran toward her grandmother and hugged her. "But I want to help. We closed the gate!"

"I see that, dear. Well done. I knew you would." She pinched Azalea's cheek, did a double take when she spotted the dragon, but didn't say anything, just poked her head in the orange door of the ger. "Welcome back, Torin, dear. Is that the goddess?"

"Yes. She got shot up pretty bad," Torin called out.

Azalea stepped inside, followed by Van and Isaac, who leaned against an empty bed.

Azalea swallowed back a sick feeling. This reminded her so much of her first day at the Tower of London. It seemed so long ago when Maiken had requested she see the effects of burnout and watched Erik lying there writhing in pain. This was no less disturbing.

The goddess lay so still and silent on the small table while blood leaked out of her, dripping down the side and all over the floor.

Still, it was the same as before; Maiken stood on one side of her and Torin on the other. He didn't need to hold her down with shadow ropes, but he and Maiken held their hands and elemers over her, and a warm light spread over the goddess's chest.

Azalea didn't know what this magic was; Torin hadn't taught her. But she could see the colors spiraling around each other doing something to the goddess's body. Whatever it was, the bullets popped out. Maiken's eyes squeezed shut as the blood flow slowed and then stopped.

"That wasn't too bad." Maiken took a step back, looking dizzy, but quickly recovered. "She should wake up soon."

"She shut the gate for us. Even after she got shot, she kept her word," Azalea said quietly to no one in particular. She hadn't realized how worried she had been about the goddess until that moment. Surely she couldn't die, but even so, the experience couldn't be pleasant for her.

*"Don't worry. She'll be fine,"* Torin said in her mind.

*"I know."* She smiled, then realized Van was staring at her, grinning.

"You seem different. I wonder why that would be?" Van whispered and nudged her in the side. "Everyone knows about you and Torin. You don't need to keep pretending."

"You don't know the half of it, and a lot of people are not happy, so we aren't going to make a show if it," she hissed, trying to keep her voice low in the quiet ger.

"You need to tell me! Come on, there might not be time later," Van pleaded.

Azalea dragged Van out the door and down the path away from other people. Fortunately, the rain had stopped; now everything smelled like mud and other farmy smells.

"I can't believe you kept all this from me! A soul bond." She whacked Azalea in the arm. "You sly devil, going after your teacher."

"I didn't go after him, Van, you know that." Azalea rubbed her temples.

"Can't say I'm surprised. I knew it from the start," Van said, clearly not listening.

"No you didn't." Azalea's hands went to her hips.

Van smirked, pleased with herself. "Ever since that Saturday night when you were 'studying' at his place. I knew."

Azalea flinched as another explosion hit the wards. "Nothing was going on then."

"But there certainly is now. I can see it all over your face." Van waved her hands in front of Azalea.

Azalea's cheeks heated, and she bit her lip to stop herself from smiling and giving Van the satisfaction.

Fortunately —or unfortunately— a deafening explosion interrupted them. The shield crackled, then shattered with an earsplitting crash, followed by a blast that shook the ground. Azalea raced up the path. The left corner of the manor where the swimming pool was had been hit, crumpling like a deck of cards into a pile of smoking stone.

"They're in!" Azalea yelled.

"Azalea, get under the house while you still can," RoRo ordered.

"Where are you going?" She grabbed RoRo's arm, not wanting her to leave.

Her grandmother's eyes went dark. "I'm going to fight."

Azalea knew better than to say she was as well, but she had a new idea. She let RoRo kiss her on the forehead and watched as she marched off.

Rushing into the ger, she nearly banged into Torin. She led him outside and toward the dragon, where no one would hear.

"We can undo the magic on the army. If we use our light powers, maybe it will take away the mind control," Azalea blurted out.

"Good thinking. It's possible and worth a try." Torin gripped her arm. "Just stay away from my father. Promise me that."

"I promise." She had no intention of going anywhere near that man.

Torin leaned down and kissed her, sending a kaleidoscope of butterflies through her stomach. They were in front of people! He didn't even care he was kissing her.

She was still in a daze when he pulled away.

"I know I should be more scared. Is it wrong that I'm also really happy?" she said, unable to stop smiling.

"Same." A smile tweaked at the corner of his mouth, and he stared at her lips as if he wanted more. "They'll be plenty of time for this later."

"If we don't die or get locked up." She looked down.

"Hey, you're supposed to be the optimist, not me." He held her chin and gave her one last kiss. She was left speechless and felt the eyes of people around them watching.

"Come on Mageling, let's go take down an army." He put his arm around her and guided her back to the healer's ger.

Azalea glanced back at the dragon as Faraday trotted up. "You stay here with the dragon," she ordered. Hopefully, they would be safe there together.

Torin poked his head in the door. "If Ereshkigal wakes up, tell her we will be back. Don't let her go looking for the dragon's egg."

"I'm not sure we'll have a say in that." Maiken eyed the goddess warily.

Isaac and Van stood on the path, Isaac looking particularly terrified at the thought. Van grabbed her hand. "You two look so right together! I'm happy for you." She pulled Azalea into yet another hug.

"She's right, Zaels. I'm happy for you too." Isaac grinned.

Azalea blushed; she'd been doing that a lot in the last day. "Thanks. Be safe, okay?"

Another explosion hit the house. Hopefully, everyone was safe underground. Fabian would have made sure of it.

"Come on, it's now or never." Torin took her hand as he walked past, and she fell into step with him.

"Bye guys! See you soon." Her heart pumped with adrenaline as they headed for the front line.

# Chapter 45

They neared the front gate, and the yelling intensified. Blasts sounded in the distance, and Azalea flinched with every hit, imagining the house collapsing into nothing with every sound.

"It's going to take us too long to walk there, and it's too open. What if we go into the Hollow and into the forest? The wards are down now." Torin's steps slowed. "Plus, we need to see if our magic is going to work on reversing whatever is wrong with the army."

"What if it isn't magic?" Azalea chewed on her lip.

"It has to be. Her Majesty's Armed Forces do not have any affiliation with the magical community. It just isn't possible."

"Okay, let's sneak a few soldiers off and test it on them before we start blasting people."

"Agreed, but I'm going to tell Kira to meet us near the gates soon." Torin slipped his phone out of his pocket and started typing.

"Why? I don't trust her." Azalea clenched her jaw.

Torin frowned at the phone. "*I* trust her. She helped us escape, didn't she? And we needed to get into the Tower of London, anyway."

"I suppose. Though she did poison us as well..." Azalea added. Something about Kira made her uneasy.

"We need to know what we're getting into." Torin slipped his phone back into his pocket.

Azalea inhaled slowly. "I said it's fine."

Torin cut into the Hollow, and Azalea cut out in the forest at a safe distance from the road. She followed Torin's lead, trying to keep her footsteps as silent as his as they neared a group of soldiers standing by a line of army trucks.

*"I can see it on them. A trace of Owl magic."* It was gold and white, just like House of Owls' colors, and it was the same on all of them.

*"You can see it?"* Torin studied her face.

She nodded. Sure of it. *"Yes. Ereshkigal's magic."*

*"I wondered what you were going on about with the colors before."* Torin frowned at her.

She hadn't meant it to be a secret, but she hadn't explained it either. *"Sorry, there's been a lot going on. Let's distract them with shadows, then pick a few off."*

*"Those two, at the end."* Torin was already moving down the tree line to two soldiers blocked from the other's sight.

Azalea sent out tendrils of shadows like vines that crept along the grounds. The movement caught one man's attention. She reeled them back into the forest like a slow fishing lure. The men spotted the strange phenomenon and didn't hesitate to follow it into the woods. It was clear they knew nothing about magic.

Torin signaled her to keep moving back, and she led the men through the trees on a rough track until they were out of sight and hopefully out of earshot, muffled by the thickening undergrowth of brambles.

Shadow ropes shot from Torin's elemer and bound the men faster than Azalea could even summon the power symbols in her mind.

Torin nodded to Azalea. "Do it now."

Azalea's heart raced, and her palm warmed as the light magic drew into her hand. She shot the blast of light at both men, and they slumped to the forest floor.

Azalea let out a shaky breath. "Not much recoil, but it felt like it took something from them, and they aren't glowing now."

"Good. Looks like the Owls' mind control." Torin was scarily calm and focused.

"That was rather easy. I don't think it will be hard to do more of them."

"Only one way to find out." Torin strode onto the path, and Azalea raced to keep up with him.

They walked for ten minutes in the direction of the house, remaining hidden in the trees. Azalea followed Torin's lead when he summoned a shadow cloak around him, then crept through the thinning growth to the edge of the woods. Even when she couldn't see him, she knew exactly where he was.

They crouched behind a fallen log covered in colorful mushrooms.

"Holy crap," Azalea said as she took in the sheer number of people filtering into the estate, glad they were well hidden.

"We'll need an amplifying spell. Have you learned any power symbols like that?"

"Nope." Azalea shook her head, suddenly not liking this plan quite so much. Even the power symbols she had stolen from others with the new magic had slipped her mind. The gift of borrowing powers only seemed to be a temporary effect.

He took her hand, and she couldn't help but jump.

"*Like this,*" he said in her head, and a wavy image came into focus.

She closed her eyes and tried to make out the symbol in her mind. It was like in a circuit, a triangle with lines coming out, plus a few extra lines like sun rays.

"I got it," Azalea said aloud, and Torin confirmed it was the right symbol. *"I think we're getting better at this."*

She felt all of Torin's focus was on the lines of soldiers in front of them. *"We need to be experts, first time round."*

They watched for several more minutes.

The gates had been blasted down with some sort of giant guns on turrets with wheels. Korbyn stood next to the turret, screaming at someone. Like full on yelling, then his victim, one of his own men, was in the air being held up and strangled by shadows right in front of everyone.

The army faced forward, and it seemed all the mages were inside the gates at the front, watching the house falling and waiting for Korbyn or the Archmage to give orders.

Fabian and his defensive force had set up barricades halfway up the driveway. Giant walls of earth protruded from the ground. RoRo was behind there along with Danni. She hoped they knew what they were getting into.

Korbyn threw the man to the ground with his shadow ropes, and Azalea turned away, not wanting to see the man hitting the earth.

Kira walked out of the fallen gate as if she were on a mission and crossed the bridge to their side, following the creek toward them.

Torin let out a bird call that Kira seemed to recognize. She changed her course, walking straight into the forest.

"Thanks for meeting us. What's he planning?" Torin shuffled between his feet.

"It's clear you're outnumbered, so he is over-confident and plans on making a good show of it," Kira said without emotion.

Torin didn't take his eyes off his father. "Good, he'll be distracted with what's in front of him. We can take care of the army."

Azalea nodded in agreement, her hands shaking at the thought.

Kira tapped her finger against her lip. "Small problem. Korbyn knows about Cassie, and he's set on going to find her before he destroys the house anymore."

"How did he find out?" Torin asked.

Kira kept looking around. "I'm not sure. Maybe Livia overheard something?"

Azalea didn't trust her and was sure she told Korbyn, but turned her focus to studying the group at the front and realized she couldn't see Korbyn anymore. "I think your dad might have already gone."

Torin's gaze darted around. "We can't let him find her, or the others. I've got to go."

Azalea agreed and knew what he was going to say next. "It's fine. I've got this. Don't worry about me."

"What are you planning?" Kira asked, as if Azalea couldn't be trusted on her own.

"Azalea is going to take down the army," Torin stated as if it were a sure thing.

A spark of pride beamed in her chest.

"You sure about that?" Kira stared at Azalea, and she stared right back.

Torin put his arm around Azalea's shoulders. "I wouldn't just leave her here if I thought she was going to get herself killed."

Azalea kept her expression neutral but was smirking on the inside.

"I wouldn't put it past you," Kira said under her breath.

Torin ignored her comment. Stepping closer to Azalea, he tilted her chin toward him.

"*Do not let yourself get killed. It will make me look bad,*" he said in her mind.

"*I have no intention of doing so.*" She smiled as he kissed her softly. "I had a great teacher, after all," she said aloud.

"*Have* a great teacher. This isn't goodbye." He released her chin and squeezed her shoulder as he stepped away.

"Okay, later then." She couldn't help but smirk, feeling a little bit smug that he had kissed her in front of Kira. "Bye, Kira."

She watched as Kira marched off, and Torin donned a shadow cloak, melting into the forest background. She doubted anyone would notice the extra shadow following Kira into the estate.

Taking a deep breath, Azalea focused her whirling thoughts and buzzing nerves. She was ready to prove herself, and she didn't need Torin there watching or assessing her. This was for her, and she was ready. Everything she had trained for had built up to this day—that was what she told herself to stop her from running back into the woods like a scared puppy.

Azalea focused her whirling thoughts and buzzing nerves while striding to the gate.

# Chapter 46

Torin kept close to Kira as she marched toward the house. After about six minutes, they stopped at the pack of House of Raven operatives closest to the barrier Fabian had set up.

"I'm going to assist Korbyn," she told the soldier at the end.

The man turned. Torin's breath hitched—it was Conner. It had been over eight years since Torin had seen him. He still had the same dirty blond hair, but the childish smile was gone now. His expression was severe, the angles of his face more refined, his jaw sharper.

"Be safe, love," Conner said, then he glanced at the space where Torin stood. "Good luck." He turned to face the front.

Torin's heart raced. Conner had clearly known he was there. Maybe Kat was right. Maybe they did want him back.

Kira marched forward. Torin took note of the mages in the front line. He didn't recognize the commander of the unit: he was a solid man with brown hair, a crooked nose, who stood well over six feet, and looked like someone you wouldn't want to mess with. He nodded at Kira as she marched past. It seemed she had a lot of respect here and that his escape hadn't set her back.

Most of the soldiers were House of Raven mages dressed in black combat gear. Some were from the House of Owls, dressed in obvious white and gold robes—the opposite of combat gear. House of Phoenix guards were scattered around the edges dressed in the red and black of the Tower of London; they carried guns, so he wasn't sure if they were aware that they could use Echo Magic here. Hopefully, they didn't work it out.

He looked for the Archmage but didn't spot her. She wouldn't be too far away, knowing her.

Kira surrounded herself in shadows, and they made their way up the hill on the grass instead of the driveway, steering clear of the barricades Fabian had set up. It was too easy to sneak in. Fabian didn't have enough people, and they weren't trained like the House of Ravens.

The house in front of them was half-standing. The cannon fire had stopped for now and it seemed they had just wanted to do damage for the sake of it. Causing fear and panic was one of his father's favorite tactics. It was how he had driven so many House of Snakes families from their homes.

The pillars of the front door had lost their tops, and the door hung open, half shattered, with shards of wood sticking out. Kira pushed it open, and Torin followed.

"Head for the kitchen." He brushed past her and ran for the kitchen with the trapdoor underground.

It was open.

For once, he hoped Fabian would be there when he arrived. But he knew that wasn't the case. Fabian would never have left the trapdoor open.

No longer caring about the shadow cloak, Torin raced down the stairs, along the low hallway, and past the storeroom he had been kept in until he came to the tunnel at the end.

Whimpering echoed up the long stone tunnel, and the gate at the end was open.

He raced into the massive room, an old cellar that had bunk beds around the edges and tables at the center. There were people filling every space, at least fifty of them. Children were crying, and several adults were sniveling and pleading. His eyes fell on his father at the center of the room and on Mrs. Yates tied up in shadows lying on the ground, screaming silently through her bonds.

Torin stopped and slipped his elemer into his belt, holding his hands up to show he was unarmed. Kira skidded to a stop at his side, keeping her elemer out.

Korbyn pressed his elemer to Cassie's throat and held her tight to his chest, one hand gripping her arm so tightly it would bruise.

Every muscle in Torin's body tensed. "Don't hurt her."

"You've decided to join us again, boy? You finally chose the winning team, ay?" Korbyn pulled Cassie closer to him.

"You're not the winning team. Hand her over." Torin clenched his jaw.

"You're as bad as she is, siding with the enemy. Lying to me. But I'm giving her a second chance, an opportunity to be great."

"Cassie, whatever he says, don't listen to him, okay?" Torin held eye contact with her.

She nodded. There was fear behind her eyes, though, she looked calm and unpanicked. He just hoped she would trust him.

"You, boy, have been nothing but a disappointment. And to think I gave you chance after chance to come back," Korbyn spat.

"You clearly didn't get the message last time when I told you no and threw a chair at you." Torin knew it was immature, but it had felt good at the time.

A whimper came from the corner where families were huddled. Korbyn ignored them. "You are a lost cause. Weak. This girl is a gift, a chance for my legacy to live on. The gods look down on me with favor."

Torin knew for sure that was not what the gods were doing. Most of them didn't give a shit about any of this.

"Will someone please explain to me what's going on?" Cassie said clearly.

Torin had to commend her bravery in the face of a man with a knife at her throat. "Cassie, I don't know how to say this... but—"

"If you're going to tell me he's my father, I already know," Cassie said. "Fabian told me, he also told me you're my brother. I just want to understand why this is happening." She risked grazing the knife on her throat to look up at their father.

Torin tensed, ready to lunge for her if Korbyn made a move, not that he'd be able to make it in time. He thought about blasting them both with the light magic, but again, he couldn't be sure Korbyn wouldn't hurt Cassie. She had to be clear of him before he acted.

Korbyn tightened his grip on Cassie. "Because I want you to come home with me. I can offer you everything—everything your brother threw back in my face. A grand legacy and a place in our new order."

"Why couldn't you just ask me like a normal person?" Cassie swallowed.

Torin saw his father's grip on the girl's slim arm grow tighter. He had to do something soon. If she kept talking like this, Korbyn would only make things worse for her, he knew from experience.

Torin took a step toward her, and Korbyn slid the knife closer to her throat, drawing tiny droplets of blood.

"Because you're an insolent girl." Korbyn let her arm go, and with a loud slap, he struck her face, then grabbed her arm once more. "You grew up with Blackbourne and these *snakes* in your ear. I knew you would hate me no matter what I said."

A tear slipped from each corner of Cassie's eyes, but she didn't make a sound.

"Whatever Fabian told you about him is true, Cassie." Torin inched closer.

"He said *you* killed his brother, Azalea's dad. Is that true?" Cassie asked.

Korbyn chuckled, and for a microsecond, Torin saw a flash of fear in Cassie's eyes. She might appear brave, but she was holding a strong front. He needed to find a way to end this soon.

"Yes, it's true. It's something I regret every day," Torin answered honestly.

"See that, girl." Korbyn pointed his elemer at Torin. "Weakness. He should be proud, but he chose the life of a traitor and a coward."

Cassie's deep brown eyes locked with his. Silently pleading.

"Azalea has forgiven me, and I have forgiven myself," Torin said. "I am free of my father, and I will make sure you are, too." Suddenly feeling lighter, he realized at that moment he truly had forgiven himself. Saying it aloud made it feel so much more real.

He didn't need Fabian's or anyone else's forgiveness. He could move on and make up for the things he had done by making the world better. Starting with Cassie.

"You will let me pass," Korbyn demanded. Family time was clearly over.

"Like hell I will." Torin stepped forward, but Kira's hand fell to his arm—a warning.

Korbyn took a step toward them. "You will let me pass or I will kill her."

"Let him go," Kira whispered. "Trust me."

He had to trust her. She had helped them escape, after all.

"Good, don't fight me." She spun around and kicked Torin's knees out from under him. He was on the floor before he could react. Kira was on his back, holding his hand to his spine while his face crunched into the gritty concrete floor.

"Good girl, Kira, and to think I doubted you there for a moment." Korbyn strode past them, and like a light switch, his mood shifted from anger to glee. One of the many things Torin hated about the man.

"Let me up, Kira," Torin growled as his father marched Cassie out of the room.

"Not until they're safely upstairs. There are too many people down here that could get hurt."

Eventually, she let him up and raised her hands. "Sorry, Tor. I had to."

"Fuck you." He knew that was true, but she was making it very hard to trust her. "Lock this gate behind me," he yelled back as he sprinted up the stairs, and Kira didn't stop him.

He burst outside the kitchen door to the courtyard lined with mosaic pots and herbs. His father was lashing shadow ropes around Cassie's arms, and she was thrashing frantically. She stopped moving when she spotted Torin.

"Go find Fabian," Torin ordered Kira. If there was ever a time for that man to appear, it would be now.

Korbyn spotted Torin and shoved Cassie in front of him as a shield. Real classy.

"I'm not going to tell you again. Let her go," Torin said as magic surged into his palms. It wasn't the new light magic, it was dark, and it wanted to kill.

"Let her go or what? You don't have the balls to do anything, and I've given you enough chances." Korbyn started backing out of the courtyard.

"Let her go, or I'll kill you!" Torin yelled. Shadow Magic streamed from his fingers, sending darkness rushing through the courtyard and up the house's walls.

"Dramatic. But I think not."

Cassie's gaze darted to the courtyard entrance. Fabian sprinted in, his eyes wild and seeking blood.

"I might not have been able to save Mum, but I sure as hell won't make the same mistake twice." Shadows exploded from Torin's hands, pitching the entire courtyard into inky blackness, so dark even he couldn't see.

He charged into the space where his father was and collided with the man. He felt Cassie break away and fall to the side. Hopefully, she'd been trained how to take a fall and her leg was safe in its cast.

This time he would end it, once and for all.

# Chapter 47

Azalea crept closer to the bridge leading to the gate, her shadow cloak strong and her feet as silent as cats' paws. The afternoon had disappeared, the sun now low on the horizon. The dark shadow of the crumbling house was long across the lawn.

Azalea took some much-needed breaths. There was no one to watch, no one to applaud her success. It would be silent and subtle, and she would be the one to know she had done her part in protecting her family and friends.

Crossing the bridge, she slipped through the gate. Hardly daring to breathe as she walked, she followed the fence behind the rows of soldiers glowing with faint golden magic until she got to the very end. She wasn't sure how many she could get in one go, so she prepared to do this quickly.

She waited until Kira had made it to the house in the distance, not wanting to give Torin a chance to turn back and help her. He needed to help Cassie and be the one to face his father.

Taking several deep, calming breaths, Azalea went over her plan, then opened her eyes.

She was ready.

She checked her shadow cloak was strong, then took her time walking all the way along the edge of the soldiers so she was in line with the front row. Cutting into the Shadow Dimension, she summoned more power than she had ever attempted before. She combined it with her and Torin's magic for control then blasted out a solid stream of shadows, shaping it into a dark wall between the army and the House of Ravens mages.

Yelling started from the other side. She ignored it and stretched the wall as far as she could in either direction. Breathing heavily, she pushed more and more magic into it and was still nowhere near burnout.

She knew Torin wouldn't approve. He wanted her to take them all out in secret. If there were two of them, maybe they could, but this way was better for her.

She made sure her shadow cloak was still concealing her, then dashed to the side of the army. Their orders must have been drilled in pretty well because they didn't fall out of line. But there were mumblings circulating, and many stared up at the height of her shadow wall.

It was now or never.

Azalea summoned the amplifying symbols in her mind and pulled in as much Shadow Magic as she could, then tucked away her elemer, holding the magic in her chest like a dam waiting to burst. She took in a breath and pooled the soul bond magic in her belly.

Holding out both palms, she screamed as the magic ripped out of her. Sweat poured from her forehead, stinging her eyes as she focused all her energy on weaving together the magic as it flooded the army.

The recoil wave hit her like a lorry, and her feet slid out from under her, the force sending her skidding across the wet grass. She rolled over and wiped her eyes with her sleeve. A third of the soldiers were on the ground. They were no longer glowing with magic. Hopefully, that meant they would think for themselves again and run off once they woke up.

The remaining two-thirds all had eyes on her, and a small group had guns pointed at her. She didn't think, just stood up slowly and started the process again. Her lungs screamed, and her veins burned with both ice and fire of the combined magic.

Gathering the magic faster this time, she held in a scream as the power ripped from her. She ground her feet into the earth and leaned forward as if she were pushing against a door with all her magic then forced her arms to sweep in a wide arc to cover more people.

The recoil hit harder this time. The blast threw her back further, and her shoulder screamed as it collided with something hard. She gasped for breath and forced herself up once more, ignoring the pain blooming all over her body and the mud and grass caked down one side of her.

"Someone stop her!" a voice yelled. Her wall had fallen, and the mages were running toward her.

Just once more. She had to do it. The remaining soldiers raised their guns and fired. The machine gunfire was deafening.

She sent up a shadow wall all around her. The thud of bullets into her barrier was as loud as if they were going right through her, and her whole body shook with the force of holding the wall. The chill of the Shadow Magic and the sheer power felt so right even as it scorched her veins.

As she forced out the Shadow Magic, the light magic simmered in her belly. The bullets stopped. This was it. She ground her feet into the earth, one foot in front of the other, and dropped the shield.

Determined eyes stared at her. There were fewer soldiers than she thought, but their guns all pointed at her. She didn't know how long it took for them to reload.

Almost without her permission, the light magic rose again. She was quick to throw her hands out and aim it at the soldiers, this time forcing her eyes to stay open against the blinding light as the beam spread across the remaining brainwashed soldiers.

She was prepared for the recoil and fell to her hands and knees before it could throw her back.

"Take her down!" She heard the commander loud and clear.

Her hands were muddy, and her body howled at her to give up, to just lie down and have a nice sleep in the mud.

"No. This one is mine."

She knew that voice. Azalea's eyes shot open, and she was on her feet in seconds. The Archmage marched through the bodies of the unconscious soldiers as if they were nothing to her.

The commander of the mages followed close behind.

"What are the orders?" The tall man checked the pulse of one of the men on the ground then caught up to the Archmage.

"I believe it is time to attack. We can't wait any longer."

Azalea stood, frozen in fear. Her magic was weak, but she could already feel it recharging. She just needed more time, but there was nowhere she could run, and the last person she wanted to face was the Archmage.

"Shouldn't we wait for Mage Dumont to return?"

"Korbyn clearly has better things to do. I believe he left already. You will follow my orders and attack," the Archmage said.

Only Azalea saw the golden magic stream from her staff into the commander.

"Yes, Ma'am," he agreed without question.

"No!" Azalea cried out.

The Archmage's cold eyes pierced into her soul. "Quiet girl. You have been more trouble to me than I ever could have thought. I should have killed you alongside the elemer-smith's boy."

"His name was Erik," Azalea said through ground teeth.

"Your new powers may be impressive, girl, but mine are all-natural. Yes, I heard about your little soul bond with Mage Dumont. You think yourselves quite the pair of rebels, don't you?"

Azalea wasn't going to argue with her. The woman was trying to make her angry to lose control. She would not let that happen.

"Don't take any of this personally. You and Dumont were merely pawns in a plan for the greater good."

Azalea held out her hand, ready to react. "You do realize *you* were just a pawn in Korbyn's plans, right? How did he even get you to think opening the Echo Dimension was a good idea when it fucked up all your own House's magic and not his?"

"You may be pleased to know that no one from my House died of burnout. We had it under control. As you see, I used Echo Magic to control this army. I have my ways." The Archmage smiled a thin smile, then it vanished as if she suddenly remembered Azalea had fucked up her brainwashing scheme.

Azalea bit her tongue, desperately wanting to have a go at the old witch but knowing making her angry might not be the best path forward.

"Now the gate is shut, the world is in chaos as planned, and I have the upper hand once more. I control the High Council just as my parents wanted for themselves. I did what they could not. My family will live on, and I will live on in legends."

"I hope it was all worth it," Azalea said bitterly, her legs barely holding her up as she stood in a sea of unconscious bodies.

The Archmage snorted in disgust. "You're still hung up over that boy? Erik was it?"

She knew very well his name was Erik. Azalea clenched her fists. Her magic was coming back, and now she had to keep it in.

"He never loved you. Never even liked you, you silly child." The Archmage stood creepily still, holding her owl-headed cane, which appeared to double as a staff for magic, in front of her.

Azalea took a calming breath. She wouldn't rise to this.

Azalea had been so focused on the Archmage, she hadn't noticed the battle begin in front of the house. Piles of dirt shot up in the air as fireballs pelted the earthen wall. It seemed they had worked out that they had Echo Magic again.

Azalea flinched as fireballs shot back, and shadow projectiles soared through the air from both sides. Flashes of light and shadows flickered all around as shields were drawn and lowered and creative elemental attacks were flung in all directions.

"I don't care if he loved me or not. He didn't need to die." Azalea stood her ground, waiting for her magic to settle, to be ready to use.

A chilling smile tightened the Archmage's lips. "Oh, but he did. You witnessed it yourself. His sacrifice was the catalyst to our rise."

She called this a rise? This woman was delusional to do all this to prove to her dead parents she was better than them. She was nuts.

The Archmage looked up in thought. "You know, I'm glad I sent you to work with Dumont. I admit, you were very good together, and without you, we wouldn't have all the relics. The gate would never have been opened. Once again, I thank you for your contribution."

Azalea couldn't hold back much longer. But she knew how powerful the Archmage was, and even with all her new gifts, this could end badly. Torin would tell her to run. But she wasn't going to let this woman get away with anything else. She would get what she deserved.

"You're just a petty old woman who wants to control everyone and everything around her. You're a monster." Azalea took a step toward her.

"You're an insolent girl. Let's see how you like being under my true control." Her eyes blazed, and she raised her cane-staff.

Azalea held out her hand, and her blast of light hit the Archmage's stream of magic as it blazed toward her.

She stumbled backward but caught her footing before she fell. The Archmage's magic pushed against her, thrusting her back with power that felt like she was standing next to a solar flare with its flames whipping all around her.

Azalea pushed back, her light magic flaring out of her, meeting the magic from the Archmage. With this sort of force, she knew that if it hit her, she was done for; it wasn't brainwashing coming for her, it was death.

Every muscle in Azalea's body rippled with the force of her magic. The edge of burnout hurtled toward her, but she would go past it in order to rid the world of this woman.

She summoned the last of the magic in her and took a step forward, then another. She let out a scream and took one more step. There was a loud CRACK, as her magic overpowered the Archmage's.

Azalea tumbled forward, face-planting into the mud. She rolled over, groaning. Scraping the sludge from her eyes, she searched for the Archmage. She wasn't there.

Checking her hands, she poked a finger into her palm to make sure she wasn't dreaming. She wasn't brainwashed or brain scrambled, at least.

Clambering to her feet, she found the Archmage lying half on top of an unconscious soldier, her staff fallen from her hand, her legs spread wide, and her mouth hanging open. Azalea crawled along the ground and touched her shaking hand to the frail-looking wrist.

Azalea's heart nearly stopped when she felt the faint pulse and found she was actually glad she hadn't killed her. She climbed over the soldiers until she found one with handcuffs on their belt. Rolling the Archmage over, she cuffed her hands together and did the same to her feet. Then used what felt close to the last of her Shadow Magic to bind her in shadow ropes and cloak the old woman.

No one was watching her. No one had seen what she had done. For good measure, she stripped the jackets off a few nearby soldiers and hid the Archmage under them.

Now she had to find Danni. She'd know how to lock her up so she couldn't escape.

# Chapter 48

A zalea stumbled up the hill with a shadow shield tight around her; the house and the battle seemed so far away. With every step, she regained a little more magic, and she had a little extra she'd absorbed from the Archmage, including so many horrible power symbols for mind control and torture. She hoped those faded quickly, as she had no intention of using them.

The battle raged all around her. Mages, all with solid black eyes, were dueling each other in whirlwinds of fire, water, shadows, air, and any combination of elements one could imagine. It was nothing like her elemental battles in class. There was screaming all around her. People on fire thrashed on the muddy grass, limbs flew through the air, and tornadoes and blasting winds appeared and disappeared in terrifying feats of localized magic.

The smell of burning flesh hit the back of her throat, mingling with smoke and the salty taste of her sweat pouring from her face. Azalea stuck close to the ground, desperately looking for Danni or someone who could help. She hid behind an earth mound until she caught a glimpse of Danni's fiery red hair, not to mention the fire surrounding her like a defensive cloak. Azalea swallowed her fear and sprinted toward Danni, hoping she wouldn't set fire to her before she recognized her.

"Danni! I need help!" Azalea waved out.

Danni turned her head at her name and stopped herself right before she hurled a fireball at Azalea. "Get out of here. I'm a little busy."

"I've got the Archmage," Azalea said.

Danni lowered her hands and looked at Azalea in disbelief. "Lead the way and tell me what happened quickly."

Azalea shielded them both with a shadow cloak and blurted out the story. They dodged to the edge of the main battle and raced down the hill. Azalea was breathless by the time she and Danni arrived at the army of unconscious soldiers.

"Did the Archmage do this? Where is she?" Danni glanced around.

"No. I did this. I hid her over here somewhere." Azalea darted over several groups of slumped bodies before she found the hiding place. "They aren't dead if that's what you're wondering. I just took away the mind control."

Azalea peeled the coats off the Archmage to reveal her awkwardly laid-out form.

"By the gods, you were right," Danni said as if she hadn't believed Azalea's story.

"I don't know how long she'll be out. Please arrest her or lock her up somewhere, so I don't have to do this again."

"Certainly." Danni whipped a pen out of her belt and stabbed it into the Archmage's neck.

"Did you just kill her?" Azalea stared in horror.

"No. It's a tranquilizer. She'll be out for a few hours at least. Maybe more with whatever magic you used." Danni covered her in the coats again.

"Good. You need to get to safety." Danni pushed her along forcefully.

Azalea looked over her shoulder. "I need to find Torin. Korbyn was going after Cassie again. Do you know where she was?"

Danni continued to hustle her along. "In the underground shelter. Let's go."

They ran back up the hill that went on forever while she maintained a shadow cloak. Azalea was breathless; she hadn't done any training in the last week, and it showed.

RoRo was in full battle mode in the center of the fight. Her grandmother looked like a goddess glowing all green. Shields of vines surrounded her with terrifying thorns that flowed around her like armor. Whips of plants shot out from her sides, lashing at anyone who attacked her. She had four mages surrounding her, and she appeared to be winning.

Her control of air and earth magic was masterful. Azalea couldn't help but stop to watch.

"She's a terror, isn't she?" Danni said.

"She's amazing." Azalea scanned the horrific scene in front of her which was also disturbingly captivating. There were so many colors; every mage lit up like Christmas lights with their particular brand of magic.

"Come on, we're no good standing here." Danni pulled Azalea down as a fireball shot out from behind Azalea's shadow shield and hit a nearby raven mage.

"Wait." Azalea reached for Danni's arm, so she knew where she was. "Some of the House of Raven and Phoenix mages have the Archmage's magic on them."

Danni narrowed her eyes. "How do you know that?"

"I can see it?" Azalea squinted, suddenly doubting her vision.

Danni rubbed her chin. "Can you reverse it?"

Azalea held out her palm, lining up one mage that was about a football pitch of distance away on the edge of the fighting. She'd never tried it that far before but took a breath and let the magic surge out.

The beam shot toward her target, but accidentally hit a House of Snakes mage who flopped to the ground.

"Crap." Azalea waited for the power recoil to hit, then ducked alongside Danni. "Sorry. That didn't go well."

"You need to get closer." Danni's eyes darted around.

Azalea thought she spotted some Ravens fighting against their own, hopefully, ones on Kat and Kira's side, but she wasn't sure with all the noise and chaos. She wanted to get to Torin but had to trust that he and Kira had it under control. Cassie had to be okay.

"You go find Torin, and I'll pick off as many of them as I can," Azalea said, not wanting Danni to leave her, but she had to do this alone, anyway.

"Are you sure?"

"Yes. I'll stay hidden."

Danni sprinted off, raising a shield of fire along her side as she ran.

Azalea crept around the outskirts of the battle, trying to block out everything but the magic clinging to people. A Phoenix guard was her first target. She ground her feet and blasted him. As he collapsed, his fire magic slammed into her along with the mind control spell.

She spotted several more just like him and blasted light. People were starting to look toward her. She moved. Every time she took someone out, she sprinted to a new spot and kept her shadow shield strong, and it grew stronger with every House of Raven mage she took down. Having their powers was intoxicating, and the sheer number of options she had for magic was giddying.

She fought the urge to use the new magic to join the fight. It would be so easy to take anyone down using any combination of Echo and Shadow Magic. She took down mages from various houses: White Deer, Ravens, Phoenix, Owls, even a Winged Bull.

Focusing on the light magic, she wove through the crowd, getting bolder with each take-down until there were hardly any left with the golden glow.

The smell of blood and singed flesh filled the air. The fighting was more brutal than anything she could have imagined and until now, she had tried to block out any details around her. But the people lying on the ground writhing in pain and sobbing were hard to ignore.

She knelt over a woman; her clothes were singed off revealing bubbling flesh with only a tiny patch of a tattoo showing on her arm—a snake. Azalea gripped her elemer with sweaty hands and instinctively put her hand and her elemer to the woman's chest.

Closing her eyes, power symbols of the House of White Deer flooded into her mind, and silvery magic flowed out of her. The burns shrank and pulled inward, revealing the fresh skin complete with a snake tattoo. Azalea screamed as pain flared up her arms like her skin was melting off. Then it vanished. Sweat poured down her forehead and soaked her shirt. Her shield had vanished around her, and she'd used most of the healing magic.

"Thank you," the woman said.

"I've got to go now." Azalea stumbled up, scanning the field for RoRo. She wasn't fighting anymore but leaning over someone in the center of the battle.

Azalea strengthened her shield and wound through the bodies, many just unconscious thanks to her.

"RoRo," Azalea called. Her grandmother looked up with fear in her eyes, and Azalea realized she couldn't see her. She lowered the shield, hoping her grandmother wouldn't attack her out of reflex.

"Hold this." RoRo placed Azalea's hand on a cloth pressed into a wound of the person lying on the ground in front of her. Azalea looked over the body and gasped.

"Mum!" Azalea cried out and nearly let go of the cloth. "What happened to her?"

"A House of Owl Mage hit her with something, and they stabbed their elemer into her." RoRo's voice shook.

Azalea's gaze ran over the faint light of weak green magic that barely tinged her mother, then saw the glow of gold in one area over her abdomen.

"I can help," Azalea said, fighting down the building panic. Her mum shouldn't have even been out here.

"You need to leave, Azalea. It isn't safe for you here," RoRo ordered.

"I'm fine. I can heal her." She moved the blood-soaked material and placed her hand and her elemer blade on the wound as her mother's bright blood flowed between Azalea's fingers, oozing down her arm.

"Azalea, you need to get out of here. The High Council is going to arrest you and Torin."

"I need to do this," Azalea said as blood squelched between her fingers.

She cut into the Shadow Dimension to get more power, then pressed both hands and the flat of the elemer blade back over the wound and did her best to summon the healing magic she had just used. But only the dregs of it remained, and the power symbols in her mind were growing fuzzy.

*Come on, Mum. Don't give up.*

Forcing the magic through the elemer and into the wound, she felt the skin knit together, but it didn't feel right, not like the last one. When she pulled her hand away, the bleeding had stopped, and a shiny pink line was left.

"You're a wonder, my love. I'll take care of her. Just get yourself out of here, okay?"

Azalea nodded. "Love you, RoRo. Keep her safe."

She glanced around to see the battle was nearly over. Only a few enemy mages were still fighting, and they were cornered and outnumbered.

She had to find Torin. She slipped on her shadow cloak, turned, and ran toward the house.

*"Torin, where are you?"* she called in her mind as she ran.

There was no answer.

# Chapter 49

Torin's full weight collided with his father, sending him backward. He held down his chest and landed one good punch in the side of his face. It was a bloody good feeling.

Magic surged into Torin's palm, calling for death, but he jerked his hand back in time. It wasn't going to be that easy. He wanted it to last. Rage burned through his veins alongside his magic, bubbling like a stream of molten iron.

The air cleared of shadows, and he heard Fabian's voice somewhere, but it was distant. All he could see was his father and that smug face. The man who had made his childhood a living hell, the man who had killed his mother.

This was for her.

Torin stood and stumbled. Shadows coiled around his ankles, yanking hard, threatening to toss him. He sliced them apart with light magic and danced back, sending a barrage of razor-sharp shadow points toward his father as he did so.

Korbyn was on his feet. He was agile for a man his age. He never stopped training, always expecting enemies around every corner. He threw up a shadow wall and avoided Torin's shots.

Torin's vision narrowed. Everything around him was black, non-existent. The world was no longer there until he took down this nightmare of a man.

He blasted away the shadow wall with light. It would be too easy to just steal his father's powers with the light magic, and if he did, it was just another thing the council would use against him to prove he was dangerous. He had to do it the hard way. The right way.

Korbyn's face dripped with blood. Some of the shadows had hit their target.

"Just kill him!" Fabian's voice echoed around him.

Torin circled his father. The battle escalated as they threw more and more spells at each other. Elements of Echo Magic: fireballs, air laced with ice crystals, a barrage of rocks from the gardens. None were Torin's strong suit, but they were wearing down his father, and Torin's magic felt limitless. They were both equally skilled in combat with shadows, so anything with Shadow Magic, both easily thwarted.

Korbyn's movements were slower and his Echo Magic weak. His father had to know by now how serious he was, and he should be worried. He also knew better than to engage Torin in hand-to-hand combat; he was avoiding getting close. Torin was bigger, stronger, and, more importantly, his father knew what would happen if Torin was touching him and lost control.

It was time for this to be over.

Torin sucked in a breath. "Father, just stop. Give yourself over, and you will be treated by justice fairly."

Korbyn threw a single shard of shadow at Torin that sliced dangerously close to his eye as he ducked. Blood trickled down his face, blocking his vision as rage rose in his body before he could contain it.

He charged at his father and knocked him hard to the ground with a low tackle. Shadows streamed from Torin's elemer and latched onto his father. Locking him in place as Torin straddled his chest, it took everything in his power not to pummel his father's face into the stone.

"Look at me," Torin growled and gripped his father's chin, forcing him to look straight up at him.

Korbyn clenched his jaw. "Why should I? You are no son of mine."

Torin fought the hand of death. "Do you remember how I got the scar on my eyebrow?" he asked calmly.

His father let out a disgruntled huff. "Why should I care? I gave you everything to become great. This is how I am repaid. A whinging son who cares about a stupid cut."

Torin tightened his grip on his father's jaw. "You threw a teacup at me when I was six. Is that something a good father would do?"

"You ungrateful sod." Korbyn spat in his face.

Torin released Korbyn's jaw, shoving his face back hard as he fought his rage. "You're nothing but a small, hateful man."

Torin's hands shook as he got up.

"You can't even do it. Can you?" his father taunted.

"I could easily kill you. But I'm choosing not to be like you. Goodbye, Father." Torin lashed him to the ground with shadows and got up.

He forced himself to walk away and spotted Danni already on her way over. Cassie was in Fabian's arms.

"Please take him away before I kill him," he said to Danni between gritted teeth.

A sharp pain shot through his back and sliced across his arm. More shadow shards. He spun around to see his father out of the shadow restraints and marching straight toward him.

"I say when it's over, boy." He raised his hand to hit Torin. But Torin was faster. He dropped his elemer and reached out, shoving his palm hard into his father's chest and blocking the other one midair. Time stopped. Torin was aware of his breath, the chill of the breeze around him, the warmth of his father's skin beneath his jacket.

He made a choice in that moment. He could explain later that it was a reaction or instinct, but in that second, he chose to kill his father. The magic surged into his hand, and he felt the heartbeat beneath his palm, slow and steady, the heartbeat of a psychopath.

With the hand of death, Torin slowed that heartbeat further, pressing into his father's chest, waiting for what was probably only a few seconds, but it was all it took to draw the life out of him for good.

Torin took the full weight of the man in his hands, laid his father down on the ground, and watched as he drew his last breath.

"Know that you made me do this," Torin said.

Then it was over.

# Chapter 50

With the sun below the line of distant trees, Azalea ran inside the house. The entryway stairs were collapsed, and the chandelier smashed across the tiles.

*"Torin, tell me where you are."* Still no answer.

She dashed in and out of the rooms she could get to. Everything beyond the kitchens had crumbled into a mass of rubble and dripping pipes. She ran down to the underground rooms and didn't find him there, but Jade updated her on what had happened. She sat safely with the dragon's egg, which Azalea was grateful for.

"Just stay down here until someone comes to get you, but it should be over soon. I think we won. Just don't come back through the kitchen, it's not safe, go to the outside exit."

A cheer rang through the huddled group, and Azalea straightened, not expecting that. Hopefully, she hadn't just gotten their hopes up to have them smashed again.

She waved goodbye and ran upstairs, her breath burning in her chest from the dust and smoke now thick in the air.

A horrible feeling washed over her. It was like her chest was being crushed, no, it was grief, a horrible, hollow sadness, and it wasn't coming from her.

"Torin," she whispered aloud, then broke into a sprint and burst into the courtyard.

People were everywhere, but she didn't see faces. Her head was whirling, trying to spot Torin. Finally. There he was in the center of the courtyard standing over a body.

"Torin!" she cried out, and he looked up.

His face was blank, but she could feel his pain, so deep it bled beyond the new barriers that separated their feelings.

His shirt was torn to shreds, and he was covered in blood but still standing. She threw herself into his arms, and he buried his face in her hair.

"He's dead. I killed him." Torin's breath brushed over her ear.

Azalea glanced down to see Korbyn's eyes staring up at her. She squeezed Torin tight, then guided him away from the body, half expecting it to jump up and try to kill them.

Danni and Fabian moved the body, and Danni confirmed that Korbyn was dead.

It was finally over.

"You did the right thing," Azalea wiped a tear from his cheek; she'd never seen him cry. "It's the only way he would have let it end."

"I tried not to, but he had to keep pushing." He put his arm around her and squeezed her to his side. His grip on her shoulder was tight, possessive even. Then she saw why.

The council mages marched their way. Their faces were not triumphant, but serious and determined.

"Remember when we were in Cyprus, and we had that really nice hotel room?" Azalea turned to face him and to distract him from what they both knew was coming and took both his hands in hers.

"Wish we were there right now?" His eyes locked on hers.

She twisted the green demantoid garnet ring on her finger with her thumb. "I wish we were anywhere else right now. But yes, we should go back there when this is over."

"Deal. I'll teach you how to make a flock of shadow birds." His finger traced small circles on the palm of her hand. "We could escape right now. Overpower everyone in this courtyard."

She nodded. "I know. Which is exactly why we have to stay and show them we won't."

"For once, I think you're right." A brief smile touched his lips.

"Hey!" She hit him playfully. Without warning, he pulled her into a kiss. She closed her eyes, sinking into the warmth of his body like there was no one around them. Her heart pounded against her rib cage; they didn't need to say anything, but it felt like goodbye. He broke away and kept her hand in his.

Everyone was watching them, all the House of Snakes mages, everyone from the tent village who'd been fighting, RoRo, who was grinning ear to ear, Danni who looked conflicted, Kat, looking pleased with herself, and Fabian, who for once didn't look like he wanted to kill Torin—which was the most surprising of all.

Azalea's cheeks heated to what was probably a deep red, and she squeezed Torin's hand tighter.

*"Just do what they say, okay? Don't resist,"* Torin said in her mind.

*"Don't they have bigger things to worry about than us right now?"* she replied.

*"Right now, we are the biggest threat. So don't be threatening."*

*"You're the one frowning like you want to kill them all."*

They broke eye contact and faced the old mage at the same time.

"Mage Torin Dumont and Apprentice Azalea Sharp, you are both under arrest by order of the High Council and Paranormal Justice Unit for use of illegal magic and the forging of an illegal soul bond," Mage Skeffington said looking a little too pleased with himself.

Azalea and Torin didn't move.

"If you do not cooperate, you will be taken into custody by force." He adjusted his jacket which was a little too clean to have been in a battle.

"We will fully cooperate," Torin said with a hint of a smirk. Azalea smiled.

"You can't arrest them. They're the ones we should be thanking," some random Snake mage called out.

"She took down the whole army. We'd be fucked if it wasn't for her."

She silently thanked whoever said that, then remembered the Archmage. She couldn't be left out there to escape. "Danni, Danni!" Azalea waved her hands to get Danni's attention, ignoring the unimpressed scowl of Mage Skeffington. "The Archmage, you need to go get her."

Panic rustled through the crowd. "It's fine." Danni hushed the crowd. "I'll go get her; we left her tranquilized. You and you with me," she ordered two of Fabian's people.

"Before you leave, would you be so kind as to arrest the prisoners?" Skeffington said to Danni.

Danni waved off his request. "It seemed like you had it under control."

"It is your job as an agent of the PJU to take orders from High Council members, and I order you to arrest these two." Shadows curled around the old mage.

*Old Skeffington was on the High Council?* He must have been the only member cowering here while it was taken over.

Danni sighed. "Fine. But just so you know, it was Azalea who took down the Archmage, and Torin took down his own father. It's these two you have to thank for everyone here remaining alive." Danni got out two pairs of handcuffs and marched toward Azalea and Torin. They held out their wrists without protest, and she slapped on the handcuffs.

"Sorry, guys," she mumbled.

Skeffington rocked back on his heels, pleased at his handiwork. Azalea was surprised he wasn't high-fiving his mate, Russ, who was standing beside him like a good dog. Mage Stone glared at them with a thin smile of triumph.

Azalea suspected she would never be accepted by the House of Snakes because of Torin, but she didn't need them.

"We'd just like a word with Torin before you run off," Kat said, more of an order than a request. Azalea smiled at the look on the mage's face. He wasn't enjoying the lack of respect or control he had around here.

"Who let all these House of Raven people in here? Someone arrest them!" Skeffington yelled as more House of Raven soldiers made their way into the courtyard.

Fabian rested his arm on Kat's shoulder. "It's fine, mate. These ones are on our side. They've rounded all the bad ones up out there. You can take them with you on your way back to jail," Fabian said as more House of Raven operatives followed behind Kira as she walked over to stand behind Kat. It was evident that Torin had numbers on his side, just as Kat had said.

"We knew you could do it, Torin." Kat put a hand to her heart. "We'll be waiting for you at the Rook." She smiled and kissed Torin on the cheek.

Kat stepped out of the way, and Kira stepped forward and did the same. "You always said you would do it. I'm sorry I didn't believe you Tor. You know I never hated you, right?" A tear slid from her eye, and he brushed it away on her cheek with his handcuffed hands.

"Do you know how long I've wanted to hear you say that?" He smiled.

Azalea couldn't help but prickle at Kira's closeness to Torin.

"Enough of this drivel," Skeffington barked. "Take them away."

# Chapter 51

Azalea stared straight ahead, blinking as she tried to get her bearings. Three days she had been in a cell alone, and now the noise of the stirring courtroom was almost too much. They were in the House of Eagles Tower, which had somehow remained standing while the rest of London fell to all forms of looting, fires, and attacks by mysterious creatures and magic.

She scanned the all-white courtroom, an amphitheater of shiny surfaces topped by a pyramid ceiling of glass and steel beams at the very top of the skyscraper. Above, the sky was gray and cloudy. Seated in a curved row at the very front were the surviving mages of the High Council. Behind them were stands of spectators and media.

This appeared to be a very public event.

Azalea shuffled in the hard chair. The handcuffs were heavy on her wrists and bound with charms to block magic, though she was sure she could easily break them if she wanted to. But she followed Torin's lead and did everything to cooperate.

He sat two seats away to her left. They'd been kept apart the whole time they'd been there. He was right. If they had any chance of getting out of this, they had to cooperate and prove they were not a threat to the magical world.

She was exhausted from not sleeping, despite finally having the time to do it. But she couldn't stop worrying. Was Isaac okay? Had Van recovered? Had Ereshkigal taken the dragon egg? No one told her anything while she was here, with the exception of one note from Danni saying her mum was doing better and not to worry. Not even Faraday or Sita had gotten in. And she couldn't help the niggling unease that the Archmage was locked up somewhere nearby. Was she in the cell next door? The weight of it all made sleep impossible to come by. At least she'd had Torin to talk to in her head.

Her palms were sweaty as she stared out across a sea of unfamiliar faces until her eyes fell on RoRo, who gave her a confident nod. She could do this. She couldn't see her mum anywhere, but Fabian was there with Cassie at his side, and Danni and Maiken were next to them.

*"Don't rise to any of their attempts to set us off."*

Azalea's head snapped toward Torin. *"They'll do that?"*

*"Don't look at me, and don't tell them we can mind-speak. Be as honest as possible, and hopefully, they won't go into our heads."*

Azalea stared forward as a wash of dread filled her, and she had the urge to knock out everyone in the room and run. They wouldn't really use mind magic on them, would they? She forced herself to remain seated with her back straight and her mind spiraling over the outcomes of this trial.

Worst-case scenario, they were both locked up—surely they didn't still execute people over this anymore? Best case, they were set free for shutting the Echo Gate and saving the day. Either way, she still had to go back to the Shadow Dimension. But leaving Torin in prison was not an option. She knew how hard he had worked to be free and wasn't about to let him go back in.

The proceedings started, but Azalea couldn't concentrate. The judge was not a judge, but the Head of the High Council, a

House of Eagles mage named Harriet Williams who seemed to have a lot to say. She was a petite woman with gray hair tied back in a tight bun who went on about laws and historical examples of soul bonds. Of course, none of her stories ended favorably for the soul-bonded couple. Azalea had to admit if this power was in anyone else's hands, she would be worried too. They should consider themselves lucky she and Torin were being cooperative and responsible.

Azalea sighed. It was tense in the room but also incredibly boring. All of Mage Harriet Williams' research and yammering were probably to do with losing the High Council to Korbyn Dumont; she was trying to establish her place. She couldn't blame the woman, but Azalea felt like they didn't need to be the scapegoats this woman used to get on top.

They called the first witness on their side to the stand. Azalea clasped her hands tight in her lap as Rowena Sharp rose from her seat.

RoRo's dress of blue flowers swished around her as she walked to the stand carrying an air of authority and the glow of bright green power along with her. She stood at the front behind the raised white podium, her expression grim.

Azalea swallowed as the High Council turned their questioning to RoRo.

"Do you agree to tell the truth?" Mage Williams asked.

"Yes."

"And if you withhold information, you agree for the truth to be taken by force?"

Azalea's heart plummeted. They couldn't do that.

"I agree," RoRo said without hesitation.

"We will proceed. Mage Sharp, you knew your daughter, Leda Sharp, was having a child with Samael Blackbourne before Azalea was born?"

"Yes. She told me."

"And you did not encourage them to marry?"

RoRo's face was cold, unreadable. "It was not my place to do so. Leda is a forest guardian, and it was important she fulfilled her duties. It was what she wanted."

"Did Samael Blackbourne offer, at any point, for Azalea and her mother to live at Blackbourne manor?" Mage Williams asked.

"I believe he did. But both agreed it was not what was best for Azalea."

"What was the reasoning behind this?"

Azalea didn't move. These were things her family refused to discuss with her. She was kind of pissed off that it came to this to find anything out.

"Leda did not like Shadow Magic, and even back then, the House of Snakes was under threat from the House of Ravens. It was not safe."

Mage Williams looked down the glasses balancing on her nose. "And you believed this threat to be real?"

"Yes, of course. Did you not see what just happened?" RoRo glared at Mage Williams, shaking her head as if the woman had no common sense. "They decided Azalea was safer having a normal childhood."

Azalea nearly snorted out loud. Was it normal for a child to see ghosts and have everyone tell her to ignore them? If she'd grown up with her father, at least she would have understood those things, not been kept in the dark until it was too late.

Mage Williams narrowed her eyes at RoRo. "There was another reason, yes?"

"Are those not good enough reasons?" RoRo said.

"I am referring to a prophecy. A prophecy you failed to report."

RoRo stood with her hands folded in front of her. "It was not clear that was about my granddaughter."

"But you believed it to be. You told Archmage Norwich." Mage Williams narrowed her eyes.

RoRo remained silent.

"Will you recount the prophecy for the court?" A clear order.

RoRo cleared her throat and didn't once look toward Azalea. "When the fallen raven returns to the tower, a young azalea will bloom in darkness. Only when they destroy the balance will a new era of magic dawn. A dark book will guide their path. Only as one can they undo the great destruction. As one, they will bring new light."

"There have been other prophecies like this in the past, yes?"

RoRo gave a short nod. "Yes."

"And they always foretold a powerful soul bond."

"Yes."

"You knew who this prophecy referred to, didn't you? The seer from the House of the Winged Bull, Mage Sarah Pike, told you this directly."

"I could not be sure."

Mage Williams tapped her fingers on the podium in front of her. "But you took measures to ensure it came to pass?"

RoRo pursed her lips as if choosing her words very carefully. "Azalea's mother did not want it to pass. She wanted to protect Azalea."

"But you did not agree."

"No," RoRo said.

Azalea's mouth went dry. RoRo knew all this and never told her. She knew something would happen to her, and she didn't give her a heads up, or training, or anything.

"So you set your granddaughter up to cross paths with a 'fallen raven who would return to the tower?'"

"No. I did not. The prophecy played out on a natural path. That is how prophecies work. You cannot change or manipulate them." RoRo glared at Mage Williams like her eyes might set her alight.

Mage Williams ignored the stare. "But you arranged with the Archmage since Azalea was a girl to have a place in the initiate program at the Tower of London?"

"Yes. This is common knowledge." RoRo's voice grew louder.

"But no one knew who Azalea's father was?"

RoRo raised her eyebrows. "No, it was not something Leda wanted to be known. I'm sure you can understand why."

"But her mother still didn't want her to go?"

"No."

"If that was the case, how did you convince her?"

RoRo paused and for the first time, her expression flickered with a microsecond of fear. Azalea couldn't have been the only one to see it.

"You will tell the court, or we will take it from you." Mage Williams' voice echoed around the chamber.

RoRo took a breath. "I sent a flock of ravens with poisoned talons after her to prove to her mother she was in danger."

Hot anger rose through every inch of Azalea, and she stood up. "You could have killed Isaac! We were on motorbikes for fuck's sake."

RoRo's eyes snapped toward her. "I'm sorry, Petal. I didn't know that at the time."

A guard pushed Azalea back down in her seat. She was shaking all over.

It was all so clear now. RoRo had given her the Shadow Atlas. She had been there after Azalea and Isaac were attacked by ravens. She had been the one to call Fabian to take Azalea to the Tower of London. RoRo knew all along who Torin was and never said anything.

# Chapter 52

Azalea's eyes grew blurry and hot, fighting off tears. RoRo had set her up. She bit the inside her of lip to snap out of it and stared straight ahead, blocking any thoughts that might come through from Torin. If she looked at him, she would start crying, and that was the last thing she wanted.

"I have done nothing illegal. I don't see the point in this questioning," RoRo said without a hint of remorse.

Mage Williams' lips curled at the edge like she had something to say. "The point is, you told the Archmage of this prophecy, and she used this to plan to overthrow our council and the magical community with Korbyn Dumont."

"That is not what this trial is about," RoRo said coldly.

Azalea wasn't even sure she recognized the woman she thought she knew as her grandmother. This was not the woman who taught her how to make calendula salve after she got stung by a bumblebee dragon, took her to the meadow to pick wild skullcap, or went to the village market every weekend to sell remedies and chat with the locals about sheep and how horrible the weather was.

This was the mage who chose power over being a forest guardian. This was the mage she'd seen on the battlefield.

Azalea's heart grew tight, almost like a spirit had gone through her, but this was worse. This was betrayal, and she suddenly missed her mum. Why wasn't she here? Had RoRo kept her away on purpose?

"No. It is not, but it paints the full picture we need. You may be seated. Thank you, Mage Sharp." Mage Williams gestured for her to take a seat.

RoRo's face was blank of emotion as she took her seat next to Fabian in the stands.

Fabian shook his head at her as she sat down, clearly disgusted, but she didn't even look at him. He hadn't been in on the whole thing, and that made Azalea feel a little better.

"Azalea Sharp, please stand," Mage Williams said.

Azalea stood and was guided to the front by the guard, her cuffed hands clasped together to hide the shaking. She took the same oath as RoRo and felt a flush of magic like a cold shower for a split second, and then it was gone. She eyed the House of Owl mage to the side.

Mage Williams cleared her throat. "Is it true you entered into a soul bond willingly with your apprentice master, Mage Torin Dumont, of the House of Ravens?"

"No. Neither of us knew what it was." A pain shot through Azalea's head, and she doubled over.

"You are lying."

"No, I'm not!" Azalea said. It was the truth. Why was it doing that? Her head pounded, and she was forced to shut her eyes.

Mage Williams glared down at her from her stand, tapping her bony fingers. "The only way to enter a soul bond is willingly. To do so, Mage Dumont called you back from death, and you agreed to the bond. Yes?"

"The goddess Gula made the bond under orders from Ereshkigal." Azalea glared right back at her.

"So that is a yes. You would have died had they not done so?"

"Yes," Azalea answered.

"Then you agreed to it willingly."

Azalea swallowed. This was not how it was supposed to go. "If you put it like that, then yes. But we tried to undo it after that. We found a way. It wasn't like we were trying to use the power."

"But when given the chance to break the bond, you did not." Mage Williams raised her thin lips in a sort of smile. "Instead, you escaped custody after your bond was discovered and made a consensual choice to seal the bond with your apprentice master. Is this true?"

Azalea clasped her hands together tightly. "Well, yes. But we did it so we could close the Echo gate and help fight the House of Ravens and the Archmage."

"But you both wanted to do it?"

"Yes," Azalea said, knowing this was not going well.

"Then the reason does not matter. You made that choice."

Power was building under Azalea's skin. She struggled to push it down, focusing all her energy on not proving their point. She felt Torin's eyes on her but ignored him. Looking at him wouldn't help.

Mage Williams continued. "You will recount all instances leading to the sealing of the bond."

Azalea's cheeks flushed. No way was she sharing all the personal details. They would twist her words, her nights studying with Torin would suddenly sound dirty. They would make her relive everything with Erik and make Torin look like a jealous lover. She would have to share things that were better kept between them.

"No. I won't do it." She set her jaw.

Pain shot through her head again. Whatever she said would make them look worse, and then they'd bring up Torin killing her father, and he would have to relive all of that. It wasn't worth it.

"Very well. Pull the truth from her," Mage Williams ordered the Owl Mage.

"No!" Torin was on his feet, glaring at Mage Williams. "Touch her and I *will* kill you."

Azalea groaned internally. That was not going to help their case.

"Ask me. I'll do it," Torin said as if that would help them forget the death threat.

"You will both recount the events. This is not optional for either of you, Mage Dumont. Now sit down."

Fuck. She was going to have to do it. She was glad her mum wasn't here. One thing was for sure, if they got free, she was going to go live under a rock and avoid people for the rest of her life. Maybe being in jail would be the better option after this since that was what way it seemed to be going.

A rush of wind filled the courtroom. Papers twisted into the air, and a great black dragon appeared above them beneath the glass pyramid roof.

Azalea let out a breath. She had never been so glad to see Ereshkigal in her life, and never thought she would be.

"She is mine. You dare lock your savior in chains?" Ereshkigal bellowed then stretched her wings and glided off the dragon. The goddess landed next to Azalea, and the dragon stretched out in front of the High Councilors, taking up the full length of the row. Its legs folded under, and it began licking its front foot like a cat.

Without warning, Ereshkigal ripped Azalea's shirt and spun her around to show them her back. "She is marked as mine. A demi-goddess. She is above your laws, above your weak magic, and above your judgment."

Azalea clutched her shirt to her chest, her face burning hot as she felt eyes on her exposed back.

"Why do you not recognize their triumph?" Ereshkigal's voice boomed.

The courtroom remained silent, and Ereshkigal turned Azalea back around and undid her handcuffs with a flick of her hand. They dropped to the floor, and Azalea kept holding her shirt to her front.

"These two traveled to the realms of the gods! Despite the gift I gave them, they went on separate quests to save your world, neither expecting to see one another again, and this is what you do to them?"

Mage Williams sunk in her seat looking tiny.

"I placed my favor on them for a reason, and you condemn them for this?" Her voice echoed around the chamber.

Azalea's heart raced, daring to hope there was a way out of this where Ereshkigal didn't kill or curse everyone somehow. The goddess was terrifying and magnificent, her black wings spread wide, and her gold crown with stars glinted in the harsh lights of the room.

"This girl defied me for you. She escaped my realm for you. She tracked an escaped god and returned him to the Echo Dimension for you. And she convinced me to close the gate for all of you."

Ereshkigal's eyes wandered, lingering on certain individuals for seconds at a time, making them look like they shit themselves.

"She bound herself to me and the Shadow Dimension. She is bound to her role to ferry spirits to my great city. You should bow down to her as a new goddess because everything you have is because of her and this man." She pointed at Torin, who hadn't taken his eyes off Azalea.

Azalea hoped Ereshkigal would end this soon and whisk her and Torin away on that dragon. She still had a month here to collect spirits, so hopefully the goddess would hold up that end of their bargain.

"It is your fault she fought my gifts in the first place. You are ungrateful creatures who do not deserve the blessing of the Anunnaki. It is clear why Enlil has forsaken this world and his own House." Ereshkigal spat on the floor.

"You will absolve them of these absurd crimes and revere them as new gods on earth."

Azalea did her best not to wince. That was the last thing she or Torin wanted. Torin's handcuffs clattered to the ground, and he rushed over to Azalea, moving very strategically between her and Ereshkigal. He took off his sweatshirt that was a gray prison-wear type thing with a white t-shirt underneath, and she gladly accepted it.

Ereshkigal stepped off to the side and stood by the guard, who had been looming over Azalea and Torin. He didn't look so big and tough now.

"You will continue," Ereshkigal ordered.

Mage Williams' eyes were wide when she stood back up. Azalea bit her lip, but this time to hide the smile.

"It seems new evidence has come to light," Mage Williams' voice shook. "Does anyone have an account of Mage Dumont's or Apprentice Sharp's actions from the battle?"

"Azalea took down the army the Archmage brainwashed!" Jade called out from the back somewhere. Azalea hadn't even seen her in there.

"Can anyone else confirm this?" Mage Williams asked.

Hands raised all over the room.

Fabian stood up and Azalea tensed. "I witnessed Mage Dumont battle his father, Korbyn Dumont. He tried to take him into custody, but his father turned on him, and he had no choice but to kill him."

"You saw this firsthand and vouch for Mage Dumont?" Mage Williams said.

"Yes. He tried to do what was right but was given no choice but to take down the man. He used the hand of death."

A reverent awe settled across the crowd. Azalea's heart leaped at the fact that Fabian had defended Torin. He had finally seen the good in him.

Mage Williams looked defeated. "Very well. The High Council acknowledges the achievements of Apprentice Azalea Sharp and Mage Torin Dumont in their part in closing the Echo Dimension gateway and in the defeat of the House of Ravens and House of Owls, resulting in the restoration of the High Council." She paused and wet her lips like there was a sour taste in her mouth. "However, the fact remains that they have powers beyond anything or anyone in this world. Therefore, they are dangerous."

A murmur rumbled through the crowd. Ereshkigal looked like she might shoot Mage Williams down with some terrible curse at any moment.

Mage Williams went on. "If they are allowed to be free in this world, they must abide by restrictions placed upon them that will be upheld by the High Council and the Paranormal Justice Unit."

Her gaze moved to Azalea and Torin. Azalea held her breath. There was always a catch.

"Azalea and Torin will remain free, but they are prohibited from working for the Council or any administrative or government body in any country in the world. They will not seek to tip the balance of power. Can you agree to these terms?"

Azalea and Torin both nodded.

"Then you are free," Mage Williams said with a halfhearted wave of her hand. Azalea was surprised the woman didn't throw all her research papers and have a tantrum. She certainly looked like she wanted to.

A cheer rang through the crowd, though it was noticeable that many people remained seated, notably, Mage Skeffington and several High Council members. Azalea suspected no one would ever be fully accepting of their powers.

Torin's hand curled over her shoulder, and she looked up at him.

*"Can we go now?"* she asked.

*"As long as it isn't on that dragon."*

"Come," Ereshkigal ordered and walked toward the dragon.

# Chapter 53

Fabian stood in the ruins of his family house and shook his head. It was fucked. The pool was filled with rubble from the level above where his bedroom used to be. The glass lay shattered, white bricks were scattered everywhere, and the weathervane lay abandoned on the lawn, which was now more mud than grass.

He'd felt it as the wards shattered, like they'd taken part of him with them. He rubbed his chest, then froze as movement in the rubble caught his eye.

Noodle slid out from under a pile of overturned bowls.

"Noodle! You made it." Fabian didn't realize how much he'd missed that stupid skeleton snake. He wound the cold bones around his neck, and the snake vibrated happily, its ghostly tongue tickling his ear.

Kat navigated through the piles of loose stone and shards of broken furniture and art that had somehow been blasted beyond the inner walls.

"Come to witness my downfall, I see." Fabian gestured to his crumbling empire.

Kat shook her head. "Don't be such a sook. It could be much worse, and you know it."

"I s'pose." He absentmindedly petted Noodle's bony head. All those renovations; what a waste. He hadn't the money to keep it running, let alone rebuild it.

"Everyone underground was safe. But there were many casualties on both sides from the battle," Kat said.

Fabian nodded in understanding; he had seen too many of them himself. "How are your people doing?" he asked, staring with unfocused eyes at the mess.

"About half have come over to our side. The rest have been left to the PJU. The Archmage's brainwashing wore off the agents who had been on her side, so it seems relatively corruption free."

Fabian snorted. "As if that was possible. But I'm glad it's working out for you," he said, meaning it.

"You're a good man, Fabian. You know that right? And now other people can see it."

"I did it all for you, love," he said with his best seductive smile.

She slapped his arm. "Oh, come off it. You did the right thing, and you bloody well know it."

He smirked and started gathering bricks into a pile. "Just don't expect me to sit down with Dumont for Christmas dinner anytime soon."

"I think you're safe there. Anyway, he's going to be busy for a while." Kat kicked some bricks toward him.

"So he agreed to come back to the Rook?" Fabian did his best not to sound too interested.

"Not yet. I still need to talk to him, but I have high hopes."

Secretly, he hoped he did. Torin might not be so bad after all. And if he was at the Rook, he was away from Fabian. Win-win. He might have warmed up to Torin a little, in the sort of way he didn't want to kill him anymore, but he also didn't want to see his face every day and certainly not that close to Azalea.

"He's supposed to be teaching Azalea, and look at what happened to her. She's a bloody demi-goddess somehow and bonded to the bloke. Good luck with him running your show."

"You're cute when you're all protective. You know that?" Kat said, then quickly changed the subject. "You haven't seen Torin, have you?"

Fabian's eyes lit up. She said he was cute again.

He shook his head. "Not since he flew off on that dragon with my niece."

Something tumbled from the second story down to the ground, and he caught Kat's arm to steer her away. It was clearly not safe here.

They walked across the grass that had been littered with bodies just days before. Most of them had been knocked out by Azalea when she reversed the Archmage's magic. Some had been very dead, killed by all means of elemental magic and shadows. He tried to block the images from his mind.

Several of them had appeared as ghosts, lost and wandering the battlefield looking for their friends or wondering what the hell was going on. He ignored them and walked the other way. He'd get Azalea to clear the grounds once he reset the blood wards.

"What are your plans now?" Kat asked as they headed back toward the camp. The evening already smelled of wood smoke from the chimneys of the gers, coiling lazily into the still air. Everything was calm and quiet.

"The House of Eagles put out a bond for collecting these mythical creatures on the loose. I guess I'll go back to hunting."

"But not for gallu again?"

"Not this time. I was thinking the world could do with a tidy-up."

"What are they doing with the creatures?"

"Apparently, they've staked out a nice little island somewhere to make a sanctuary. Kind of a Jurassic Park scenario or something."

"Because that went so well." Kat smiled. It was lovely to see her smile. "But it sounds great, Fabian. You'll enjoy it."

"You can come with me, you know. I know you'll miss me."

She raised an eyebrow at him, and he caught her hand. "Come with me, Kat."

She stopped and studied him. He was serious. She had to know that.

"The offer is tempting..." She didn't pull away or slap him.

She did her best to hide her smile, but he saw it. He pulled her closer.

"I knew you wanted me." He leaned into her, the warmth of her body pressed against him, her head tilted toward him expectantly. This was his chance.

But darkness fell over them. She pulled away, already in a defensive stance with her elemer out. A shadow blocked out the sun, and a huge dragon appeared above them.

Great timing...

The dragon landed close to the house—well, what was left of the house—and Azalea jumped off. She was grinning ear to ear, and he couldn't blame her. Riding a dragon was a rare thrill. Perhaps if he found a dragon, he could train it to give rides to people for money...

His chance with Kat had gone, but now he was sure there would be another, and he wasn't too worried.

Dumont slid off the dragon behind Azalea and stumbled forward. It was clear he was not suited to dragon flight. Good to know he had at least one weakness... or two.

He was glad he hadn't noticed it before. Or maybe he had and blocked it out—the way Dumont looked at his niece was unmistakable; they were infatuated with each other, and it was not something he wanted to witness.

*Be nice.* This was his chance to make amends with Azalea, and he couldn't fuck it up like every other time.

Ereshkigal stayed atop her dragon, and Fabian and Kat walked closer to meet them.

"There are new spirits here," Ereshkigal stated, scanning the area like an eagle.

"I'll get them, don't worry," Azalea said as if it were nothing. Something must have changed. A chill ran through Fabian. He'd seen the pain in her eyes that time a spirit went right through her and disappeared. It hadn't made sense then, but now that he knew what she had been subjected to, it was even more disturbing.

Ereshkigal looked disapprovingly at the house. "I will return in one week, clear this area, and we will hunt more spirits."

"I'm allowed to stay!" Azalea shot a gleeful look at Dumont.

"One week then we hunt for three weeks, then we return to the City of Stars." Without another word, Ereshkigal took off into the sky on her dragon.

Dumont's arm fell over Azalea's shoulder, and Fabian tensed as they turned around and saw him and Kat standing there.

"What did she mean about leaving again?" Fabian asked.

Azalea tensed noticeably.

"I made a deal with her. I have to spend six months in the Shadow Dimension and supply her with spirits. But it isn't as bad as before. It doesn't hurt me now," she said.

Fabian's heart sank. "She did this because of you," Fabian said to Torin.

"And you, you idiot." Azalea marched toward him. "I wanted all of you to make it back from the Echo Dimension, and I did what I had to do. I have no regrets."

Kat moved away from Fabian's side and hugged Azalea. "Thank you. I'm sure we couldn't have done it without you."

She strode to Torin next and hugged him. "I'm so proud of you. You will come back to the Rook, won't you?"

Dumont smiled as he hugged her. The relief on his face was apparent. Strange... before this he hadn't thought of Dumont as having any feelings.

He pulled away from Kat. "I have some ideas about that I'd like to discuss with you later. I have something I want to talk to you about too, Fabian, once things are more settled."

Azalea looked excited at the prospect. Fabian couldn't think how this could be good, but right now was his moment to make things right, to free himself of the hatred he'd held onto for so long. But it was hard, and the words stuck to his mouth like peanut butter.

He nodded and cleared his throat. "Sounds good, mate." He glanced at Azalea with her wide gray eyes staring up at him expectantly. He wasn't sure what he'd done to deserve her.

"Look, Torin, I just wanted to say to you—that I'm sorry for um, trying to kill you and whatnot, and I retract my death threats."

Dumont gave a sharp nod in acceptance. "Thank you, Fabian. I appreciate that."

Azalea grinned from ear to ear like she'd won a horse race, not that he'd ever seen her out betting.

Fabian cleared his throat. "I still don't like you, but I saw you take down your old man, and I know that couldn't have been easy. You have my respect and my thanks." He held out his hand to Torin, something he never in a million years would have pictured himself doing.

Torin took it and gave it a firm shake.

"That means a lot." He made eye contact, and his words were heartfelt and genuine.

"Thank you, Uncle Fabian," Azalea said and rushed in for a hug as soon as his hand dropped. He had to admit it felt good. He'd finally done something right by her.

She squeezed him tight and finally broke away, then caught a glimpse of the house in ruins. "Oh my gods, how are we going to fix the house?"

"We? I'm quite certain I'll be the one going down in history as the shitty owner who destroyed the place. I guess we're all living down in the ger camp now." Fabian's shoulders slumped.

"I'm sure there is a way to rebuild it," Azalea said. "There's magic in the walls. I can see it."

"You can see it? A soul bond perk, I suppose?" Fabian frowned. Then checked himself. He was trying to be supportive.

"Um, no. It's actually Ereshkigal's magic. I can see magic now. It's quite beautiful. The house is all tied together with webs of purple magic." Azalea tapped her chin, staring at his pile of bricks. "I think if you got enough people to put everything back, it would knit together."

Azalea placed a brick on top of another brick, and they joined instantly.

"Aren't you just full of surprises? Maybe we can recruit some weather mages to help with moving things around," Fabian pondered aloud.

"Has anyone seen my mum?" Azalea suddenly said, looking around.

Fabian hadn't seen Leda in a while. "Haven't you talked to Rowena?"

"No. We just got back, and I'm not talking to her." Azalea's eyes darkened.

He couldn't blame her. He hadn't seen any of that coming either, the scheming witch. "Oh, yes. Sorry about that. I had no idea."

"I didn't think you did. My mum?"

"Sorry, I didn't think to tell you. She's down in the healer's ger."

Azalea rested her hand on Torin's arm. "I better go check up on her."

"Would you like me to come?" Torin asked.

"No, you talk to Kat about your thing and go find Cassie. I'll come find you." She kissed Torin, then ran off.

Fabian ignored the lingering remnants of anger toward Torin. She was so grown up. He couldn't help but be proud, despite not being able to take any credit.

"Do you mind if I talk to Cassie?" Torin asked Fabian.

"Go for it, mate. She has too many questions for me to answer anyways. She's a curious blighter."

Torin looked relieved. He had never noticed how young Torin was before. He was always his brother's murderer. Even when he was sixteen, he saw him as nothing else, but now he saw he was scarred from his ordeals. He vowed to be nicer, but only a little.

"You know where I can find her?" Torin asked.

"Yeah, she's down at the cemetery. Odd girl. Loves it down there." He was about to add *at her mum's grave,* but Torin probably didn't know Yelena was down there. Maybe it would be best if Cassie was the one to tell him.

Torin picked a few bricks up off the emerging path to add to Fabian's pile. "Thanks. I'll be back for a chat with you, Kat, if you've got a minute soon."

"I'll come find you," Kat said with a wave.

Torin wandered off.

Kat turned to Fabian with a smile he'd never seen before, a true smile.

This was relaxed Kat. He'd only ever known her as a House of Ravens operative under the thumb of Korbyn Dumont, all the while reporting as a double agent to the PJU. He'd never appreciated how much pressure she must have been under until now.

"You didn't answer me before. Want to come on a few adventures?" he asked.

"I need to help Torin get on his feet. He needs to take over the Rook. But yeah, I reckon I could swing some weekend trips."

"I knew it." He caught her up in his arms and spun her around. He kissed her just the way he had imagined for so long. But this time it was real, and she kissed him back.

# Chapter 54

Torin walked around the crumbling house and down to the cemetery next to the garden where they'd had Azalea's apprentice ceremony. He spotted a tuft of Cassie's hair around the side of a gravestone and swung open the creaky gate, glad of the noise to give her some warning he was coming rather than sneak up on her.

She poked her head around the gravestone and waved when she saw him. So far, so good.

"Hey, Cassie. I wanted to talk to you." He stopped next to the grave she was hanging out at. She was sitting cross-legged on a blanket, leaning against the headstone with a book in her lap.

"Good. I was worried Fabian was never going to let me see you again after... you know."

After he killed their dad in front of her, plus every other thing Fabian had against him. "Same, but against all odds, he seems to be warming up to me." Torin sat down at the end of the slab of stone that covered the grave. "So, you like hanging out here?"

She nodded. "It's nice. I come here to read. But I was just talking to mum, telling her all about you and how you saved us all." She grinned.

"Mum?" He glanced around, looking for Mrs. Yates.

"I mean *our* mum. Here." She patted the gravestone behind her.

Torin's heart dropped to his feet. "Our mum," he repeated. All those years ago, in his apprentice ceremony, his mum had told him to find her, and he finally had. Well, Cassie had.

"You didn't know she was here?" Cassie said softly.

He shook his head as he swallowed hard. Cassie shuffled to the edge of the slab and slid off to stand by Torin.

*Here lies Yelena Dumont*

*Guided by shadows, now free to dream her dreams*

He couldn't help but wonder if she was in the Shadow Dimension somewhere.

"Don't feel bad. They lied to me too. I didn't know I had a father or brother, but I'm happy I've found you now." Cassie wrung her hands.

He realized she was as nervous as he was but hiding behind her confidence. "Me too. I'm sorry I didn't know."

"It's okay, I know it wasn't your fault. So you're a Shadow Mage like Fabian? Maybe you can teach me when I'm older," she blurted.

"I'd like that. If Fabian allows it," he said, doubting he would, but that would fit in well with an idea for the future of the Rook he'd been toying with.

Cassie picked at her sleeve. "Good. So are you moving to the Rook? Fabian told me it was our father's home. Did you grow up there?"

How was she so open, so welcoming after finding out the truth, after witnessing so much death and destruction?

"Yes, I grew up there. But it wasn't a nice place then. I'm hoping I can change that." Hoping the people left would forgive him for abandoning them for so long. Would they accept him back like Kat said? He was dreading finding out. He'd tried so hard to push that place into the furthermost recesses of his mind and lock it behind a wall.

Kat appeared at the gate to the cemetery, waiting for him.

"Where are you staying?" he asked.

"In the camp with my mum and dad. We're hoping Fabian is going to repair the house. Some of it is fine. Our rooms are fine, but we're waiting until it's all safe. I can't really go back to school. I dunno if it's still standing. Hopefully, my friends are safe."

"I'm sure they are. Fabian would have picked a very safe school for you, knowing our father. It kept you hidden this long, so it'll be fine."

"Good point." She smiled. "I think Kat wants to talk to you."

Torin glanced toward the gate. "Do you want me to walk you back to the camp? It's getting cold."

"No, I'll be fine. I'll read a little longer. But will you take me to see the Rook one day?"

Torin's throat grew thick. "I'd love to."

"Thanks, Torin." She leaned forward and wrapped her arms around his middle in a brief hug he didn't even have time to react to, then nestled back in her blanket against the headstone.

He walked toward Kat, knowing what she was going to say, and he was ready.

"Will you come to the Rook now? With everything falling apart, the House of Ravens needs guidance. We need new leadership to undo everything Korbyn did. We need you, Torin." Kat said, her eyes pleading with him.

"Okay." Torin swung open the gate and kept walking, so she had to catch up with him.

"What? That easy? I was sure you were going to fight me on it."

"I always said I would go back and set things right. This is my chance to do something good in the world."

"*Torin, my mum's really sick. I think I need to take her back to our forest,*" Azalea's voice blared in his head.

"Shit." He upped his pace. "*Hold on, I'm heading your way now. I'll come with you.*"

"What is it?" Kat kept up with him.

"Azalea's mum is sick. She needs to take her back to their forest."

"Just don't forget about your people, Torin. We need you too," Kat yelled after him.

# Chapter 55

Azalea felt Torin enter the room before she saw him.

"She isn't healing." She wiped a cold flannel over her mum's brow. "She was stabbed with an elemer in the battle, and I tried to heal her. I had some magic kicked back from a healer, but Maiken says some of the magic of the person who attacked her might be stuck inside. I can see the magic in it."

Torin moved the gauze covering the wound and frowned.

Azalea already knew it was bad. It was inflamed, angry red, with black lines creeping out from the scar. But worse than that, Azalea was the only one who could see the glow of golden magic in the wound, creeping into her mother's veins. It was something from the House of Owls that was poisoning her.

RoRo stepped into the ger and marched over, glancing over Torin's shoulder. "She needs to go to the heart of the forest."

"I am well aware of what she needs," Azalea snapped. She knew that because Maiken had mentioned it ten minutes ago. But she wasn't going to say that to RoRo. She was still pissed off at her. Her heart physically hurt when she thought of all the lies her grandmother must have told her over the years. But it was setting the ravens on her and Isaac that was unforgivable. Isaac could have died.

RoRo didn't budge. She moved to stand at the end of Leda's bed with her arms crossed, her face furrowed in a frown.

Azalea felt Torin's gaze shift and focus on the two beds across the other side of the ger. "Is that Van and Isaac?"

"Yes. They're okay. But Van went full vampire after overdoing it on the healing magic, and there weren't enough supplements. Isaac must have been in the wrong place at the wrong time because she almost drained him." Azalea's hands shook. There had been too many shocks already today. She had to focus on her mum.

"She doesn't need you." Azalea glared at RoRo. "I'm going to take her now."

RoRo put a hand to her heart. "Please, Petal. Let me help."

"No! You've done enough already. She was the one protecting me while you were throwing me straight into the fire. We don't need you."

"I'm sorry, love. I did what I thought was right. And look how it turned out. Everything was for the better."

"For the better? My mum is dying, Fabian's house is half destroyed, the world is in chaos, and I have to live in the Shadow Dimension half the year. Is that what you envisioned from this prophecy? Was it all worth it?" Azalea screamed.

"You formed a soul bond; you have powers others would kill for—have killed for. You should be more grateful," RoRo snapped.

Azalea clenched her fists to her side. She was not going to react. "You're starting to sound a lot like the Archmage."

"What a horrible thing to say. I'm nothing like her."

RoRo hid behind a guise of wanting to protect Azalea, but nothing she had done was protective. It was so Azalea could one day be her puppet. To have some form of control over the power.

"You're just like her!" Azalea said.

"There is no reason to raise your voice. This is a hospital." RoRo's hands went to her hips.

Azalea's hands vibrated with the strain of keeping her magic in. But she took a breath, and, with control, she pulled it back. She wasn't worth it. She turned back to her mum. "We're leaving now. Can you help me carry her, Torin?"

"Gladly." He shot a dark look at RoRo, scooped Leda into his arms, and followed Azalea out the door.

☽ ☽ ☽ ● ☾ ☾ ☾

It was dark by the time they were in the forest. Faraday ran along in front, and Azalea's senses were alive, being back in her old stomping ground. As they trudged along, she breathed in the familiar scent of the damp forest floor littered with sodden leaves and the loveliness of decaying logs. She'd never appreciated the old forest as much as she did right now.

Her eyes adjusted to the darkness as they went further into the woodland. The mushrooms lit up the path with low blue light like fairy landing strips. The path grew narrow, and low-hanging branches creaked out of the way. They were close.

She was grateful for the clear night and filtered light of the waxing gibbous moon. It was so different from her last experience here, being dragged along reluctantly in that horrible rain, the kind that soaked you to the bone, and her mum so focused on fixing her. Though now she knew how her mum must have felt.

This time, it was her chance to fix things.

"I think we're nearly there," she called back to Torin, who was silently trudging along behind her, her mum between them on the stretcher. She'd tried to go through the Hollow to the heart of the forest, but it seemed to be too protected by the forest's magic.

She decided to enjoy this walk. It might be the last time she came here in a while. Behind them, she sensed spirits following, but they wouldn't be a problem. At least that was one thing she knew how to deal with now.

As they neared the clearing, Azalea went over the ceremony in her mind. She had grabbed one of her mum's old kits from their cottage, and she'd scanned over the items briefly, but she could easily have left something out.

Suddenly, they were there, crossing the line of silver birch trees into the open space. She felt exposed among the standing stones that formed the sacred circle.

They lowered her mum in the center of the stones, and Azalea rushed to pour a salt circle around them. Without speaking, Torin and Azalea set up the ceremony.

Leda was deathly silent and hot to the touch. But this wasn't a fever or infection that any concoction of herbs or antibiotics could fix. They needed the forest.

"Can you get some wood?" she asked Torin, realizing her mum had prearranged a fire the last time.

She got out her mum's worn chopping board scarred with years of hard work. Next, the old earthenware bowl that was chipped, but functional; she placed it on the board and retrieved a fresh white candle, a white feather, and a bundle of sage mixed with dried rosemary, balm of Gilead, thyme, and vervain.

Digging into the bag, she found matches and a wad of old newspaper. She started scrunching up pieces, so by the time Torin came back with enough kindling, she was ready to arrange it on top.

"Hang on, Mum. Nearly there," she mumbled as she worked.

The fire sparked to life on the first try and hungrily ate the kindling. Torin arrived with larger bits of wood, and the fire was ready for them. Her front sweltered beneath her thick jacket, though her back remained freezing.

"There's a fair few spirits gathering now," Torin said as he sunk to the ground to sit next to Azalea.

She relaxed as his knee rested against hers.

"They won't get past the salt. I think I'm ready." Her mum's chest rose and fell, her face serene in the stillness of the night.

Torin's hand closed around Azalea's as she took in a long, slow breath and closed her eyes.

She dropped into deep meditation. It felt so natural now, like coming home or sinking into a safe place.

The energy of the forest welled around her. For the first time, she felt what her mother had gone on about all those years. She instantly wanted to tell her mum, then remembered what she was doing, and her breath hitched for a second.

"Great goddess, we call upon you. In the light of the waxing gibbous moon, we draw upon your ancient power. As protectors of this ancient forest, we ask that you protect your loyal guardian. Aid her in the battle against this corrupt magic and give her strength. We honor you."

Azalea opened her eyes to see a shimmering green glow settle across everything within the standing stones like a veil of emerald silk.

Letting go of Torin's hand, she filled the bowl with water and set the feather across the top. She lit the candle, then touched the flickering flame to the bundle of herbs which curled greedily with red edges quickly turning to black, filling the air with aromatic smoke tinted with green magic.

Waving the sage over her mother's body, she silently prayed to the goddess Ninhursag to heal her.

Occasionally, Torin added to the fire, and Azalea kept lighting bundles of herbs. The moon trailed from one side of the clearing, then dipped below the trees on the other.

The goddess never came, but then again, she never had in any of her mother's ceremonies, and she always swore they had worked.

Bright embers glowed in the fire as the flames died down low.

Azalea lifted her mum's shirt to check the wound and let out a sigh of relief. The gold magic was nowhere to be seen. The green magic soaked back into the earth and into Leda, and Azalea let out a breath.

"It worked," she breathed.

"My demi-goddess." Torin kissed her cheek, and she leaned onto his shoulder and nearly collapsed backward from exhaustion.

He caught her and set her upright.

"No more Mageling?" she cuddled closer to his side, trying to get warm.

"I think you're well past Mageling now. How about Magelet?"

"Is that better?"

"I have no idea. I like demi-goddess."

A weak groan came from Leda's lips.

"Mum! You're awake!" Azalea nearly jumped on her mum with excitement.

"Blimey, I feel like I've been hit by a herd of elephants." She leaned up on her elbows.

"You're fine, Mum, we're back in the forest. I did your ceremony, and it worked."

Leda looked around and rested her head back down. "Ah, so we are." She smiled to herself. "I'm proud of you, Azalea."

"I'm not sure I did anything. I think it might have been the forest."

"We are part of the forest. Always remember that." She licked her lips, and Azalea rushed to get her water. She must be thirsty after all that.

Leda took a long sip of water. "Ninhursag gave me a job."

"You saw the goddess?" Torin asked.

"What did she say?" Azalea added.

"I am to take the seeds and give them to the right people, people who will nurture them and protect them. The balance of the world will reset."

"Let's not worry about that now. For now, rest and we'll get you back home." She eyed the spirits gathering around the edge of the salt ring. Funnily enough, she was looking forward to sending them off.

"The cottage?"

"Yes, Mum. It's safe now. You can go back."

She sat up and pulled Azalea into a big hug. "What a clever girl you are."

"Okay, you can let me go now. I've just got one thing to do before we leave, then we can go home."

Azalea stepped over the salt circle and embraced the spirits as they walked toward her. She was ready to see their stories and send them on their way.

# Epilogue
## *One Month Later*

The smell of Shadow Magic permeated the very walls of the Rook. The hallway lined with tapestries and statues felt shorter, narrower than Torin remembered, and it didn't seem as dark or as cold as it had when he was a boy. He half expected his father to walk out of his office and yell at Torin to get his arse in there. Thank the gods he didn't and never would.

Torin pushed open the door to his father's office, feeling rebellious for not knocking. His foot hovered over the threshold, then he stepped in. The stench of old cigar smoke lingered in the air; it was ingrained in the walls, the leather, probably even the books. Hopefully, he could save the books.

He went straight to the windows and threw them all open to reveal the dull gray sky—back the way it should be. People were already arriving outside, but he'd wanted to come in here first. See the place and know his father wasn't still there. It was silly but necessary.

The sword in his hand was heavy, and he wasted no time and conducted no ceremony as he placed it back in the mount with the House of Ravens family crest. He slipped his father's elemer into his belt and patted his jacket pocket to make sure the relic he'd taken was still there.

"It's good to see you be the one to place that back in there." A voice sounded from the doorway.

Torin's head whipped around. "Sampson. Gods, it's good to see you." He marched over to the old butler and shook his hand.

"I knew you'd make it back, Master Torin."

"You can just call me Torin."

"I know, but I still see you as a wee lad, even though you've grown to be a strapping fellow. It's good to have you back here." Sampson gave him a firm slap on the back.

Torin took a last look around the room, this would be first on the agenda for redecorating. "I would say it's good to be back, but I'm still not certain about that."

"You'll come right with time. But in the meantime, everyone's waiting for you. Better get outside."

"I'm glad you're here, Sampson. I'm going to need a lot of help." He held his hand out to Sampson.

Sampson took it in both hands and shook vigorously. "Anything for you, Master Torin, all you need to do is ask."

Torin nodded in thanks as footsteps sounded in the hall outside.

"We thought you might need a kick in the bum to get out there," Kira said, then marched into the office and looked around with disgust. "That arsehole got what he deserved."

"He deserved a lot worse. It almost seems like he got away with it," Torin said bitterly.

"Well, he didn't." Kira went into the drawer, pulled out a bottle of brandy, took a swig, and handed it to Torin. "Come on, he's not here."

Torin took the bottle from her and swallowed a mouthful of burning liquid. "Cheers, Dad."

Kira took back the bottle grinning. "I've always wanted to do that." She nudged him. This was the Kira he remembered.

"Hiya, Torin." Matt bounced into the room, followed by Torin's former squad mates, Dev and Conner. Matt hugged him so hard he could feel the excitement bubbling out of him. Dev was next with a back-slapping hug, then Conner sauntered over.

"Thank fuck you're back, mate." He threw his arms around Torin, and he knew Conner meant it. They handed the bottle of brandy around until they'd all had a swig.

Conner put the bottle on the desk. "Come on, mate. We've come to force you outside."

Torin smiled. "I'm not going to run away. I'm ready."

"Good, because you can't get out of this now." Conner gave his shoulder a friendly, though firm, squeeze.

He followed his old friends outside and marched across the gravel driveway to the podium set up with the backdrop of the Rook and all its castle glory in the background. It would look good in the photos, Danni had said.

Torin nodded and shook hands with people as he waded through the crowd to get to the front. There were a lot more people than he'd expected; hopefully, it wouldn't rain. It was the first time the doors to the Rook had been open to outsiders in over one hundred years. He supposed many of them were just curious.

A wide smile spread to Azalea's eyes as soon as she saw him. He could never get enough of that.

She stood at the front of the crowd, wearing a simple black dress and a red coat with black lace-up boots. She looked stunning. *"You were nearly late."*

Torin stopped in front of her and kissed her on the cheek. *"I'm here now, Mageling, be patient."*

She rolled her eyes but smiled as he stepped up onto the makeshift stage. He studied the crowd, a mixture of all Houses, but mostly Shadow Magic houses: Ravens, Snakes, Winged Bulls, and White Deer.

His eyes fell on individuals, lingering for slow seconds as he made eye contact. Their backs straightened, and he caught that glimpse of fear in their eyes, a remnant of his father's rule.

A hush formed over the crowd. Everyone he knew was there—even Fabian, who he suspected was dragged along by Kat. Mergen, the shaman, stood with some of the House of Snake mages and High Council members. Cassie was with her parents. Danni and Maiken were in the front row with Ava and Zoe. Azalea's mum looked much better than the last time he'd seen her, and he noticed that she wasn't standing with Rowena. Van and Isaac were together, which was nice considering she'd tried to eat him, and Jade sat in a chair at the front cradling that bloody dragon's egg they still needed to give back. He wasn't quite sure why Ereshkigal hadn't claimed it yet. There were even people from the Tower of London, ones who had proven not to be in league with the Archmage.

"Thank you all for coming." Torin forced confidence into his voice. "This is a chance for new beginnings and to honor the dead. We have all been through a lot, but it is up to us to learn from this and reshape the world in a way that can make a difference."

Applause followed his pause, which he hadn't been expecting. Azalea beamed from the side of the stage. The rest of his speech included acknowledging as many people as he could in hopes of bringing them all together to be a catalyst for cooperation in the future. After he spoke, Torin stood in the crowd next to Fabian. As the next speech started, he slipped the jade dragon relic into Fabian's hand without saying a word.

Fabian looked down at his hand, and his eyes grew wide.

"Keep it safe," Torin whispered.

After several more speeches, they unveiled a memorial obelisk next to the flag poles on the front lawn. Everyone stood around admiring it, and Torin took the chance to seek out Mergen. "You should have this to bring back to your people. I'm sorry for all the pain my father caused." Torin held out the bone elemer his father had taken from the shaman Altan so many years ago.

Mergen nodded in approval, accepted the elemer with two hands, and bowed his head. "I thank you, Torin Dumont, you are the leader this House needs. Use your powers well."

The old man studied the elemer before tucking it into his belt.

"There is one more thing," Torin yelled to get the crowd's attention once more. Azalea came to stand next to him and took his hand. They stood in front of the obsidian monument with the dull gray backdrop of sky behind them. Danni, Kat, and Fabian joined them in front of the crowd.

"We would like to announce that the Rook will be reopening in a few months' time as a new school for magic."

A quiet mumbling surged through the crowd.

Torin continued, "This will be a magic school run with the cooperation of all Shadow Magic houses and open to all students." He heard his heartbeat over the crowd's silence.

He swallowed back his nerves and continued, "Though Shadow Magic will be the focus, we will also incorporate Echo Magic into the studies and will be open to all students who wish to study here. We already have one student on the list." He nodded to Cassie, and she waved to the crowd, grinning. "We hope more of your families will join us."

He explained it would include primary through university level, teaching normal school curriculum until they reached sixteen when they could start their magic studies.

He took a breath, hoping this wasn't going to be a bust.

"And with that, I officially announce the establishment of the Shadow Magic Academy."

Fireworks shot into the air, and a wall of fire sprung up behind them. He suspected Danni was behind it.

Vigorous clapping competed with the fireworks and shrill whistles of support.

Azalea squeezed his hand, and he let out a breath of relief. This was the part he had been nervous about. His grand idea that now seemed like a monumental task. But seeing the enthusiasm made him think that maybe it was the right thing to do after all.

A great black dragon descended from the sky as the fireworks died down. Torin's heart sank. The goddess could have picked better timing.

*"I was hoping we had a bit longer,"* Azalea said in his head.

Torin pulled Azalea away from the crowd as everyone watched the dragon circling above. *"She already gave us an extra week. Let's hope she's in a good mood."*

Azalea gripped his hand tightly and spoke aloud. "There's so much I want to say to you."

He tucked her hair behind her ear. "You don't need to. We can still see each other in our dreams, and it's not forever." He brushed his thumb across her jawbone and kissed her hard. Her breath danced over his lip as she pulled away.

"I know, and you'll be busy starting your YouTube channel—*Prophet Torin of the House of Ravens.*" She grinned.

"And when you're back you will be helping me with that—and it won't be called that."

"*The Word of Torin.*" She grinned.

She had an endless supply of name suggestions. "No. Just remember I'm still your teacher, and we will be continuing your apprentice training so you can become a mage, even if you come back thinking you know everything about Shadow Magic. And you can get back into your uni studies." He was reminding himself more than her. *This wasn't the end.*

"Which I may have to start again..." She winced.

"And when you're away you can get to know your dad, and you are a demi-goddess, I'm sure that comes with some perks." He squeezed her hand.

She smiled. "Living in a palace wouldn't be the worst thing. And you're right, it's not forever." She looked up at the sky but continued to grip his hand tightly as they stood in silence, leaning on one another as the dragon circled elegantly until it reached the ground.

Ereshkigal spread her wings and flew from her dragon, ignoring the crowd.

"It is time to go." Ereshkigal's gaze homed in on Azalea.

"Ooo, it's hatching!" Jade cried out. She set the dragon's egg on the ground, and everyone moved back as the goddess glided toward her.

Azalea pulled Torin along to Jade's side.

The shell had tiny glowing fractures that spread all around it. A loud TAP TAP came from within. Then shards flew everywhere. The egg shattered in a mini explosion, and when Torin looked back, a tiny blue dragon sat on the grass staring up at Jade with wide eyes that were all black and as round as the obsidian orbs the seers used.

It shimmered with iridescent blue scales, so tiny you could hardly see them, and was about the size of a Jack Russel. Jade held out her hand for the dragon to sniff, and it offered a tiny chirp in return.

"It has chosen you, human," Ereshkigal did not sound pleased.

"She says her name is Immaru." Jade held her hand steady while the dragon rubbed the top of its head on it. Jade was beaming.

Ereshkigal towered over Jade, her wings sending shadows across the crowd. "You are now bound to be guardian of this dragon. Do you accept this role?"

"Yes," Jade squeaked, but her gaze was on the tiny dragon puffing steam and trying to climb onto Jade's lap.

Ereshkigal clapped, and a shower of sparkling darkness fell over Jade and Immaru then disappeared. "So it is done. Your task with the dragon is to travel to the City of Stars every full moon."

Jade's mouth fell open as the dragon began licking her cheek.

"You may remain in the city and bring one guest." Her eyes fell on Torin, and a lightness flooded him. Ereshkigal was doing this so he could see Azalea. She'd had a plan all along with the dragon's egg. He didn't speak, fearing that saying anything aloud would make her retract her offer.

Ereshkigal pulled something from inside a bag that appeared from nowhere. "You can have this back. I am sick of it," Ereshkigal handed Azalea the Shadow Atlas, Sita, back in his book form, and she instantly set him free again. Torin had been wondering where he had gotten to, but Azalea hadn't seemed worried about the demon.

"About bloody time." Sita shook himself out and uncrunched his ears.

Azalea ruffled his head. "Don't be such a grouch."

"Say goodbye," Ereshkigal ordered.

Torin was starting to realize this was the goddess being kind.

Azalea took his hand as they walked to the dragon together. Stopping, she took both his hands in hers. "The school will be brilliant."

"I hope so. Have fun in the Shadow Dimension." He didn't want to let go of her, despite knowing she would be fine.

"I'll see you on the next full moon. I can't wait to show you the palace and the City of Stars." Her eyes lit up. Her excitement was contagious. This wasn't a front to make them both feel better. It was a new beginning.

"I can't wait to see it." He let go of her hands as she said goodbye to her mum and their friends. He smiled to himself at the prospect of visiting Azalea in the Shadow Dimension. He could see Licorice again, maybe find his mum.

Suddenly, it was time.

She stood on her tiptoes and kissed him, softly at first, then with an intensity that made him think they shouldn't be doing this in front of people. He found he didn't care and kissed her back like they were the only people on earth.

A loud *reooow* sounded, and they parted lips to see Faraday standing at their feet looking unimpressed.

Azalea giggled. "I think he wants to go."

"I think you're right." Torin bent down to pat the little cat's head. Faraday rubbed along his leg then stood on Azalea's boot.

She picked up the cat and hugged him to her chest, and Torin helped her onto the back of the dragon, then handed her the bag she had been keeping with her at all times. Faraday hopped up and nestled into the spare bag she pulled out.

"See you soon. Love you." Torin waved, but it didn't really feel like goodbye.

"Love you too," Azalea said as Faraday's head popped out the top of the bag.

Ereshkigal flew onto the dragon's neck and launched them into the sky without another word. Azalea squealed as they took off, waving and beaming from the dragon's back with Faraday and Sita tucked tightly in front of her.

Torin watched as the dragon got smaller and smaller until it was a tiny black spec in the blanket of clouds. Danni appeared next to him and put an arm around his shoulders, and for the first time in his life, he felt surrounded by family.

# Shadow Atlas Glossary

**Abigale Shepard-** Teacher at the Tower of London Initiates Program. Mind and water mage. House of Owls.

**The Anunnaki-** Pantheon of Sumerian Gods.

**The Archmage-** Esther Norwich. A powerful mind mage. Head of the House of Owls, Master of the Tower of London.

**Apprentice-** Level of magic training after initiate.

**Aqrabuamelu-** Also known as Scorpion People. Guardians and warriors of the Echo Dimension, with the body of a giant scorpion and the torso of a human.

**Azalea Sharp-** Student of Shadow Magic and Echo Magic. House of Snakes and House of Bees.

**Barghest-** Giant hounds from the Shadow Dimension.

**Bashmu-** Giant horned serpent.

**Blackbourne Manor-** Country house owned by Fabian Blackbourne. Headquarters of the House of Snakes.

**Cassie Yates-** Fabian Blackbourne's ward. Daughter of Colin and Mary Yates.

**City of Stars-** City in the Shadow Dimension mostly inhabited by spirits. Ruled by Ereshkigal and Nergal.

**Colin Yates-** Groundskeeper at Blackbourne Manor.

**Conner Stewart-** Torin's squad mate from the House of Ravens.

**Damu-** God of healing. Son of Gula, goddess of healing. Resides in the Shadow Dimension.

**Danni Fletcher-** A powerful fire mage. House of Phoenix. Works for the Paranormal Justice Unit as an agent. Is married to Maiken Hawthorn.

**Dev-** Torin's squad mate from the House of Ravens.

**Dumuzi-** Husband of Inanna. Echo Dimension Shepherd God. Was trapped in the underworld by Ereshkigal.

**Echo Dimension-** Dimension above the mortal world. Populated by gods and mythical creatures. Source of Echo magic.

**Echo Magic-** Magic sourced from the Echo Dimension. Used by mages and students of the four Echo Dimension Houses. Includes discipline of elemental magic: fire, water, earth, and air. Plus more refined disciplines of weather control, mind magic, and plant magic.

**Elam Frost-** Initiate at the Tower of London. House of Owls. Grandson of the Archmage. Twin brother of Livia.

**Elemer-** A magical dagger that is used to channel magic. Has a blade on one end and a key on the other.

**Enki-** God of water and mind magic. Patron of the House of Owls. Creator of mankind. Resides in the Echo Dimension in the Palace of the Waters.

**Enlil-** God of air and weather magic. Patron of the House of Eagles. Resides in the Echo Dimension.

**Ereshkigal-** Queen of the Underworld. Goddess of death and the dead. Patron of the House of Snakes. Ruler of the Shadow Dimension alongside her husband Nergal.

**Eridan-** River that runs through the Shadow Dimension.

**Erik Faber-** Azalea's classmate at the Tower of London. Training in Echo Magic, specifically in fire magic and metalwork. House of Phoenix.

**Evangeline Grey-** Healer apprentice. Shadow Magic. House of White Deer.

**Fabian Blackbourne-** Head of the House of Snakes. Gallu hunter, shadow mage, previously employed by the Paranormal Justice Unit. Azalea's uncle. Samael Blackbourne's brother.

**Faraday-** Azalea's pet cat.

**Gallu-** Spirit monsters from the Shadow Dimension that have become fully corporeal. Are dangerous and capable of killing humans to absorb their spirits.

**Geshtinanna-** Goddess of agriculture and sister of Dumuzi. Controls the seasons on Earth.

**Great Desert of Dreams-** Dream realm ruled by the god Zakar.

**Griffin-** Creature with the body of a lion and the head of an eagle.

**Gula-** Goddess of healing. Patron of the House of White Deer. Mother of the god Damu. Resides in the Shadow Dimension.

**House of Bees-** House of magic founded by the goddess Ninhursag. Specializes in plant magic. Magic comes from the Echo Dimension.

**House of Eagles-** House of magic founded by the god Enlil. Specializes in air and weather magic. Magic comes from the Echo Dimension.

**House of Eagle's Tower-** House of Eagles headquarters in London. A large skyscraper that contains apartments, offices, a mall for magic users, a giant indoor forest and lobby area, scientific labs, a courtroom, and meeting place for the High Council.

**House of Owls-** House of magic founded by the god Enki. Specializes in mind and water magic. Magic comes from the Echo Dimension.

**House of Phoenix-** House of magic founded by the god Utu. Specializes in fire magic. Magic comes from the Echo Dimension.

**House of Ravens-** House of magic founded by the god Zakar. Specializes in sleep and dream magic. Magic comes from the Shadow Dimension.

**House of Snakes-** House of magic founded by the goddess Ereshkigal. Specializes in necromancy and spirit magic. Magic comes from the Shadow Dimension.

**House of Winged Bulls-** House of magic founded by the goddess Nanna. Specializes in divination. Magic comes from the Shadow Dimension.

**House of White Deer-** House of magic founded by the goddess Gula. Specializes in healing magic. Magic comes from the Shadow Dimension.

**The Hollow-** Sub-dimension between the mortal world and the Shadow Dimension. Used by certain shadow mages to travel between any two places.

**Inanna-** Queen of Heaven. Goddess of war, sex, love, and fertility. Her city is Erech where she is ruler of the Echo Dimension.

**Initiate-** First-level magic trainee.

**Isaac-** Azalea's best friend from home. Non-magic.

**Isimud-** Two-faced God. Enki's messenger. Resides in the Echo Dimension.

**Jade Pike-** Initiate at the Tower of London. Studying Echo Magic. House of the Winged Bull and House of Eagles.

**Kat Emerson-** Shadow mage and assassin from the House of Ravens. Torin's trainer from the Rook. Trusted adviser of Korbyn Dumont.

**Kira Reid-** Torin's best friend from childhood. House of Ravens. Shadow Magic.

**Korbyn Dumont-** Head of the House of Ravens. Powerful Shadow Magic. Torin Dumont's father.

**Kur-** Land in the Shadow Dimension ruled by Ereshkigal and Nergal.

**Land of Light-** Another name for the Echo Dimension. Used by the gods and residents of the Echo Dimension.

**Leda Sharp-** Azalea's mother. Forest Guardian. Uses small amounts of ambient Echo Magic for plants, but is not a mage.

**Licorice-** Torin's pet raven from his childhood.

**Livia Frost-** Initiate at the Tower of London. House of Owls. Granddaughter of the Archmage. Twin sister of Elam.

**Maglium Boat-** Boat used to cross the river Eridan to enter Kur in the Shadow Dimension.

**Maiken Hawthorn-** A powerful healer mage of the House of White Deer. Wife of Danni Fletcher.

**Matt-** Torin's squad mate from the House of Ravens.

**Mary Yates-** Housekeeper at Blackbourne Manor. Married to Colin Yates, mother of Cassie Yates.

**Mrs. Young-** Cook for the House of Ravens at the Rook. Unofficial healer, originally from the House of White Deer.

**Mushussu Dragon-** Rainbow dragon of Enlil. Has a long serpent-like body, iridescent wings, and a pointed muzzle with whiskers.

**Nabu-** The Scribe. Grandson of Enki. Resides in the Echo Dimension.

**Nergal**- King of the Underworld. God of death, war, and destruction. Husband of Ereshkigal.

**Neti**- Guardian of the Seven Gates of the Shadow Dimension.

**Ninhursag**- Goddess of plants and earth. Patron of the House of Bees. Creator of mankind. Resides in the Echo Dimension.

**Palace of the Waters**- Enki's Palace in the Echo Dimension.

**Paranormal Justice Unit (PJU)**- Magical police force. Tasked with keeping magic a secret from the non-magical population in England. Law enforcement, investigation of magic-related incidents, control, and concealment of magical creatures, detainment of dangerous magic users. Funded and heavily influenced by the High Council and the House of Owls.

**The Rook**- Estate of Korbyn Dumont and base for the House of Ravens. Military magic school for Shadow Magic training.

**Rowena Sharp**- A powerful plant mage from the House of Bees. Azalea's maternal grandmother.

**Samael Blackbourne**- Shadow Mage of House of Snakes. Azalea Sharp's father. Deceased.

**Scorpion People**- Also known as Aqrabuamelu. Guardians and warriors of the Echo Dimension.

**The Shadow Atlas**- A mysterious magical book that speaks in riddles and maps.

**The Shadow Dimension**- The dimension below the mortal world. Populated by gods, demons, and spirits. Source of Shadow Magic.

**Shadow mage**- A mage that uses Shadow Magic.

**Shadow Magic**- Magic sourced from the Shadow Dimension. Used by mages and students of the four Shadow Magic

Houses. Includes disciplines of healing, manipulating shadows, Hollow travel, divination, spirit magic, and dream magic.

**Sitaddaru-** 'Sita.' A Wayfinder demon from the Shadow Dimension.

**Spell cloud-** forming a spell in one's mind by drawing power symbols into their thoughts.

**Taniwha-** (Ta-nee-fa) Mythical shape-shifting reptilian guardian of a cave in New Zealand.

**Torin Dumont-** Powerful Shadow Mage from the House of Ravens.

**The Tower of London-** Base for the House of Owls. A popular tourist attraction in London, also home to a secret community of mages.

**Utu-** God of fire magic. Patron of the House of Phoenix. Resides in the Echo Dimension.

**Wraith Gallu-** Spirit monsters from the Shadow Dimension in their weakest form. They seek to feed on human spirits.

**Zakar-** God of sleep and dream magic. Patron of the House of Ravens. Resides in the Great Desert of Dreams.

# Also By Jenny Sandiford

**Read The Shadow Atlas Prequel for Free!**
Go to jennysandiford.com

**The Shadow Atlas Series**

# Acknowledgments

The biggest thanks to those of you who took a shot on a new author and picked up the first book, stuck by me through the second, and now find yourself at the end of this magical journey with Captive. I truly hope you enjoyed it!

A special thanks to everyone in my advanced reader team. Your reviews always make my day.

A huge thank you to everyone has supported me, even in the little ways. You have no idea how grateful I am for every book review, every post shared, and every word-of-mouth recommendation you give to your friends and family. Your enthusiasm makes the hard work all worthwhile!

To my wonderful husband Michael, thank you for your love and support and for putting up with my weird writing hours and editing-induced near-meltdowns. Thank you for carrying all the heavy boxes of books to sell at stalls and for everything you have done to make my writing dreams come true. I couldn't do this without your encouragement.

A massive thanks to Liz Highland, for beta reading this book so quickly! I promise to have more friendly deadlines in the future!

My deepest thanks to Mandi Oyster, my meticulous and insightful editor. Your magical editing skills and constructive feedback have shaped not only this book, but the whole series into what it is today. Thank you for sticking with me and delving so deep into the Shadow Atlas world alongside me.

To my proofreader Amy McKenna, your keen eye has saved me from many a blunder. Thank you for seeing the things that I cannot and for your commentary as you read—it always makes me smile.

Thank you to my critique partner, Bethany Arliss, for being on this publishing journey alongside me. I'm so glad we found each other. Can you believe we both made it to the end of our trilogies?!

Thank you to the groups here in Darwin, Write Now and Co-Working Darwin, that got me out of the house and gave me new friends to work alongside. A special thanks to Yasmin, Nikki, Sean, and A'Mhara.

Last but not least, to the family and friends who have been so supportive, bought copies of my books and encouraged others to do the same. Please continue to do so! I love you guys!

*Woohoo, we made it it to the end! If you loved this book, please leave a review on your fave book seller page, or on Goodreads.*

Bye for now, I'll see you in another magical land soon...

# About The Author

*Jenny Sandiford*

Jenny grew up in small town New Zealand on a steady diet of fairytales and fantasy books. She lived in Mongolia for nine years with her husband where they spent the unfrozen months of the year living on the edge of the Gobi Desert mining gold. When she isn't writing, Jenny enjoys hiking, meeting new animals, and loves to curl up in a sunny corner with a cup of tea, a cat, and a book. She lives in Darwin, Australia, with her husband and their two street cats from Mongolia.

# CONNECT WITH JENNY ON:

**Website**: jennysandiford.com
**Instagram**: instagram.com/JennySandifordAuthor
**Facebook**: facebook.com/JennySandifordAuthor
**Goodreads**: Jenny Sandiford

# WANT THE LATEST BOOK RELEASE NEWS?
*Sign up for monthly updates!*

jennysandiford.com/subscribe

www.ingramcontent.com/pod-product-compliance
Lightning Source LLC
Chambersburg PA
CBHW050103120726
47904CB00004B/1197